The White Iris

A novel by

Sandy MacDonald

DREAMCATCHER PUBLISHING

Saint John ● New Brunswick ● Canada

First printing, September 2006

TITLE: The White Iris

DreamCatcher Publishing acknowledges the support of the Province of New Brunswick.

ISBN: 1-894372-59-X

PS8625.D66W48 2006 C813'.6
C2005-900177-1

Cover Art: Hardy & Associates

Author's Photo: David Duchesne

Editor: Shelley Rogers

Typesetting: J. Gorman

Printed and Bound in Canada

55 Canterbury St, Suite 8
Saint John, NB, E2L 2C6
Canada
Tel: 506-632-4008
Fax: (506) 632-4009
www.dreamcatcherpublishing.ca

For my Grandmother

Author's Note

"I think it's good," said Tennessee Williams, "for a writer to think he's dying; he works harder." Thanks to those who have given me palliative comfort: my editors, Brenda Conroy, whose eagle eyes can spot a flaw at a thousand feet, and Yvonne Wilson who performed brilliant surgery in separating the conjoined twins of volumes one and two. My family, especially my mother and her financial support. Mr. MacDougall's endless supply of wood to keep my fingers from freezing to the keyboard. Mrs. Eleanor Mutimer for her Latin translation – maximo auro. My grandmother, Annabel, who boldly believes in everything I do. A.E. Roland's many years of discovering the flora of Nova Scotia and his meticulous studies. Tom Roach for his reviews and encouragement. Jean Vanier whose Bronfman lecture made me realize just who Fiddy is. And my Lord and God Who gives me my purpose and the strength to do it, how great You are.

White-flowered irises, known as forma *murrayana,* are exceedingly rare. The last plant of this variety was collected in 1922 near Louisbourg and is now believed to be extinct.

– **Wilson and Smith:** ***The Flora of Nova Scotia***

[ONE]

Oh, Adam was a gardener,
and God who made him sees
That half a proper gardener's work
is done upon his knees,
So when your work is finished,
you can wash your hands and pray
For the Glory of the Garden,
that it may not pass away!

– Rudyard Kipling, *The Glory of the Garden*

THE VILLAGE OF WINTRY HOPE begins at the edge of the Northumberland Strait among groups of pink-red volcanic rocks. They slumber like stone dragons in the shallow waters and use their jagged backs to defend Wintry Hope's swampy banks from Northeast swells. In late spring, however, the dragons sleep in gentle waters as mussels bloom in the creases of their armour, the sun bakes their backs and periwinkles move slowly across their toes.

The beach is wide and varied, comprised of streams of rock, pebbles and sand, all lumpy where mounds were left by stranded ships of melting ice. Above the slumping, soppy banks, the swamp steeps its tea and gives way to pastures, which in turn give way to rolling hills beyond which the highlands rise in wooded mists.

The village of Wintry Hope is a few houses at the foot of the hills, farms, barns with fishing boats next to them and at its centre, an enormous church. Built by ambitious settlers, it can hold two thousand people even though Wintry Hope, the surrounding villages of Krydotan and Cleaving Antom, together with all their farm animals, number under two hundred.

In the hills of Wintry Hope, where she could, if she were to look, take in a panoramic view of the village, the pastures of Wintry Hope, the church and the silver Northumberland, Mirabella Stuart walked briskly from her trailer to the garden, carefully avoiding the view. Gawking was for people who didn't have enough work to do. She threw herself to her knees beside a row of kohlrabi and started plucking weeds. Each one she plucked she shoved into a plastic garbage bag which she pulled behind her as she moved down the row. She cleaned up the kohlrabi and moved to a bed of comfrey, and was tugging impatiently at a dandelion root when she heard a door slam. She looked up to see a short, slim man crossing the lawn toward her from his truck.

"Nice spinach," he said. He introduced himself as the provincial Agricultural Representative.

"It's not spinach," Mirabella said. "It's a different species altogether – comfrey."

"Oh." He hesitated. "Our department deals in commercial vegetables like carrots, potatoes, tomatoes and turnips." He gave a strained smile.

Mirabella stared perturbedly.

He pointed to a row of green stalks. "But we do handle celery," he added.

"Celery?!" She looked around indignantly. "Just where do you see *celery*?"

He pointed to a row of stalks, a foot tall, wet, crisp, green, sinewy, with feathery-tipped somewhat transparent leaves on short spreading branches, all of which looked conspicuously like celery.

"Florence fennel," she spat. "It doesn't look like anything remotely similar to celery. Look." She pointed to the underside of the fennel's papery leaves.

He came over cautiously, like a mule wary of a violent owner and bent to look.

"See?" she said. "Small white spots. Celery doesn't have those."

"I don't see them," he said.

"There!" she barked. She pushed some leaves almost into his nose.

"Oh," he said. "They're kind of beige, aren't they?" He smiled weakly.

Mirabella said nothing. She put her hands on her hips and waited for him to get his business done.

"I organize the Eastern Fair," he announced. "Maybe you

could use some advice. You could win a prize." He looked around at the garden, his face hopeful, perhaps, that he would identify a commercial vegetable. The garden, of modest size, had rows, patches and beds of plants, a trellis holding vines, crawling plants that looked like spiders, plants growing in cages like mysterious deadly animals, their branches reaching through small openings and sprouting green fruit. Another plant grew prickly on the ground. One looked like a cross between a watermelon and a cabbage. The Agricultural Representative stood awkwardly in front of Mirabella, who was by now thumping her foot impatiently on the ground.

"Your Department of Agriculture told me it couldn't be done north of the Carolinas," she snapped. "But you've been proved wrong. Look." She indicated a small miserable sickly plant teetering on the edge of survival. "Dasheen. It doesn't look like much now, but it'll have large sweet tubers by mid October."

He still said nothing.

"You do know what tubers are, don't you?"

"Of course. And I know what *dashings* are too." He pointed to a plant with white blossoms. "What's that?" he asked.

"Dixie butterpea. When they mature and are dried in the sun, they're something like lima beans, but you can boil or steam them like peas. Excellent source of fiber."

He moved to five long rows of leafy, lettuce-like plants and Mirabella kept an eye on where every single one of his work boots landed. "Is this some type of lettuce?"

"Witloof chicory."

"Is this the lettuce?"

"Generic fetticus."

He continued up the line and Mirabella listed the names, none of which were lettuce. "Pepper grass, which the rabbits love, and I can't seem to shoot them fast enough. Garden cress, which has a nice hint of mustard flavour, good in salads but most people can't handle too much of it. Watercress, which is self-explanatory. Witloof, endive, there's nothing mysterious about endive, I don't know why I bother with it. My Asian varieties begin here. Wong-bok, Pe-tsai, chi-hi-li . . . "

As Mirabella listed off dozens of other salad vegetables, the Agricultural Representative examined the soil. There were subtle changes in the colour, texture and humus content in each sector of the garden. At one end, near the *dasheens*, the soil was light red, while at the other end, near what looked like bean stalks, the soil was black. Mirabella saw him looking toward the stalks, short plants no more than a foot tall anchored to poles rising twelve feet high. "I've only just planted them," she said. "And they're already a foot high. By mid July they'll be two feet and by the end of September they'll be ten."

"Incredible. What variety of beans are they?"

"They're girasoles. The blossoms are like Black-eyed Susans and the tubers are starchless. If I wait for winter and dig out the tubers from the frozen soil, they'll be sweetest." She couldn't wait. She'd have to use a hammer and chisel to dig them out of the cemented soil.

"How interesting."

She sensed his boredom and resented having shared her garden with him. "I don't know why your department doesn't try marketing these vegetables," she said. "They're far more nutritious than the mass-produced roughage you call food."

"Consumers don't like anything different."

"Maybe you should invest in a marketing campaign. People's tastes change."

"We've tried. It never works. People just eat the same things, year after year. They're like robots. Once they're programmed, they can't be changed."

"What's advertising for, then?"

"They might try a different carrot, but not a different vegetable. It's been tried and we've found that it is impossible to change people. They will never change, no matter how good the alternative."

Mirabella shook her head in disgust. There was no market for her unique, disadvantaged vegetables, not even for such interesting ones as luffa and scorzonera. Because people can't be changed, he'd said. What did he know? He couldn't even tell the difference between lettuce and fetticus. She wondered if she should tell him that she'd been able to make a perfectly edible marmalade sauce out of green gourds. If she could convince him to try it, he'd have to realize there was a market for it.

She declined. This man was a neanderthal when it came to vegetables. "Well, what do you want?"

"Oh, yes. MacDougall's farm. Can you tell me how to get there?"

She gave him the directions and, with a sigh, resumed weeding. Her vegetables had no commercial value, he'd said. The three hundred jars of green-gourd-marmalade-sauce in the storage space under her trailer, therefore, had no value. Because people couldn't be changed.

She'd have to see about that.

AT THE EDGE OF MIRABELLA'S property, the Wintry Hope brook, a small but dependable stream, led the way through a stand of hardwoods, down Wintry Hope's hills, across the plains, avoided the marsh, and tumbled into the Northumberland – from there, to the world. Downhill from Mirabella's trailer, the APT Agent stood at the edge of the stream, about to arrive at a vast conclusion which she'd been threatening to make for two years.

The Agent had been introduced to the brook because of her acquaintance with the great marsh of Wintry Hope, a soggy nest of thousands of rare species of Nova Scotia flora, sprawling from one side of Wintry Hope near the edge of Applefern Mansion to the brook on the western side. The Agent loved the marsh nearly as much as the brook and roamed it every weekend, arriving from the nearby town of Tina Shingo with her lunch, sampling equipment, sketch pad and recording device.

She'd befriended the brook slowly, according to her APT Society manual for studying Earth's treasures, and one day had mustered the courage to lower one booted foot down into its depths. The soft mud in the gentler part of the brook had swirled slightly in the current. Then: nothing. The brook had been indifferent. The contented, gurgling sounds, like a baby's cooing, continued as before, making no allowance whatsoever for the foot. She'd relaxed and felt overwhelming jubilation at being accepted. She hadn't expected shrieking. A sigh perhaps?

Gradually, after months of studying the crystal clear water running over perfectly clean rocks, she learned the brook's deep secret: it was sick. Or, more accurately, it was completely sterile, utterly devoid of life. She set out with meticulous patience and the skills of a scientist to find out what was wrong. She collected evidence from every botanical class, microbial life, insect life, invertebrates, fish, amphibians, fungi. She found a few discoloured frogs and fish, dead and rotting. Chemical analysis revealed elevated amounts of phosphates, sodium hydroxide, alcohol ethoxylates, dimethyl benzyl ammonium chloride and abnormally high levels of nitrogen, phosphorus and potash – all chemicals used to make industrial cleaners. She recorded the details, graphed the concentration of chemicals in the various topographical regions from the hills to the plains to the strait and gradually closed in on the source. Now she was sure she'd found it: an outtake pipe overhanging the brook from an embankment in the hills of Wintry Hope.

She stood at the edge of the brook, clicked a few pictures of the protruding pipe and struggled up the embankment with her pet, a toy dog she named Twig, tucked neatly into a pack on her back. She reached the top and, between the trees, could see a property just beyond. She stepped past some hardwoods and looked through the tree trunks, carefully eying the home of the likely perpetrator.

On the eastern side of the property was a rambling, decrepit house, its electric wires dangling disconnected from a nearby hydro pole. On the western side, closer to where the Agent was hiding, was a small, neat trailer with steel siding, an older model with tires on the roof. It was well-kept but barely managing to keep its status above that of a hovel. A thin, wiry woman was weeding the garden.

The Agent settled down in the leaves, next to the trunk of a tree to observe. She was close enough to the woman to hear her muttering to herself and so, very quietly, she rubbed soil and leaves on her face, neck, arms and in her hair. She also covered her pet with the camouflage and they stayed as still as salamanders to watch.

The woman seemed to have finished weeding and moved to the woodpile at the edge of her trailer to start another chore. She took a few minutes to sharpen an axe with a file and arrange large blocks of wood. "Surely she's not burning wood this time of year," the Agent whispered to her pet. She took out her camera, snapped a few pictures and removed a pad of paper and a charcoal pencil from her pack. She began sketching the scene before her, trying to capture the hard lines on the woman's face, the determination of her eyes, her intensity, her concentration on her chore, all the details that couldn't be captured in film.

MIRABELLA FINISHED SHARPENING THE AXE and arranged a block of wood on the stump. She lifted the axe and with a grunt brought it down. The block of wood, a gnarled piece left from the winter and full of impossibly dense sinews, remained. She stood back to examine it. It was from the part the tree where, it appeared, a dozen limbs had grown. It reminded Mirabella of textbook drawings she'd seen of the human heart. Muscular, with atria and ventricles, severed arteries and veins all drawn tightly into a twisted cyst, it could have been the tree's own heart. She selected the optimal place to strike with the axe and brought it down again. Impenetrable. A few more strikes and a blister broke on her hand, spilling watery blood into the dry axe handle. She kept striking at the block of wood, refusing to stop but wincing from each flash of pain. She struck again and again and with consistent strikes on the same groove, the wedge moved into the wood. The longer it took, the more her fury grew. When it finally broke, a thrill of victory moved through her and intensified her destruction. Halves became quarters, quarters were split and the pieces were reduced under her power until they were no more than slim pieces of gnarled kindling. She stacked it at the back of her shed, raked the splinters and fragments into a dustpan, tossed it into her bag of weeds, and took out her list to see what was next. Dishes. She went inside.

Mirabella washed her dirty dishes almost as she ate from them but unused dishes in the cupboard had to be cleaned too. Sometimes once a month. Although she didn't keep exact track, she knew instinctively when it was time for them to be done. Sometimes, the warning came in the form of a premonition, as she'd received the night before. In a vivid dream she'd seen waves of dust collecting on the plates, saucers, cups and glasses, filtering through the closed doors of the kitchen cupboards like the fingers of dirty imps. As she'd watched through the eye of her dream, armies of bugs had come to feed on the dust: mites, scavenger ants, sow bugs, earwigs and beetles. Then came small white worms to feast on the dead bodies of the insects, spawning a city of larvae, a twisting writhing mass filling up the cupboards and spilling out to her counters, sinks and floor. She awoke screaming, undid the straps holding her into her bed and came to the kitchen to see if what she'd dreamed was true. She'd stepped up to the cupboard, listened for movement within, and in a quick motion threw open a door only to see silent dishes. She knew, however, that her subconscious had somehow detected the microscopic dust and was simply alerting her that it was time to wash the dishes.

It seemed dark inside the trailer, after being in the sunshine all morning. Mirabella took off her steel-toed boots, brushed the dirt and sawdust into the garbage can and placed the boots in plastic bags at the back of the closet. She put on her white orthopedic support shoes and took a glass of water at the sink, her fourth of the day. Doctors suggested eight glasses per day, but she'd read in a newspaper that some health organizations suggested ten to twelve. She'd settled on the average, ten, and sometimes it was one minute to midnight before she would manage to swallow the last of them. She kept track of the number of glasses she consumed with sharp lines at the top of her daily list of things to do, just beneath the lines she etched to keep track of the number of cigarettes she smoked. She allowed herself six of them. Six cigarettes, ten glasses of water, no cholesterol, lots of fibre, eight servings of fruit and vegetables, and she was guaranteed to live until she was a hundred, after which she would die peacefully in her sleep.

Six cigarettes wasn't an addiction.

She finished the glass of water and with pride marked the line on her list. Only six more to go and it wasn't even lunchtime yet. She washed the glass, dried it and put it back in the cupboard.

She emptied the cupboards and the small china cabinet in the corner of the kitchen, placing the dishes on the counter in the order in which they would be washed. Water goblets and wine glasses first, followed by cups, saucers, salad plates, dessert plates and dinner plates. Next, the cutlery which she had polished only two weeks ago but which nevertheless could use a good washing. She examined every dish for signs of dust. She found none, but, she reminded herself, dust was microscopic and couldn't be seen or felt even though it was everywhere all the time and surely coated every surface of everything. Dust, Mirabella knew, was comprised of flaked skin, hair, dead bugs, cobwebs and free-floating germs. It was a microscopic city of filth that caused disease and corrupted every inch of her living environment.

Suddenly she found it difficult to breathe. She covered her nose and mouth and turned away from the dishes. With dead skin and hair – her own dead skin and hair – covering the dishes, she was breathing in – maybe even eating with her food – her own rotting corpse. She coated everything. She leaned against the counter to steady herself, breathed deeply to offset her nausea and tried to think clean, sterile thoughts. Breathe. Good. Clean. That's better.

She straightened. She was in control. She turned on the taps and the hot water sent up a cloud of steam. She added three cups of bleach and half a cup of industrial-strength cleaner to the water and started washing. She washed and dried the dishes in shifts, gently setting a few at a time in the washing sink, quickly and vigorously scrubbing each one, inspecting it thoroughly for signs of skin, hair and dead bugs, rinsing with water so hot it seemed to have been skimmed from pools of molten lava, and setting each dish in the drying rack. She polished each piece individually and carefully placed them in stacks on the kitchen table. After she had washed the cutlery, each piece front and back, and between the teeth of every fork, she began the miscellaneous items: the silver platter her mother had received as a wedding present from her grandfather; the crystal tray for condiments she'd picked up for seventy-five cents at a flea market in Tina Shingo twenty years ago and hadn't used even once; the Scottish Thistle china pieces for cream and sugar with their matching tray which she'd bought at Aunt Olive's estate auction and had never used.

But the Scottish Thistle set was hers, she thought with covetous pleasure. Old Mrs Crowe had wanted it for her own collection, which she'd been working on for at least sixty years, but every time she'd raised her black talons to bid for them, Mirabella had growled like a hungry wolf. The long low rumble was a warning to Mrs Crowe that if she dared bid on them, she'd better be prepared to offer her throat in sacrifice as well. Mrs Crowe, her small black eyes smarting from Mirabella's fierceness, had acquiesced. However, she blamed Mirabella for the ensuing bout of persistent acid reflux gurgling in her throat. Mirabella had taken the set home that day, placed it in the china cabinet in the corner of the kitchen and hadn't used it since.

She pulled the plug in the sink and let the water run out.

OUTSIDE, THE APT AGENT heard a gurgle behind her. She put down her sketch pad and, keeping an eye on the trailer, crept back through the trees to the edge of the embankment. She peered over just in time to see, in apoplectic astonishment, a flood of fluorescent fluid and suds gush out of the outtake pipe. The effluent dribbled down the embankment and seeped into the brook – her brook!

MIRABELLA PUT THE DISHES AWAY, scrubbed the sink with steel wool and cleansers mixed with sand for extra abrasive power, and sprayed bleach on anything that might have become contaminated by the dust. She polished with vinegar. She cleaned the drying rack. The counters were disinfected, the handle on the refrigerator sterilized, the floor next to the sinks mopped and finally she was finished.

She went outside again. Coming down the steps she stopped to poke through the leaves of her geraniums, twisting off all the infant buds she could find. She pulled the buds apart, ground them into small pieces and mixed them into the soil of the window box to fertilize the plants for future blooms. When more buds would come she would pinch them off and return them to the soil for more future blooms – which meant, of course, that she would never have full blooms of geraniums. But what staggering potential they had! This year, she had counted more than three dozen buds at one time. And she'd plucked every last one of them. It was to her tremendous credit, she thought, to forego a current pleasure for the sake of a future one.

She straightened the mat at the bottom of the steps and went across the crunchy pebble path to her garden. It was still a mess, a complete mess, and the Agricultural Representative, as empty-headed as he was, had seen it like that, with dozens of infant weeds advancing like an army between the rows and beds of fledgling plants. She'd already scratched it off her list, however, thinking it had been completed and she couldn't put it on again after it was scratched off. She'd put it on tomorrow's list and keep to the strict order of today's list for today. The lawn was next and to exchange it so that she could revisit her garden work would be like committing adultery. She headed for the shed and her lawn mower.

[TWO]

Ah, I laugh to see myself so
beautiful in these mirrors . . .

– Gounod: Marguerite, *Faust*

GOWNED IN RED, with diamonds and pearls at her ears and neck, Desdemona Pacifico-Rossini, star soprano, stood in the middle of a polished black stage at the Royal Albert Hall. She sang from one of the most difficult pieces of her repertoire: *Der Hölle Rache*, in the original German:

Der Hölle Rache kocht in meinem Herzen,
Tot und Verzweiflung flammet um mich her!
Hell's Revenge cooks in my heart,
Death and despair flame about me!

The Queen of the Night went up and down her scales, defying the impossible transitions, her high C-sharps coming from some other world not made of earth and mud but of the air of music. Perhaps, she thought, the enraptured audience were afraid she'd topple from the impossibly high notes. Never! But Desdemona Pacifico-Rossini was known to test her limits. She swooped through the voice manouevres, an angel, she imagined, dancing from spire to spire at the top of a great basilica. Her aria built to *crescendo*, descended and built again, flooded its banks and hit newer and higher climaxes.

When she finished, the audience sat before her in a silent gasp, unable, no doubt, to comprehend her brilliance. They were reluctant to intrude on the sacred moment with something so clumsy as applause. But since it was all they could do, she allowed them their vulgar expression of approval.

The applause sounded throughout the auditorium like thunder. They loved her. They loved her! Shouts of adulation came from everywhere. *Bravo!* They shouted for more, they demanded more, they needed to have more lest there be a riot. And so Desdemona Pacifico-Rossini gave them more. She gave it freely, out of her inexhaustible abundance of talent. She sang three more selections from her repertoire and the applause began again. *Bravissimo*, they shouted in a fury. *Bravissimo!* The applause was like a great storm surge. Hooves and chariots pounded across a desert. How long could it continue? Two minutes? Three? It seemed as though they'd been adoring her for hours. Desdemona Pacifico-Rossini glowed as if her skin had been rubbed with the rising sun. Could she give out more? She would try.

But as she took a breath to start again, from a distant place an ugly noise intruded. A high-pitched, atonal hum. She gave the orchestra a perturbed glance but they only looked to her, all their instruments poised to begin. It wasn't them. It wasn't the air-conditioning. Terrorists? When the walls, the stage, the curtain and her audience began to fade, Desdemona Pacifico-Rossini realized what was happening. Her jewels fled into the dazzling morning light, she sat up in bed and screamed: "Mirabella!"

The lawn mower buzzed from the adjacent property. "Damn you, Mirabella. Enough is enough!" She could reach the window from her bed and so shoved it up and leaned out. "Give the grass a chance!" she shrieked, her voice clear and shrill despite the night of performing.

From her lawn at the other side of the property line, Mirabella saw Fiddy's second-storey window open and her enormous wigged head stick out. She saw the mouth moving rapidly, the plump fist shaking. She couldn't make out the words over the droning of the lawn mower but she knew what Fiddy would be saying. She'd heard it all before and wasn't about to compromise her mowing to listen to the babble again. Taking her eyes off the grass even for a moment could cause her to veer away from her invisible lines and miss part of the unmown lawn. With so little difference between mown and unmown grass, Mirabella had to keep the lines clear in her mind or else she would lose her place. The inefficiency resulting from redoing already mown lawn was just as treacherous an error as failing to completely cover every part of it. She ignored Fiddy and turned a corner so that Fiddy was at her back.

"Give the grass a chance, I say!" Fiddy bellowed. She shook

her fist again. "Bloody rot! Five times this week, Mirabella! Enough is enough!" She shook her fist a few more times, but, hating to be ignored, pulled herself back inside and closed the window.

"Humph!" she pouted, and hopped from the bed as though she were only sixty years old. "Trailer trash. That's what you are, Mirabella Stuart. Trailer trash."

She stood in front of her full length mirror and looked herself up and down. Suddenly her anger melted and she had to smile. She was beautiful. Even when she was pouting. Or at least when she drew back the skin from her face and got rid of some of the wrinkles. And it helped to pull some of her chestnut curls down over her forehead to cover it up. Of all her features, she hated her forehead the most. If she looked at it for any length of time, it seemed to expand into a wide monstrosity. And if she dared look longer, her head would seem too fat and her cheeks too plump. Even her elegant nose would look squashed and pudgy.

The only thing to be done was to glance quickly at herself, fleetingly, then to look away so that the truest picture came into focus among the purple orchids of her wallpaper. This she did, several times, blinking rapidly to improve the effect. She moved sideways in front of the mirror and assumed a standing crouch, her ample behind thrusted out. She blinked rapidly. Marilyn Monroe appeared among the orchids on the wall.

She waved at herself, straightened, slipped into three-inch heels, pulled on a *faux* silk housecoat and flounced into the hallway, muttering curses at Mirabella under her breath for disturbing her sleep, while she clopped her way down the hardwood hallway, grasped the railing in her right hand and began descending the staircase. "By the devil's teeth, Mirabella. This time, you've gone too far."

Her shoes made a most satisfactory *clop clop* on the steps to accompany her mumbling. She pranced to amplify the effect. After all, the faster one stepped, the more important one was.

She stopped on the landing midway down the stairs and looked at herself several fleeting times in a mirror hanging on the wall. "What a Banbury cheese you are, Mirabella. You have no idea how my heart stirs among these breasts." She swooned and fell against the bannister as one dying, all the while watching herself in the mirror. "Oh, how my soul rots within me by your poison, Mirabella! A thousand deaths I shall die because of you!" She gasped for breath as if her tongue were as parched as desert sands. She pressed her face against the cool wood of the bannister, feeling tired and defeated by the thought of confronting her nemesis.

"No!" the woman in the mirror yelped, surprising her. "I'll not be stabbed in silence behind the curtain to fall, a simple croak, to the floor!" She folded her hands above her head and leaned back to gaze toward the ceiling where another mirror stared down at her. Blinking, she watched herself become enclosed in the centre of a white floral tomb. "I shall wither away slowly like the last of summer's lilies, folding up my intricasate tender virgin petals in a cathedral-grave, to spend eternity frozen alone in timeless beauty, forever hidden from a world that would shun and scorn me."

She continued to stand with her hands arranged in a cathedral above her head and blinked at the mirror for a long time – until her stomach gurgled. "After breakfast, perhaps," she said, and pranced down the remaining steps. She danced her way through the livingroom without incident but when she came to the downstairs bathroom, she stopped, took off her heels and tiptoed past the door, ajar just a tiny crack but wide enough for her to see and smell the brown fluid overflowing from the toilet. Once past, she allowed herself to breathe again, slipped her heels back on and resumed her joyous promenade until she entered the kitchen. There, she punched the play button on the ghettoblaster, turned up the volume and waited for the music to strike like a shockwave from Hiroshima: *Fortuna Imperatrix Mundi.*

Carmina Burana was one of her favourite pieces and she could approximate nearly every Latin word of it. She didn't understand what the words meant but she knew they were sinister. The melody spoke of risking, losing, winning and death. What better elements of drama could there be? Besides, it closed with bells and trumpets and Fiddy loved bells and trumpets more than anything.

She swung open the refrigerator to see what food she had left but slammed it shut as a putrid stench emerged. "Cookies, then," she announced, even though she knew she didn't have eggs, or, if she did, they were unreachable in the refrigerator.

Substitutes in cooking were one of her specialties, however. A jar of mayonnaise would do the trick. She opened the cupboard next to a dirty, encrusted stove, which smelled of the very bottom of the propane tank. She squinted to see what was there. Ketchup, barbecue sauce, Grey Poupon, olive oil and a dozen or so plastic containers of tapioca pudding. She considered the Grey Poupon for a moment. It was the colour of beaten eggs but tasted nothing like them. Did tapioca pudding have eggs in it? She didn't know. Olive oil was like fat, she knew, and there was fat in eggs. A bit of olive oil and tapioca pudding then. What the heck, she'd throw in some Grey Poupon for colour.

She turned on the oven and with the gusto of a great chef tossed the ingredients into an enormous steel bowl. Without measuring, of course. None of the great chefs measured. While she was mixing the batter, the music ground to a stop. She stared at the ghettoblaster in disbelief. Surely that wasn't the end of her batteries? She could bear anything but the loss of her music. She punched the machine. Perhaps the tape was stuck. Nothing. Then she shook it. A slow, painful sound emerged from the box, a demon's voice growing through various stages of agony until, with one more punch from Fiddy, it sped up to its normal pace. She smiled. She still had some time left.

She poured one large cookie with her improvised batter onto a baking sheet and placed it in the oven, licking her lips, hungry for fresh cookies. But then she noticed, by waving her hand inside the oven, that there was no heat. She examined the temperature knob, turned it a few times and looked at it from different angles to make sure it was on. It was. She groaned. She was out of propane. To make matters worse, the music came to another exhausted stop. She nearly wept. Silence filled the kitchen.

Suddenly, Fiddy noticed how dirty it all was. Even the portrait of the Queen Mother in the corner was soiled with grease or chicken gumbo or something. The wallpaper behind it was faded to a black grime. The garbage needed to be emptied; it buzzed with flies. She could hear the whiz and whine of insects outside in the happy sunshine, but the air inside was stagnant. She could almost feel the house rotting around her, pulling her down into the basement into which it was all gradually sinking.

In the livingroom, near a window that faced Mirabella's trailer, she slumped down in a chair with the cookie sheet and the last of her brandy. As daintily as she could, she licked cookie batter from a finger and washed it down with gulps of brandy. The batter tasted like mustard mixed with olive oil but she was so hungry she ate it, although with revulsion. The artist must suffer, she told herself. Painters ate their paint. Sculptors ate their clay. Sooner or later she'd be forced to eat her false teeth.

After a while the lawn mower stopped and she strained to look through the dirty window to see what Mirabella was doing. It looked as though she were picking tiny strawberries out of the grass. Or perhaps she had lost something – like a needle. Fiddy held up her glass of brandy in a toast. "Here's to you, Mirabella." She laughed at the irony of toasting Mirabella, who hated liquor and actively advocated for a return to Prohibition. "To Mirabella Stuart," she continued, "the only one in the world who's worse off than me." She gulped down the brandy, winced and tossed the glass toward the fireplace. The glass, however, struck the lampshade, veered off course and smashed against the window. Drops of brandy dribbled down the pane, wobbling Mirabella's form.

AFTER CLEANING HER LAWN, Mirabella noticed the driveway was a mess too. Large, sharp rocks in the inferior gravel annoyed her when they crunched and cracked under the bald tires of her car. And since she was nearing the end of her chores anyway, she might as well do something about the annoyance. She had already filled two garbage bags with grass clippings from the lawn so she started a third for rocks. She was weighing a stone in her hand, trying to decide whether it was too big for the driveway, when Fiddy came out the back door of her house. She headed toward a dilapidated shed, which had been an outhouse at one time, at the rear of her lawn.

"Hi, Mirabella, la, la, la!" Fiddy sang to her neighbour and waved. Mirabella stopped her examination of the stone, glared at

Fiddy and resisted the urge to throw it at her. Fiddy waved again, excitedly, but still Mirabella responded only with a steely stare.

Long ago Mirabella had decided to be perfectly honest with Fiddy. As a consequence she showed Fiddy nothing but disdain. It took far too much energy to match Fiddy's incessant bubbly cheer and the extremes to which she would go for dramatic effect. From experience Mirabella had discovered that ignoring her worked best, conserving energy for her own harsh life instead of wasting it on Fiddy's alternating turmoils and tragedies.

Fiddy's high heels were designed for many things, including thrusting out the breasts, accentuating smooth curvy hips and giving the body more pleasing proportions, but for trekking through the jungle of her own back lawn, they were not. While trying to maintain her broadest, superstar smile to Mirabella, she yelped each time her ankle twisted or she was forced to swoop to catch her balance.

Mirabella wondered what nonsense Fiddy was up to. She winced at every one of Fiddy's steps, not for the pain they were causing but for the hideous holes they were making in the lawn. Mirabella wanted very badly to fix those holes. She tossed the stone into the bag and watched as Fiddy swooped her way to the shack.

From the shadows of the hardwoods at the edge of Mirabella's lawn, the Agent also winced with each of Fiddy's haphazard steps, thinking of the worms under the sod being impaled with each spike. She cried out in her mind: poor worms! And she imagined the wretched, solitary creatures in the black, loamy earth attempting, fruitlessly, to dodge those depth charges from above. How could humans be so cruel? Why didn't anyone ever think of the worms?

Fiddy's shack hadn't been painted in a century. Its original colour had been red-copper, the same used by fishermen to seal the hulls of their lobster boats. Now it was dark grey, covered in moss and lichen, and struggling to hold itself up as if drunk. Gradually it was losing the battle. Sinking, dissolving, it was little by little being swallowed up by the dark moist wormy earth. Maybe, with their infinite patience, this was how the worms were fighting back.

Fiddy reached the shack, entered and immediately came out again carrying a gas can. She waved to Mirabella again as though she were entering centre stage at the Metropolitan Opera. Mirabella continued to glare, crossed her arms and gave a disgusted *humph.*

"Just doing some cooking," Fiddy offered, as if Mirabella had politely inquired. "I'm making a cookie. Ouch!" One of her heels stuck and when she pulled out her foot, she lost her balance and stepped on a thistle. She limped back to the house, shoe in one hand, gas can in the other. Mirabella still said nothing and when Fiddy's door closed, she resumed work on the driveway.

FIDDY HOBBLED INTO the kitchen so as not to put pressure on her impaled foot. She dropped the sloshing gas can, settled into a chair, removed her pantyhose and tried to bring her foot close enough to see. Her eyes didn't have a chance. Fortunately she always had a litre or two of bikini wax on hand, which she retrieved from underneath the sink. She heated some with a lighter under an empty spam tin, applied it to the afflicted area with a spatula and quickly peeled it away. The thistles came out.

Comfortable again, she took a deep breath, picked up the can of gas and began dousing the kitchen. She spilled gasoline inside the oven, across the floor and around the base of the refrigerator, which reminded her of a frumpy old maid. Why on earth didn't she do the dishes? She spilled gas across the counters and liberally doused all the dirty pots and pans. Then she backed her way out of the kitchen, went down the hall, quickly passed the revolting bathroom and went into the livingroom. She doused the dusty chesterfield she had always hated, the one the St Vincent De Paul Society had burdened her with thirty years ago. She covered the floor, coffee table, lampshades, the rotten and ragged horsehair love seat she also despised, and in a flurry of movement twirled around quickly to let gasoline spray out on the walls and curtains, ensuring that everything she despised received at least a few drops.

She tossed the empty can aside and found a book of matches on the mantle. She tried to light one but with her stubby fingers it wasn't easy. After the fifth try she succeeded. A flash and then the match settled into a gentle flicker in front of her eyes. The flame crept toward her fingers.

She couldn't take her eyes off the flame, such a mysterious, hypnotic power it held over her. One tiny flame, or even one small spark, had the concentrated power to blow things up. It could even blow her up. It could ruin lives, save lives, bring light to lives. All it needed was the fuel, the effluvium and, strangely, it didn't matter how much of it there was. One tiny match could set an ounce of gasoline on fire – or a supertanker. One match is all it took. Perhaps there were even unignited stars in the universe that one spark could set ablaze.

"Ouch!" she yelped as the flame reached her fingers. She gasped when the match hit the floor. She expected to be set on fire and waited for it. But the match merely sent out a small puff of smoke and died. It had missed gasoline by an inch or so. That was close, she thought. She could have set the house on fire without getting properly attired for the occasion. And what an awful last word for her to utter: ouch! The great Desdemona Pacifico-Rossini couldn't die with such a word on her lips. No. If Fiddy Washburn were to have a glorious end to her glorious life, her last words would have to be better than that. She would have to think though. Perhaps a rhyming couplet put to music would be suitable. She strained to come up with something but the fumes were making her thoughts difficult to string together. She went to the kitchen for her ghettoblaster. Another performance from *Carmina Burana* perhaps, if the batteries were up to it.

OUTSIDE, MIRABELLA SCRUBBED her garden hose in a washbasin full of soapy water. The hose was *filthy*. Badly in need of a good cleaning. From the woods, the Agent observed with horror, the suds overflowing the basin. She was considering calling the police on her cell phone when Mirabella suddenly stopped scrubbing and looked directly at her.

The Agent froze and could only stare back with wild, frightened eyes. Had the woman picked up her scent? As if in answer, Mirabella seemed to sniff at the air like a grizzly bear. But then she turned her face away from the Agent and looked toward Fiddy's house.

It was gasoline Mirabella smelled. What was that stupid nitwit doing now? She wiped her hands on her apron, left the garden hose to soak and walked to the eastern limit of her property from where she could survey Fiddy's decrepit house. The windows revealed only streaks of white among reflections of the sky. She paced the line dividing their properties like a foot soldier on duty, careful to keep her feet a few inches away from Fiddy's property so as not to trespass. That would have been a sin.

UPSTAIRS IN HER BEDROOM, Fiddy sat down at her mirrored boudoir and added mascara to her fake eyelashes. Her voluptuous red curls looked, appropriately, like the flames of a funeral pyre. Her lips were scarlet and her skin was white. She dabbed a hint of pinkish blush at the top of her cheeks, careful not to make herself too daring. She didn't want to be greeted at the gates of heaven looking like a tart. The only slight problem was her eyebrows. She had no real ones. Not a hair. It was a wonder of superior genetics. So she had to draw them in and she'd aimed a bit too high. The neat black lines swept in arcs almost halfway up her forehead. She had no more erasers though; they would have to do.

She put on rhinestone earrings and pinned a shiny brooch to her green gown which was missing sequins in a few places but if she folded her hands over strategic locations the gown shimmered like an emerald. Around her neck she fastened a black choker clasped in front with a silver-coloured heart. Finished, she stood up and backed away from the mirrors, blinking rapidly and smiling at herself. She was more gorgeous than the Queen of the St Patrick's Day Parade.

She swept across the room to her bureau upon which she had placed the ghettoblaster, pressed play and gave it a small punch with her fist while keeping her long fingernails carefully away from the impact. *Carmina Burana's* discordant *Olim Lacus Colueram* began.

She lit a candle, wrapped it in newspaper and tossed it through her bedroom doorway. It sailed over the railing and into the livingroom below. She slammed the door and pattered over to her bed where she leapt to the bedspread among her most valuable possessions: a collection of uncut diamonds, the Miss Wintry Hope tiara she won in 1945 and a black and white picture of herself winning the pageant. She carefully placed the tiara in her hair and while she waited for the gas to ignite downstairs, sang along with the *Carmina Burana* piece as if in great travail:

Once I dwelt on lakes,
once I was beautiful,
when I was a swan.

This is it, she thought. Soon she would have her shroud of smoke and the fire would come to set free the bright spark of her soul.

The gasoline ignited in an explosion that shook the bed. Downstairs, windows shattered and wooden beams splintered. The floor shook and buckled but Fiddy kept singing and only hugged her picture harder. The ghettoblaster was nearly shaken from the bureau but it kept on playing. Fiddy could hear the roar of the fire and the air being sucked out of her room. The house whined like a rising demon. Its labour pains came sharply but Fiddy kept singing:

Wretch that I am!
Now black
and roasting fiercely!

Smoke burled into the room and flames licked at the door. Fiddy coughed but refused to recoil from the smoke. She breathed it in, gave herself over to it and, in her mind, followed it as it escaped from the roof of the house. *One tiny spark is all it takes, you know.* That's who she was. That's what her voice was. A spark.

She soared above the house and into the sky, past the blueness and into the black of space. *One spark is all it takes*. She looked for the sad grey pallor of an unlit star, to strike it with her spark and set it ablaze . . .

The batteries were giving out in the ghettoblaster. Perhaps the song was finished. Should it be this hot in space? Or perhaps the swan was dead, its flesh black and burnt.

Where was her waiting star? Fiddy was suddenly frantic. She moved through the dark of space in search of the unlit star, flew past planets with red storms raging on their surfaces, past ghostly moons, until finally she saw it: round, vast, as smooth as cream, so white it seemed blue, luminescent even though it gave no light, like new snow that could be seen on a lightless, moonless night.

The star was all alone at the edge of the universe waiting for her. She smiled and moved toward it, anxious for the blaze of light. She knew it meant her end but soon the universe would finally see who she really was. She could even hear the applause beginning, like dry wood crackling under advancing flames.

MIRABELLA WAS STANDING near the property line, sniffing the gas on the air and watching the house, when the bottom floor exploded and showered her with glass, nails and wood. She hit the ground as a flapping Chippendale's calendar escaped the house like a lecherous bat on one wing, narrowly missing her. When she looked up, the bottom floor of Fiddy's house was in flames.

She ignored the property line and ran for the house. "Fiddy!" she screamed and made her way beneath Fiddy's bedroom window. "Fiddy, your house is on fire!"

Over the sound of burning she could just make out the distorted music. She ran for a ladder from Fiddy's shed, pushed it against the side of the house and climbed up.

Fiddy's muffled singing escaped from her bedroom:

The spit turns and re-turns,
My funeral pyre burns me fiercely;
And I cannot fly away . . .

"Fiddy, you idiot, your house is on fire!" Mirabella yelled outside the window. She rapped against it with her fist but Fiddy continued to sing. She strained to see inside but could only see black smoke swirling like swarming flies against the glass. "Fiddy!" she yelled once more. Nothing. The music stopped. Mirabella formed a fist, closed her eyes, turned her head away and with bare knuckles punched through the glass. Smoke surged into her face. The house seemed to sigh and groan. She took a deep breath and screamed through the broken window: "Fiddy, your house is on fire!"

Then, the air reversed and the house seemed to take in a breath from the broken window. The smoke in Fiddy's room cleared and Mirabella saw her on the bed, eyes closed as if in sleep, and within reach. "Fiddy!" she hollered.

She pushed the remaining shards of glass out of the window, leaned inside and slapped Fiddy hard across the face. "Wake up, you idiot! Your house is burning down!" The door and the floor near the boudoir were in flames and the fire was spreading quickly toward the bed. The house groaned again. Mirabella shook Fiddy's shoulder.

Fiddy stirred groggily, felt her cheek and looked directly into Mirabella's face. "Mirabella, what on earth have you done to my window?"

"Your house is burning down, you fool. Get out of there!"

"You're trespassing on my property." She turned her back to Mirabella and snuggled into the bed clothes. "You interrupted the most wonderful dream," she complained. "I was in outer space and –"

"You fool! Get out!" Mirabella leaned inside as far as she could and managed to grab hold of the largest piece of Fiddy she could reach: her hair, tiara included.

Fiddy shrieked when she felt her wig lifting and held to it. "My hair! My hair! Don't touch my hair!" But Mirabella refused to let go. The fire was beginning to exhale again and smoke spewed out of the window and into her face. She kept her fist on Fiddy's hair, pulled, and Fiddy came with it.

By now the entire room was in flames. Almost as Mirabella pulled Fiddy outside, the bed fell through to the bottom floor. They were only a few steps down the ladder when, with a violent roar, flames leapt from the window. The roof was on fire. Joists and beams crashed down inside the house. Fiddy shrieked all the way down the ladder but Mirabella kept a firm claw on her hair.

At the bottom a short pudgy fireman doused them both with a burst of dirty water. Fiddy wailed as though, like the wicked witch, she were made of brown sugar and would melt away. She cried miserably and would have climbed back up the ladder to throw herself into the flames had Mirabella not knocked down the ladder in anticipation of such a possibility.

Mirabella went back to her own lawn, upon which a fire truck had parked next to her garden, blocking it from the sun. A burly man who identified himself as the Fire Chief informed her that in emergencies the fire department could park on properties adjacent to burning houses and that, in fact, he could even park in the middle of her garden if necessary. Then he asked after the owner of the burning house, found Fiddy and drew her away. To Mirabella's annoyance, they stood on her property to watch the fire.

FIDDY'S HOUSE WAS LOST. There wasn't anything the firefighters could do except watch as it twisted and writhed against the flames. "Was there anyone else in the house?" asked the Fire Chief, although it didn't much matter since the house was fully engulfed.

"No," said Fiddy. She'd changed moods and was now happy to have the attention. She smiled at the Fire Chief winsomely, noticing his thick arms and ringless fingers, and straightened her tiara. "I'm single."

He looked perplexed. She swooned slightly and he held her up. She coughed demurely. "Are you sure you're okay?" he asked. "You may have had too much smoke."

"Of course she's okay," said Mirabella before Fiddy could reply. She gave Fiddy a heavy slap on the back to clear her lungs and inserted herself between Fiddy and the Fire Chief. "She's fine. There wasn't anyone else in there. You might as well let the old eyesore burn down. And maybe you could set that shed on fire while you're at it." She pointed and they all looked at the shed. It sat at the edge of the lawn like a stray dog that had wandered onto the property, knew it was in the wrong but hoped it would be fed anyway.

Suddenly realizing she'd been pushed out of the way, Fiddy became insulted by Mirabella's meddling. She stepped in front of Mirabella, where the Fire Chief could see her. "Can't you please save my house?" she pleaded.

The Fire Chief looked at it doubtfully. "I'm afraid it's too far advanced."

"What about my diamonds?!" she cried.

"Diamonds?"

"Yes," she pleaded. "I have a fortune in diamonds in my bedroom. Couldn't you please send someone in after them?"

The Fire Chief looked at the house again and as they watched with him, the top floor collapsed and crashed down into the bottom level. Several firefighters shouted and ran for cover amid flying embers and debris.

"Well?" Fiddy asked again, her face vacant. She waited for an answer.

"Of course not, you idiot," Mirabella snapped.

WHEN IT LOOKED LIKE the fire was contained, Mirabella left and went to her trailer to clean it of the soot and ash falling on it from Fiddy's house. The firefighters remained to ensure the fire didn't spread to the woods. The Fire Chief extricated himself from Fiddy to supervise the work. Fiddy went to her dilapidated shed, which had been spared for the time being, found an old lawn chair, opened it up and sat down to watch the last of her house burn away.

She also watched the firefighters. She noticed them occasionally glancing at her with dark pity in their eyes, at which she winced. She despised their misplaced pity. They obviously didn't know who she was. If they only realized how many people around the world worshiped her, they would ask her to sing right now, next to her burning house. Something near the end of Mozart's *Requiem* would be appropriate, she thought, or *Don Giovanni*. And then they would clap and cheer and be amazed that Fiddy Washburn could sing so beautifully. *I had no idea*, someone would say in an astonished voice. *I can't believe I've known her all my life and never heard her sing. Simply breathtaking! What talent!*

She wondered where she would be sleeping that night. She considered the shed next to her but there were nests of snakes and wasps and mice in there. She could ask her friend Mrs Crowe if she could stay with her, but Mrs Crowe hated her and was prone to violent tantrums. Perhaps she could stay with her nephew Johnny and his wife Martha. They were rich and lived in Applefern Mansion only a short distance away in Wintry Hope proper. Their house contained at least ten spare bedrooms.

Fiddy, however, had never been able to wiggle her way into their luxurious exclusivity, despite hundreds of creative attempts. The last one had involved a bomb threat and a series of notes threatening to seize her unless a ransom was paid. She managed to stay at the mansion for three nights before her plans were exposed. She'd made the mistake of exaggerating the ransom demand. Any specific sum of money had seemed to cheapen her value so she'd listed some of the greatest artistic achievements of human civilization, including a Michelangelo, a Cezanne and the original score to Verdi's *Falstaff*. She really had no idea how rich Johnny and Martha were and she'd wanted to ensure they couldn't complete the ransom. In any event, despite her deft touch they'd twigged and confronted her. She'd admitted it all in a performance which ended only when she was forced from their premises by their security company.

All her bridges, it seemed, had been either burned, blown up or sold. But she still had one resource left: her talent. She had twisted sows' ears into purses before. She would create magnificent sublimity from her tragedy. It's what all the greatest actresses did.

After hours of watching the fire depart into the sky as smoke and steam, someone handed her half of a cheese sandwich. She rejected it at first because dairy products were harmful to her voice but, feeling hungry, she asked for it back. She pulled off the cheese and ate the bread while watching the firefighters douse. Ash and water streamed down the smouldering beams – like dragon's tears, Fiddy thought. The plumes of wafting steam reminded her of white ghosts over a black corpse. When the fire was completely out, the firefighters left and a long flatbed truck pulled up with a bulldozer. While men unloaded the bulldozer, an inspector and the Fire Chief sorted through the ruins.

The house, at last, was silent. Fiddy left her chair and went through the ruins in search of her diamonds. She kicked over pieces of metal and searched under fragments of burnt wood for anything valuable, carrying with her the plastic grocery bag she'd been given with the sandwich. Beneath the place where her bedroom had been she found fragments of glass that had probably come from her window. She searched among the steel coils of her bed springs and found burnt plastic from makeup containers and a compact but no diamonds. Not far away she found broken pieces of the mirror that had been in her now dissolved boudoir. She dug through ashes with the stump of a brass lamp and overheard the hushed voices of the Fire Chief and the inspector in what used to be her kitchen. She looked up from her work to see the Fire Chief pointing at her. The inspector fixed a cold skinny gaze on her.

"Ms Washburn?" he asked.

"This is she," Fiddy answered with dignity, as though she were answering the telephone. She pointed to herself with the stump of the lamp. "I am her."

"Ms Washburn, what do you think happened?"

She wondered if perhaps he was asking the question in the same fashion that doctors in the hospital did when attempting to determine her mental health. *Do you know where you are? Do you know who you are? Do you know what day this is? How many fingers am I holding up?* "My house burned down," she said, hoping it was the correct answer.

"Yes, but how?"

"I don't know. I was in the deepest embrace of Morpheus when it happened."

"You told me before there was no one else in the house," said the Fire Chief, a concerned look coming on his face.

"Yes."

"Who's this . . . Morpheus?"

"It's an expression. It means I was asleep. One simply closes one's eyes and the world, darkness, the body, the mind, all disappear."

"In that?" The inspector pointed to her soiled green gown which, since the fire, had lost more of its sequins.

"What do you mean, 'in this'? Of course in this."

He exchanged glances with the Fire Chief. Fiddy noticed her burnt curling iron nearby, scooped it out of the soot and stuffed it into her bag.

"You don't remember hearing anyone enter the house after you went to bed, do you?" the inspector resumed, and Fiddy couldn't tell if he was asking her or telling her.

"No," she answered, cautiously.

The inspector motioned for her to join them. He held up a

sliver of blue paper. "I want you to see something." He rubbed the blue paper on the edge of the burned-out stove and it turned a vibrant red. "Do you know what this means?" He held it up for her to see.

It was a very pretty red, Fiddy thought, and the transformation was quite magical but other than that she knew nothing of its significance. "No. What does it mean?"

"It means someone was trying to kill you."

Fiddy gasped. "No!" She teetered on her heels but the Fire Chief didn't move in to steady her as she'd hoped.

"This is my theory, Ms Washburn," said the inspector. He paced in front of her. "Someone was watching your house. They learned your habits. They discovered you go to bed for a nap every day at around the same time . . ."

"I feel so violated," Fiddy interrupted, looking around in case they were watching her now. At this very moment they could be admiring her fine lines and physique. Or perhaps they were waiting until she found her diamonds.

The inspector cleared his throat and continued. "They decided to make their move today, when you went for your nap. When they thought you were asleep, they sneaked into the house . . ."

"An intruder!"

"Yes. And while you were sleeping, they doused the downstairs with gasoline and set it ablaze."

"Goats and monkeys!"

"There's no doubt. The fire was deliberate. Do you know anyone who would want to kill you?"

"Mirabella Stuart!" she blurted. "I know it was her! You've got to protect me! You've got to arrest her now!" Fiddy rushed forward and tried to fall into the Fire Chief's arms but he backed away from her and she had to cling to the inspector, a less attractive man, being thin and pale, but she had to cling to someone.

The inspector looked into the damsel's eyes. "But she's the one who saved you from the fire, Ms Washburn." His voice was low and cold.

Fiddy let go of the inspector and straightened herself up, feeling spurned by his coldness. "Oh yes, I'd forgotten about that."

"You can't think of anyone else?"

"I'm an actress. It could be anyone."

"I don't agree, Ms Washburn. I don't believe that it could be just anyone."

"Whatever do you mean?"

"I know who did it."

"Who?"

He pointed at her. "You."

"Me?" Fiddy had never been so outraged. "You scoundrel! You rascal! I was upstairs in the arms of Morpheus!"

"Do you deny it then?"

"Deny what?"

"That you're the arsonist!"

"I am no such thing! I am a lady. No, I'm a duchess. And I'm unaccustomed to that sort of language, young man!"

The inspector rolled his eyes. "Do you deny, my fair duchess, that you poured gasoline all over your house and set it on fire?"

"Of course I do! What kind of fanatic do you take me for?"

The inspector smiled. He gestured behind Fiddy to where the back door had been. Fiddy saw a young woman standing here. She'd never seen her before in her life.

The woman was wearing the most primitive clothes Fiddy had ever seen. They looked as though they'd been woven from the grass clippings Mirabella picked off her lawn. Her hair had twigs, leaves and bugs in it, and her thin white lips were pursed angrily shut. She reminded Fiddy of magazine pictures of frozen cave people or even a small Sasquatch. It was the APT Agent.

"May I introduce," the inspector said, "Ms Garden Twinkle."

"I've never seen this woman before."

"I assure you, Ms Washburn, she's seen you. In fact, she saw you today. She saw you leave your house, enter your shed, procure a can of gasoline and return –"

"To blast greenhouse gases into the air and destroy this beautiful planet!" shrieked the Agent, almost crying with rage. She'd seen the house explode from her hiding place in the woods and had been the one to call the fire department.

"Yes, Ms Twinkle, thank-you."

The Agent was far from finished. "You monster!" she seethed at Fiddy. "Do you think this planet exists solely for you?!"

Fiddy put a dainty hand to her breast, affronted by the Agent's violent chastisement. This wasn't a Sasquatch at all. It was an uncouth environmentalist. "I didn't destroy this planet," she said.

"Don't you know what's happening? Carbon dioxide destroys our atmosphere. You've released thousands of tons of it in only a few hours. Don't you realize what this has done? We're burning up! The sun is going to kill us all and we're running out of time!"

The inspector nodded to the Fire Chief, who went to the Agent, gently took hold of her arm and escorted her back to where the door had been. The Agent struggled against him. "The sky is scorching the grass!" she screamed. "Plants are dying! Think of the grass! Think of the grass!"

The Fire Chief almost succeeded in pulling her through the doorway when she broke free, hopped over a pile of rubble and made a dash for Fiddy. She was about to reach her when he caught her around the waist but she was able to stick a finger accusingly in front of her face. "You're a murderer! Murderer! You have no right to enslave the animals and kill the grass!"

The Fire Chief pulled her back toward the door while she squirmed and struggled in his arms like an eel. "J'accuse! J'accuse! J'accuse!" she shrieked in French, as if unable to give voice to her concerns within the limits of the English language. The Fire Chief managed to pull her through the doorway.

Fiddy was suddenly morose. "She's right," she said into the distance. "I am a murderer. I've killed the grass."

"I'll be informing your insurance company that you caused the fire," said the inspector. "They won't be covering your loss."

Fiddy looked at him quizzically. "What on earth makes you think it was insured?" Then, noticing something at her feet, she knelt down and picked up a dirty rock. She wiped it clean on her gown, looked at it closely, nodded, and looked up at the inspector with a victorious smile. "This is my insurance," she said.

[THREE]

Charity upholds and purifies our human ability to love, and raises it to the supernatural perfection of divine love.

– Catechism of the Catholic Church

BY NIGHTFALL Mirabella was exhausted and nothing could have made her happier. She loved sore muscles, the result of her physical labours. She would sleep well tonight instead of listening to the trees creaking in the woods behind her trailer or staring into the darkness for hours, watching for the moonlight to strike the window, fall to the floor and scamper across the room.

She had washed her hair, added blue rinse and rolled it tightly into dozens of tiny curlers to form a wiry crust on top of her head. She'd filled in the tracks left by the fire trucks in her lawn. She'd swept the broken glass and debris from her driveway and washed the ash from the side of her trailer. She'd washed her clothes and hung them outside on the clothesline. Now she sat at her kitchen table with her lists to check off the items. She ensured every chore was completed, shredded the lists and sprinkled the confetti into the garbage can. Walking by the window, she happened to notice a light glowing red from Fiddy's front lawn: a small pup-tent flickering with a candle within. She sighed, shook her head, wrapped herself tighter in her housecoat and stepped outside.

"Are you in there, Fiddy?" she said when she reached the tent. She stood outside, waited for a response and when she received none, she pulled down the door zipper, stuck her head inside and surveyed what remained of Fiddy's life.

Fiddy was sitting with her rump on a pillow at the head of a sleeping bag, waving the broken curling iron over a solitary candle to heat it up. Her tiara and several cleaned stones glittered in the light next to the candle. "What on earth are you doing out here?!" Mirabella demanded, so harshly that Fiddy flinched and nearly dropped the curling iron.

"Hello, Mirabella," she said with regained dignity. "So nice of you to stop in. Would you like a cup of cherry tea? A scone? How about some baked Alaska?" She drew out a lock of hair and wrapped it around the hot iron.

"Where did you get this tent?"

"Johnny's children loaned it to me."

"You should stay with me tonight. I have room."

Fiddy put down the curling iron and grimaced. "In a *trailer*?"

"Yes. In my trailer. You can't stay out here. It might rain tonight and this tent isn't waterproof. You'll freeze."

Fiddy shook her hair out of the curling iron and looked at herself in a small piece of broken mirror. Her hair had a bit more tousle to it but she would need more time to make it *glamourous*. She sighed and waved the curling iron over the candle to warm it up again. "Mirabella, you really should know by now that the eternal summer rages in my heart and will never fade. The eye of heaven shines with light upon me and floods my soul with warmth. I shall always glow with a golden heat that sweeps me into endless –"

"Would you stop with that ridiculous gibberish! You can't stay out here!"

Fiddy calmly wrapped a string of hair in the heated iron. "I can, I will and I shall," she said.

Mirabella pointed to the stones. "Aren't you afraid someone will steal your diamonds?"

"Of course not." Fiddy put down the curling iron and reached under the edge of her sleeping bag. "That's why I have this." She pulled out a double-barreled shot gun, aimed it at Mirabella's face and cocked it.

Mirabella howled and dropped the flap between them. "Put that thing away! You could hurt someone!" She waited for a moment and peered back inside. Fiddy was still aiming it at her.

"I said put it away!"

Fiddy placed the gun within easy reach on her sleeping bag, picked up her curling iron and resumed curling. "I do say, Mirabella, you can be positively precocious."

"You don't even know what that word means."

"I do so. It means simply terrible."

"Where did you get that gun?"

"The children borrowed it for me from their father."

Mirabella gasped. "From Johnny? He's going to kill them. Does he know you have it?"

Fiddy shrugged.

Mirabella tried to make her voice sound less harsh. "Listen, Fiddy. You can stay in my spare room until you figure out something more permanent."

"Stop trying to force me into the bridle, Mirabella. I'm to be free like a dove with seven extra wings, flying higher than the swallows and soaring over the seas, across plains and –"

"Fine then." Mirabella let the flap fall and marched back to the trailer. At the top of the steps she stopped with her hand on the door. "You've given me no choice," she warned. "I'm calling Adult Protection to have you committed."

Inside the tent, Fiddy put down the curling iron. "Committed to what?"

Mirabella played her trump card. "To a nursing home."

A pause. Mirabella watched the tent. It began to shake.

"Wait a minute, Mirabella! I'm coming!"

Fiddy struggled to get out through the flaps, her two hands cupping her stones and her foot attempting to open the zipper. The tent quaked and shifted violently as she tried to force her foot out. "Don't call Adult Protection! I'm coming!"

As Mirabella continued to watch she saw Fiddy's shadow dip and swoop. Then the shotgun went off and one of Mirabella's kohlrabi exploded in the garden. "You killed one of my kohlrabi!" she cried.

Silence. The tent no longer moved. "Fiddy? Are you all right?"

There was a long pause before Fiddy started screaming. "I'm hit! I'm hit! Dear God, I'm hit!" She wailed like a sparrow caught on barbed wire.

Mirabella waited with arms crossed until the wailing became a whimper. "Well? Are you dead or do you want me to finish the job?"

Fiddy groaned and finally managed to get a foot and some of her body through the door of the tent. "You don't care a figment about me or my wants, do you?" she pouted.

Mirabella moved through the door. "If you were hurt, you'd be screaming like a stuck pig," she said.

"I was!"

"You weren't. That was no more than a hamster getting a bruise. Besides, I could see your shadow next to the candle."

"Hmpf." Fiddy finally escaped the tent and trotted across the lawn. She stood at the bottom of the steps, cupping her diamonds in her hands, her tiara dangling from her wig. "I could have been frozen in terror, you know."

"When people are shot, they don't freeze in terror. They're just like animals. Didn't you ever see a wounded rabbit? They wail, whine, scream, moan and sob when they're suffering. Last winter I had to chase one to the top of Black Mountain. It was dragging itself by its front paws. It cried, sobbed and shrieked until I whacked its head against a rock ten or twelve times. Finally, the neck broke."

Fiddy looked at her in horror. "Papa used to call me Bunny."

"I know what death looks like," Mirabella concluded. "It isn't nice." She held the door open for Fiddy.

Fiddy looked as though she wasn't entirely sure she wanted to stay with Mirabella now. While Mirabella waited, Fiddy looked across the lawn at the tent still glowing red with the candle flickering within. While she watched, the tent exploded in a *poof*, presumably catching a spark from the candle. The sleeping bag and pillow smouldered for a few seconds and went dark. "I suppose I could stay with you for a while," Fiddy sighed. "I'll help you get back on your feet. Then, however, I must take my leave."

Mirabella held the door for her. "Don't you know you aren't supposed to have candles in tents?"

"Don't be so dreadful phlegmatic." Fiddy entered and Mirabella came in behind her.

Fiddy stepped into the kitchen and sat down at the table with a small sigh. "Did you eat yet? I'm farmished."

Mirabella was already regretting her charity. She took the kettle from the stove and ran the tap. "It's *pragmatic*, not *phlegmatic*. And there's no such word as *farmishe*d. It's *famished*."

Fiddy rolled her eyes and adopted her British accent. "Words aren't what they mean, dearest Mirabella. It's what they're *attended* to mean."

"You mean *intende*d – what they're *intended* to mean."

"That's precisely the point you're misting."

Mirabella resisted the urge to knock Fiddy's head with the kettle and instead dropped it to the stove with a crash, turned on the heat and pressed the kettle into the burner to make it heat up faster.

Fiddy looked around. "This is such a . . . charming . . . little place." The kitchen opened up into the adjoining livingroom where there were four straight-backed chairs, a chesterfield, a coffee table with several pictures of dead relatives on it and a small television set. The walls were covered with what looked to her like needlework. One was of a bluebird on a yellow flower. Others included a barn with a fence, a green field with a pony, an old-fashioned well with a hanging basket of green plants, one of a squirrel in a tree, and dozens of others which were combinations of these themes. It was Mirabella's July collection, a week early.

"They're simply lovely," Fiddy remarked. "Needlepoint is so . . ." She struggled for the words while Mirabella waited for them to come scurrying across the kitchen floor like mice so that she could jump on them. "*Provincial.*"

"It's not needlepoint. It's crewel."

"A more fitting name for it, I should say. I've got a far too delicate constitution for such things."

She continued to survey Mirabella's dwelling. The chesterfield was a dark floral pattern of browns and yellows. The end tables held ornate lamps with needlepoint – or crewel – lampshades under protective plastic wrap. There were crewel doilies, crewel coasters, crewel picture frames, crewel covers for the arms of the chesterfield and a crewel cover for the pot of a dreary plant on the coffee table near the small bay window. Ribbed plastic mats designed for extra grip covered the burgundy carpet in front of the chesterfield and the chairs, all of which were arranged at right angles to each other. A path of mats led to the tiny television set.

Mirabella found Fiddy's silent inspection insulting. "What are you looking at?" she demanded.

"Why do you have plastic mats on the floor?" asked a careful Fiddy.

"To protect the carpet from wearing of course."

"Oh. Capital."

Mirabella pressed down harder on the kettle and it sizzled for a moment. She lifted it off and poured some of the water into the sink and put it back on the burner where it sizzled again. She went back to the sink, dried the beads of steaming water with a piece of paper towel and discarded it into the garbage can. She went to the refrigerator. "I have some cold chicken. I suppose you want to eat it."

"That would be simply gorgeous, Mirabella. But you don't have to do it for me." She continued to sit still, however, hoping Mirabella would.

Mirabella did. She constructed a sandwich in a flurry of motion, made tea from the not-quite-boiling water, threw an assortment of condiment jars on the table, presented the meal to Fiddy and hovered over her to watch.

Fiddy slowly lifted a piece of the sandwich to her mouth and watched Mirabella out of the corner of her eye.

"Why don't you have some green-gourd-marmalade-sauce?" Mirabella asked suddenly, just before Fiddy could get the sandwich to her mouth. Mirabella lifted the bottle from the table and placed it next to Fiddy's plate.

"I don't think so," said Fiddy, looking unfavourably upon the green paste.

"It's very good."

"I don't like green marmalade." She lifted the sandwich to her mouth.

"It's made from green gourds. It's very good. You should try it."

Fiddy sighed and looked up at Mirabella. "I'm fine," she

said.

"You don't even know how good it is. You should try some of it."

"I don't want it!" Fiddy wailed. "Won't you just let me eat in peace?!"

"You don't have to yell. I'm only right beside you."

Fiddy shot a dirty glance at her.

Mirabella couldn't help but watch the unopened, neglected jar of green-gourd-marmalade-sauce. She picked it up and removed the cover.

"I don't want any," Fiddy said with her mouth full.

Mirabella put a dab of it on her plate. "Just try it. It's very good. See how good it is." Fiddy sputtered with fury.

For the next fifteen minutes, Mirabella stood over Fiddy and asked her why she wasn't trying the green-gourd-marmalade-sauce. She told her it was a sin to waste. She reminded her of all the starving children in the world. She told her how very good the green-gourd-marmalade-sauce was. Finally, with Fiddy weakening, she scraped the green-gourd-marmalade-sauce from the plate with a spoon and held it to Fiddy's face. "Just try it."

"What are you going to do, feed it to me?!"

"Take the spoon yourself then." Mirabella handed it over. Fiddy held the spoon and glanced up at Mirabella, her face a wonder of disbelief, then back at the spoon. "It looks like pond scum," she said.

"You don't have to worry," Mirabella added. "It's not sweet. It's just pure, mashed, boiled gourds." No cholesterol. No fat. No sugar. No taste.

Fiddy's eyes went back into her head and she swayed queasily. Then she sighed in defeat, forced the spoon into her mouth and swallowed. "There," she said, her mouth frowning. "I tried it."

Mirabella took the spoon, a flash of victory on her face. "I told you it was good." Fiddy nodded miserably. Mirabella held up the plate with the second half of the sandwich. Fiddy took it and Mirabella suddenly began clearing the table. Jars of condiments went back into the refrigerator, the salt and pepper back to the cupboard;

the margarine went, as did the milk, the napkins, the cutlery and Fiddy's glass of water. Her plate gone, Fiddy held her sandwich aloft with one hand until Mirabella came back to the table from washing the dishes at the sink. "I can't finish this," she said, surrendering it.

"Well, you're not going to waste it. Think of all the starving children in the world. Think of children searching crates of rotten tomatoes for something to eat."

"It's only a bit of crust and some chicken. In England they never eat their crusts."

"That's a damn lie."

"It isn't! I swear!"

"Then they're all going to hell." Mirabella went to the cupboard, returned with a zipper bag and made Fiddy put the remains of the sandwich inside. She sealed it on her way to the refrigerator where she deposited it on the top shelf. "While you're in my house, you will eat your crusts," she said. "You could have been one of those starving children with nothing to eat but rotting garbage. Ingratitude towards God, that's all that is. When people lose the things they take for granted, like food or –" She glared at Fiddy – "*shelter,* that's when they discover how fortunate they really are." She slammed the refrigerator door and the jars inside rattled together as though in fright. She went into the livingroom, straightened the plastic mat near the chesterfield and stepped back into the kitchen. "If you look after the pennies, the nickels will look after themselves."

Fiddy took a sip of tea. "Who on earth cares about nickels?"

"Oh, I forgot. You're far too rich to be worried about nickels."

"Wealth speaks for itself. Or, when it's old money like mine, it need only whisper." She rose from the table with her tea and moved into the livingroom. Mirabella swooped down on the kitchen table to remove the lone remaining spoon. She took it quickly to the sink to sterilize it.

"That's my seat," she said without looking, as Fiddy was about to sit down on the chesterfield. "Sit over there." She pointed with the back of her head to a straight-backed chair in the corner. Fiddy complied, carefully keeping to the path of mats.

Mirabella finished washing, drying, polishing and putting away the spoon. She cleaned the sink, wiped her hands with half a piece of paper towel and deposited it in the garbage. Then she went to the seat which Fiddy had almost appropriated and fell like a landslide to her knees on the plastic mat. The trailer shook with the impact.

"What in the name of the Kingdom of India are you doing?!"

"We," Mirabella hissed, "are going to say our bedtime prayers."

"Oh," said Fiddy. "My knees are too sore from praying in the chapel all morning so I'll stay here."

Mirabella glared at her for a moment but then took a deep breath and bulldozed into sets of prayers and novenas with unrelenting speed, without taking another breath for a full seven minutes. Words, words, and more words lashed out of Mirabella's mouth like machine gun fire, riddling the air with thousands of syllables every second. Her tongue moved so fast it was a blur within her mouth. It was like an enslaved sprite which knew what it had to do and did it without any help at all from Mirabella's mind. Or from her heart for that matter.

When the prayers were over, the trailer was filled suddenly with a vacuum of silence. Fiddy blinked a few times, as if coming out of a matinee into bright sunshine, and wondered if she shouldn't contact the Guinness people. Surely to pray every Latin prayer followed by the entire litany of the saints, followed by every known prayer and injunction in the English language, all within seven minutes, was a world record.

"I'll make up your bed," Mirabella said, getting up. She went down the hallway and returned with sheets and pillows and began removing the cushions from the chesterfield.

"I thought you said you had a spare room."

"That's Mama's room."

Fiddy looked at her in confusion. Mirabella's mother had been dead for at least fifteen years. Had Mirabella kept her mother's corpse? A dead, dried, wrinkled mummy with empty eye sockets, lying in the bed, covered with cobwebs and dust? "Mirabella," Fiddy asked sweetly. "Isn't your mother dead?"

"So?"

"So, I do say, is she still in there or what?"

Mirabella pointed a finger at her. "Don't you mock the dead!"

"Mirabella, darling, sweetheart, with as much drama possible, I simply cannot sleep on a chesterfield. My back won't take it, and if I'm in pain, my voice will suffer. I'd be nothing but the softest of deranged whimpers. I'm called to be an orchestra, not a whimper, and the four winds that await my whistles in the morning dew will never –"

"Oh, shut up." Mirabella had no idea what Fiddy was talking about but she would endure no more of it. At the same time, a seed of doubt had inserted itself into her mind. Was she being unreasonable about her mother's room? She looked to the hallway. No one had slept in the room since her mother had died there. The bureau was still filled with her mother's clothes. The silver bell her mother had used to ring for her was still on the night table, beside the same small shot glass she'd used for the water she took with her medication. The red wool blanket Mirabella had placed every night over her mother's tiny frame was still folded neatly at the bottom of the bed. Letting a nosy and noisy intruder such as Fiddy into the room would be to defile the place.

But perhaps she was being sentimental and sentimentality was an impractical emotion. She mustered up her strength. "Fine," she said. "If you don't want to sleep on a perfectly good chesterfield, fine with me." She shoved a cushion back into place. "I'll make up Mama's bed, but if you touch a single thing in the room, I'll cut off your fingers and feed them to the crows."

Fiddy followed Mirabella to the room and watched from the doorway as Mirabella stripped the corpseless bed and remade it with clean sheets. After that, Mirabella moved the silver bell and shot glass to the bureau in case Fiddy should knock them over and left the room with the red wool blanket over her arm.

"You won't need this," she said. "If you need air, open the window. I'll wake you before I leave for work in the morning."

"This is simply delightful, Mirabella. I will never forget your kindness. You are a gem in the firmament of love."

Mirabella winced.

Fiddy stepped into the room and gently closed the door. "Goodnight!" she sang through the last crack.

Mirabella shook her head on her way down the hallway to the livingroom where she began her bedtime ritual. On all fours, she checked the mats and carpet for signs of smoke or heat in case an ember from her last cigarette had fallen there. She swiped her arm underneath the chesterfield, carefully palpating for signs of heat. She unplugged the television set and lamps in case a sudden lightning storm struck in the night and they exploded. She turned the plant on the coffee table thirty degrees clockwise so that the morning sun would strike new leaves. She tightened the taps in the kitchen and bathroom. She went back to the kitchen to make sure she'd turned off all the burners on the stove. She unplugged the microwave and toaster, checked that the refrigerator was still running and then stood in the middle of the kitchen floor looking and listening for any signs of impending disaster. All appeared to be okay. She straightened the plastic mat next to Fiddy's chair and headed to her bedroom.

On her way, she noticed the light under Fiddy's door and stopped. Not in years had she seen that light and it made her feel odd. She listened to Fiddy's soft noises – hanging up her clothes, shoes hitting the floor, soft humming, the bed springs as Fiddy lay down. It all made her feel somehow violated and angry at Fiddy's presence. Then she remembered her charity and went to bed.

FIDDY SAT ON THE EDGE of her bed and was perfectly contented, despite the small drab cell she found herself in. The walls were made of trailer material, a substance not quite wood and not quite plastic, covered in a wallpaper that was remarkably similar to most of Mirabella's blouses – grey pinstripe in navy blue, brown and beige. Fiddy clicked off the light, pulled the covers up around her chin, groaned softly with pleasure and closed her eyes. She was in a tomb but at least it was a warm and comfortable tomb. She was safe from marauding animals. Her stomach was full and tomorrow would be a new and glorious day.

Everything had gone so well, she thought. True, her house had burned down, at the hands of some rascal. Perhaps he was the one who had burned down her tent too. Her possessions were gone, but she had her tiara and her diamonds, thanks partly to Mirabella who had rescued her. What a friend!

She was sleepy and began releasing herself to the sweet suitor of the night. As she dozed toward the happy state she wondered if Mirabella would ask her to stay – perhaps for as long as she wanted while her new house was being built. That would be just the thing a friend would do.

The comfort of the bed drew her deeper into the land of dreams. Mirabella presented her with a bouquet of roses. *Please stay*, she begged.

Then she was pleading on her knees in the hallway. *Fiddy, you've brought such joy to my home, I don't know how I could live without having you here. Could you stay? Just for a year or two?*

Fiddy promised to think about it. She struggled her way down the hallway with Mirabella clinging to her legs. In the bathroom Fiddy was able to open the closet. "Oh, Mirabella, you shouldn't have!" There, among the towels and pressed linens, Mirabella had concealed an orchestra. "Sing for us Fiddy!" they chimed.

"Yes, please," begged Mirabella from the floor. "Just one song."

Desdemona Pacifico-Rossini walked onto centre stage and began to sing.

[FOUR]

Air is emptiness: man has weight.
Unsupported I drop like lead
To where my body awakes in bed .

– C.S. Lewis: *After Vain Pretence*

THE AUDIENCE HAD NEVER HEARD anything like it. Desdemona Pacifico-Rossini sang her signature pieces from *I Pagliacci* and *La Bohem*e, and Milan fainted before her. Her notes sought out the highest limits of La Scala, and as she finished, they froze in mid-air like leaves of crystal so delicate the audience couldn't breathe lest they shatter. Next she sang the greatest *mezzo* pieces from *Turandot*. That brought them to their feet with cheers. She went on to Handel's *alto* piece, *But who may abide the day of His coming*, and they raged like a thunderstorm. Such splendor, such deftness, such finesse! Even a thunderstorm was insufficient exaltation for her. They stomped their feet and threw flowers and money at the stage. They shook their fists and screamed and writhed against each other like frenzied animals. And when they realized there was nothing else they could do to applaud the majesty, they wept. Desdemona Pacifico-Rossini wept with them. She didn't understand it either. She was just the one who delivered the Voice.

She was standing at centre stage, wondering what she could do to comfort the weeping audience, when the air was split with a series of gun shots, as loud as cannons. She shrieked and quickly felt her arms and gown for the wound but found none. When she looked up, however, her audience had vanished.

Fiddy opened her eyes and sat up in bed. "Mirabella!" she screamed. She stumbled out to the hallway.

Mirabella was in the kitchen with her gun aimed out the door. "I won't miss the next time!" she hollered and let another shot go.

It was so loud Fiddy could feel it in her rib cage.

A cloud of dust rose up from a quickly departing vehicle.

"By God's hounds, what are you doing?!" cried Fiddy.

Mirabella pulled the gun inside, closed the door against the dust and released the shell from the barrel. "Protecting my property, that's what." Her eyes were blazing blue.

"From what, prithee?"

"That pig."

"A pig?" Fiddy asked in amazement. "And it was driving a car?" She'd heard of flying pigs but never driving pigs.

"No, you ninny. Gorble Gote."

"Gorble?" Fiddy went to the window and scanned the driveway. "You should have woken me. He probably wanted to see me. What did he say?"

Mirabella put her gun in the closet. "Nothing. He's just a nuisance."

"He must have said something."

Mirabella didn't answer. She went to the sink and ran the water. "It's about time you're up," she said. "You can't sleep away the whole day."

Fiddy put her hands on her hips. "I want to know what he wanted!"

Mirabella started scrubbing her hands. "I have some things to go over with you before I go to work," she said.

"Stop!" Fiddy screamed. She stomped a foot on the floor. "I know what he wanted! Now why won't you just admit it to me?!"

Mirabella stopped scrubbing. "What did he want?"

Fiddy thumped her foot impatiently. "I'm not stupid, Mirabella. Gentlemen come calling on me all the time. In the future I would appreciate it if you would direct them to me."

Mirabella nearly laughed. Gorble Gote was a short, whiskered, pot-bellied bootlegger who belonged to the breed of locals known as *scruff.* He'd come looking for Fiddy to give her his condolences for the fire, and had hinted that to get through the tough times, perhaps Fiddy should partake in some of the pleasures of life. When he'd attempted to hand Mirabella, with his greasy hand, a half pint of whiskey to give Fiddy, she'd gone for her gun.

"You're right," said Mirabella, willing to win the argument by losing it. "Next time I'll let you handle it."

"Good," said Fiddy. "I hope you learned your lesson. You should never assume that I wouldn't be interested in entertaining gentleman callers. In fact you can expect that for the duration of this time I've agreed to stay with you that a great many of my admirers will be stopping by to see if they can catch a glimpse of me . . ."

Fiddy continued her lecture at a hypertensive pace while Mirabella turned from the sink and faced her. Mirabella didn't listen to the words – she simply tried to bore holes in Fiddy's head with thoughts of unmitigated hatred. Soon, Fiddy lost track of what she was saying and fumbled for words. She warned Mirabella not to drop the watermelon, then corrected herself, backed up, tried again but strained against Mirabella's stabbing glare. Suddenly Fiddy saw herself in a headlock and being pulled by the neck out the door; Mirabella pushing her down the sandpaper-covered steps to the ground; Fiddy trying to scramble away on her hands and knees across the lawn; Mirabella raising a large weapon, like an oar, over her head. She closed her eyes on a flash of blood and hair. "I'm too young to die, Mirabella!" she shouted.

"Then keep your mouth shut."

Fiddy shut her mouth.

Mirabella finished at the sink and handed Fiddy five lists. "I'm going to work. Follow these lists and don't do anything that's not on them. If you have a question about whether you should touch something, taste something, poke something or use something, read the lists and if you can't find the answer in the lists, the answer is no, you can't touch it, taste it, poke it or use it. Do you understand?"

Fiddy looked at the lists in confusion.

"Do you understand?!" Mirabella shouted.

"Yes!" Fiddy shouted back. "I understand completely! Do nothing. Touch nothing. Follow the lists. I get it. Do you take me for an imbecile?"

Mirabella took up her purse and headed to the door. "I won't answer that." She left.

Fiddy went to the window to watch her leave. She looked for Mirabella and was startled when a hand, like a club, reached into the window box directly in front of her and snatched a geranium bud.

"What the . . . why won't you let them bloom?"

Mirabella pretended not to hear from the other side of the glass.

"Let us bloom, why don't you!" Fiddy hollered but Mirabella calmly got into the car and took off down the drive. "Ingrate!"

What a trial this was, thought Fiddy in despair. Helping dear Mirabella was a challenge meant for a god. Mirabella should be thrilled with having Desdemona Pacifico-Rossini staying with her. How many times did Gorble Gote visit otherwise? Probably never.

Maybe, now that Fiddy thought about it, she would only stay with Mirabella for a few months instead of years. One year at the most, but only if Mirabella mended her ways and began to treat her better. And if she begged – convincingly. Then maybe Fiddy would stay with her, for a year at most, while having her new house built, perhaps somewhere near the beach where she would always hear the Northumberland. Maybe Johnny and Martha would let her build on a lot next to them, not a house as big as Applefern Mansion, but slightly smaller so they could still claim supremacy in Wintry Hope.

She snapped out of her reverie and looked at the lists in her hand, surprised that she could actually feel Mirabella's writing on them. Mirabella's razor-sharp, serial-killer lettering was etched into the paper as if she'd used a nail to write. The first list was entitled Prohibitions. She was prohibited from setting fires, entering or watering the garden, cleaning or doing any housework, mowing the lawn, using the blue towels, chopping wood or doing any other chore exclusively reserved as Mirabella's. "Not a problem, sweetheart," Fiddy said, tossed the lists on the table and headed to the bathroom.

She avoided the woman in the mirror for the time being and attempted to turn on the hot water. The tap wouldn't budge. She tried with both hands but it still wouldn't move. She took a deep breath, contorted her face, put as much of her hip into it as she could, and when she felt as though her arms would detach at the shoulders, let out an agonized squeal and pushed even harder. Nothing. She tried the cold water tap and it turned easily with the effort of two fingers.

She washed quickly with the cold water and to get even with Mirabella, brushed her dentures with Mirabella's toothbrush.

She couldn't remember whether to use the blue or green towels but decided on the blue. After a thorough, yet unsuccessful, search for makeup in Mirabella's medicine cabinet, she confronted the pale, wrinkled face looking back at her from the mirror.

She needed makeup. Badly. The fiery red hair was still beautiful and had held its curls throughout the night, but the small brown eyes looked like squashed raisins. Too bad she hadn't saved her boudoir and the makeup it contained from her burning house. If Mirabella had any ambition at all, she would have picked up the boudoir, slung it over her back and taken it down the ladder to save it from that horrible fire.

With no boudoir and no makeup, her natural beauty would have to do. She sucked in her cheeks and opened her eyes as wide as she could. Her skin was dusty white. Her cheekbones disappeared somewhere within the wrinkled skin sagging down from her eyes. Her forehead had swollen to a monstrous size during the night and she needed to paint some eyebrows in there somewhere to break up the vast distance. With no lipstick, her thin lips disappeared when she smiled. Her cheeks were already cramping with sucking them in and her eyes were watering from being held open too wide. Perhaps her natural beauty could use a little embellishment after all.

She headed to Mirabella's bedroom. Surely Mirabella had *something* she could use. She opened the forbidden door slowly, exhilarated by the danger of entering Mirabella's lair. The room was as dark as a deep pit. The curtains, which looked like black burlap, kept out every hint of sunlight. Fiddy found the light switch and a small lamp came on next to a bed, surprisingly small for Mirabella's dragon size.

The bed sat close to the floor as though its legs had been cut off. It was comprised of steel bars painted white and reminded Fiddy of a self-contained insane asylum. She stepped toward the eight-drawer bureau and rifled through the items on top. She found an eyebrow pencil and a surprisingly attractive shade of lipstick. She furtively applied them both without the assistance of a mirror as if they were items of precious food and she'd just spent six months in a concentration camp. Relieved, she moved on to Mirabella's closet to begin sorting through her clothes.

There was nothing, not a single gown, cocktail dress or swan suit. Only navy blue, grey or brown slacks and blouses, all drab, all utilitarian, all old. The polyester slacks were shiny with ironing and the blouses were threadbare from continuously fierce washing. Poverty, thought Fiddy, should be illegal. "No wonder she's such a crab," she muttered and tried to concentrate on making a selection.

AFTER BREAKFAST Fiddy sat, in Mirabella's tight clothes, in Mirabella's place on the chesterfield, with Mirabella's phone in hand, and tried to establish her social calendar for the day. She clicked the receiver a few times, wondering if the line had gone dead. Mabel MacIsaac had been disconnected, it appeared, for the third time. Fiddy would try her friend Henrietta Gillis. She dialed and it rang. Twice, three times, four times. At a hundred and six, Henrietta Gillis was the oldest person in Wintry Hope, so Fiddy let the phone ring, and ring, and ring, in case dear old Henrietta needed extra time to get out of the bathtub, come down from a ladder or push her walker up the stairs from the basement. After the twenty-third ring, an elderly woman's feeble voice came on. "Hello?"

"Hello, Henrietta. It's Fiddy. I was wondering if – "

The phone was slammed against something solid – perhaps a wall or a stone bench – four or five times and, apparently, also disconnected.

Undaunted, Fiddy dialed another number. "Who is this?" demanded Mrs Crowe, picking up the phone midway through the first ring as if ready to accuse whoever it was of indecent assault.

"Fiddy Washburn."

"What do you want?"

"I just wanted to chat with you. It's been so long. How are you today?"

"I've got rheumatism and cancer of the spine. What do you want?"

Fiddy shifted nervously. She hated having to get to the point of any matter. "Do you happen to be going to Achievement Day?"

"Of course I am. I haven't missed an Achievement Day in

fifty years. Did you think I was going to miss this one?"

"No, of course not. That's why I'm calling. I was wondering if I might get a drive with you."

"But you live on the other side of Wintry Hope."

"It's only a couple of miles."

"But I might not go until later."

"That's okay."

"But I might go early."

"That's okay too."

"But I might not go at all. I've got a headache and I might be taking a stroke. Besides, my feet are too hot and the sun hurts my eyes and I chipped my tooth on a piece of toast this morning and now" – her voice lowered to a croak – "my voice hurts from talking so much and having to explain myself. My knees are cramped and I've got a congenital hip that makes it difficult to go to the bathroom and I may need some help to have a bowel –"

Fiddy slipped the phone onto its receiver and pulled her hands away from it as though it were a snake. She could tolerate almost anything except talk of bowel movements.

She wondered who else she could call for a drive. She went down a mental list of her other friends. Most of them were either dead, legally incompetent or were never her friends to begin with. "Won't anybody listen?" she scowled, stood up from the chesterfield and let full frustration take root. "Sugar!" she yelled into the ceiling with fist upraised. "Sugar!" How was she supposed to get to Achievement Day? It was at least three miles away. Perhaps it was only two, but she couldn't walk even one mile in her heels.

She went to the window and looked out across the lawn to the charred ruins of her house. The bulldozer had finished leveling it off. Nothing remained of Fiddy's past except for a blackened foundation and a pile of rubble. "All I want is a drive," she said dismally. "In a nice car. With air conditioning and a handsome driver. And maybe a glass of *merlot*. Is that too much for the prettiest girl in Wintry Hope?"

No one answered. All she could hear was the annoying drone of the refrigerator. She hummed softly from her favourite musical,

The Sound of Music, in her opinion the greatest piece of musical theatre in history:

Rainbows on kittens,
and six pounds of codfish . . .

She grasped the curtain, like Julie Andrews did in the movie version, and wished she had a wig of short blonde hair.

A fortune in rubies . . .
and small, wrinkled raisins . . .
Brown paper sandwiches,
Tied up with string.
These are a few of my favourite things . . .

She smiled. Singing always brought her back to life and she knew that if she were to rush to the bathroom to visit the woman in the mirror she'd find her smiling too, and beautiful. She broke away from the window with a burst of new energy and was about to sing out more music when she stopped. Her mind munched on a possibility. Indeed, she thought, it just might work! She laughed. Now she knew how she would get to the community centre. She pranced her way across the kitchen, bounded out the door and headed across the lawn toward her property.

Surely, driving a bulldozer wasn't that much different than driving a car.

She was surprised, when she got it going, that a machine as large as five elephants could only go at the pace of an ant. Mirabella's driveway was nearly half a mile from the highway so it took what felt like a long time for the bulldozer to inch its way down. On the way, she sang a Wagner piece she felt harmonized beautifully with the bulldozer's rumbling bass. She didn't know how to stop the bulldozer, nor how to turn it, so when she reached the highway she pulled the only lever she hadn't yet pulled. The bulldozer drifted to the right and demolished three mailboxes, including her own and one ornately decorated like a miniature trailer. She discovered another lever, pulled it and the bulldozer shot across the highway into the ditch. She screamed in terror as she entered the great marsh of Wintry Hope, clinging for all she was worth to the levers and knobs around her.

[FIVE]

> Whippoorwill – First proven to breed in Nova Scotia in 1930 but is very scarce. The whippoorwill is best known for its long, ghostly song which it only ever sings at night. It is unlikely to become more common, unless with the impact of global warming, and it could disappear without most people ever noticing its absence.
>
> – **Johnson and Schwartz:** ***Maritime Atlas of Birds***

THE MARSH OF WINTRY HOPE slouches in the middle of the village and takes up more than half of the community between the western plains and the land claimed by Applefern Mansion in the east. Black puddles begin, like the footprints of water nymphs, among humps of grass at the edge of the mansion's gardens, form small moats around brambles and berry bushes, grow as big as the occasional pond in the middle of the marsh and thin out near the plains on the western side of Wintry Hope beyond which the brook teases.

The Agent had studied every inch of the marsh. She entered it usually from behind the community centre and loved to roam at random, sometimes ending up at the shore of the Northumberland, sometimes at Applefern which she was forced to shrink away from, sometimes at the extinct volcano overlooking the road to the wharves and beach. Sometimes she ended up at the brook which she could follow downstream to the Northumberland or upstream into the wooded foothills of the Sgairian mountains where Mirabella's trailer was. Today she planned to stay in the heart of the marsh, as far from the mansion, the wharves, the highway and all other forms of human civilization as she could get. She needed respite from noisy cars, groaning lobster trucks, fire engines, radios, sirens and all people intent on destroying her planet.

In the marsh, she was free to be with her friends, the birds that alighted among sedges and grasses, diddled in its ponds or nested among the cattails. She used a digital recorder to capture their songs, like the eastern phoebe, kittiwake or, if she were exceedingly lucky, the whippoorwill. She had only one recording of the whippoorwill as it was a rare, evasive bird. She'd had to stay in the marsh all night, many consecutive nights in order to catch the song. Sitting motionless for endless hours among peepers, crickets and all manner of slithery things, on the fourth night, she'd been rewarded. Just before dawn, before the birth of the sun, the bedlam of the marsh went mysteriously quiet. She listened. She waited. In the movement from dawn to morning, the world had stalled so that nothing moved, nothing sounded. Only then did the whippoorwill's song emerge into the misty air, a long lament. A moment later, the lonely cry had faded away in the sunshine and the willets were soaring, the bitterns gulping and the ditty of sharp-tailed sparrows announcing the reveille. The Agent had fumbled with her recorder to find out whether she'd simply imagined the song or if she'd actually caught it. She listened. She'd caught it. Her skin tingled as though she were hearing a phantom that had appeared briefly and left. A singular triumph.

The Agent loved her marsh. She loved everything in it. She even loved the four-toed salamander and the surly brown toad covered in dark warts.

The sun was shining hot overhead, the bees were humming busily on the blossoms and a breeze carried floral scents in airy streams around her. With Twig on her back, her recorder ready, and her sketch pad in hand, she moved through the marsh. She took in every flower, shrub, and blade of grass. She saw the flash of a frog disappearing into a puddle. She found an iris and touched its tightly bound bud carefully between two fingers, marveling at the delicate elegance of its stem. Another bud had opened to reveal downward arching petals, dripping toward the ground like tears. She took out her pad and sketched it. In her sketch, however, she made the petals white instead of blue. It was foolish, she knew, to pine after the white iris but she couldn't help it. She searched for it every spring, and she would continue to search for it despite the fact that it was most likely extinct. In the meantime, it grew to life on her paper.

As she sketched, she heard nearby ducks chatting. She moved some sedges aside and saw to her delight a pair of mergansers building a nest in the open water. She shaded the busy mergansers into the page, with the white irises in the foreground. As she sketched, her feet sank slowly into the black mud. She didn't mind. It was comforting to have a part of her grasped or even trapped by the muck of the marsh. She trusted the marsh. It could do with her what it pleased.

The mergansers' eyes were the most difficult to sketch. They had a strange quality about them, as if they should be blind. Black points of glimmering onyx that flashed like lost coins. They had an empty essence she tried to capture, a quality of lacking . . . pretension? Motive? Thought? Whatever it was, the Agent found it impossible to uncover it in her charcoal.

She was making a third attempt when her hands and the usually stately cattails started to tremble. She looked to the sky in search of the rumbling, wondering if perhaps it was a surveillance plane the police used for detecting marijuana. The rumbling, however, grew too loud to be an overhead plane, and she could feel the marsh shivering nervously where it held her feet in fright. The birds went quiet. The rumbling grew to a roar until it seemed to surround her. She tried to step to higher ground to see beyond the cattails but the marsh wouldn't let go of her feet. Like someone drowning, the marsh had seized her in its fear.

She saw the blade of Fiddy's bulldozer come down on her just in time to scream.

BY THE TIME FIDDY found the highway again with the bulldozer, she had become an expert at bulldozer operation. She turned into the driveway of the community centre, missed the fencing around the softball field by at least two feet, scraped part of the vinyl siding off the building and parked neatly in the middle of a flower bed. She turned the key and the bulldozer sputtered, coughed and died. She stepped down gingerly, said a secret Hail Mary that Mirabella's slacks wouldn't split, and when they didn't she made her way like a penguin to the entrance.

Hector MacInnis was standing outside the door smoking. "Since when do you have a driver's license?" he growled as Fiddy waddled by.

"Excuse me?" she asked, the buzzing of the bulldozer still in her ears.

"The bulldozer," he growled again, pointing at it with his cigarette. "You're supposed to have a licence to drive that thing."

Fiddy looked with feigned surprise from Hector to the bulldozer and back to Hector again. "My dear old man," she said, "I have dramatic licence. I can drive anything."

She swept into the community centre and entered the main floor as if strolling into the lobby of the Waldorf Astoria. She was immediately enfolded by the sounds and scents of the local 4-H Achievement Day. The bleating of sheep, mooing of calves and squawking of poultry. Dishes rattled from the kitchen where home-cooked lunches were being served. Between the open doors and livestock at one end and the kitchen at the other, tables displayed the children's projects or sold locally produced goods. In an open area near a temporary stage, locals mingled while an auctioneer sought a bid of three dollars for a strawberry shortcake.

Fiddy stood under the welcome sign and felt a wave of pleasure. She loved the local fair, even if it was essentially rural. A celebrity from the city had an obligation to foster the arts in rural areas. She started by touring the children's projects: knitted mittens and hats, wooden toys, book shelves, macramé and découpage, lampshades made from popsicle sticks. After the crafts, she visited the animals – rabbits, chickens, ducks, hens, goats, sheep, pigs and cows. After exhausting all of the free entertainment, she stood alone near the washrooms to watch all the glorious forms of entertainment that could be purchased.

A fish tank for children guaranteed a surprise every time and only charged a dollar. Straws stuffed with pieces of paper were twenty-five cents for five and promised winnings of up to fifty dollars. There were draws for crocheted afghans, quilts, cakes and lobsters, guesses for an immense jar of jellybeans and silent auctions on everything from bottled preserves to an exhaust system for a tractor.

Fiddy coveted everything in sight and felt the surging desire within her to consume recklessly. With some effort she managed to wedge her hands into the pockets of Mirabella's slacks in the hopes of finding a forgotten bill. Nothing. Not even a nickel. She considered borrowing someone's hat – Hector Gillis had been wearing one – putting it down on the floor and singing for money. That, however, might be perceived by the Achievement Day committee as unlicenced competition. There were ways of obtaining money other than earning it, she told herself.

She could borrow. The twelve-year-old girl selling homemade fudge refused to advance her credit of any kind. Neither would the boy taking money for guesses on the jellybean jar. And by that time everyone who handled currency in the community centre had been notified of her poor credit and promptly shook their heads at her on sight. She spotted Mrs Crowe's small, hunched frame negotiating for a set of steak knives at a hardware table and made for her.

"I thought you weren't coming," Fiddy said, trying to sound hurt. She tugged at Mrs Crowe's black shawl.

"I told you I didn't know when I was coming," Mrs Crowe clipped.

"You told me you were going to die."

Mrs Crowe clutched her wrinkled throat and coughed. "Yes, my throat is so sore and every bone in my body throbs with pain. I shouldn't even be talking to you." She turned and walked away, abandoning her attempt at the steak knives for the time being.

"Mrs Crowe!" Fiddy shouted.

Mrs Crowe stopped. Under her black shawl, the feathers on her back bristled like the needles of a cactus. She turned around and aimed her pointed nose at Fiddy. "What do you want?"

Fiddy pattered over to her. "My dear, Mrs Crowe, you will never guess what terrible calamity has befallen me. It's simply devastating. I was in my bedroom sleeping like a lily under the moonlight and a vicious intruder stole into my house, poured gasoline all over my beautiful livingroom and kitchen, set it all on fire and left me to burn. I was almost murdered – murdered! Can you imagine?!" She lowered her voice to a whisper. "They're investigating Mirabella. You know the Stuarts. A vicious streak in them. And now I've lost everything. Everything except, of course, for my diamonds. Diamonds can't be burned, thank goodness."

"Could you just get to the point?" sighed Mrs Crowe.

"I wanted to tell you about the Washburns and the Crowes. Did you know we fought together on Culloden Moor?"

"The Crowes are Welsh. We weren't anywhere near Culloden Moor."

"I wasn't talking about Culloden Moor. I was talking about the Battle of Waterloo."

"I thought you said Culloden Moor."

"You heard wrong. It must be your cancer. As I was saying, we Washburns, being a noble family, saved the Crowes in the Battle of Waterloo."

"So?"

"So, you owe me."

"Go to hell." Mrs Crowe turned to walk away.

"Wait!" Fiddy screamed.

Mrs Crowe froze and noticed that people from all over the community centre were watching them. She turned back and whispered harshly to Fiddy. "You're better off with no money at these things. The children are such thieves."

Fiddy yelled, "But you owe me!"

Mrs Crowe's eyes darted left and right. "Just the likes of you to throw a fit," she seethed. "I should have let your siblings kill you years ago when I was babysitting you. You're the one who owes me. Remember the strychnine? They wanted to use it to keep you quiet. I should have let them."

Of course Fiddy remembered the strychnine and she told Mrs Crowe how appalling it was that she would bring up something from so long ago. As the people around them looked on, Fiddy began to whimper. "I can't believe you wanted my siblings to poison me with strychnine," she moaned. She mumbled accusations against Mrs Crowe through sniffling and tears. Tears, Fiddy knew, were the most powerful weapon in any battle and even more so for a public one.

But Mrs Crowe suffered a tragic handicap on this front: she was one of those people who could not cry. She could manufacture no remorse of any kind for any occasion, and Fiddy knew it. Mrs. Crowe viewed even her own misfortunes with firm detachment, focusing any unsteady emotion into cold, steadfast hatred. In her ninety-five years and counting, everyone knew, she had been able to gush rivers of tears on only one triumphant occasion: when her husband had been found dead under a crate in her cellar with indentations on his forehead matching her cast iron frying pan. The police had at first looked at her suspiciously but the tears had kept them from asking questions.

"How much do you want?" Mrs. Crowe sighed, defeated.

"Twenty dollars."

"Twenty dollars?! That's highway robbery!"

"Waterloo changed the course of history. And prices this year are plenty high."

"I'll give you two and not a penny more."

"Ten."

"Five."

"Seven."

"Five. Take it or leave it."

"I'll take it." Fiddy held out her hand for the money and smiled winsomely.

Mrs Crowe slid a thin claw into her purse, slipped out a crisp five-dollar bill and gave it to Fiddy. "Take your money," she spat and went back to the hardware table to negotiate for the steak knives.

Fiddy quickly spent the five dollars and sat down on the bleachers next to the softball field. She ate a hotdog loaded with double the works and cheered the winners of a three-legged race with mouth full and sputtering relish. Father Francis came by and asked if she would be a judge for the children's skit competition and she shrieked with glee.

Mrs Crowe was sitting at the judge's table when Fiddy entered, trotting behind Father Francis like a happy puppy, and took her seat next to Mrs Crowe. Mrs Crowe looked down at the new set of steak knives at her feet – as if considering whether to stab Fiddy to death – but caught sight of her great-nephew next to the stage adjusting his costume. She smiled weakly at Fiddy, who fraternally returned the smile and settled in beside her.

The skits began. The first group of children were, by Fiddy's estimation, very good. Toward the end of the skit, however, one of the participants, who was dressed in a thick rabbit costume, started screaming uncontrollably for his father. One of the spectators, presumably the father, jumped up to the stage, dragged the boy outside, stripped off the costume and hosed him down with cold water. The unfortunate claustrophobic child eventually stopped screaming but the dramatic impact of the skit, to Fiddy's mind, had been considerably undermined.

The second group mimed their skit, a very artistic touch, Fiddy thought, but wholly inadequate as, in the end, a voice was necessary to truly see into the artist's soul.

The third group was disastrously disorganized. Comprised of some of the older boys, they didn't take the exercise seriously enough for Fiddy's taste. Their acting, if one could call it that, was stilted, with no heart.

The fourth group, Fiddy decided, she would mark last. It wasn't just because she knew Mrs Crowe's great-nephew was in it but because of the unprofessional conduct of their prop: a chubby pig which alternated between bored sighs and unrestrained flatulence. Fiddy was horrified by the uncouth spectacle and couldn't understand how any civilized person would find it funny. But the crowd, including Mrs Crowe, went wild with laughter and the skit ended with raucous applause. It was a strange mystery to Fiddy.

The fifth group was unremarkable except that it had superior costuming. It was no small accomplishment to have designed and created convincing characters made entirely of different types of lettuce. Fiddy made a mental note to tell Mirabella.

When they were finished the three judges formed a conclave in the kitchen to determine the winner. Father Francis agreed with Fiddy that group four should be marked last. One of the children had blurted out the Lord's name in vain while stifling a laugh and waving a hand to disperse the smell of the pig. Mrs Crowe felt that the comic relief of a pig's flatulence was not only a brilliant touch but impossibly difficult to coordinate. She insisted group four should win. After a heated exchange and much wrangling over elements of delivery and oratorical technique, Mrs Crowe gave up. She couldn't sustain disagreement with a priest for very long. They made their collective decision and Fiddy accepted the task of informing the waiting audience.

The announcement wasn't intended to be an overly involving task. No one could have considered the possibility of Fiddy doing anything other than taking centre stage and blurting out the number of the winning group. But when she ascended the three steps to the stage and looked over the heads of the four or five dozen people watching, she felt the rush of a thousand bodily chemicals compelling her to perform.

"When you act," she began, as everyone in the audience rolled their eyes, "you must offer yourself completely – body and soul. You must feel the blood of your characters flowing through your own veins and arteries. You must feel their blood pumping through your heart and feeding your mind with their thoughts. You must love as your characters love, hate as your characters hate and suffer as your characters must suffer." She looked around the room and wondered how they could possibly understand someone with her level of dramatic experience. Impossible, she thought and changed tactics. "Let me demonstrate."

Ignoring their moans, she cleared her throat, wagged her red wave of hair to shake loose the inner cobwebs and adopted a posture befitting one of her favourite Shakespearean figures: Cleopatra. She looked to the ceiling and called for some hidden sprite, the audience following her eyes:

Where art thou, death?
Come hither, come! Come,
Come and take a queen
Worth many babes and beggars!

"Just tell us who the winner is!" Hector suddenly shouted from the back where he was standing to listen while holding his cigarette outside the door.

A large woman holding a soup ladle shushed him. "It'll be over in a second," she said. "Let the poor little thing try."

I am fire and air; my other elements
I give to baser life. So, have you done?
Come then, and take the last warmth of my lips...

She screamed, startling a baby into crying in the front row:

Come, thou mortal wretch!

She applied an asp to her breast and shrank back from the pain of it. She winced again as the snake bit. She applied another asp to her arm and the poison made her stumble to the edge of the stage. While she teetered, she let out another long scream of pain. Then she looked into every pair of eyes in the audience and asked:

What . . . should I stay?

She lingered for a moment, teetered, stumbled, regained her footing – and collapsed. She fell like a block of granite to the stage. Stone dead. The audience looked on.

The woman with the soup ladle nudged Hector Gillis. "Ask her now."

Hector threw away his cigarette and made his way through the crowd to the stage. He nudged Fiddy in the rump with his cane. She didn't move. He leaned in to take a closer look and noticed Fiddy's eyes were still open, glassy and unblinking. He couldn't see if her chest was moving. He whacked her with his cane. "Fiddy, wake up and tell us who won the contest!"

Fiddy was in a warm, dark far off place where nobility still reigned, soldiers fought for beauty and audiences applauded. One of the greatest queens of history had just killed herself before them, and all they could do was sit and watch. Would no one defend her against Caesar? Would no one attempt to take away the asp? She felt Hector Gillis's cane strike her again and returned to reality with a flinch. She focused her eyes and saw people looking at her. Some were glaring at her impatiently. Some only looked disinterested. Why, she wondered, hadn't they applauded? What were they waiting for? Was it her costume? She sat up, moved to all fours and struggled to get to her feet.

It wasn't until she heard the horrifying sound that she remembered her wardrobe limitations. In the passion of her performance, she'd forgotten all about Mirabella's precarious slacks.

Scrip.

The sound was heard from one end of the centre to the other. Even worse, her bottom end was aimed in the general direction of the audience. She glanced around to see if perhaps she had only imagined the sound. Every face gazed at her, eyes wide open, registering surprise that seemed to have frozen on every face. A few miserable seconds passed in silence. Then the laughter erupted. The children laughed freely while the adults made an effort at stifling themselves, which only made it worse. Tears flowed down eyes, chests heaved and they gasped desperately for breath.

Fiddy aimed her behind at the wall and watched the hysteria in bewilderment. "It was just a rip," she told them. "Not a fart." They howled with laughter and Fiddy watched them in confusion. So unsophisticated, she thought. So provincial. What could one do? She waited until they were able to collect themselves, held the paper up to her eyes and read the winner. "Group five," she announced.

A woman in the front row shrieked and the crowd exploded in applause. There were whoops and cheers and whistling and again Fiddy was awestruck by the response. Even the losers were applauding enthusiastically. Four beaming children dressed in wilted lettuce took to the stage to bask in the community's praises. Cameras flashed. Parents' eyes misted. The foam ceiling reverberated, and the animals were all quiet with fear.

Fiddy slid to the side of the stage and delicately climbed down, careful not to show anyone her backside, which she kept to the wall. She was sliding her way inconspicuously toward the door when Father Francis arrived with a white tablecloth. "I don't think anyone noticed," he said as he handed it to her with a safety pin the woman with the soup ladle had given him.

"Notice what?"

"The very slight tear in your slacks."

"Oh, my!" She took the tablecloth, wrapped it around her neck like a cape and pinned it in front. "I wouldn't want to be indecent!"

"Your performance was . . ." Father Francis appeared to be struggling for the words. Fiddy listened carefully. "Sublime," he finally said.

"Oh Francis, you shouldn't gush! But you know, I do it for

the people."

"It's too bad they couldn't applaud."

"Why on earth not?" she wailed. "They have hands. It's the polite thing to do, even if they couldn't understand."

"They were being polite," Father Francis explained slowly, "because this is the children's day and they wouldn't want to make them feel left out."

Fiddy was pensive for a moment. "You're absolutely right. I hadn't thought of that." She pulled the cape around her and admired the dignity it gave her. "This is simply gorgeous," she said. "I will treasure it always." The gift didn't quite make up for the lack of applause, but it helped.

[SIX]

The heavens forbid but that our loves and comforts should increase even as our days do grow!

– Shakespeare: *Desdemona, Othello*

MIRABELLA LEFT APPLEFERN MANSION at four thirty-one after making a casserole for the family of salsify and parsnips with a garnish of witloof chicory. She was in a good mood, having completed every task on every list, but when she aimed the great steamship of her car into her driveway, her heart sank. Her mailbox was gone. She sat, aghast at the injury, her hand grasping at the air where her mailbox should have been. When she came to her senses she got out of the car to search for it. She found the wreckage in the bushes, together with a shredded electric bill and a renewal notice for her subscription to *Northumberland Catholic*. She shook her head in disgust.

Her mailbox, a small replica of her trailer, was a landmark in Wintry Hope. People had called her from Thorn Grant to Tanderlush Delta to compliment her on it and ask where they could obtain one. She hadn't obtained it anywhere, she'd told them. She'd built it herself. Anyone could do it. She gave them the list of ingredients: a dozen or so cedar shingles, needles instead of nails, a good set of pliers, a steady hand to drive in the needles, a few litres of various colours of paint, the dexterity of a surgeon and three thousand hours of solitary confinement. Now, reduced to carnage, even the little window boxes with pansy buds about to bloom had been crushed. "Darn kids," she said to herself and dropped the mailbox into her trunk. She drove the rest of the way up the driveway.

Fiddy was sprawled on the chesterfield eating jellybeans in her white cape when Mirabella entered, stood at the doorway and glared. The timer on the stove was ringing. The lights were out. Crumbs on the table. Mats crooked. And Fiddy, a walrus, lounging in the middle of it all. "So now you're Superwoman?" Mirabella quipped.

"Why do you ask?"

"The white cape."

"This?" Fiddy looked at it as though noticing it for the first time. "This isn't a cape, it's a tablecloth."

Mirabella waited for more explanation but when none came she moaned loudly, went to the stove and fixed the timer with one twist of her hand. She washed her hands in the kitchen sink and went to the electric panel in the bathroom to replace the blown fuses.

"You'll never guess what," said Fiddy cheerfully when Mirabella had returned with a casserole from the freezer, put it in the oven and was washing her hands again at the sink.

"You won the jellybean jar at Achievement Day."

"Right!" Fiddy popped another five into her mouth. "I've got nine hundred and twelve left. But that's not all." She got up from the chesterfield with an agility that defied the two hundred and sixteen jellybeans she'd eaten. She met Mirabella at the sink.

"What?" said Mirabella, not in the least interested.

Fiddy pointed out the window and whispered, "I won a lamb."

Mirabella stopped scrubbing her hands, looked at Fiddy through ever widening eyes and looked out the window. On her back lawn stood a languid lamb, munching grass.

"Isn't he beautiful?" said Fiddy. "His name's Shaemis. I won him in a raffle."

"You've got to be joking." Mirabella turned her full attention on Fiddy. "You stupid idiot. Don't you know how the animal raffles work?" Mirabella knew. She'd organized them herself in years past. Prizes nobody wanted were the best money-makers. Everyone bought tickets and would write someone else's name on their ballot so as to curse them with the prize. Obviously, everyone had put Fiddy's name on their ballots and sent her home with the burdensome beast.

"You're an idiot," Mirabella said again. "A complete idiot. You can't take care of yourself, let alone a lamb. Are you going to feed and water it every day? Will you make sure it gets exercise? Brush its fleece? Don't you know how much work an animal is? And with the way the law is, if you neglect an animal they'll throw you in jail. How can you take on that kind of responsibility?"

Fiddy didn't answer.

"Look at it," continued Mirabella. "Look at the mess it's making of my lawn."

Fiddy looked at the lawn of which Shaemis was eating. She smiled. "He's adorable. Look. He's eaten out the shape of a heart. He just wants you to love him, Mirabella."

Mirabella didn't look at any imagined hearts in her lawn. She felt like choking Fiddy. "Animals aren't capable of love, you moron. They have no souls. When they die, they go to the dinner table. That's it."

"You don't know everything," said Fiddy. "There's enough room in heaven for animals."

"There isn't even enough room in heaven for most people," Mirabella snapped back. "And there isn't enough room for a lamb on my property. There won't be any grass left by the time he's ready to butcher."

Fiddy gasped. "Butcher?! Shaemis isn't for killing!"

"What on earth else is he for?"

"He's a pet!"

"A pet?" The word slipped from Mirabella's mouth with disgust. "I'll not have a pet on my property. Pets are nothing more than a form of disguised gluttony and, I might remind you, gluttony is a capital sin which leads to thousands of other sins like theft, addiction, drunkenness, idolatry, licentiousness and murder. I'll not have the gates of hell opened up on my property for the whole world to fall through. If you want to keep it you'll remove it from my lawn." She wagged a finger in front of Fiddy's nose. "Hear me?"

"Yes!" said Fiddy, exasperated. "Yes, Mirabella! I hear you. The monks at Monk's Head can hear you."

Mirabella handed Fiddy two pieces of folded paper towel to use as napkins. "I'll not tolerate foul language in my house either, or denigrating men of the cloth." She resolved to add the detail of her own foul language to her list for the confessional. "Now, hurry up and set the table."

Fiddy took her teacup to the table, sat down and pulled her cape around her. "I had a wonderful day," she said, in case Mirabella was wondering. “Achievement Day was a magnificent success. They asked me to judge the children’s skits. I couldn’t very well say no. They were marvelous. Then I showed them how a *professional* actress does it. They were utterly thrilled. I performed a delightful little Shakespearean piece from *Antony and Cleopatra*.” She added conspiratorially, “She dies, you know.”

Mirabella opened the oven door and peered inside. She prayed fervently that the casserole would quickly bubble. It didn’t. She closed the door, turned up the heat and stared at the ceiling to look for stains while Fiddy continued to babble on about the bake table, the furry rabbits, Mrs Crowe’s steak knives and the *simply delicious* hotdogs. She talked about the extra relish on her hotdog, the remarkable fact that condiments were free, and Father Francis presenting her with the tablecloth after her performance. “It was a gift,” she said. “They had no roses. It makes me look like a bishop, don’t you think?”

Mirabella didn’t answer. She had her face pinned to the oven door seeking any sign of a bubble in the casserole. When one broke through, she whisked the dish out of the oven and placed it in front of Fiddy. She said grace and told Fiddy to shut up and think of all the starving children in the world who have eaten nothing for weeks. “And take some green-gourd-marmalade-sauce with it. It’s good for you.”

Fiddy poked the casserole with her fork. “Are you sure it’s done?”

Mirabella felt like pouring the entire sticky mess over Fiddy’s silly red head. That would show her how done it was. She spooned some on her own plate, added a spoonful of green-gourd-marmalade-sauce and, as was her custom, took her plate to the counter beside the sink to eat while standing up.

“Do you think Mrs Crowe is a witch?” Fiddy asked. “She kind of looks like a witch, doesn’t she?”

Mirabella took a forkful of her casserole. It was dry, not nearly hot enough for her palate and the apples were sour. But it was good for her so she forced herself to swallow. She noticed Fiddy hadn’t taken hers yet. She went to the table and spooned casserole onto Fiddy's plate together with a generous dollop of green-gourd-marmalade-sauce.

"Thank-you," said Fiddy, although she'd rather not have had the green-gourd-marmalade-sauce. She'd decided it looked and tasted like mashed frog brains.

Mirabella returned to the counter. "You shouldn't be uncharitable," she growled.

"I'm not uncharitable."

"You are. You said Mrs Crowe looked like a witch. You'll have to remember that when you go to confession."

Fiddy laughed. "Confession? I only go to confession twice a year." She shoved a mouthful of casserole into her mouth and immediately spat it out to the edge of her plate. It was hotter than molten lead. "Do you think it's a mortal sin?" she asked, blowing out air to cool her mouth.

"Every sin is serious, and charity is the most important virtue. Without charity we'd all go to hell."

"I don't want to go to hell," Fiddy said. "No one sings in hell. Only screaming and that's not much as far as singing goes."

"And after a few days, the worms will have eaten away your throat."

Fiddy grimaced. "Do you think I should go to confession right now?"

"What would you do if you had a piece of lint worth a billion dollars?"

"What?" Fiddy was confused by the sudden change in the conversation.

"I asked what you would do with a piece of lint worth a billion dollars!"

"I don't know – sell it for a billion dollars?"

Mirabella sighed. "You'd be very careful with it, that's what. You wouldn't drop it. You wouldn't get it mixed up with pieces of worthless lint, and you'd probably carry it in one hand with the other hand making sure the wind didn't blow it away."

Fiddy's face registered no comprehension. "So I wouldn't sell it?"

"No!"

"Why on earth not?"

"Because then you'd go to hell, you nut!"

"Oh." Her brow furled in perplexity. "I don't remember getting my piece of lint. Perhaps I'm not Catholic at all. But why would I go to hell?"

Mirabella rubbed her temples and hoped her migraine wasn't the beginning of a stroke. "Ask Father Francis."

Father Francis had used the metaphor in his last sermon. The point was that a soul was worth much more than a billion dollars, and yet most people treated theirs with far less care than they would a piece of lint worth a billion dollars or a winning lotto ticket. The analogy had been lost on most but Mirabella had remembered it.

"I most certainly shall ask Father Francis," said Fiddy. "Indeed, I will demand my piece of lint too." She scooped up casserole from her plate, took a bite and spat it out. "Mirabella, this casserole is simply –"

In one quick movement Mirabella was at the table with her fork at Fiddy's throat. "What? My casserole is what?!"

"I'm sorry," Fiddy choked. "I meant to say . . ." She fumbled nervously for a moment. "I meant to ask, in a polite and charming manner, what this simply delightful medley is comprised of." She pointed to the casserole and Mirabella backed off, returning to her position by the counter.

"Apple, girasole, cinnamon, ginger and paprika, baked."

"It's quite nice." She stuffed in another forkful and winced while holding it in her mouth without swallowing. She watched and when Mirabella wasn't looking, delicately spat the remnants on the edge of her plate. Then she noticed the dessert. "And what in the name of the kingdom to come is that?" She pointed to it with her fork.

"Merry Bran Delight," said Mirabella, disconsolate with the whole affair and feeling exhausted all of a sudden. "A cup of prunes, a cup of bran, a half-cup of unsweetened applesauce and a cup of dates, ground up together in the blender and chilled for an hour. It's good for you."

"Dear God," said Fiddy breathlessly. "A maggot living on the gut truck wouldn't eat that."

Mirabella glared at Fiddy with eyes that blazed with grey-blue flames. "Would you shut up?! Why don't you think of all the starving children in the world, for one bloody cotton-pickin' minute?" She aimed her fork at her again. "Or do I have to stab you in the throat?"

Fiddy nodded slowly, her eyes widening in fear. "Fine," she squeaked and shut up. She tried to imagine the emaciated faces of children staring at her longingly for a morsel of food. It didn't help. They wouldn't eat it either.

Silence at last, thought Mirabella, even though the price of it was to utter a death threat. She made a mental note to add that tiny sin to her list for the confessional. And she had called Fiddy an idiot or the equivalent thereof at least twelve times in the past twenty-four hours. Then there were the dozens of violent thoughts relating to Fiddy, the curses under her breath and possibly countless other sins. Dear God, Mirabella thought. Living with Fiddy would be the ruination of her soul. Her piece of lint would be carried by the winds of Fiddy's idiocy to the nearest volcano where it would be sucked into hell and tormented by flames forever.

"I noticed you used the blue towel in the bathroom this morning," she said when she was washing the dishes and Fiddy was having her tea in the livingroom, squirming to get comfortable on the hard-backed chair. "I told you, they're for guests."

"*I'm* a guest."

"No, you're a charity case, and if you want to continue receiving my charity I would appreciate you following my rules. Including –" She glared at her from the sink. "Not wearing my clothes."

"Would you prefer I walked around in the nude?" From the safety of the livingroom, Fiddy felt she could be saucy. "Those rags of yours make me look dowdy, dumpy and common. Do you think I like that? Do you think I enjoy that?"

Mirabella clenched the salt shaker she was washing.

"I don't know if you realize this, Mirabella, but I lost

everything in that horrible fire – everything! All my wonderful trend-setting clothes renowned for setting the world's fashion scene on its head. And now look at me: a disgrace. A fallen doe run down by a cement truck. A gorgeous vixen trapped in a quagmire of perpetual fashion faux-pas. An exquisite chameleon forced to live on plaid. An exotic gypsy stripped of her bangles and tiara. A gallant lioness forced to wear a dog collar of plastic bells . . ."

"And somewhere, in the distance," Mirabella barked, "a toilet flushes. No one takes you seriously when you exaggerate."

"You must understand my position, Mirabella." Fiddy paused for extra effect. "I simply have nothing to wear."

"I know, I mentioned that to Johnny and Martha and they gave me some money to get you some things, until your insurance money comes in."

Fiddy wept. "Mirabella, you're wonderful!"

"You should thank Johnny and Martha. It's their generosity, not mine."

"When do you think we could leave?"

"After supper and before choir –"

"Choir practice!" Fiddy shrieked. She looked to the ceiling gratefully. "Who says our dollars don't fall from heaven? This is simply marvelous. Shopping and singing. Oh, Mirabella. What a magnificent gift of God you are."

"I told you, it was Johnny and Martha."

"I will never forget your generosity," Fiddy said passionately. "Never! I shall have a monument built in your honour when you die. In the shape of a great lioness with a heart of pure gold." She rested her teacup on her lap, leaned back in her chair and basked in the pleasure of her sudden good fortune. "Can Shaemis come too?" she asked wistfully.

"Of course not, you idiot."

[SEVEN]

> No torrents stain thy limpid source,
> No rocks impede thy dimpling course . . .
>
> – Tobias Smollett, *To Levin Water*

THE SOFT BLACK MOIST MARSH saved the Agent and her dog. When the steel blade of the bulldozer came down, the marsh enclosed them in its warm darkness until the gleaming, silvery blade had gone by, followed by the rattling tracks.

When the trembling stopped, the Agent remained motionless in the safety of a dark womb where there was no sound and she could feel only the comforting pressure of the black mud around her. She couldn't breathe but she felt no fear or worry. The muck, under the sunshine and perhaps because of the properties of decomposition, was as warm as bath water. Even as her lungs pumped uselessly for air, she felt only a detachment from herself and union with the marsh. She couldn't go back to a world that poisoned her, that voraciously consumed her, that cut into her skin with sharp silvery blades and pounded her with rattling steel.

Then she felt Twig's legs struggling against her back, pushing for the surface, fighting to reach the air. Twig wanted to live.

The Agent's head came out first, then a hand, and the rest of her wet and sticky body slid out of the wound. Her mouth, nose, ears and eyes, her hair, her entire body was covered in black slime. She coughed it out, gulped at the precious air and wailed. Twig came out next and the Agent helped deliver her. The dog was a skinny dripping mess with four dangling legs and a flitting pink tongue.

The Agent sat in the mud and cried. She was in the middle of a twelve-foot swath of destruction slicing through the marsh. The wound continued to ooze dark blood; the mergansers and their nest were gone; flies buzzed over the frogs and salamanders dying under the scorching sun, their pale undersides drawing crows to feast on them. Even an eagle defied its nobility by swooping down and carrying off a crushed frog. All of its joints broken, the legs dangled from around the eagle's beak as though they were made of wet paper.

Still crying, the Agent searched the mud for her backpack but couldn't find it. She soon gave up looking. She found a few scraps of moist paper but nothing of her sketches. Her lunch was gone. The recordings she'd made of birds' songs, including of the whippoorwill, were gone. The sketch of the white irises and mergansers was gone.

After a long time in which the sun crossed into the northwest sky, she let Twig down, wiped away her tears, took a deep breath and stood up to survey the devastation. The lane, if paved, could easily have landed a commercial jet. Not a plant or fragment of a bush were left where the bulldozer had gone by. The black soil was already drying into a hard cake in the sun. Twig, the Agent noticed with alarm, was eating a large beetle. "Stop!" she scolded, and the dog dropped the insect, licked its black lips and stared at her vacuously. The beetle began circling, only half of its legs functioning, the other half broken. What a fallen world she lived in, she thought. Even her own pet was prone to the temptations of the carnivore lifestyle. She clutched her dog to prevent it from feasting on other wildlife.

The world was corrupt, she knew. All had fallen short of the glory of the tree. But having learned her activism in the elite school of the APT Society, her knowledge had come from books of theory, not practice. The level of disorder of the planet, the level of disorder of human beings, was beyond anything she could have imagined. What would it take to bring order to this disorder?

Impossible, she thought despairingly. She could participate in protests, she could hold information sessions, she could lobby politicians, but what could be done to change the heart of man? The planet was immense but human beings covered it like an infestation of lice. They were everywhere. How could she defend the brook, the marsh, the trees and the strait all at the same time? How would she choose where to be and what to defend? If she couldn't defend the brook at the same time as the beach, how did she decide which to save? Was one creature worth sacrificing in order to protect another? She didn't know if she was capable of making that choice.

The beetle continued to circle uselessly at her feet, half of its body dragging the other half, enduring incomprehensible pain, she knew. Unable to watch its torment, she clenched her eyes shut. She told herself to be strong but she could feel a vicarious tingling at her shoulder as if her own arm had been broken. She groaned with her decision. "It's not fair!" she wept. She lifted a foot, clenched her eyes shut even tighter and stamped her foot down.

Snap. The shell broke cleanly and the beetle's movements, which she could feel under her foot, ceased. The tingling at her shoulder, however, continued.

MIRABELLA CLEARED OFF the table, finished washing and polishing the dishes, wiped Fiddy's fingerprints from the back of her chair and put every item of leftover food in appropriately sized zipper bags. Fiddy watched with galloping impatience from the livingroom. "Do you think you could do that later?" she finally had to ask.

Mirabella dropped to her knees in front of the open refrigerator and tried to reorganize the bottom drawers. From the livingroom Fiddy caught sight of her zipper-bagged dessert, the Merry Bran Delight, and her stomach lurched. Tomorrow morning she would have to find it and flush it down the toilet where it belonged in the first place.

Mirabella finished the rearranging and slammed the refrigerator door, rattling the contents. "A chore undone means the devil's won," Mirabella said.

Fiddy stood up. "Great," she said. "You beat him. Now, let's go." She crossed the kitchen with the tablecloth following along behind her like the train of a wedding dress and stood beside the door.

Mirabella went to the sink and washed her hands. She washed the taps. She turned them as tight as she could. She wiped the beads of water from the sink. She put the tea towel to dry on the handle of the stove. She straightened the little clothesline on which she hung tea bags to dry. She felt the tea bags for dryness. In the livingroom she straightened the chairs and the plastic mats in front of them. She rearranged pictures on the coffee table. On hands and knees she carefully palpated every square inch of the carpet, while sniffing the air like a hound.

Fiddy could stand it no longer. "What are you doing?!"

"What does it look like?" Mirabella snapped.

Fiddy thought about it. "Are you looking for spare change?"

"I'm checking for fires, you moron."

"How on earth could a fire begin under the chesterfield?"

Mirabella hollered from beneath the chesterfield where half of her had disappeared. "An ember could fall from my cigarette and be pushed underneath with my foot." She continued her sweeps to the end of the chesterfield, stood up and sniffed the air. "Do you smell smoke?" she asked.

Fiddy shook her head, even though she could still smell the smoke from Mirabella's after-dinner cigarette, the end of which was now under a layer of water in the ashtray on the counter.

Satisfied there was no smoke, Mirabella unplugged the lamps at either end of the chesterfield, together with the telephone, television, radio player and the crewel-covered electric clock on the wall above the chesterfield. She straightened the plastic mats on the floor again and a crewel picture on the wall. Back in the kitchen, she unplugged the coffee maker, microwave, food processor and toaster-oven.

"Why are you unplugging everything?" Fiddy asked.

"Why are you questioning everything I do?" said Mirabella testily. "If there's a lightning storm the surge will ruin the appliances." She glared at Fiddy. "Not to mention set my trailer on fire."

Fiddy rolled her eyes.

Mirabella made sure the switches for the oven and stove burners were turned off. She opened and closed the oven door just to make sure and tapped all four electric burners with her hand in case one of the switches was broken or her eyes were deceiving her. Sighing nervously, she looked around the kitchen for anything else she should check.

"You forgot to unplug the refrigerator," Fiddy offered.

"Do you think I should?"

"Only if you're crazy."

"You're making fun of me."

"Oh no, Mirabella. I wouldn't do that."

"A refrigerator is an expensive appliance. I don't want to lose it. On the other hand," she added pensively, "warm food is a breeding ground for salmonella." She took a deep breath. "I'll risk leaving it on. Let's go." She would close her eyes to the other disasters that would happen in her absence.

"Finally," Fiddy grumbled and fled for the car. She slid into the back seat, pulled the door shut and watched as Mirabella stepped cautiously out, checked for her spare key in her coat pocket and stuck her head back inside to take a last look. She seemed to be sniffing the air again. With deep nervous breaths she pulled the door closed. As Fiddy watched in amazement from the back seat, Mirabella tucked her purse under her arm, grasped the outside doorknob with both hands and pulled it furiously, looking to Fiddy like a shark caught on a hook. The trailer quaked and the windows rattled. Finally, apparently satisfied that the door would hold, Mirabella let the storm door close and came down the steps. On the way down, she felt inside the box of geraniums, found a bud that had dared to creep out and plucked it off.

She picked at a flake of paint on the last step with her fingernail. She inspected the skirting of the trailer. She squashed a caterpillar with her shoe and pushed the smithereens under the step. She tugged at a weed in the grass. She examined the underside of her eaves. She rubbed a dent in the trailer's siding. Fiddy nearly wept with rage.

After what felt to Fiddy like months of agony, Mirabella finally came to the driver's side of the car and got in. Fiddy let out a relieved breath and sat up like a proper lady, ready to get on with it. "Front seat," Mirabella ordered.

"Can't you indulge me even a little?" Fiddy pleaded.

"I will not indulge your vanity. If you want to go to Glen Gowsaw, you will sit in the front seat like a normal human being."

Fiddy groaned but quickly moved to the front. Mirabella put the key in the ignition. Fiddy waited for the roar of the car. When it didn't start she looked miserably at Mirabella who still had her hand on the key, continuing to look intently toward the trailer door.

"What's wrong now?!" Fiddy said.

"Did you notice if I put out my cigarette?"

"Of course you put it out. Is there something wrong with you?"

"Are you sure you saw me put it out?"

"I didn't actually see you put it out but I'm sure you did. Please, Mirabella," Fiddy implored, "you simply must proceed with the most urgent dispatch. I cannot wait any longer. I shall die. I really shall, and you will go to pieces, and then your trailer really will burn down."

Mirabella continued to look at the door of her trailer. "I don't remember putting it out."

"What in the name of time do you think you could have done with it? Left it smouldering underneath your bed? Hurry up and let's go!"

Mirabella unbuckled her seatbelt. "I'd better check just in case."

As Mirabella got out and went up the steps to the trailer, Fiddy hung her head and pleaded for God's mercy. The emotional ups and downs were too much for her tiny sparrow's heart. She would explode in horse feathers. She knew it. Or she would go the other way and dissolve into small fragments of dust – or lint – and slide ignominiously into the creases of the car seat to be forever lost in a graveyard of misplaced pennies and sticky things. She consoled herself with the thought that history's greatest artists suffered as she suffered. It was nearly seven o'clock before they left.

FROM THE BUSHES, the APT Agent and her pet watched as Mirabella and Fiddy took off down the dusty driveway. The marsh mud had dried on the Agent's face, arms and clothes and in her hair. She was covered with small twigs and leaves and the wool of last winter's cattails, all of which made her indistinguishable from the bushes and rocks around her. After retrieving her spare backpack and an assortment of equipment, including her camera, from her jeep, the

Agent had followed the bulldozer's tracks through the marsh to find their point of origin. Along the way, she'd taken pictures of the dead creatures, the trenches filled with muddy water, the destroyed nests and the disorientated birds. When she reached the beginning of the bulldozer's rampage, it was just as she suspected: Mirabella Stuart. The enemy of her brook was also the enemy of her marsh.

She headed up the driveway cautiously, keeping to the sides of the road, where she melded invisibly with the dirt. When she reached Mirabella's trailer, however, she was surprised to see that the bulldozer tracks went further – to the remains of Fiddy Washburn's house. She reassessed the evidence: the pyromaniac and enemy of the sky was also the enemy of her marsh.

She photographed the origin of the bulldozer's tracks and also Mirabella's septic pipes above the brook, together with the seeping effluent. She took specimens of the contaminated mud from the embankment and went back to Mirabella's lawn in search of other violations of environmental laws. She saw the neat garden and the perfectly symmetrical woodpile. Rocks from the beach had been painted white and placed in a perimeter around the driveway. The walkway was swept clean and the trailer, although a small, older model, was fastidiously well-kept.

Finding nothing more, she packed up her camera and specimen bottles and was leaving when she thought she heard a noise coming from behind the trailer. Almost indiscernible at first, it was no more than a whimper. She walked slowly around the corner and listened. In coursing down the western sky beyond the strait, the sun was beginning to cast shadows behind the trailer. The Agent could make out nothing to which she could attribute the noise. She waited and listened. There, she heard it again. She strained to see through the shadows and saw a small creature beneath the hardwoods. The lamb.

The Agent nearly wept at the sight of the animal. No bigger than a small dog, it was attached to a stake by a rusty chain. It's spindly, black legs were tucked up underneath it and its head was resting miserably on the bare ground. When it saw the Agent, it bolted to its feet, immediately afraid – as if it had already been beaten several times, thought the Agent. Tears spilled down her face, leaving streams of pale skin where the mud washed away.

"What have they done to you?" she asked. Of what physical and emotional neglect were Fiddy Washburn and Mirabella Stuart capable? It horrified the Agent to see a lamb in the possession of two such cruel people – their *possession.* The Agent took off her pack and searched it. "I'll rescue you, don't worry," she told the lamb. She found what she was looking for: a bottle of fake blood she used, from time to time, for embellishing protest signs.

She approached the lamb. "It's okay," she whispered and the lamb didn't bolt against the chain. The Agent patted its head and it nuzzled the underside of her hand. She could feel its hot breath on her palm. It seemed to crave the touch.

"I'm going to spray a bit of this on you, okay?" she asked. In the lamb's eyes the Agent saw it was okay to proceed. She shook the bottle a few times and sprayed the blood on the lamb's hind quarters. "Good," she said when the trusting lamb hadn't flinched.

She took the rusty chain, carefully wrapped it around both hind legs and stood back to take pictures from different angles. She nearly wept at the representation of the probable neglect of Mirabella Stuart and Fiddy Washburn. When she had enough pictures, she freed the lamb's legs from the chains and washed away the fake blood with Mirabella's garden hose. Before she left she hugged the lamb. "I'll save you, I promise," she whispered. The lamb's breath quickened. She took one more look into the endless eyes and, seeing more pain than she could endure, she left.

FIDDY LOVED long summer drives. She rolled down the window and the hot wind rushed through her fiery hair, tousling the red waves into what she imagined were rivers of flames. She longed to hang out the window with her face full in the wind and allow her cape to sail behind her. She suspected, however, that Mirabella would object to that much fun.

Instead, she pushed back into the seat, closed her eyes on the green fields of Krydotan and imagined herself on the back of a motorcycle in tight white leather, clinging to an enormous, tattooed, swarthy mass of a man – the drummer for her band. And he liked to drive fast. The air lifted her bleached blonde hair and shook it like the mane of a wild horse. She laughed, took a swig of vodka and sang along with Joan Jett & the Blackhearts, *I love rock 'n roll!*

"Put up your window," Mirabella ordered. "You'll ruin my perm."

Fiddy's eyes remained shut. Her lips moved and guttural sounds trickled from her throat. The tablecloth had been lulled by the breeze toward the window and was in danger of being sucked out.

"I said put up your window," Mirabella said louder, "before it's –" Too late. The wind sucked the tablecloth out in one gulp. Fiddy opened her eyes and felt her neck where it had been fastened. "Serves you right," Mirabella said. "Now put up your window."

"You must go back for it!" Fiddy shrieked.

"I'll not go back for it. You're the one who was careless enough to lose it. Serves you right, daydreaming all the time. If you weren't so bloody foolish, maybe you wouldn't be losing things."

"I need it!" Fiddy wailed.

"If it's on the road on our way back, we can stop and pick it up."

"That'll be nice," said Fiddy sarcastically. Her favourite cape would be marked with black tire tracks. She would look hideous in it.

When the car stopped on the main street in Glen Gowsaw, Fiddy leapt from the car and sprinted to the Thrift Store before Mirabella could even remove her seatbelt. When she looked up she groaned as Fiddy's bare rear end, hanging out of Mirabella's split slacks, entered the store.

Fiddy blew into the store like a hurricane and planted herself in front of the lone worker, a young woman with a shock of blonde hair tied at the top of her head. The hair fanned out in a miraculous spray that greatly impressed Fiddy. The girl's lips were frosted with pink, her cheeks were a deep rouge, her fingernails had blue daisies on them and her hazel eyes were dusted all around with blue. She was sorting through a large bin of discount socks.

"Excuse me, dahling," Fiddy began in her best British. "I do say. How much?"

The young woman put down the socks and chewed her gum a few times. "For what?" she asked slowly.

Fiddy swept her hand across the array of used clothing. "For everything."

The Thrift Store worker appeared to be mulling over the request. Mirabella entered and stood next to Fiddy who backed up to a rack of bras and panties.

"I don't know," the worker said finally. "I'd have to add it all up."

"Add what up?" Mirabella nearly shouted.

"Balderdash!" Fiddy blurted, startling the worker who flinched like a frightened parakeet. "Tell me, darn it! I demand an answer to my inquiry! How much, I say, in pounds and pence?"

"I don't know," said the worker. "A couple hundred dollars at least?"

"Then I'll take it." Fiddy turned to Mirabella. "Pay the woman."

"Your budget is thirty dollars," Mirabella growled.

"Thirty dollars!" Fiddy cried in disbelief. "What on earth? I can't buy one flip-flop for thirty dollars."

"A pair of flip-flops is only twenty-five cents," the worker offered.

"Is that right?" said Mirabella, interested. "Could you show me?"

The worker was about to show Mirabella the flip-flops when Fiddy, sensing the loss of her audience, exploded. "I need help!" she shouted. "I'm going shopping and I need a cart!"

Mirabella and the worker looked at her. She was red in the face and looking very much like Napoleon about to throw a tantrum. "I'll find them myself," Mirabella whispered. "If she explodes we'll be buried in jellybeans."

The worker raced for a shopping cart and followed the trail of destruction left behind by Fiddy, who was tossing clothes and accessories on the floor for the worker to pick up. Shoes, sandals, pantyhose, socks, underwear, two girdles, bras, skirts, dresses, jumpsuits, leg-warmers, hats, gloves, blouses, underclothes, an umbrella, plastic jewelry, purses and accessories, all went into the air like the proceeds of a tornado and landed all over the store. When the cashier had filled the cart, Fiddy crushed the contents down and dumped an armload of cosmetics on top. On top of that she loaded a bale of wigs and the cart nearly toppled. To the cashier's amazement, and Mirabella's shame, Fiddy tore off her clothes and pulled on a floral gown she thought would be fitting for choir practice. She discarded Mirabella's clothes on the floor and kicked them under a clothes rack. "Do pay the woman," she commanded on her way past the counter. At the door, she paused. "And of course, do tip conspicuously."

Mirabella helped the Thrift Store worker remove the clothes and accessories from the cart and pile them on the counter. She looked skeptically at a pair of pink tights. "These wouldn't cover even one ankle," she muttered. The Thrift Store worker nodded.

Fiddy was sitting on the curb next to the locked car when Mirabella arrived under five bags of clothes. She was painting daisies on her fingernails with a bottle of polish she hoped the tip had covered. "What on earth took you so long?" she asked, her voice sweet but with a hint of indignation that barbed at Mirabella. Mirabella, with surely more arms than any average human being, handled the five bags expertly, removed the car keys from her purse, opened the trunk and tossed them in. She didn't answer.

"My goodness," Fiddy continued, "I do hope you had enough money."

"Of course I had enough money." Mirabella unlocked her door, got in and unlocked Fiddy's door. Fiddy struggled to her feet from the curb, keeping her nails free of harm and climbed into the car.

"I suppose it was very expensive," she said hopefully.

"Not really."

"How much was it?" she finally asked, outright.

"Twenty-eight dollars even."

"That's it?"

"We only had thirty dollars to work with, you idiot."

Fiddy wasn't so sure she even wanted the clothes any more.

How could one have glamour if it wasn't expensive and wasteful?

"I bargained the cashier down from thirty-two," Mirabella said with pride.

Fiddy gasped. "You *what*?"

"Bargained. I don't believe in paying full price."

"Have you no sense of class at all?"

"If you look after the pennies the nickels will look after themselves."

Fiddy shook her head. "What a life of misery you must live, clamouring after the *nickels* as you like to call them. Surely you tipped her well?"

"Tip?" Mirabella snorted. "For what? Doing her job?"

"For doing an exemplary job. Didn't you see how I exploited her? Isn't that worth something?"

Mirabella rolled her eyes. "I don't tip cashiers, gas attendants, hair dressers, porters, bus drivers, waiters, airline stewards or anybody else who should darn well do their jobs and be happy about it. No one ever tipped me when I was at the factory. Johnny and Martha don't tip me for keeping the mansion and their children clean. Nor would I accept a tip. It's my job and I am paid to do it to the best of my ability. People use tips as an excuse for treating people like dirt, like you did to that poor girl. You should be ashamed of yourself. I hope you're keeping track of all these sins for confession."

"You're the one who didn't tip her. That was supposed to be my penance. Now I'll probably go to hell and it'll be all your fault."

"That's not the way it works, you brainless moron. It wasn't your money to begin with. If you go to hell it'll be your own fault."

"Do you really think any of that matters?" Fiddy asked listlessly.

"Your immortal soul doesn't matter? The Church doesn't matter? The blood of the martyrs doesn't matter? Two thousand years of doctrinal development doesn't matter?" Her face was flushed with anger.

"Whatever," said Fiddy.

Mirabella shot glances at her but after sitting in silence for a while it was apparent that Fiddy did not want to fight.

When they entered Tanderlush Delta, Mirabella kept her eyes on the road and her hands locked on the steering wheel. Fiddy craned her neck to take in her first view of the Northumberland. A warm haze rose from the motionless silver-blue mirror, an expanse of liquid pewter stretching to infinity.

"How does it do that?" Fiddy asked.

"How does what do what?" Mirabella growled.

"How does the ocean turn into sky?"

"Don't be so damn stupid."

Fiddy settled down into her seat but didn't take her eyes off the Northumberland. She squinted her eyes, searching for the horizon but the water and sky somehow had conspired together to hide it. How did two such vastly different entities blend together without a seam between them? It was a thrilling mystery. Why didn't Mirabella wonder about it? Why didn't she try to find that point where the water became the sky?

Impossible. Fiddy looked at the strait but her eyes could find no horizon. Somewhere, deep in the midst of the strait, despite its heaviness, the water became air and sky. Perhaps from the elevation of Mirabella's trailer she would be able to see it. If only she could discover that secret place, where water became sky, maybe she could become part of the sky too.

[EIGHT]

Obviously, a good choral ensemble results from a demanding director.

– Lewis Gordon: *Choral Director's Complete Handbook*

AS THE CHOIR DIRECTOR of St Margaret of Scotland parish, Mirabella could trace her authority in an unbroken line of succession as far back as the founding of the parish in 1792 when Pope Pius VI occupied the seat of St Peter. The struggle to attain the venerated position was, like many offices of power and influence, marked by connivance and treachery. Mirabella had beaten her way past no fewer than nine qualified rivals for the position.

Mrs Crowe had been her greatest threat. She'd started a rumour that Mirabella supported a modern version of "Amazing Grace," leaving out the words "*That saved a wretch like me*," and replacing them with "*That saved and rescued me*." Furious, Mirabella had printed and distributed leaflets calling for a return to classic favourites from the Latin Mass, together with an unequivocal denial of the rumour. At the bottom of the leaflet she'd scrawled a stirring message to the effect that she most certainly believed, as she had always believed, that all people were wretches. No one had difficulty believing her.

This required Mrs Crowe to abruptly change gears and insist that Mirabella was far too conservative to be choir director. But the sudden change in direction destroyed her credibility with the congregation of St Margaret's, who, at election day, firmly condemned Mrs Crowe for her misanthropic tactics. And of course everyone in the parish knew Mrs Crowe had killed her husband by smacking him on the head with a frying pan. They couldn't very well have a murderer for choir director.

The other contenders were too young and guileless to have been any real competition. Mirabella was presented with the baton of the position, which she would hold until death tore it from her white-knuckled clutch.

The early years of Mirabella's tenure were marred by turmoil and division, but now, as she drove to choir practice in her purring car with Fiddy in the passenger seat next to her, she had no fear of the unexpected. The road twisted its way to Wintry Hope from Glen Gowsaw along the contours of the Northumberland. Mirabella saw that the turns, like the curves of a sandy beach, were making Fiddy drowsy. She nearly fell asleep, which would have allowed Mirabella, possibly, to leave her in the car during choir practice, but as they came down Thism's Hill into Wintry Hope and in sight of the church, Fiddy suddenly perked up. "I know what I could do to make it up to God," she said. "I could sing a solo at the Bishop's Mass. What do you think: *Morning Has Broken?*"

"You're not singing a solo in *my* choir."

"But I'll go to hell if I don't do penance for stealing the nail polish!"

"Go and make a humble confession, renew your baptismal calling, express sorrow for your sins, do the penance the *priest* tells you to do, try not to sin any more and – "

"I can't do all that!"

"That's the only way to avoid going to hell."

"But I want to sing."

"Tough." Mirabella firmly shook her head and would have wagged a finger in Fiddy's face if it wouldn't mean removing a hand from the steering wheel. "I'll have no non-Christians singing solos in my choir."

Fiddy slumped in her seat. "Oh, Mirabella. If you only knew what it was like to have a voice such as mine."

"What's that supposed to mean?"

"Oh, I didn't mean –" she stammered. "You have a very nice, somewhat . . . scratchy voice, but *my* voice . . ." Fiddy took a deep breath as if she were about to sing and Mirabella shuddered. "My voice, is like an Arabian stallion gnashing at the bit. Human reins cannot contain her! I need to run, Mirabella, nay, to gallop, to gallop like lightning across the savannah, to feel my hooves pounding the earth like thunder! Oh, Mirabella," she pleaded with a passionate gaze, "the stallion must run! I can hold it back no longer! Sing I must! Sing I must!" She let out a long, shrill note, nothing like those found in *Morning Has Broken*.

"Okay, okay!" Mirabella shouted lest the note continue. "I get the picture." It took every ounce of her strength to keep her hands in their proper positions instead of covering her ears or choking the voice out of Fiddy. Either way, if she didn't stop Fiddy from singing, they would both end up dead in the ditch. "We'll see how it goes at practice."

They pulled into the church parking lot at one minute to nine o'clock. The choir was already assembled in the loft, whispering to each other in conspiratorial tones in the ineffectual way servants do in the absence of their masters. Fiddy elbowed her way into the third row near a microphone in the midst of the sopranos, cleared her throat and began her voice warm-ups. Mirabella arranged her hymn books and glanced quickly at the five rows of singers before her to see who had dared to be present and who had dared not to be.

The choir of forty vocalists, representing all ages, was arranged on either side of the massive pipe organ, which reached with golden flutes toward the church's upper reaches and the heavens beyond. The children, both boys and girls, stood on the bottom steps, followed by three rows of altos and sopranos on either side of the organ. Further up the steps were the rows of male voices, with the basses behind the altos and the tenors behind the sopranos. Further back, behind the vocalists, where they could neither see nor be seen, were the violinists and trumpeters, six in total, all on loan from the university in Tina Shingo. They were a defeated and miserable lot who had been promised extra credit for their extracurricular effort. In two years of practicing with the choir, they hadn't yet performed during a single Mass. Neither had they received their credit.

Their only purpose, and the reason Mirabella had made the arrangement with the university, was for performing Handel's No. 51 Chorus, *Worthy is the Lamb*. The musicians sat silent and bored for the whole of choir practice, as they were not permitted by Mirabella to sing, and for the duration of their own practice endured the harassment of Mirabella's caustic tongue. In two years, they had managed to get through No. 51 in its entirety only twice. It had been a regrettable indulgence on Mirabella's part. When they looked up up to see what approval, if any, they could glean from her, she only shook her head in disgust, after which she railed against them for their dismal timing and lazy stroking. "You sound like sick ducks," she'd told them. "We're lucky we weren't attacked by migrating geese."

But the day was coming when, like Wintry Hope's extinct volcano perhaps, they would send forth their fire. Mirabella had most recently acquiesced to the violinists attending Sunday Mass just in case the choir was doing extraordinarily well and, if there weren't too many people present, they just might risk it. The promise had been like a shot of cocaine to their blood streams, swelling their hearts with sweet hope. That was the day one of the violinists decided, after all, that he wouldn't throw himself over the edge of the choir loft to certain death.

Virgil MacPhee was Mirabella's prodigious organist, nineteen years old and, she suspected, already eyeing her position. He was well liked, naive, innocent. Of all the members of the choir he was therefore the most dangerous. He sincerely loved the music and had refused a prestigious position as assistant organist at a basilica in the city. But Mirabella had caught him stroking her director's baton. She'd snatched it away and scolded him with it. He hadn't touched it since, although Mirabella had, as a test, placed it next to his music on occasion. In any case, Virgil could never be choir director. He wasn't harsh enough. Vocalists, like rebellious slaves, had to have their spirits constantly broken to be really good.

Despite the brutality of choir practice, members arrived optimistic that this week they would get it. This week they would exceed Mirabella's expectations, make her smile slightly and maybe even give them a compliment. *Good. That was good.* Or give them a noncommital shrug. *I suppose that wasn't awful.* Maybe this would be the week Mirabella would let them sing No. 51, and the congregation would go wild with cheering, clapping and stomping of feet.

The hope was an illusion. The congregation never did respond to the choir's impeccable musicality. They always remained the same: bodies with only slightly flickering souls trapped in motionless marble. They stared straight ahead, stood or sat when appropriate and left the church at the ordained time. Polite, pleasant, but infuriatingly untouched by the choir's praises to the Holy One.

Mirabella tapped her baton on the bannister. "Attention. Everyone listen." She spoke in her crankiest schoolteacher's voice. The choir hushed. "Sunday's performance, as I'm sure you are all aware, was humiliating." She stared at forty shocked white faces. "I know you're all quite ashamed, or at least you should be." Still blank faces except Fiddy who gave a cheery smile since it was never her who failed in singing.

Mirabella was shocked by their shock. "Did you actually think you were good?" she asked rhetorically. No one ever doubted that all of Mirabella's questions were rhetorical. "They felt sorry for you, that's what. The performance was worse than amateurish. You embarrassed yourselves, this parish, our community and your families. Instead of improving, you've been developing bad habits which will take you down the path of destruction. Soon you will be hated. Is that what you want? To be detested? Despised? Or do you want something a little bit more?"

She gave them a moment of silence in which to repent of their incompetence. There was no easier way to turn the tide on mediocrity than to rub their noses in it. A dark pallor came over the choir and Mirabella waved the truth in front of them like a bloodied murder weapon she'd just discovered in their possession: "Sherry, you sounded like a hyena in heat. Marcie, on the A you sounded like a rusty old seesaw. Fiddy, wipe that grin off your face, I'll get to you. Arthur, your voice cracked three times in the *Ave Maria*. You sounded like a coughing cat." The blood went out of Arthur's face. "The rest of the tenors," she continued, "were no better. The altos were wobblier than water. I want to hear the *natural* vibrato. *Natural*. Not forced like a disgusting fart. Basses, I could hardly hear you, and when I did, you sounded like cars being mashed up in a metal compactor. I want to hear a *throaty* rumble, not a train wreck. One collective voice, not a cock fight. We might as well forget about No. 51. I'm not sure I could even stomach you singing *Twinkle, Twinkle Little Star.*"

She sighed, looked from face to face and saw that all were

thoroughly disheartened. Perfect. "But I suppose you are a choir and we'll have to sing something. Begin with *Panis Angelicus*. Heads up, remember to breathe, straighten your voices. I said *straight!* Relax your abdominal muscles, tighten your diaphragms, an egg in your mouth, project through the top of your head and – " She whipped the baton against Virgil's knuckles and he winced with pain. "We're not doing this *a capella*, Virgil. Hurry up and begin. We need the notes."

Virgil played. The members of the choir raised their faces, breathed deeply, relaxed their abdominal muscles, tightened their diaphragms and projected the first notes.

Panis . . .

"No, no, no!" shouted Mirabella. "Far too emotional. We're looking for sincerity, not sentimentality. I don't want all that flowery crap. Sing the damn hymn, don't embroider it." She tapped the baton on the bannister and they began again:

Panis . . .

"Stop, stop, stop!" Mirabella covered her ears. "I've heard snakes hiss better music than that!" In the front row, little Sarah Gillis, nine years old, wiped away her tears.

Mirabella paced in front of them. "Someone's horribly off. Horribly off. It's like a broken siren. Who is it?" She glanced around at the choir with a vulture's eyes. "Who is it? Who's making that awful noise?" She shot a glance at Fiddy.

"Not I!" Fiddy said.

Mirabella marched in front of them like an SS officer about to decide who was to live and who was to be tortured and killed. "It's one of the male voices." Half of the choir visibly relaxed and exhaled while the other half stiffened like a cramped muscle. "Arthur, give me your F sharp."

As a practicing barrister, Arthur Stuart had been rebuked publicly, at least in his earlier days, by the fiercest rudest and most ignorant and unforgiving judges in the province, but none of their blasts compared to his aunt's choler. He took a deep breath and gave the note. It was dead on. Mirabella nodded. "Maybe you should try singing like that at Mass."

She moved on. "Ernie, give me the soprano G." Eight-year-old Ernie MacHattie gulped, swallowed, took a deep breath and gave the note as well as any archangel could. "Alright." Mirabella moved on. "Virgil – give me the A!"

He had his back to Mirabella but she could see his face in the mirror above the keyboard on the organ. A flash of red leapt to his neck and the muscles in his face twitched. He cleared his throat and opened his mouth but nothing came out. He coughed, cleared his throat again, took a deep breath and managed to give the correct note, although it lacked confidence.

"Ha ha!" Mirabella rejoiced, "our culprit is caught!" With the quickness of a witch, she moved to the other side of the organ where she could see his face close up. "Now, try again, Virgil, but this time, softer."

He gave the note again, this time softer.

"Now, even softer."

He gave the note even softer.

"Softer," she said again.

The note he gave was imperceptible.

"Now try closing your mouth."

Virgil closed his mouth and stared at her, confused.

"There," Mirabella said and smiled, her teeth more white and perfect than the keys of the organ, owing, no doubt, to their nightly soaking in bleach. "Perfect."

She went back to her position behind the bannister and snapped the baton against it a few times. "Alright, begin again. Heads up thirty-five degrees, breathe, project, straighten, relax, firm your voices, an orange in your throat, no wobble or chordal fuzz, Virgil with your mouth shut, now, sing!"

The choir breathed in and sang out. With so many contradictory commands, most of which were an utter mystery to the younger singers, the choir couldn't help but sing with total abandon. So they forgot everything Mirabella said and flew through their hymns with nothing more than hope to guide them. They soared over the fields and mountains of their music, across rivers and through wooded glens, and at the end, each hymn dissipated into the air like wisps of white mist. They sang the *Celtic Alleluia* in nine harmonies, and in the Gloria Fiddy and the first sopranos flew out above everyone else with the descant:

Lamb of God
You take away
the sin of the world . . .

after which the tenors and altos answered like a great wind following them,

Have mercy on us!

The church felt as though it would burst. Fiddy cried. When the last hymn was finished, the singers gasped to catch their breath and looked to Mirabella hopefully.

"I guess there's nothing more we can do tonight," Mirabella said, the sting of defeat in her voice. The violinists waited for a moment to see if they would be permitted to attempt No. 51 but Mirabella only gathered up her books. "That's it," she muttered. "Be here on Thursday. Dismissed."

The instrumentalists packed up their unused instruments and with the singers, sauntered away, grumbling their useless complaints against Mirabella among themselves, but taking care that she didn't hear them.

"What about my solo, Mirabella?" It was Fiddy, still standing in her position in the third row. As if on cue, those of the choir still lingering quickly fled like moths under the sun.

"There isn't time," Mirabella said, pushing a hymn book into her satchel.

"There is so time!"

"There's no accompaniment."

"I can do it *a capella*."

"No one will sing *a capella* in my choir. The bishop will be here in two weeks, and that isn't enough time for you to prepare properly. You can bring out your raging bull some other time."

"You said I could sing a solo at the Bishop's Mass."

"I did not. I said I would see. And that was before I heard how awful they were. You heard them. They sounded like strangled chickens. It was murder."

"I thought they were fine."

"Well they weren't. They need a lot of work. And I think we need a new organist. Virgil's performance has been lacking."

"He was simply gorgeous, Mirabella. And so were we. When will I get to sing?"

"I think you should give someone else a chance."

"But I'm the best!"

Mirabella latched her satchel, hoisted it to her shoulder and sighed impatiently. "No, Fiddy. You aren't the best. You aren't even in the top half."

Fiddy gasped. "How dare you! I've sung for audiences all over the world!"

"You have not."

"I have too!"

Mirabella jabbed her baton into its velvet glove and glared. "I'll not get into this with you, Fiddy. You're not singing a solo at the Bishop's Mass and that's final." She headed to the stairs.

"But I'll die!" Fiddy cried, into the emptiness of the church. Her voice echoed back: *Die! Die! Die!* She said it again even more miserably: "Die!" And the upper reaches of the church answered her back: *Die! Die! Die!* She could hear Mirabella's soft-soled shoes heading with careful, methodic determination down the stairs.

She moved to the edge of the choir loft. For a moment she considered jumping over the railing and killing herself just to prove to Mirabella how much she needed to sing her solo. With her luck, however, she'd fall on a pew and injure only her larynx and never be able to sing again. Then she really would die. Her limbs she didn't care about. They could all break and snap off. She didn't need her toes to sing. When she took to the stage they could always distend her arms, legs and neck with steel rods. She'd look like an immense, unwieldy, marionette, singing with only her lips and jaw moving, but at least they would hear the voice from heaven.

Mirabella stuck her head out from under the choir loft directly below her, near where Fiddy would have landed had she jumped. "Are you coming or do I have to knock you over the head and throw you into the trunk of my car?" Fiddy resisted the urge to spit.

MIRABELLA COASTED TO A CLEAN skid-free stop in her driveway, turned off the engine and applied the emergency brake. "Mirabella," Fiddy persisted, "why don't you come inside and I'll have a cup of tea and some cucumber sandwiches made for us. We need to talk about this."

"I live here, you idiot!" Mirabella shouted.

"What?" Fiddy looked out the window and saw Mirabella's trailer. "Oh. Yes. Right."

Mirabella stepped out of the car, retrieved Fiddy's shopping packages from the trunk and headed up the steps to her trailer with her arms loaded.

Fiddy followed. "You can make the tea then, Mirabella. And do please cut off the crusts of my cucumber sandwiches. I still think we should talk about this."

While juggling the five large bags of Fiddy's clothes together with the satchel of hymn books and her velvet encased baton, and while struggling for the keys, Mirabella still managed to give Fiddy a cold hateful stare before she opened the door and pushed inside.

"Why are you ignoring me?" Fiddy pleaded from behind her.

"Maybe it's because I've already told you – I'm the choir director and my decisions are final."

She tossed the keys on the kitchen table and went down the hallway to Fiddy's bedroom where she placed the packages at the foot of the rumpled bed. She shook her head in disgust, resisted the urge to make it, closed the door and went back to the kitchen. She filled the kettle with cold water, put it on to boil and went to the freezer. She took off the lid of a metal can, removed a plastic container from inside and dislodged the zipper bag which held her package of cigarettes. She bought her cigarettes by the cart-full in the city twice a year, a special Russian variety with black paper, filter-free and extra tar. Even though it was nearly ten-thirty, she'd only had four of the six she allowed herself each day. That meant she could have two more before going to bed. That wasn't an addiction, she told herself, as she made a notch to indicate she was taking one. She also recorded the time it was taken. She wrapped up the package again and put it back in the freezer. She lit the cigarette, puffed out a billowy haze of soot and waited for the comfort of slight disorientation to take hold in her head.

"How long before your insurance money arrives?" she asked, leaning against the small space of counter between the sink and refrigerator where she ate her dinner.

"What insurance money?"

"On your house, you ninny!" Mirabella hissed like a bobcat.

"Oh. Yes. The insurance. It shouldn't be too long."

"HOW long?"

"Two weeks? A month? Two months?"

Mirabella shook her head miserably and took another deep drag. "And then what?"

Fiddy shrugged. "Maybe I'll build a new house," she said, somewhat daringly.

"A new house?" Mirabella said in disbelief, letting the smoke drift out of her mouth as she spoke. It floated from the edges of her mouth, suspended like a moustache.

"A beautiful house," Fiddy said dreamily, buying fully into her fantasy. "A Cape Cod overlooking the Northumberland, with pink shutters and a sunroom and five bedrooms and a fireplace with a mantle for my pictures and a hot tub where I can drink blueberry wine and a studio with mirrored walls where I can practice my lines."

Mirabella filled her lungs with smoke again and kept it there until she almost passed out. "Fiddy," she said blowing the smoke out in wild eddies. She firmed up her voice in case Fiddy should misunderstand her words for compassion. "You know you can stay here if there's nowhere else for you to go. But you can't stay here for that long, certainly not two months." Or even two weeks, she thought. "I can't stand it already and it's only been one day. It isn't anything personal. That's just the way things are. You'll have to find somewhere else to live until your insurance money comes in." Her tone was defiant.

"You're the one who asked me to stay here," said Fiddy.

"I couldn't allow you to freeze to death out there."

"*Now*, it's perfectly alright for me to freeze to death?!"

"I was just being charitable."

"Charity? You kicked me out of my condominium and burned it to the ground, and now you want me to find somewhere else to live? My insurance will take at least two weeks to come in and who knows how long to build a new house. I may not even choose the architect for six months. Until then, I have nowhere else to live."

"That's not my problem." It wasn't, she told herself. Fiddy's problems were of her own making. She would have to find somewhere to live on her own. Of course Johnny and Martha were the only ones with enough room for her, personality included, but they wouldn't be able to slow down enough to pick up the lowly lost Fiddy. Mirabella could imagine their uncomfortable excuses for not wanting to take her: *She wouldn't like it here . . . It's too big . . . Maybe she could move to Tina Shingo . . . Why don't you keep her for a while?*

"Maybe you could get some quick money from the insurance company," Mirabella offered reasonably. "Before your final settlement. Most insurance companies do that. It would tie you over for a while, and you could get an apartment in Tina Shingo until your house is built." She continued to keep her voice harsh to make sure Fiddy didn't confuse her advice for kindness.

"You don't want me here?"

"I can't take care of you. You're too old. And moreover, I shouldn't have to look after you." She crushed out the last of the cigarette between two fingers, poured water over the butt in the ashtray and set it on the counter to soak. She faced Fiddy and crossed her arms. "I wouldn't want to see you starving to death, or freezing on my doorstep, or being eaten alive by wild animals at the end of the lawn, or anything like that. But we're too different, Fiddy. It's only been one day and I can't stand it anymore. You're impossible to live with. You're impossible to be around. You're incessantly annoying and incorrigible. You've ruined my clothes, you've burdened me with an animal, you've pestered me to no end about the solo." She waited a moment. "And you went on a joyride with that bulldozer and destroyed my mailbox."

"I thought you enjoyed my company," Fiddy said in a

whimper.

"The sooner we're out of each other's hair, the better." Mirabella stood at the counter and waited for a response, watching Fiddy carefully. The red hair was ridiculous, she thought. As was the vast floral gown. A geriatric clown, Mirabella concluded, with four eyebrows, two of which were in the middle of her forehead. Fiddy was far too old to be behaving like the spoiled brat she was. What on earth was she to do with her?

Fiddy squirmed under her searching eyes. "We'll see," she said at last. "Perhaps I'll take a place in New York or London. I have an obligation to my fans, after all. Perhaps I've been in Wintry Hope for too long."

Mirabella continued to glare, searching Fiddy's face, her gestures; analyzing, probing and evaluating. She'd known Fiddy her entire life. There was nothing hidden in Fiddy that Mirabella couldn't find. "You don't have any insurance, do you?"

Fiddy raised her chin proudly. "Insurance is for pessimists." Meryl Streep had said that in *Out of Africa*, and Fiddy had been trying, for twenty years, to find an occasion to say it.

Mirabella exploded. "Are you insane?! Why the devil wouldn't you have insured your house?"

"I have no intention of living my life as though disaster is my destiny. What do the rich and famous need insurance for?"

"You're not rich. You're not famous. You don't have a cent. Just what do you think you're going to do?"

"Something will come up," she said. "Just like the tide. First thing you know, I'll have the loveliest castle built of sand. You'll see."

"I know exactly what will come up. MY charity. This time, I'm finished holding your head up above the water. You can't stay here for the rest of your life." Mirabella decided to level with Fiddy. "You'll have to go to a nursing home."

Fiddy gasped. "You wouldn't!"

"I would. I will."

"Surely you can give a person in need a roof over her head," Fiddy pleaded. "Just give me a few months. Even a few weeks. I'm sure if I wait a little longer, something will come up."

"Like what, Fiddy? The Cirque du Soleil? You're old, you have no skills and you have no money. The only realistic option you have is to go to a nursing home."

"I have lots of other options!"

Mirabella promptly took a pad of paper from the top of the refrigerator and readied a sharp pencil in her right hand. "Okay Fiddy, list your options and I'll write them down."

Fiddy sat back in her chair, crossed her ankles and laughed. "Ha, Mirabella! If you only knew to whom you were speaking. I could move to Turkey or maybe to Bali or the Greek Isles." She paused and her brow furled. "Then again building codes in Turkey are simply deplorable and they don't have pistachio ice-cream in Bali. The Greek Isles are uncommonly hot this time of the year and they are reported to have enormous lizards. I simply despise lizards, Mirabella. Perhaps I should join the Cirque du Soleil after all." She gave a despairing sigh. "I'll never be able to decide all these choices! I need time!"

"You have only one option, Fiddy and that's to go to a nursing home. If you don't consent, I'll call Adult Protection and have you committed. If you consent, I'll help you make the move. I'll plan everything. I'll do the paperwork, file a request for financial assistance and make any other arrangements. I'll drive you there with your belongings and even pick you up on the occasional weekend so that you can come to Mass here and sing in the choir. In the absence of your own plan that's what you're going to have to do. There's no other way."

"I can't go to a nursing home," Fiddy whined. "I hate hard-boiled eggs and creamed corn."

"There's nothing pretty or glamourous about growing old. All you can do is offer up your suffering and hope you don't go to hell forever. I can't possibly be expected to look after you for the rest of your life. You need virtually constant care. You have no money and no one will put up with you. You've made your bed, now it's time to sleep in it. You have no one to blame but yourself. Tomorrow after work I'm going to the nursing home in Toome, and you're coming with me. If you weren't so congenitally incompetent, you could have avoided this disaster, but I'm afraid the only destiny you have is in a long-term institution. I've said my piece now I'm going to bed." She disappeared down the hallway before Fiddy could respond.

MIRABELLA CLOSED the bedroom door behind her and disrobed in the dark. She pulled on a thin nightdress, crawled into bed and buckled together the safety straps across her legs, waist and chest to prevent her from falling out of bed during the night. She stared into the darkness above her. "Surely, that's all that can be expected of me," she whispered. She received no answer. She struggled against the straps and squirmed until she was comfortable.

She was right, she told herself. She couldn't be expected to look after Fiddy. She'd already looked after her mother during her final years. Long, difficult years of emptying and cleaning the commode, giving sponge baths, cooking special foods, feeding, washing clothes, keeping track of and administering the dozens of medications. Her lists had been endless.

No, she couldn't be expected to do the same for Fiddy, a woman she wasn't even related to. They shared Johnny, Arthur and Father Francis as nephews, Mirabella on their father's side, Fiddy on their mother's, but that was it. Mirabella had a hard enough time ensuring her own survival let alone taking care of Fiddy.

She was at perfect peace with her decision. She closed her eyes, squirmed into her pillow and waited for sleep to knock her out. She clenched her eyes shut in an effort to force sleep in. She struggled against the straps. She heard an owl in the woods. She opened her eyes again and sighed. Sleep would not come. Damn her! Damn Fiddy!

She unbuckled the top strap and sat up. It wasn't fair for her to feel guilty. Fiddy, the flibbertigibbet, had floated through life like an aimless cloud and now that it was time for the rain to come Mirabella was the one who was forced to hold everything together. And how could she hold together a cloud?

Fiddy had never worked for anything in her life. She had never made a list to organize herself. She had never saved any of her welfare payments or the money she received from the people who felt sorry for her. She had spent lavishly what little she had and gambled away her security on foolish dreams.

What a curse dreams were, thought Mirabella. A curse! They had destroyed Fiddy's life like a cancer. The dreams of fame and wealth were nothing more than an addiction sent by the devil to bring Fiddy's life – and probably her soul – to eternal damnation.

At least Fiddy had no one to blame but herself. Mirabella, over the course of at least fifty years, had done all she could to discourage Fiddy with the reality of her lacklustre talents. She'd told her how ridiculous she looked. She'd called her a brainless idiot. She'd informed her in a thousand various ways that she had no talent. She told her she couldn't sing. She told her she couldn't act. She told her that her voice was flat, that she was tone deaf, that she was homely, that her forehead was enormous, that she had absolutely no talent. She had no talent!

Mirabella lay back down and fastened the upper strap again. She was right, she told herself. None of this was her fault. She had done everything in her power to destroy Fiddy's dreams. She had done nothing but discourage her. It wasn't Mirabella's fault if Fiddy had wasted her life. It was a tragic example but Mirabella was completely blameless. She closed her eyes and ordered sleep to take her quickly. Quickly!

MEANWHILE FIDDY SNEAKED outside into the warm summer night. In bare feet, she crossed Mirabella's lawn to her own property, lay down in the long grass and looked up at the sky. She breathed in the heavy scents of crushed mint and wild strawberries, thankful she hadn't accepted any offers to have her lawn mown. Above her, someone had sprayed the sky's black velvet with silver glitter. Larger stars hung like pregnant bulbs to form the constellations, twinkling and blinking at her like distant cameras flashing. She smiled and posed for the pictures. At that distance, of course, they wouldn't turn out very good.

After the pictures she dug into a pocket in her gown and took out her pouch of diamonds. She placed one in front of her and tried to look through it to the stars. She couldn't see anything at first. She aimed it in different directions until its crystalline chambers caught a star's struggling light and magnified it. She gasped to see so many cathedrals with angels dancing and laughing inside them.

After a while, her back began to ache against the earth, but she couldn't return inside yet. She put the diamond back in the pouch and searched the sky for a falling star, promising herself she wouldn't go back inside until she had seen one. A good one. Watching, she wondered how it was that something so vast and beautiful as a firmament filled to the brim with stars could have no sound at all. It should have a dull roar, she thought, like a waterfall or an earthquake. Or perhaps it actually did have a very quiet sound, like a distant violin, and she would only hear it if she were extremely quiet.

She held her breath and listened. Nothing. Only the rapid beating of her heart in her ears. Perhaps the sound of the firmament was even quieter than her heart's beating. How could she make her heart stop beating so that she could hear the heavens? It would only stop when she was dead. Only then, perhaps, would she hear the sky – in that moment when her body had stopped living but her mind was still alive and waiting to be taken. Then she would hear the heavens: stars like a soft wind through guitar strings, growing gradually into an orchestra of violins. Handel would take her by the hand and usher her into the best of heaven's choirs, where she would sing her solo, and God would laugh and clap for her with the sounds of thunder. She couldn't wait.

Her back, however, throbbed from one end of her spine to the other, as if she were a piano and the devil was playing her with a hammer. She was almost driven to sit up when her eyes caught it: a light over the northeastern Northumberland, toward the Cape and St George's Bay. The flash came toward her and seemed almost to linger as it etched a hairline fracture in the black sky. Then it was gone.

She'd seen it though! She'd seen her falling star. If she hadn't been looking exactly in that part of the sky, however, she wouldn't have seen it. Probably no one else in Wintry Hope had seen it. Probably no one else in the entire world had seen it! What a thought.

She relished the gift of being the only one to have witnessed the final, glorious moments of a particle of cosmic dust. It could have been roaming the lightless empty universe for thousands of lonely years in search of its chance to be seen.

And weren't all those dark and empty years, traded for one fleeting flash of light, worth it? Even now, in its invisible death, did it not smile in knowing one set of eyes had seen it? There had been a plan in the silence and darkness at the outer edge of the universe from the very beginning. A plan indeed! The level of design necessary to bring the flash of light to Fiddy's eyes at just the right moment, just when she was about to give up, was incomprehensible. Any planet or asteroid or moon or star in the universe, if it had been slightly bigger, slightly smaller, in the wrong part of its orbit at the wrong time, could have swayed the particle from its target and the moment it had shared with Fiddy would never have happened. The universe had, instead, bent and twisted to allow it through, allowed it to journey for millennia, to find Fiddy, to give her its joy. It was a staggering effort on God's part. Such an effort deserved applause. Fiddy clapped her hands and cheered.

Suddenly, she didn't care that she was destitute and homeless. She didn't care that she was alone. She didn't care that her only friend hated her and spoke to her with cruel harshness. She didn't care that she was getting too old for life, that her bones ached, that she felt tired all the time, that she dreaded a glance in the mirror. She didn't care that she had nowhere to live. There was a plan. The universe would move and twist and allow her through. She wouldn't be finished until the last drop of her life was spent and had produced a glorious flash of light for all to see. Then her heart could stop and the violins of heaven embrace her. All she had to do was wait with patient hope and be ready with her song to sing.

[NINE]

67(1) No person shall knowingly release or permit the release into the environment of a substance in an amount, concentration or level or at a rate of release that causes or may cause a significant adverse effect.

– *Environment Act,* Revised Statutes of Nova Scotia

DESPITE HER BEST EFFORTS, Mirabella barely slept. The night was too hot. There were too many noises – rustling leaves, hooting owls, creaking tree trunks, a city of peepers – all, seemingly, in the woods directly behind her trailer. She could hear Fiddy's laboured breathing and intermittent mumbling. She saw the hallway light come on every time Fiddy got up to go to the bathroom. She watched until she heard the toilet flush, saw the light go out, heard Fiddy's heavy steps return and, moments later, the sound of Fiddy's sleep resuming. Mirabella took Fiddy's easy entry into and out of sleep as a personal slight. She became more frustrated, hot, sticky with perspiration, and lost nearly the entire night. What sleep she did achieve was only a thin semblance of the real thing, which denied her all of its comforts but took all of her time – another fact she resented. If she'd known she wouldn't sleep, she'd have found something to do.

At five o'clock, somehow she awoke from a dream, screaming and sweating. She'd dreamt that her trailer had been knocked on its side by a tornado and that she'd been thrown from her bed into the closet – despite the straps. The closet was a boiling mass of tar that wrapped her in its strong black arms and pulled her under. She flailed against it, trying to find the surface but quickly became weak as it suffocated her. She noticed, however, that if she stopped fighting it, the tar seemed to relax. She let herself go freely into its arms. It covered her gently, caressed her, loved her. She tasted it and found it was a sweet burn to her mouth. Suddenly, she was drinking it in greedily, taking hungry gulps, even though she knew it was killing her. She couldn't stop. She awoke screaming.

She blinked in the dim light until she realized by the emptiness inside of her that she hadn't drunk anything. She held her breath and listened. The trailer was silent except for Fiddy's aimless mumbling in the next room and the low hum of the refrigerator in the kitchen. The world outside was silent, awaiting the morning reveille. She let out a cautious breath and felt for the straps holding her into the bed. They were still taut. The trailer hadn't been blown over by a tornado and she hadn't been thrown into the closet. She wondered why her straps hadn't worked properly in her dream. She looked at the closet doors. They were closed, quiet and looked back at her like highly disciplined prison guards. No poisonous pitch to burn, blind or tempt her. She was safe. She hadn't tasted it. She hadn't drunk it.

Now that she was fully awake, she decided to get up. She unbuckled the strap at her chest and clicked on her light, under which her lists were ready to begin issuing their orders. The lists would know what to do. They would keep her safe from wasting the day, keep her mind sharply focused on the real. Not the unreality of straying thought. On work and dirt, not on closets and tar and the sweet burning taste.

She unbuckled the strap at her waist, sat up with the lists on her lap and read the top items: *Write column. Write letters to the editor. Do laundry. Clean kitchen. Make nursing home arrangements. Kill Little Fiddy.*

Kill Fiddy?! She blinked and strained to make out her writing. *Fill kitty litter*, it said. She breathed relief. She'd run out of kitty litter last week and had put it on her list as a reminder. She always kept a good supply of it on hand at the mansion. It was a useful, all-purpose item she used for soaking up oil and for grip on the steps in winter. She also used it for extra abrasive power when she was cleaning particularly difficult objects like the lobster pot or the inside of a chimney.

She read over the remaining dozen or so items. It wasn't a bad list. Along with her regular chores, she'd have enough to make it through the day. She unbuckled the last strap around her feet and got out of bed. After washing and dressing, she made herself a cup of decaffeinated tea which she drank with half a biscuit and a cigarette. She retrieved her typewriter from her closet and sat down with it at the kitchen table just as the sun was beginning to test the eastern sky.

She'd been writing her "After the Fall" column in *The Northumberland Catholic* for almost twenty years along with at least three letters to the editor per week to various other newspapers. She wrote mostly in defence of Church teaching but she also wrote apoplectically on modern-day atrocities such as the paucity of journalistic integrity, the lack of grammar skills, the global-warming illusion and the subversive activities of the United Nations which she refused to refer to as anything other than the *Fourth Reich.* She detailed the ridiculous and entirely subjective basis for wind-chill figures, condemning the premise that somehow a scientific numeral could be calculated to indicate what the temperature *felt* like. The temperature was what it was. How could it feel like something else?

With words that cut like the edges of a diamond one of her best columns, and one for which she'd received the most mail, had been on the indolent practice of *cutting one's food with one's fork.* The abomination had made itself known to her one day when she'd seen a young woman in a restaurant carving a Salisbury steak in just such a fashion. She'd been appalled to see the woman's elbow cranking like an ice-cream machine. She'd sat watching, unable to eat, as the young woman continued to use only her fork to crush apart the food and to eat it – *with the same fork in the same hand!* Was she too lazy to use the knife with her other hand to perform the function properly? Did she think that by crushing the patty with the side of her fork she was actually saving time and effort? Did she not know how ridiculous and stupid she looked to everyone in the restaurant? Mirabella's face had gone aflame as she'd felt heaps of vicarious shame for the woman.

On her return home, Mirabella had promptly written a stirring piece and the next week received dozens of letters from people all over the province who had lived years of frustration with spouses or other family members who had insisted on cutting their food with their fork. Mirabella had given a welcome voice to their anguish and perhaps had even caused some perpetrators to repent of the maddening habit. After that article, Johnny had begun referring to her "After the Fall" column as her "Eau de Vitriol."

Mirabella had no ideas, however, for what she would write in this week's column. She searched through a recipe box full of index cards she kept for miscellaneous column ideas and finally found an issue that made the gall rise in her throat: parents encouraging their children to say the magic word: *please*. Outrageous!

She began writing. First of all there was nothing magical about the word *please*. One could string it along in a hundred incantations and unless it was aimed at the Lord God, it would never lead to anything magical, let alone supernatural. Second, magic was expressly forbidden by the Bible and Catholic tradition. Third, to encourage children in magic was also a scandalous sin for which parents could expect to pay dearly in extra decades of confinement to purgatory. Magic, divination, the occult, idolatry – these were not laughing matters. She stabbed away at the keys of her typewriter until the seven hundred word column had been belted into place. Satisfied, she whipped the page from the typewriter with a *yap*, folded it into an envelope and placed it in her basket for outgoing mail. Johnny should like this one, she thought.

THE NIGHT WAS FILLED with angst and sleeplessness for the Agent too. Her nightmares, however, were of Mirabella Stuart. Unable to move from where she was chained to a tree, the Agent watched as Mirabella attacked the lamb like a hungry lion. With bared teeth, Mirabella tore the defenceless creature into a thousand pieces while its bawling pierced the air. The Agent awoke covered in fur and blood, which with much screaming and flailing she managed to cast away. The lamb's bawling, however, was not so easy to erase from her mind. At three o'clock in the morning, she found it impossible to seek sleep.

Her subconscious, she determined, was trying to warn her about danger. The lamb was at risk and she had to do something about it. The evidence against Mirabella Stuart was ready but what about in the meantime? What if she were to neglect or abuse or – she could hardly even think about it – *murder* the lamb? The Agent couldn't let that happen. She bounced from her bed, pulled on some clothes and went to the APT Society offices.

She rummaged through the vast equipment room on the sixth

floor, found what she needed and drove to Wintry Hope, arriving before four o'clock. She parked her jeep on an old logging road and trekked through the woods to reach the stand of hardwood trees at the northwest side of Mirabella Stuart's property. She installed four small video cameras to survey the property from four different angles: views of the garden, driveway, lawn and where the Wintry Hope brook cut through the western side of the property near a picnic table. Velcro straps held the cameras securely to the trunks of their host trees without marking or harming them. A small solar panel detached from each camera and extended up the tree trunk toward the sun, where it could gather rays to power itself. The Agent also placed two cameras in the bushes behind Mirabella's trailer where they would directly watch the lamb. If anything illicit were to occur, the Agent would be able to act quickly.

It was after five o'clock when she sneaked away. She thought she heard distant gun shots but when she stopped to listen, she realized it was the *snap, snap* of a typewriter from inside the trailer.

She returned to the offices of the APT Society to get the surveillance system up and running. The six video feeds downloaded digitally by satellite into the APT Society's computers. All six frames came up on a large television screen in the media and communications room. The Agent could manipulate the cameras any way she desired in order to observe the property from every angle and magnification.

She watched the sun come up on Mirabella's lawn. Blue jays came and went, carrying away worms and grubs they dug out of the grass, much to the Agent's horror. At six-thirty she watched Mirabella leave the house with a bucket of water and the Agent leaned closer to the monitor to watch. Mirabella came into view behind the trailer and placed the bucket in front of the lamb. The Agent held her breath, expecting Mirabella to do something cruel to the lamb – like kick it or strike it with a stick – but Mirabella merely gave it the water, watched it drink and fed it grain and millet from another bucket.

Then she watched as nothing happened for several hours. At seven-thirty Mirabella came outside carrying five items which the Agent noted: an empty casserole dish, a bucket with mop, her purse and a super-sized jug of bleach. While coming down the steps,

Mirabella managed to free a hand from the items she was carrying in order to pluck something from a box of geranium leaves at the window. She put her items into the passenger seat of the car and in a storm of black smoke sped off down the driveway. The Agent wailed into her sleeve when she saw a butterfly fly into and become entangled in the radiator of the car. Why, oh why, did the insect world have to suffer so much? She pacified herself with the thought that soon Mirabella Stuart would be paying for her crimes.

FIDDY AWOKE AT TEN-THIRTY with the sun shining in on her from the top of the window. The light was too bright to be the stage-lighting in her dreams and so she pried open her eyes and got up. She went to the bathroom and washed her face quickly in cold water without even bothering to try the hot water taps. Back in her bedroom, she decided it was a day for black and white. She pulled on a pair of cream-white pantyhose, a black skirt and blouse, a white belt and white suit coat. She finished the ensemble with a pair of white gloves, a large heavily starched bonnet and black heels. She looked in the mirror at the finished product. Jackie Onassis smiled back between blinks. On her way out she remembered her diamonds from the dresser and tucked them into a front pocket.

She took an umbrella from Mirabella's coat closet and bounded outside, forgetting breakfast for the time being. She came down the steps with the legs, she imagined, of a prancing fairy and headed for the picnic table near the brook. She walked with extra hip, sat down at the table, opened the umbrella above her head and sighed with pleasure.

She had come for the sounds of the brook. She watched it from the shadow of her umbrella and listened carefully for the different aspects of each of its sounds. From the midst of the stream, in the faster-flowing, frothy water, she heard *wiss, hiss, shish*. Beneath the rushing current, the soft, water-worn stones slapped together, *clabber, clap, clap*. And at the edges of the brook the water chuckled and clucked as if being tickled by the tips of the bluejoint grass reaching down to dabble in it. All the sounds combined to form fresh applause and Fiddy could resist the ovation no longer. She climbed to the top of the table, held her umbrella high and sang:

A love that can hardly be spoken,
a love that I can only sing,
such a love has captured me!

She set the aria free into Wintry Hope and when she finished, listened carefully. She didn't have to wait long before she heard it: wave after wave of resounding applause coming from as far away as the Northumberland shore. She took her bows.

THE AGENT WATCHED Fiddy's performance on her monitor.

"Good thing there's no audio," said her supervisor, Jiminy Tree, coming in behind her to watch.

"Indeed."

"Is this the bulldozer woman?"

"Yes. She doesn't look it, but she's dangerous."

"I didn't realize she was so old. That might not be so good."

The Agent looked up at him. "Why?"

He shrugged. "Old people get too much sympathy."

The Agent fixed a piercing glare on him and began counting on her fingers. "She almost single-handedly destroyed a major waterfowl habitat. She murdered thousands of organisms from every kingdom and phylum. It will take years for the marsh to repair itself. I've never seen ecological havoc on such a scale. Add to that the fact that she nearly killed me and Twig. The woman is a monster. She might look old but she's still a monster. I've documented all the damage she's inflicted between burning down her house and the bulldozer rampage. The legal department agrees with me that it's time these women paid for their crimes."

"Okay, okay," said Jiminy, "I'm on your side. All I said was that if she's old she's likely to arouse sympathy."

The Agent sighed. "Sorry, Jiminy. I've been under a lot of stress lately, trying to get this case together. We have to move quickly or they may do something worse." She swallowed. "They have a lamb."

Jiminy's eyes widened. "That is serious. How close are you to compiling the case?"

"I'm finished. All I need is your go-ahead." She pleaded with her eyes.

Jiminy took a deep breath and considered the request. "Every action we take must be consistent with the overall objectives of the APT Society." It was a quotation directly from the manual.

"Please, Jiminy," she implored. "Give me this chance to prove myself. You'll never forgive yourself if something happens to the lamb."

Jiminy stood before her, meeting her gaze. He kept his hands locked behind his back and appeared to be struggling with the decision. "Okay," he finally said. "Make the call. This'll be your first case."

Her eyes flashed with delight. "You won't regret this," she said fervently.

He met her smile.

She snatched up the phone and dialed.

IN THE DINING ROOM AT APPLEFERN MANSION, from underneath a twenty foot-long solid mahogany dining table, Mirabella scraped away dried mashed turnip flakes with a putty knife. They were stuck to the underside of the table, and she had discovered them – in the shape of Connie Stuart's small hands – while polishing the legs.

Scraping was a satisfying, kinetic task for Mirabella. In the process, sound, vibration and matter were produced, which was far more satisfying than such tasks as dusting or polishing, which produced nothing in the way of sound or discernible change in appearance, owing to the fact that Mirabella dusted and polished so often. The Stuart family, in fact, assumed that Applefern Mansion simply didn't produce dust.

She finished scraping and soaked the remaining turnip particulate with a damp sponge. When it was moist enough, she rubbed it off. But having examined the underside of the dining table, she decided it was in need of a good cleaning, which she promptly undertook, after which she massaged orange seed oil into it. She finished her task by vacuuming the carpet, carefully backing her way out of the room so that none of her footprints remained.

The next item on her list was to clean the toilet plungers from each of the mansion's nine bathrooms. Most people would never think to do that – which is why Mirabella had the job and not any of the two hundred or so other workers who could just as easily have been promoted from the production floor of Johnny's factory. Then she washed and polished the set of silverware on display in a glass case in the foyer. She made Ignacio, a cholesterol-free cake from her favourite cookbook, *Recipes of the Saints*. Tara, Johnny and Martha's eight month old baby, awoke from her nap. Mirabella fed her and put her in a playpen with some toys earlier disinfected with a light bleach solution. She swept the kitchen floor again. She wiped away all water droplets from the sinks. She noticed a smudge on the refrigerator while pacing in front of it and cleaned it. She replaced Tara's clean diaper as a preventative measure.

She had finished everything. The only other item on her list was to make the nursing home arrangements for Fiddy but since that was a personal item, she couldn't do that until she finished at four-thirty. She wandered the mansion in search of something to do. She found it in the foyer. Thirty feet above her head, in the highest arches of the cathedral ceiling, mocking her comings and goings for who knew how long, was a fuzzy circulation fan. With visible dust, no less. The fan was almost always spinning so Mirabella had no idea how the dust had attached itself to the blades. Perhaps it was friction with the air, she theorized, in which a static charge built up on the blades. She would have to rub down the blades with used sheets of fabric softener to prevent them from dusting up again.

She didn't have a ladder to reach nearly that far so she devised a combination of furniture piled in order to scale the distance. She lugged the heaviest piece she could find to anchor the bottom: a Louis Seize armoire with drawers filled with what must have been paperweights. She placed towels underneath the legs to prevent it from etching the silvery marble floor and dragged it directly below the fan. On its polished top surface she hoisted a granite coffee table with legs of dwarf maple, padded with strips of felt so it wouldn't scratch the Louis Seize. On the coffee table she hoisted an eight-drawer pine bureau which she carried up the stairs from a guest bedroom in the basement. On top of that she placed her highest step ladder.

She stood back to estimate if it was high enough. Even with a twelve-foot pole attached at the end of her arm, she didn't think she could quite make it. She went to the library, loaded a box with three dozen volumes of Johnny's rare book collection and returned to the foyer. She placed ten books under each leg of the step ladder and stood back to examine the monument again. It rose before her like the Bastille, although it also had the haphazard quality of a revolutionary barricade. It wouldn't withstand an earthquake or even a strong wind but, by Mirabella's estimation, it would do the trick.

She moved Tara and her playpen to the other side of the foyer, near the telephone table and the hallway leading to the kitchen, well beyond the fallout area should the structure collapse. She picked up the twelve-foot pole, to which she had attached a clutch of vinegar-soaked sponges, and began her ascent. She climbed the Louis Seize, the marble coffee table and the bureau and leapt over the foot and a half of books to the bottom step of the ladder. The structure trembled, but miraculously it didn't topple. She climbed carefully while controlling her breathing, the cleaning pole now in her teeth so that she could grasp both sides of the ladder. Tara stopped sucking a piece of plastic orange and watched with wide-eyed wonder.

She reached the second highest step on the ladder, steadied herself and stood up to her tallest height. The ladder wobbled and she had to use the pole, now in her hands, for balance. By means of powerful concentration, she managed to hold the structure together but when she lifted the pole toward the fan, she was still about five inches short. The only way for her to reach it was to take the final step up the ladder. But on this highest step were emblazoned the words:

CAUTION! THIS IS NOT A STEP. HAZARD!

She struggled with a dilemna: she knew she wasn't supposed to stand on the highest step of the ladder. It was a hazard. The ladder told her so. She rebelled at the prospect of breaking a rule unless she could find some form of justification – a loophole around or through it. In the present case, she couldn't plead ignorance of any kind; the letters screamed out their warning barely a foot below her nose. And she would necessarily have to *stand* on the warning in order to violate it. But when she looked upwards at the fan, the fuzzy dust continued to mock.

No one would know, she told herself. Also, it was a private matter between her and the ladder. No one else would get hurt if she fell. No one had the right to prevent her from undertaking actions which bore consequences for no one but herself. Besides, what right did a ladder have to tell her what to do?

There. She had done it. She had justified the last step. She slowly lifted her foot and with eyes closed, neck straight, pole cross-wise for balance, she placed her foot directly on the warning and rose to stand at the structure's peak. When both feet were safely positioned, she opened her eyes, grasped both hands firmly on the pole, lifted it to the fan, pushed up on her toes to reach across the last inch or so, and started scrubbing.

The degree of difficulty of the task, combined with her violation of the top-step rule, sent a refreshing thrill through her. Each time the ladder wavered and threatened to collapse, a surge of adrenaline and other addictive juices coursed through every fibre of her body. They gave her the superhuman faculties necessary to carry out her task. Her heart pounded like cannon fire in her ears, pulsing through her neck, arms and down her legs. She held her breath between swipes of the sponge and gasped for a few quick ones when she had the chance.

The effort was making her dizzy but she continued to fight. Each stabbing thrust of the pole brought a tortured groan which spoke of agony, fierceness, anguish, enmity and torment and at the same time, exhilaration, ecstasy and fulfillment. Little by little the blades of the fan were being cleared of the dust. Even her Russian-made cigarettes didn't provide this much pleasure.

Then the telephone rang and broke her concentration. Stabbing at the blade, she over-reached and lost her balance. As she fell, her first thoughts were for the Louis Seize at the bottom. Under the weight of the marble coffee table, the bureau, Johnny's rare books, the ladder and Mirabella's broken body, the pressure would likely pulverize it into a mound of very expensive wood shavings. She would need to work for Johnny and Martha until the age of four hundred to pay it off, and she didn't think she would live half that long, even with the assistance of the ten glasses of water she crammed into herself every day, not to mention the bran.

She panicked, and with her panic, her reflexes flashed into action. As she fell, she threw a karate chop against the step ladder. It fell away from the structure and tumbled to the floor while Mirabella, like a hysterical cat, fell with all limbs outstretched to the four piles of books. She landed with a groan but quickly squeezed herself against the lumps of books on top of the pine dresser to hold it all together. The barricade swayed precariously but it stayed in place.

The telephone continued to ring.

After eight rings she roused slightly and pushed herself up to one elbow, where she could see the fan fifteen feet above her head. A partly cleaned fan, she decided, was infinitely worse than an entirely dusty one.

The telephone continued to ring.

She looked from the fan to the phone, as did Tara from her play pen. "You wouldn't mind getting that, would you?" Mirabella asked. Tara tasted a plastic lemon. "I didn't think so."

The phone kept ringing. Fifteen times, Mirabella counted as she lay among the lumps of books, trying to decide what to do. The ringing stopped for a moment and then resumed again.

There was nothing like an endlessly ringing phone to inspire the worst in mental machinations. Had someone been killed? Was the church on fire? Had Connie or Robert been crushed to death by improperly installed playground equipment? With difficulty, she dismounted from the barricade and caught the phone on the twentieth ring. "Applefern Mansion," she gasped.

"Hi, roomy." It was Fiddy's sweet endearing infuriatingly stupid voice.

Twenty demons rose in Mirabella's throat. "This better damn well be important!"

"I assure you, Mirabella, this is of the utmost importance. It has occurred to me that we are both in extraordinary danger."

"From what?"

"I just read in the newspaper you had under the plant on your coffee table that there are five crimes committed every second in this country."

Mirabella waited for more but Fiddy had finished, assuming no doubt that the basis of her fears was entirely self-evident. Mirabella felt like tearing the phone from the wall, running out the door with it, tossing it into the air above the Northumberland and blasting it to pieces with one of Johnny's shotguns.

Instead she took control of herself and breathed deeply. "Don't worry, Fiddy," she said, crushing the black writhing mass within her. "No one in Wintry Hope has ever been robbed, assaulted, murdered, raped or had their property destroyed. Those crimes occur only in towns and cities."

"I'm not worried about that," said Fiddy, her voice dramatically impatient with Mirabella's inability to see the *real* worry.

"What are you talking about then?!"

"Mirabella, Mirabella, my dear simple slow friend. Hasn't it ever occurred to you that we both spend a great deal of our time alone or with people who couldn't possibly provide us with a credible alibi? While all these crimes are being committed, I'm stuck alone in this dumpy trailer and you're down there at Applefern Mansion with Tara, who can provide no alibi of any kind. Any police officer with a quarter of a mind could arrest us for any or all of these five crimes per second. And what could we do? What, I say, could we possibly do? Absolutely positively nothing except to gather up our toothbrushes and take up residence in the big house."

"Don't be so foolish," Mirabella said. "The police wouldn't come after two old women for crimes that were committed a thousand miles away. Have some common sense."

"You simply don't understand me, Mirabella. It's all about having an alibi. Where were you five seconds ago? And the five seconds before that? And the five seconds before that? We have no alibis, I say! No alibis!"

Mirabella felt that, had she been there at the trailer, she'd have had the perfect opportunity, alibi or no alibi, to slap Fiddy hard across the face and tell her to get a hold of herself. Instead she ground her teeth and informed Fiddy that she had too much work to do to worry about such things. “And if you’re so frightened of being arrested, why don’t you go over and stay with Mrs Crowe?”

“You know very well that Mrs Crowe would not be a credible alibi.”

“Then come down here.”

“But who would be your alibi?”

“You would!”

“Me? I’m not going to lie for you, Mirabella!”

The doorbell rang, halting Mirabella’s rage for the moment. “Hold on,” she ordered and went to the door. She opened it. Two police officers were standing on the step. One held an open notebook.

“Mirabella Stuart?” the one with the notebook asked.

“Yes,” she answered carefully. She looked from one to the other in confusion.

The officer took a deep breath and started reading. “Ms Stuart, you’re under arrest for the extermination of an endangered species, emitting toxic substances into the environment, cruelty against animals, illegal dumping practices, excessive exhaust emissions and –” He counted through the other items. “Sixteen related charges of violating the Environment Act, Endangered Species Act, Clean Water Act, the Criminal Code of Canada, the Fish and Wildlife Act, Ecological Reserves Act, Oceans Act, Fisheries Act and the Rio de Janeiro International Convention on Biological Diversity.”

“This has got to be some kind of joke,” said Mirabella, nearly laughing. “Fiddy put you up to this.”

“I assure you, ma’am. This is no joke. Please come with us.”

“Quietly,” added the other officer, putting a hand on his truncheon. Both watched Mirabella warily. “We don’t want any trouble here.”

“This has to be some kind of joke,” Mirabella said again, refusing to believe the scene unfolding around her. She supposed it was either a mistake or some kind of charity fundraiser where local celebrities were taken to the mall in Tina Shingo and 'jailed' until released by adequate donations. Her status as a famous columnist in the Northumberland Catholic would no doubt make her a target.

Or Fiddy had somehow arranged it. She returned to the phone. "Fiddy," she seethed, "the police are here. If I find out you're behind this, I'm going to kill you, charity or no charity." She hung up without waiting for Fiddy's answer, picked up Tara and went out the front door where she was escorted by the officers to a waiting police car.

TEN

Maximo auro accepto illi peritissime perficere possunt actiones – Those who receive the greatest amount of gold achieve their cases with the greatest skill.

– Helena Fisch: *Uncommon Legal Maxims*

FIDDY HUNG UP THE PHONE and wailed. "I told you, Mirabella! It's because you have no alibi!" She rushed to her bedroom – as fast as her Jackie Onassis skirt would allow – to change into clothes more suitable for courtroom drama. She selected a pastel yellow suit with purple blouse, pink high heels, a dusty blonde wig and an enormous hat. A white veil gave mystery to the upper half of her face. She applied ruby lipstick with abundance to the lower half, some extra rouge to her cheeks to speak of innocence, a fan of dark blue around each eye to amplify her tears, should such be necessary, and eyelashes the size of butterflies' wings in case there should be single lawyers to wave them at. When she was finished, she stood back from the mirror and blinked rapidly. She smiled, satisfied with the creature she'd painted. A wealthy plantation owner with many workers at her disposal looked back at her from the mirror, a woman who would never stand for those rascals running off with poor defenceless Mirabella.

She rushed down the hallway to the kitchen and went out the door where she was halted by the police officers coming up the steps. She screamed, dropped her umbrella and swooned against the railing. One of the officers came up to help her.

He put a hand on her arm. "Fiddy Washburn?"

"Alas, this is she," she wailed, a wounded dove.

The officer read the charges, which were the same as Mirabella's except for the bulldozer infractions. He led her to the car and ushered her into the back seat with Mirabella, who had been permitted by the officers to leave Tara with her bewildered parents at SFP International.

"I told you we'd get caught!" Fiddy continued to wail.

"Shut up," Mirabella ordered in hushed tones. "This is some

kind of joke. They have nothing on us. Just keep your mouth shut and we'll be fine."

"Mirabella, I'm too beautiful to go to prison. You're going to have to take the fall for both of us."

"Why should I take the fall?!"

"What does it matter if you go to prison or not?"

"I didn't do anything, that's what!"

"Just think of all the things you could clean, Mirabella. I bet they have dozens of toilets in prison. Think of that! And laundry on a scale you've only ever dreamed of. Oh, and the pots and pans and all those iron bars and I bet they have industrial strength cleaners too."

"That's what I already use. This is all some mistake. I'm not going to prison."

"Oh, Mirabella. Don't you see? You're already in prison. Your clothes aren't much better than what they wear in prison. Your food is probably worse. You get up in the morning before the crows do and you never go anywhere except to work. What's that but prison?" She turned and clung to Mirabella's arm. "You have to save me, Mirabella! I can't go to prison! You know what they do to the pretty ones! You must take the fall! You simply must!"

Mirabella peeled Fiddy's arm from hers and handed it back to her. "Get a hold of yourself, you bumbling idiot."

"Please, Mirabella!" Fiddy sobbed. "I have so much to live for. I hate hard-boiled eggs. Don't make me go to the nursing home!"

"The nursing home? What the hell are you –"

"They'll force me to take sponge baths," she moaned.

"You're confused, you ninny. You're going to prison, not a nursing –"

"I've got to get out of here!" Hyperventilating, Fiddy clawed at the windows like a trapped bird.

Mirabella concluded that she would never find a better opportunity to slap Fiddy, so she pulled her by the hair away from the window and walloped her across the cheek with a thin hard hand. The impact drove out Fiddy's breath – and her false teeth. Mirabella shook her by the neck. "Now shut up and behave yourself! One more word and I'll whack you again, and if that doesn't work, I'll kill you. Then they can take me to prison!"

Fiddy found her breath and bawled like a turkey doomed for Thanksgiving dinner. Mirabella slapped her again but this time the officer driving the car saw it in his mirror and slammed on the brakes. For the rest of the trip, they were both quiet, simply staring at each other through their arms which were handcuffed to the roof.

AT THE COURTHOUSE in Tina Shingo, the Agent sat in a navy-blue business suit made from the wool left by free sheep in thorn thickets in the northern islands of the Hebrides. It was very expensive, but the APT Society had managed to acquire twenty-three of them to use whenever it was necessary to project an image of sophistication and credibility. She glanced down at her coil-bound notes, equipped with a table of contents and index for quick reference. At her feet were thirty-six laminated posters illustrating the crimes that had been committed against the most precious planet in the solar system by the Stuart-Washburn team of savages.

In front of her, beyond the barrister, sat Mr Trotatuch, the lawyer hired by the APT Society to litigate the personal prosecution against Mirabella and Fiddy. He belonged to a prestigious city law firm with hundreds of lawyers and support staff, all housed in a beautiful glass and steel structure towering with perfect consistency above a sewage-infested harbour. As a labour and environmental lawyer he'd fought and sometimes won against the largest corporations in North America. He had only rarely appeared in small provincial towns like Tina Shingo and knew nothing about the presiding judge in this court, but he felt a calm assurance that the most powerful legal maxim in English Common Law – *maximo auro* – would prevail. Those who are paid the most *must* win. He didn't doubt that whatever country bumpkin of a lawyer he faced would be charging less than his five hundred dollars per hour.

"All rise," the Sheriff said in a voice worn out by decades of daily repetition. "Provincial court is now in session with His Honour Judge MacKinley presiding. God save the Queen."

"God save the Queen," mumbled most of the lawyers present.

From the public gallery the dregs, criminals, journalists, societal outcasts and their fragmented families said nothing.

Arthur Stuart sat at the table reserved for defence lawyers. He had been one of the few to have sincerely prayed for God to save the Anglican Queen. He was in court representing a heavily tattooed young man whose only defence to public mischief was public exhibitionism, and although the law had become considerably whimsical in the post Charter years, it had not yet embraced the concept of using one crime as a defence for another. As the most senior lawyer present he would have the privilege of going first. He would quickly take whatever blows his client had coming to him and get back to the office to work on a stack of pre-trial briefs littering a foot and a half of the airspace above his desk.

The jail doors opened and two prisoners were escorted into the courtroom. The first one kept her head down so that Arthur couldn't see her face, but the second one, dressed as a lady of the south, grinned and waved at him. Her torn veil dangled lop-sided from her hat.

He couldn't believe his eyes. He couldn't. He watched in dismay as the officers guided what appeared to be his two aunts in small shuffling steps to seats not far from his table. As he watched them sit down, he was still unwilling and incapable of believing them to be his aunts. He wondered if he was somehow experiencing an extraordinary hallucination. He stared at them for what was only a few seconds but which felt like a very long time. He was trapped in an episode of *jamais vu,* seeing in the two women characteristics he'd never seen before: the lines on their faces accentuated by the fluorescent lights, the tired age in their eyes, Mirabella's cheap, worn clothes, Fiddy's ill-fitting wig. But when Fiddy winked at the Sheriff and Mirabella jabbed her in the ribs, Arthur knew for sure it was them. He rushed over. "What are you doing here?" he asked. "What happened? Are you okay?"

"My makeup's smudged, Arthur," said Fiddy, smacking her lips together to spread around the little lipstick that was left. "They confiscated my lipstick. Can you get it for me?"

"Shut-up, Fiddy," Mirabella ordered, jabbing her again.

She glared at Arthur. "We don't need a lawyer. This is all some mistake."

"We'll see about that. What are the charges?"

"Five crimes a second," Fiddy blurted. "Five crimes a second! And we have no alibis!"

Arthur looked at Mirabella. "She's had a stroke?"

Mirabella shrugged.

"Listen, I'll take care of everything," Arthur said. "Don't say a word unless I tell you to. I'll ask for the charges to be read, and then request an adjournment so we can get some time to sort this out."

"Thank-you for your offer, Arthur," said Mirabella. "But you know I can't afford to pay you. I can't afford even twenty minutes of your time."

"You're my aunt, Mirabella. Don't worry about the money."

"I won't accept your charity."

"It's not charity."

"It is so and I cannot accept it."

"I'll accept it!" Fiddy interrupted, risking another one of Mirabella's jabs.

"Mr Stuart?" It was the judge, growing impatient. "My courtroom is not the proper place to be conducting client interviews."

Arthur straightened and went quickly back to his table. "I'm sorry, Your Honour. Thank-you for your patience. I'll begin immediately."

The judge read from a list placed in front of him by the Sheriff. "Docket number 2131B . . . a personal prosecution . . . defendants are Mirabella Stuart and Fiddy Washburn." Mirabella Stuart? He looked over his glasses at the women, hoping to recognize Mirabella. He assumed she was the tall, intelligent-looking one who was trying, with some effort, to maintain her dignity. Not easy in leg irons and handcuffs.

So this was Mirabella Stuart, he thought to himself, the author of the controversial *After the Fall* column in the *Northumberland Catholic*, which he never missed. The other woman he didn't recognize and had never heard of before. After a brief pause, which he hoped no one had noticed, he continued with a firm impartial voice. "The defendants are being personally prosecuted by Ms Garden Twinkle and the APT Society." He looked over his reading glasses again at Fiddy and Mirabella and then to Arthur. "Your clients, I presume, Mr Stuart?"

"Yes, Your Honour."

"No, Your Honour," Mirabella interjected. She stood up to address the court. "I can't afford this lawyer or any other lawyer. I have absolutely no need of one. I'll be representing myself. I'm not guilty of anything. This is nothing but a ridiculous farce. I can't believe the justice system has come to this."

"I would caution you," said the judge, "against referring to the justice system or my courtroom as a farce, Ms Stuart."

Mirabella's eyes blazed. She could rhyme off a hundred examples of the Supreme Court's farcical incompetence. "Don't I have the right to express myself?" she stated. "Don't I have the right to defend myself? Or has the Charter of Rights been suspended?"

The judge turned his eyes on Arthur, who was keeping his head humbly lowered. "It appears your client wishes to speak on her own behalf, Mr Stuart."

"I assure you, Your Honour, Ms Stuart is unfamiliar with the criminal justice system and is in need of representation. She's nervous and upset, and if in a proper state of mind would choose to have me represent her."

"Your Honour, I'm in a perfect state of mind," Mirabella argued. She wouldn't be paying Arthur two hundred dollars an hour to argue a case she was more than capable of handling herself. "This process doesn't intimidate me in the least. I am perfectly capable of representing myself. Mr Stuart is not my lawyer. I have not retained him and do not wish to be associated with his professional services in any way, shape or form. I don't need a lawyer. I am perfectly innocent of whatever charges these insane people have trumped up."

"Your Honour," Arthur pleaded, "may I have a moment to consult with my client?"

"It seems clear to everyone but yourself, Mr Stuart, that she is not your client. Now sit down before you lose more of them."

"But Your Honour –"

"Sit down, Mr Stuart."

Arthur sighed and sat down. Mirabella was on her own. He stared at the wood paneling beneath the judge's bench where he expected soon to see Mirabella's splattered blood.

The judge nodded to the prosecution table. "You may proceed, Mr Trotatuch."

"Thank-you, Your Honour." Mr Trotatuch stood up. "I'd like to call Ms Garden Twinkle to the stand."

The Agent gathered up her posters and walked to the stand. She sat down demurely, affirmed her oath and looked to Mr Trotatuch, who cleared his throat once and began. "Ms Twinkle, could you please state your name and occupation for the record?"

"Garden Twinkle. I'm a field agent for the APT Society, an organization dedicated to establishing peaceful coexistence between our animal friends and human civilization. We are also active in freeing animals from bondage and oppression, the preservation of habitat, the education of the public and the prosecution of crimes against animal companions."

"Can you tell us what you discovered in relation to the defendant Stuart?"

"Certainly. Some time ago I discovered a large number of dead fish at the mouth of a brook which runs into the Northumberland near Wintry Hope. I traced the source of the pollutants to an outtake pipe on the property of Mirabella Stuart." She held up one of her laminated posters. It showed the rusty pipe seeping fluorescent green fluid, glowing as though it were radioactive. It brought gasps from throughout the courtroom.

"That's not mine!" Mirabella shouted, standing up. "That can't be mine. I don't use green cleaners!"

"I assure you, Your Honour," said the Agent sweetly, "it's hers. I took this picture myself."

"Please sit down, Ms Stuart," the judge ordered.

"But this is ridiculous! She's doctored the picture!"

"You'll have your chance. Please sit down."

Mirabella had no intention of sitting down. "This is

ludicrous," she shouted. "I cannot allow a false impression to be – "

"Sit down," the judge said calmly, "or I'll send you to the men's prison."

Mirabella sat down.

"Continue Ms Twinkle," said the judge.

The Agent smiled again, as sweetly as she could, and told the judge how she'd identified twenty-six toxins in Mirabella's effluent. She showed five pictures from different angles of a ferocious wolf with ghastly glowing eyes and bloodied bared teeth inches from Shaemis's lacerated hind quarters. She noted with pleasure that Mirabella had dumped no fewer than twenty-three bags of garbage in the past week and reported that analysis had shown Mirabella's household garbage had not been sorted for recycling. More pictures showed Mirabella's car spewing a hurricane of black smoke, which violated modern emissions standards by at least a thousand times. Before she finished, the Agent gave estimates of the number of organisms that had likely perished due to the impact on global warming from Mirabella's pollution – the equivalent of three thousand average insects, fifty thousand micro-organisms, two medium sized porcupines or one-quarter of a zebra.

The judge listened intently to her testimony, occasionally glancing at Mirabella, who certainly looked mean enough to commit the crimes of which she was accused. Otherwise he said nothing and listened with interest to the Agent.

After the Agent stepped down, one of the arresting police officers took the stand, was asked some introductory questions by Mr Trotatuch and activated a tape recorder. Mirabella shifted uncomfortably. Fiddy's voice could be heard, with Mirabella's:

I told you we were going to get caught!

Shut up! Just keep your mouth shut
and we'll be alright. They have nothing on us.

Mirabella, I'm too beautiful to go to
prison. You have to take the fall!

Why should I take the fall?

The officer played the rest of the conversation and didn't stop the machine until everyone in the courtroom heard Mirabella screaming:

If that doesn't work, I'll kill you! Then
they can take me to prison!

Followed by Fiddy's choking and gasping.

Mirabella put her head down and rubbed her temples. She felt the condemnation of the entire courtroom, including the row of criminals next to her who, though guilty of public drunkenness, assault, battery, drug offences, grand theft and other vices not even covered by the Criminal Code, summoned great vials of self-righteous anger against her.

After the officer left the stand, Judge MacKinley looked to Mirabella. "Well, Ms Stuart? Do you have anything in the way of a defence?"

Mirabella stood and mustered as much defiance as she could. "Your Honour, the photos of the pipe and the lamb were doctored. They had to be. I don't use green cleaners and there hasn't been a wolf near Wintry Hope in over fifty years. My grandfather shot the last one when he was seventy-one and nailed the paws above the door of our barn.

"The lamb in question has been well-cared for, and in any case I am not the legal owner of the animal. It belongs to Fiddy Washburn. She won it at a fundraiser at the community centre in Wintry Hope.

"It's true, my septic system emits pollution into the environment, but it complies with all the laws and regulations concerning such discharges and has been inspected by the Department of Health.

"The twenty-three garbage bags Ms Twinkle referred to are nothing more than twigs and lawn clippings which were picked up, not by the garbage truck but by a local pumpkin farmer to use as mulch. He pays me thirty cents a bag, and we use all the bags at least five times.

"I recycle my household garbage and claim my deposits at

the environmental depot which they will verify.

"As for my private conversation with Fiddy Washburn in the police car, I was not admitting or confessing to anything. Fiddy has insane notions which are too ridiculous to mention. She experiences delusions and is, generally speaking, a complete moron.

"None of these charges is fair. I've done nothing wrong. I expect full exoneration and an apology from this Twinkle woman and her cronies." Impressed with the sound of her defence, she added: "Together with twenty-five hundred dollars in damages to my reputation."

While Mirabella gave her defence, Judge MacKinley watched her carefully. Accustomed to spotting every guilty twitch, he looked Mirabella in the eye and she looked back at him with defiance. He knew from her demeanor, and from having read her column, that Mirabella Stuart was a relentlessly honest woman more likely to chew off her tongue and spit it in someone's face than to use it to tell a lie.

The Twinkle woman, however, he wondered about. She'd been too pleasant when showing pictures of the ghastly horrors allegedly done to the lamb. She'd been pleasant when describing the perilous deaths of thousands of insects. And she had only affirmed her oath. His instincts told him she was not telling the truth. He was about to dismiss the charges in their totality and award Mirabella damages, somewhere in the realm of two thousand dollars for inconvenience and malicious prosecution, when Mirabella interrupted his thoughts by resuming her defence.

"As I said before," she barked, "these charges are a ridiculous farce. These idiots who arrested me should have been able to see that. They're the ones who should be arrested." She pointed to the police officers, whose faces went scarlet.

The judge sighed. "I would caution you against insulting officers of this court, Ms –"

"And you wonder why no one has respect for the justice system anymore. The justice system is, I can now safely conclude, a complete farce and I will stand by that conviction. When you look at the insane Supreme Court decisions that have come down in the past twenty years, I don't know how anyone in their right mind could possibly conclude that the justice system is anything other than a farce. I can list you ten or more cases that have no basis in logic or reality – "

"Ms Stuart, you are not furthering your case by –"

"The courts are comprised of mindless simpletons who have no more morals than oversexed dogs. It used to be that judges had morals and the criminals didn't. Now it's the other way around. It's no wonder no one respects this institution. And then you drag innocent people like me in here, humiliate and harass me, and meanwhile perverts and pedophiles are running wild in society breeding like rabbits and you don't do a bloody thing."

Arthur covered his head.

The judge sighed deeply, shook his head and turned to Mr Trotatuch. "What are you requesting in terms of punishment, Mr Trotatuch?"

"Only corrective behaviour and a treatment program, together with probation for six months."

The judge thought about it for a moment. Wouldn't hurt her a bit, he concluded. "Granted," he said and held out his hand for the order, which Mr Trotatuch rushed to him. It was a stack of paper a foot thick, at least a thousand pages.

Mirabella gasped in disbelief at the quick verdict and felt her throat constrict. The judge signed a copy of the order and it was handed to her. It was so unexpectedly heavy that she nearly dropped it.

"You're sure you don't want to throw her in jail?" the judge asked.

"The relevant legislation doesn't allow us to impose incarceration for a first offence," Mr Trotatuch said sadly.

"Too bad." The judge finished signing the papers and addressed Mirabella. "You're free to go, Ms Stuart. Report to your probation officer every day and follow the rules of your release carefully, a copy of which you've just received. And stay out of trouble. If I see you back here, I'll throw you in jail, legislation or no legislation. Also –" He pointed his pen at her. "If I read about this in your column, which I otherwise enjoy immensely, I will hold you in contempt of court and have you thrown in jail. Do you understand me?"

Mirabella nodded silently and swallowed. The Sheriff unlocked her leg-irons and handcuffs and she moved like an automaton into the public gallery to await Fiddy's turn.

"Next case is Fiddy Washburn," Mr Trotatuch announced. "The charges are the same with the exception that Ms Washburn also went on a wild rampage with a bulldozer."

Arthur stood up. "Your Honour, I move for immediate dismissal of the charges."

"Objection!" Mr Trotatuch thundered, startling even the judge.

"Yes, Mr Trotatuch?" asked the judge.

"We haven't made our case yet!"

"My motion to dismiss presupposes there is no additional evidence against Ms Washburn," Arthur said politely.

"Well, Mr Trotatuch?"

"We have additional evidence on the bulldozing charge."

"I am aware of the fact that *someone* went on a bulldozing rampage in Wintry Hope, Your Honour," said Arthur. "But there are no witnesses present who can swear they actually saw Ms Washburn driving the bulldozer, and even if there were such witnesses, I would have a very difficult time believing them." He stepped back beside Fiddy and got her to stand up. "Look at the defendant, your honour. She is a very dignified woman of some status and poise who could not possibly have been capable of such an undertaking."

One look at the Washburn woman and the judge had to agree. He wouldn't have believed an army of witnesses that this small, aged lady with a look of utter vacancy in her eyes was capable of even starting a bulldozer, let alone taking one on a rampage. "I agree with you, Mr Stuart," said the judge. He turned to Mr Trotatuch. "Do you have any additional evidence regarding the animal abuse crimes and damage to the environment allegations?"

"The evidence is the same," said Mr Trotatuch. "So she should be found guilty, just like Ms Stuart."

"Your Honour," Arthur replied, "the incidents in question occurred on Ms Stuart's property. Ms Washburn is only a guest in Ms Stuart's home. She's not responsible for the effluent leaking from Ms Stuart's pipes. The lamb allegedly attacked by the wolf was on Ms Stuart's property at all times, and Ms Stuart had the care and control of the animal at the time in question. Ms Washburn hasn't polluted the environment, she has violated no dumping rules, and there is no evidence that she will. She's not guilty of any of these charges."

"I agree," the judge said quickly. "It was probably all Ms Stuart's fault." He suppressed a smile. "Ms Washburn, you're free to go."

"Thank-you, Your Honour."

Fiddy tugged at his arm and whispered something in his ear. "Your Honour," Arthur resumed. "Ms Washburn informs me she has no place to live. Her house recently burned down and she was forced to live with Ms Stuart, who is now undertaking to evict her."

The judge gazed, in shock, at Mirabella. "Is there no end to your cruelty, Ms Stuart?"

Mirabella bolted to her feet. "But it's my home!"

"I've heard enough from you, Ms Stuart. I amend the order to prohibit you from evicting Ms Washburn until such time as she decides to leave or is able to make other living arrangements."

Mirabella gasped.

"Thank-you, Your Honour," said Arthur, unable to keep a small smile from coming into the corners of his mouth. The judge couldn't help but smile back. Few days in provincial court were as entertaining as this one had been.

Good enough for Mirabella, Arthur thought to himself as he left the courtroom. What had she called him the night before at choir practice? A coughing cat?

Outside the courthouse, all three walked across the parking lot to Arthur's car. Mirabella heard Fiddy gabbing with Arthur. "You should have let me testify," she said. Mirabella followed along behind, holding her order on two arms outstretched in front of her.

"I didn't need your testimony," Arthur said. "And besides, we got all we wanted." They stopped beside Arthur's car.

"Next time I think I should testify," she suggested. "I might be able to keep poor Mirabella out of jail."

"We'll see."

Arthur looked at Mirabella. She didn't seem to know where she was. "Are you okay, Mirabella?"

Mirabella looked at Arthur's concerned face. Then Fiddy's. Then she looked down at the judge's order dragging her arms and shoulders relentlessly toward the ground. "Of course I'm not alright!" she erupted. "What the hell did you do to me?!"

"Nothing," said Arthur. "Just as you asked."

"What about this?" She held up the order. "And then you force me to keep Fiddy? How could you do that to me? Your own flesh and blood!"

"You wouldn't let me help you, Mirabella. Remember?"

"You know bloody well I couldn't afford it. You didn't have to make things worse for me!"

"Fiddy was my client. I had a duty to advance her case." He held the door of his car open, and Fiddy got in and rolled down the window, happy to be in the back seat of a luxury automobile.

"Mirabella, dear," she said like the baroness to an unreasonable servant, "it's not so bad. You'll get used to me and Shaemis in a few months or so."

A flash of anger flew from Mirabella's eyes. "I'll burn my trailer to the ground with you in it before I let it go that long."

Arthur told her she could borrow his car and held the driver's door open for her. He'd pick it up later at the mansion.

On the way home, Mirabella brooded.

"I'll be good. I promise," Fiddy said helpfully from the back seat. Mirabella had been too enraged about the other matters to demand that she move into the front. "Although . . ." she added tentatively, "you really can't get rid of me now so I don't think I should have to do any of the housework."

"What have you done?!"

Fiddy thought. She hadn't done anything. She hadn't even washed a fork. "I handed you my dessert to put in the refrigerator."

"You're going to have to eat that before it gets bad."

Fiddy's stomach convulsed and she cursed herself for mentioning it. "Sure, Mirabella. Maybe when I get home."

Home. Fiddy had referred to Mirabella's trailer as her *home*. "Let's get this straight," Mirabella said. "Order or no order, my trailer is not your home."

"Okay, Mirabella." It was easier not to argue with her. Let her have her own way. Fiddy would be as sweet as pie and maybe Mirabella wouldn't burn her alive as she slept that night. That reminded Fiddy of something. "If I'm to stay with you," she said, "I think perhaps we should do something about that wallpaper in my bedroom. Grey-green is simply putrid and reminds me of something Jezebel the cat threw up the year she started eating frogs from the pond. Do you remember? Simply horrid indigestible messes it would leave all over the place. Poor thing lived an awfully long time though. I suppose eating raw frog is good for cats. They say eating fish or chicken is much better than red meat dishes like mice, rats and houseflies. Don't you think? Is frog a fish or chicken dish? I suppose it tastes like chicken but it lives in the water so perhaps it has the nutrients of a fish. I don't know."

Mirabella didn't care. She was too busy offering up her sorrows for the benefit of the souls in purgatory. With this week's sufferings, Martin Luther would be getting his wings.

"I think we'll get along just fine," Fiddy continued. "You and I are frightfully ambidextrous. We're meant to be together." She looked out the window. "Aubergine. That's the colour for my bedroom. Wouldn't that be wonderful? I have no idea what it looks like but I'm sure it must have blue and pink in it. My golly, Mirabella, you're driving awfully fast, aren't you? You'll use less gas if you drive slow and I'll be able to wave to the natives. I'm so happy that I have somewhere to live now. I really must thank you for taking me in." She pointed ahead of them at the road. "Watch out for the puppies."

Indeed Mirabella was driving faster than the limit allowed, and three puppies at the end of three leashes were nearly flattened when she swung the car toward them. Mailboxes and dried grass at the edges of driveways flew past. They passed a tractor on a bridge and squashed a tiny chipmunk that had frozen in the middle of the road, with tiny paws trembling in fear, unable to move as the grill of Arthur's car bore down upon it.

From the back seat, Fiddy didn't see it happen. But she wasn't at all contented with Mirabella's driving or the lack of responses to her continuous commentary. As she talked about shoelaces, sunsets, diamond necklaces, Verdi, the persecution of artists and the demise of the miniskirt, Mirabella simply drove the car and said nothing. Finally beginning to run out of things to say, Fiddy began to pout. Mirabella should at least *try* to indulge her, she thought. She owed her that much. After all, Fiddy had agreed to stay with her in that miserable trailer. It was about time Mirabella showed some appreciation. And if she didn't, perhaps Fiddy would have *her* placed in a nursing home. See how much she liked hard-boiled eggs and creamed corn.

ELEVEN

> Sheep are very good at distinguishing between and remembering other animals. They can remember images of 50 sheep faces for up to two years. They can also recognize animals from their profiles after they have learned to recognize them from the front view.
>
> – *Animal Sentience*

BACK AT HOME, in the kitchen of the trailer, Mirabella made decaffeinated tea for herself and Fiddy and reviewed the judge's order while standing at the counter. On the first page, in large black lettering, was the number to call for her probation officer. She picked up the phone and dialed.

"Animals Are People Too. Agent Twinkle speaking."

"What?" roared Mirabella. "Is this the Garden Twinkle who just had me convicted? There must be some mistake."

"There's no mistake, Ms Stuart."

"But I'm trying to contact my probation officer."

"That would be me."

"But you're the one who had me convicted. Isn't that a conflict of interest?"

"It's too late to dispute the judge's order."

"I don't believe this," Mirabella sputtered. "This is unacceptable. It's ludicrous that you're the one who gets to enforce the order. It's not fair."

"Fair? You want to talk about fair? What about the trees? Is it fair to cut them down? What about the whales? Is it fair that they should choke and die in sewage-polluted waters? What about the cucumber tree? What about the eastern lichen? All it ever wanted to do was to form symbiotic relationships on property uninhabitable by any other organism. Fair? Since when is there fairness on this planet? Is it fair that the life-span of plankton should be cut short by ultraviolet light? Is it fair that gorillas should –"

"Okay, okay!" Mirabella snapped. "Alright, just tell me what to do so I can get this over with."

The Agent sighed. "Thursday morning you must attend

a seminar here at the APT Society offices. In the meantime, study the parameters of the order and call me every day to report on your status."

"Every day!"

"Yes."

"It's not like I killed someone!"

"That's debatable. Besides, you're in no position to negotiate."

"You're a bitch," Mirabella said, unable to help herself. She hung up the phone and turned to Fiddy, who was chuckling. "You're going to a seminar on Thursday," Mirabella said humourlessly.

"Me? What did I do?"

"You won a sheep at Achievement Day."

"What on earth should I wear?"

"Rubber boots and overalls for all I care. Don't you ever think about anything besides how you look?"

"Don't you ever think of how you look?"

Mirabella glared at Fiddy long and hard and wondered if she shouldn't have put poison in the tea the silly twit was now sipping. She could easily escape to Mexico before the stench reached her nearest neighbour. Or she could bury the body in the garden and claim to all who asked that Fiddy had decided to move to Broadway. No one would have trouble believing that. And no one would dare to dispute the choir director of St Margaret's.

Instead she went to the freezer, took out her cigarette can and unwrapped until she found the tar-black treasure within. She lit one and inhaled smoke all the way down to her toenails. She leaned against the counter and wondered how things could have gone so badly for her in such a short time. Only a week ago her life had been fine. Granted, she had always needed to work hard in order to keep groceries on her table and clothing on her back; she could afford very few luxuries. A cigarette now and then was just about it. She'd never taken a trip outside of the province and had eaten in a restaurant only twice in her life. She hadn't liked the restaurant experiences. One had served canned gravy and the other, cole slaw that contained barely three thin threads of carrot. Mirabella had resented spending four dollars on a meal she knew she could make better herself. And of course, there had been that woman with the fork . . .

Only a week ago she'd been in control of every aspect of her life. The garden had grown as it was supposed to grow. She'd never had to talk to Fiddy. She'd gone to work and come home, day in and day out, week after week, year after year, decade after decade. Her pay cheque had covered her bills. She'd done all her chores. She'd never gotten into trouble, let alone been handcuffed or appeared in court. She'd directed the choir, written her column, tended her garden and done her crewel work. Simple, ordered and predictable, all as dictated by her lists. What went wrong?

She glared at Fiddy. Fiddy Washburn. That's where her problems had begun, and she wouldn't be able to get her life on track again until she was rid of her. Why had she invited her into her trailer in the first place? Why hadn't she just let the idiot die of exposure in the tent at the edge of her lawn? It would have served her right. And sooner or later she'd have landed in a nursing home under the protection of Community Services. Mirabella wouldn't have had to do anything at all.

Mirabella shook her head in disgust as she watched Fiddy pour her tea into her saucer to cool it, spilling some on the plastic mats at her feet. How on earth had the mindless nut managed all these years without any thought of survival? Or any thoughts at all, for that matter. How could any practical thing fit in that brain of hers, already stuffed to the brim with the collected works of Shakespeare, Oscar Wilde, Noel Coward, Gilbert and Sullivan, Rogers and Hammerstein and the complete history of human fashion?

But Mirabella had to admit to herself that, whatever Fiddy's lack of faculties, her own defeat had been sound and complete. The question now was what to do to reverse her fortunes. She considered the weapons at her disposal. She could easily make life miserable for Fiddy in ways subtle enough that Fiddy wouldn't be able to blame her for causing them. That was a difficult skill but it came naturally to Mirabella, working effortlessly through her subconscious mind. Turning the hot water taps too tight for Fiddy had been a brilliant example. Unfortunately, Fiddy had the most inimitable shield of innocence – or unreality – surrounding her which prevented her from ever seeing misfortune or bad circumstances or negative feedback or catcalls from the audience for what they really were: reasons to give up, change or head in another direction. Preferably, in her case, down. Instead, Fiddy always persisted with insufferable, constant hope. And that was the crux of the problem: hope defied reality. It defied Mirabella's practicality. It defied Fiddy's mediocrity.

To solve the problem of Fiddy, to shake the rotten tooth loose from the sore gums of Mirabella's mouth, and to put Fiddy on a path towards practical independence, Mirabella needed to destroy Fiddy's ridiculous ill-conceived hopelessly hopeful hope. Perhaps a whole series of subtle mishaps would do the trick. Or a grand event aimed at destroying Fiddy's nonsensical and wholly unreachable dreams. Actually, Mirabella thought, all she really needed to do was wait for one of Fiddy's impromptu performances. Then she could let her have it – let her know how foolish she looked and how awful she sounded. Public humiliation. That would be the best opportunity for forcing a darkening of her conscience, to let her know the reality of her station in life: that she was only average, that she was ordinary, or even less. Who, let alone Fiddy, could stand to be *average*?

"What are you thinking about?" Fiddy asked cheerfully, looking up from her saucer with tea dribbling down her chin, unaware, it seemed, of Mirabella's poisonous glare.

Mirabella took one last drag of her black cigarette, crushed it between thumb and forefinger without the smallest wince and dropped it into the ashtray. "No one," she said.

ON THURSDAY MORNING, the morning of her seminar, the Agent nervously gathered together her notes for her presentation. She'd come to the office early after awakening from a nightmare of bungled exhibits, lost slides, an angry audience and an earthquake that swallowed up the entire amphitheatre leaving nothing but dust and silence. As animals are wont to do, Twig sensed the Agent's unease and made no demands on her attention.

Despite her nervousness the Agent was pleased with the upward surge her career was taking. After only five months on staff she'd managed her first conviction of an eco-terrorist. Jiminy's first conviction hadn't come until he'd been on staff for eighteen months. Of course his first conviction had been of a multi-billion-dollar oil transport company guilty of discharging bilge into St George's Bay, a far bigger fish than Mirabella Stuart, who had only polluted one stream and mistreated a lamb. But it had symbolic significance, and countless millions of micro-organisms would be saved, as well as fish and maybe the psychological health of a beautiful little lamb. And now the Agent had an opportunity to use education and reason to rehabilitate Mirabella Stuart into a productive earth-loving person.

At seven-thirty, with nothing to do but wait for her presentation to begin, the Agent went to the amphitheatre with her cue cards, notes, binders, reference books, slides, posters, exhibits and background music to practice the presentation for the third time. It took five hours to run through so she could only do an abbreviated version. At eight-thirty, as she was finishing her presentation to the empty amphitheatre, she felt a burst of confidence and was able to go to the lobby on the main floor to begin processing registrants.

The first group to arrive was comprised of twelve sluggish sleepy-eyed high school students. The APT Society had secured an agreement with the principal of a nearby high school to send recalcitrant students to its seminars as part of their punishment. The Society also had an agreement with sympathetic local parole officers to force criminals recently released from prison to attend. The remainder of the audience would be comprised of people whom the Society had managed to coerce into attending by threatening expensive legal action. Included in this group were people suspected of having drowned kittens, a biology professor at the local university who ran experiments on legless cats for a revolutionary drug capable of repairing spinal cord injuries, and every farmer in northeastern Nova Scotia who had spread manure or used fertilizers within ten kilometres of a body of water. Polite letters with stern threats had been sent to terrify the parties with the prospect of litigation.

The farmers came, along with the high school students, litterbugs, semi-reformed criminals, kitten-drowners, and at one minute to nine, Mirabella Stuart and Fiddy Washburn. They were quickly rushed through the registration process and ushered to their seats in the front row of the packed theatre.

The Agent entered and took the podium. She smiled to welcome them, even though she felt like running back to the safety of the bathroom and throwing up again. "Sheep, you will soon discover," she began, "are people too. Today you will discover a wonderful world of sheep people."

Insults from hecklers were hurled forward from the back. The Agent gripped the edges of the podium harder to stop her hands from shaking. "This seminar is designed to assist with the integration of sheep communities into our own. Over the course of the next five hours, you will learn how sheep people prefer to live, their amazing qualities and what we can do as concerned citizens to make their lives more fulfilling."

Suddenly, it seemed, the Agent had their attention. A sea of blank faces and wide eyes filled the field in front of her. Somehow, the truth would find a way, thought the Agent. This would be a brilliant success!

She didn't hear the astonished cries from across the auditorium. "*Five hours*!" they uttered in disbelief.

"Sheep people have amazing mathematical skills," she stated. A giant video screen lowered from the ceiling thirty feet above their heads and a sheep appeared. It stomped its foot three times and was given a carrot. "Sheep people have been known not only to play complex pieces of music," the Agent said, "but to compose it as well. I'm sure you are all aware of this famous composition . . ." On the screen, a sheep blew a mixture of air and saliva into a harmonica attached to a stick, producing the first seven notes of *Mary Had A Little Lamb*. The Agent saw the Washburn woman in the front row gasp in astonishment and whisper something to the Stuart woman, who jabbed her in the ribs. The Stuart woman, the Agent also noticed, was taking notes at a furious pace.

"And of course," she continued, "sheep people speak dozens of languages. By the end of this seminar you will be able to communicate in their local dialect, properly care for them and learn what their greatest dreams are . . ." The Agent continued to tell of the talents and virtues of sheep, including that in New Zealand acting as paid counselors to humans.

Meanwhile, the audience was becoming rebellious. Bleating and baaing broke out all over the auditorium amidst laughter and more heckling. The Agent didn't understand the sudden change. Within fifteen minutes she completely lost them. A short gentleman who looked as though he lived on the street got up from his seat and shuffled slowly to an exit.

"Where do you think you're going?" the Agent asked crossly, feeling it necessary to establish order. The audience went silent.

He stopped and looked at her miserably. "I'd rather go back to jail," he said and laughter broke out across the auditorium.

In minutes, the hitherto stationary and merely auditory rebellion became mobile. Human people left in herds of dozens, bleating and baaing. Apparently, they were willing to face the consequences awaiting them in their dysfunctional lives rather than suffer through a five hour seminar on sheep. The Agent faltered as she tried to continue with her presentation while her audience departed. No form of discipline could succeed against such a unanimous rebellion. She wished she could get her hands on a machine gun from the weapons room and spray them with bullets. That would teach them to love their fellow mammals.

In a few minutes, however, the only ones remaining in the auditorium were the Washburn and Stuart women. The Stuart woman was still taking notes but the Washburn woman was alternating between humming *Mary Had a Little Lamb* and the national anthem. The Agent sighed in defeat and looked up at her two remaining captives. "Aren't you leaving too?"

"Are we allowed?" said Mirabella, perking up optimistically and letting her arm have a rest from frenetic note-taking.

The Agent thought about it. What was the point? Two stragglers wouldn't assuage her failure. But Mirabella had asked if they were *allowed* to leave, which implied that they wouldn't leave unless permitted to do so. "Of course you aren't allowed," said the Agent.

"Well then, get on with it." Mirabella readied her pencil for more note-taking and the Agent, surprised by her power, resumed.

When it was over and the Agent had finished thanking them all for coming, Fiddy stood up and tried to applaud. Mirabella pulled her back, stuffed reading materials into her hands, told her not to be such an idiot and steered her to the nearest exit. Fiddy tried to escape so that she could congratulate the Agent on her performance but was again thwarted by Mirabella. When Mirabella finally managed to strong-arm her through the exit and the doors closed on the silent auditorium, the Agent put her head down on the podium and wept.

"It wasn't that bad," said a man's voice from the darkness at the back of the room. She looked up and saw Jiminy coming toward her. Her shame intensified. As bad as the presentation had been, at least she had clung to the hope that her immediate superior hadn't seen it.

"I'm sorry, Jiminy. I don't know what happened. I'll try harder next time."

"You did fine. Don't be discouraged. It was a good effort."

She shook her head. "You don't have to pretend, Jiminy. I know it flopped." Tears trickled from her eyes. "I don't understand why. I had statistics, I had evidence, I had film footage of sheep people doing fantastic things, and they just sat there as if a sheep person stomping out the answer to four minus one was something other than extraordinary. What's wrong with me? What is it about me that turns people away from our message?"

"You can't blame yourself for not being able to reach them. All you can do is your best. Some people simply can't or won't be changed."

The thought was incomprehensible to the Agent. She wiped away her tears as new ones came. She thought about all the organisms in the world that would have to suffer before humanity would change. "We have to change them," she said fervently. "We have to."

Jiminy shrugged. "I think you're right, Garden. Believe me, I really do. But education only works on some people."

"And the rest? What do we do about them?"

Jiminy sighed. "I didn't expect you to come this far in one year, let alone a few months." He hesitated and she waited for him to say more. He seemed to be struggling with what to tell her. "Education only works on some people," he repeated.

She gazed at him in confusion.

Finally, he told her: "Why do you think we have a weapons room?"

"WHY DIDN'T YOU let me talk to her?" said Fiddy as Mirabella loaded her into the car and nearly slammed the door on her feet. "Why didn't you let me talk to her?" she asked again when Mirabella was behind the wheel.

"I was afraid you'd encourage her and I'm in a rush. I've got to buy the mini-barn and get home to cover my kohlrabi before it gets too much sun." The car roared to life and she pealed out of the parking lot.

Fiddy wanted to talk about the Agent's performance. "She was fabulous, don't you think? Such passion."

"It wasn't an opera, you idiot, it was a seminar and it was torture."

"I suppose that's why you stayed," Fiddy mumbled.

"What's that supposed to mean?"

"You, my dear old rusty nail, enjoy torture."

"Don't be ridiculous. No one enjoys torture like that."

"I did. Of course I didn't see it as torture. I enjoyed it immensely. From now on I'm going to sing to Shaemis in his own language."

Mirabella slammed on her brakes at an intersection. "Don't be so foolish. He won't understand a word of it." She pressed her foot down on the accelerator and they were off again.

"And who would have known that Shaemis knows math? I wonder if we get him a harmonica, will he be able to practice his music?"

"The only thing I wonder about is whether we should get the entire lamb in chops or have him cut into roasts."

"Mirabella!"

"What?"

"That would be murder!"

"Killing animals is not murder!"

"It is!"

"It's not. And if it was, you'd be guilty too. You had bacon for breakfast this morning."

Fiddy gasped. "Bacon comes from sheep?!"

"No, you imbecile. It comes from pigs. You ate the flesh of a pig this morning." Mirabella hadn't had any of course, owing to her cholesterol-free diet.

Fiddy put a hand over her mouth. "You're right," she said. "I am a murderer. I'm a killer and a cannibal."

"You are not. Killing an animal is not murder. Animals have no souls."

"You don't know that."

"I do know it. All you have to do is watch them. Animals lack the capacity to appreciate beauty. Have you ever seen a goat enjoy a sunrise? Have you ever seen cows praying? Have you ever seen a dog or a cat gazing with stupendous astonishment at a perfectly cleaned toilet bowl?"

"Now that you mention it, I can't say I have."

"There you go."

"But animals are smart and they feel pain. I think in this age of advancing rights that animals can be people too."

"Animals are animals."

"No, Mirabella. People are animals."

"If sheep are people and people are animals, then sheep are also animals."

Fiddy opened her mouth to respond but got stuck somewhere in the barbed wire of Mirabella's logic. Her brain's wattage strained under the pressure. She chose not to fight Mirabella with logic but to concentrate on her strengths. "Mirabella, sheep people have feelings, just like you and me." She thought for a moment and then added, "Or at least like me."

Mirabella shot her a dirty look but refused comment.

Ten minutes later they made it safely into the parking lot of the building supplies store. Before she got out of the car, Mirabella turned to Fiddy. "This is the last word on the matter. Sheep are not people. Sheep are to be eaten by people. They don't know the difference. They have no souls and only a very minimal level of intelligence. Animals do not have the capacity to make choices. They are motivated by hunger, the need for safety from predators and hormonal urges relating to reproduction. It's a scientific fact." Mirabella stuck her finger in front of Fiddy's mouth which had opened to protest. "If you mention it again I'm going to cram your fat ass in the trunk and leave you there until we get home."

"But –"

"I don't want to hear any more of your nonsense!" Mirabella said, her face red. She slammed the door shut and marched to the entrance of the store.

Fiddy quickly rolled down her window and stuck her head out. "Mirabella, you've got to understand! You're blinded by the wool covering your eyes!"

They arrived home towing a small red mini-barn on a trailer attached to a hitch at the back of Mirabella's car. Mirabella expertly backed the barn to her back lawn, turned off the car and got out. Then she opened the trunk to let Fiddy out. As Fiddy was taking her first deep breath of air, Mirabella stuck a finger in front of her face. "Not another word about it."

Fiddy's lips took the shape of a pout. "I was simply going to say that –"

"Not another word or you're staying in the trunk for the night!"

Fiddy glared at Mirabella. A tire wrench had been digging into her back and the spare tire had stained her dress. "Okay," she said, and offered Mirabella her hand to help her out.

When Fiddy had been pulled free of the trunk, she attempted to regain some of her dignity while Mirabella detached the straps holding the barn to its wheels. She watched as somehow Mirabella managed to pull, push, lift and heave the entire mini-barn onto her back. Gasping and groaning, she took a painful laboured shuffle and brought the gargantuan mass forward a half foot. Sixteen more steps and she came around the car where Fiddy was standing in the way.

"Move, " Mirabella grunted, trying to get by.

"Oh," said Fiddy, startled. "I do say, please forgive–" Astounded by the exercise and somewhat frightened at the spectacle of Mirabella's strength, she moved out of the way. "Mirabella," she whispered. "Don't you think you should get some help with that?"

"I . . . can . . . do . . . it," Mirabella moaned and took another painful shuffle forward.

"What about your back?"

"I . . . have . . . a . . . good . . . back," she grunted. Another partial step.

"Are you sure you don't want me to call someone?"

"I . . . said . . . I . . . can . . . do . . . it . . . myself!"

"Okay," Fiddy said pleasantly. Content to watch, she pulled up a lawn chair, opened an umbrella over her head to keep off the sun and watched as Atlas carried her mountain another sixty tiny steps to the desired location, turned the entire structure around and let it gently down on the grass.

Mirabella straightened her back and brushed the dust from her hands. "I knew I could do it," she said proudly.

"Indeed you did," said Fiddy from under her umbrella. A new respect – and awe – of Mirabella shined in her eyes. "You need no one, Mirabella Stuart."

"You've got that right." Mirabella brushed a hand down the side of the barn and admired its clean symmetry and neat, finished construction. "This will make a great shed after we butcher –"

"What?" Fiddy bolted upright in her chair. "After we butcher what?!"

"Nothing."

"Don't even think about it," Fiddy scolded, with the air of an aristocrat. "Shaemis is my dearest pet."

"We'll see. After all this nonsense is over, I might sell him to a local farmer."

"But he's mine!"

"The court said it's mine."

"You can't, Mirabella! You simply cannot!" Fiddy stood up, like a small soldier. "Shaemis is mine. You can't put him in a farm. He hates institutionalized food and he'd have none of the privacy and independence he has here. Farms are horrible places where caretakers beat their patients. People go there to die, not to live."

"What are you talking about?"

"Shaemis hates baloney and creamed corn!" blustered Fiddy. "He hates being treated like everybody else. He's an individual. He wants a different breakfast than everyone else. Berries with cream and sugar in the summertime and *crêpes à la mode* with a leaf of mint in the winter. He wants to spread his wings and shine like the sun before his short life is finished, before his corpse rots in a politely marked grave with no one remembering how he once lived."

"You're insane," said Mirabella. "I have no idea what you're talking about, but I can tell you one thing –" She pointed to Shaemis munching nearby. "As soon as I get that Garden Twinkle off my back, Shaemis is going to a farm and you'll be going to a nursing home."

"Oh no he's not," a voice said from around the corner of the trailer.

The Agent appeared, unsmiling.

"I was just kidding," Mirabella said quickly. She made an attempt at smiling. Fiddy rolled her eyes. Mirabella's smile was as natural as lobster shell pie. "Ha, ha . . . ha," Mirabella continued, trying to laugh. "I wouldn't do that to dear little Shaemis. He's a part of the family now."

"You're right," said the Agent. "And article 457 (d) of the court order states you must care for him until his natural death."

Mirabella gasped. "Natural death? That could be years!"

"One can hope," said the Agent and she stepped around the barn to examine it. "Regulation width and height with not much room to spare. It could be bigger but I guess it doesn't violate the requirements. You'll need to put in another window as he needs to have more natural light and a cross current of air at night. I also recommend a skylight so he can see the stars and moon. This rusty red colour will not do at all. What's Shaemis's favourite colour?"

"Periwinkle blue," Fiddy said before Mirabella could open her mouth.

"Periwinkle blue it is," said the Agent. "You'll also need to apply a waterproof finish to the floor and add insulation to the walls. Perhaps you should make a list." She turned to Mirabella who was already scribbling and was at twelve items and counting.

[TWELVE]

The *Fata Morgana* is a mirage produced by reflections of light through layers of air of varying temperatures. Inversions are created which cause objects such as ships and islands to appear greatly expanded in size, sometimes to the point of floating in the air. Small sailboats can appear as gallant ships, tugboats as castles, and islands can hover mysteriously in the sky.

– James Finton: *Northumberland Light*

IN MIRABELLA'S KITCHEN the Agent went through the new procedures introduced to Mirabella's life. They stood at the sink and the Agent poured a clear liquid on a sponge, which she handed to Mirabella. Mirabella held it up to her nose and sniffed. "But it doesn't smell!" she exclaimed.

"It's not supposed to."

"How on earth can it clean then?"

The Agent sighed. For hours, it seemed, she had been instructing Mirabella on new ways of doing things, and she wondered if Helen Keller's teacher didn't have it easier. "The scent has nothing to do with how powerful a cleaner is," she explained. "It works the same whether it smells like lemons or not."

Apparently unconvinced, Mirabella picked up the bottle and read its contents: "Water, corn starch, palm kernel oil, cellulose and grapefruit seed extract." She laughed.

"What?" asked the Agent, visibly perturbed.

"This is useless!"

The Agent snatched the bottle away from Mirabella. "It doesn't need gasoline in it to work, you know."

"No, but you shouldn't be able to spread it on bread and serve it as a sandwich."

"It's called *natural.* And it works. Try it." She stepped away from the sink and Mirabella came forward with the sponge. The sink was already speckless except for a dried spot where Fiddy had left a tea bag. Mirabella began cleaning the residue with the sponge. After scrubbing, she rinsed. The stain was still there. She scrubbed harder, rinsed again and looked closer. It hadn't gone anywhere.

Mirabella looked at the Agent skeptically. "I might as well be rubbing it with a tomato."

"You've got to put some elbow grease into it."

"I know all about elbow grease," Mirabella snarled.

The Agent sighed. She'd covered sheep care, household waste management, energy use, disposal of waste water and composting, all of which were contained in the first two hundred pages of the court order. Perhaps Mirabella had had enough for one day without tackling the issue of biodegradable cleansers. "We'll pick this up tomorrow," she said. "And we'll talk about what you can and can't do in your garden."

Mirabella's mouth dropped open. "My garden?!" she sputtered. "What on earth do you want to do with my garden? Isn't a garden natural enough for you radicals?"

The Agent went to the door. "We'll talk about it tomorrow after you've had a chance to read the rest of the court order." She slipped out but Mirabella pursued.

"You're not touching one single leaf of my garden," she called out the door. "Do you hear me? Not one leaf!"

There was no answer. The Agent's hybrid electric jeep disappeared silently down the driveway.

Mirabella came back inside. "Do you believe that woman?"

Fiddy was sitting obediently in her chair in the corner of the livingroom, her face unable to contain her amusement as she'd watched Mirabella's lessons. "Well, dearest, you were poisoning the earth."

"I wasn't doing anything illegal," she snapped. She went to the freezer for her cigarette can and began unwrapping the necessary layers. "You aren't in the free and clear either," she said to Fiddy in a more reasonable tone. "She's going to start monitoring our water consumption, so you'll only be able to flush the toilet once a day. Toilet tissue is limited to five squares per –" Mirabella gasped as she reached the innermost layer. She pulled out a small note and read:

Dear Ms Stuart:
Cigarettes create noxious toxins which pollute the

atmosphere. I've therefore confiscated them pursuant to section 582(f) of the Court Order.

Sincerely,

Garden Twinkle, APT Agent

"I don't believe this." Mirabella tossed the note aside. "She took my cigarettes."

"I thought you said you weren't addicted to them."

"Aren't I allowed to enjoy a cigarette now and then!" Mirabella shouted.

"Sure. It's no worse than having a few champagne cocktails."

"It's completely different." Mirabella had written extensively to condemn the consumption of alcohol and to justify smoking, so she knew what she was talking about. "Drinking leads to fornication, divorce, mental disease and debauchery. There's nothing wrong with one or two cigarettes. That's not an addiction. A few cigarettes a day is nothing more than innocent entertainment, a pastime."

Fiddy batted her eyelashes. "Methinks ye doth protest too much."

"Six cigarettes!" Mirabella shouted. "That's all I ever have in one day. That's not an addiction. Don't put me in the same category as a dirty old drunk."

Fiddy shrugged. "As you like it."

Mirabella continued to stand in the middle of the kitchen floor. She hated when Fiddy agreed with her. She wanted to fight. Winning against Fiddy was no fun unless Fiddy broke down in tears, with moaning and gnashing of teeth. "I'm going to the store," she said. She gathered up her purse from the table and took her car keys from the nail beside the door. "After that I'm going fishing at Tanderlush Delta to see if I can catch something for supper." If she had to feed Fiddy, she might as well try to do it cheaply. From the broom closet she took her fishing pole, a gnarled alder branch with a string wrapped around the end with a rusty hook. She aimed the pole at Fiddy. "Sit there and don't touch anything while I'm gone. I'll be back in an hour and a half, depending on the fishing. An hour and three-quarters at the most."

MIRABELLA LEFT and Fiddy went to the window to watch the tempest disappear down the driveway. "Sit!" she said to herself, mocking Mirabella's fierce tone. She pointed to the chair as though to an imaginary dog. "Sit, Fiddy! Stay! Roll over!" Then she panted and barked.

She wouldn't sit. She had no intention of sitting. She went outside and sat down at the picnic table near the brook to take in the late afternoon breezes coming up the hills from the western Northumberland. A moist, stinging saltiness wafted up from the strait. Fresh alder shoots. The dust of willows and spruce and the sweet perfume of wild roses. The scents blended together like the harmonies of *How Great Thou Art*. Fiddy stood and sang.

When she recited all the words she knew she let her voice trail off. The brook applauded, *clabber, tickity, tap*. "Why, thank-you," she said and bowed.

She sat down again and watched the strait. The air over the Northumberland was thick with rising moisture and was beginning to weave its illusions. The distant islands, usually thin black lines, grew to lush, mountainous kingdoms. As Fiddy watched they swelled on the Northumberland in a miracle of strength, took a breath and lifted. Motionless above the waters they somehow held to the sky – the *Fata Morgana*. Fiddy watched in wonder. How did the sky hold them? Was it the water that pushed them there? What kept them in their transcendent state, in defiance of the laws of reality?

Perhaps it was time someone investigated this grand event. Someone comprised of equal parts earth and sky, earthly and heavenly qualities that allowed for insight into the transcendent hidden world. Someone like Fiddy. She could swim or sail to the islands, watch them come so close that they would suddenly be towering before her, a wall of wavering blueness, not water, not sky but something else. Then she would be beneath the island and the cold shadow would be over her. She would look up at the heavy mass looming dangerously overhead. It would be moving slowly, a gentle mountain dripping with brine. She couldn't resist – a hand went up to touch. She could feel the power vibrating within. And then the mystery would include her. Changed, she would leave the water's tenuous grasp and join the island in the air. Now, beyond the constant paralysis of weight, she would see everything as it truly was. She would be free.

She continued to watch the strait dreamily, singing her tunes and rejoicing to live in a land where even islands could become part of the sky.

"The next time we're at the beach," she told Mirabella when she'd returned from fishing. "I'm going to swim to the islands."

Mirabella dropped a sloshing bucket on the picnic table. "You couldn't swim ten feet without drowning." A domestic cigarette dangled from her bottom lip.

"I'll be as light as the air."

"Stop talking like a crazy person. I caught twelve smelts. You can help me gut." She placed her fishing pole across the table, the end of it directly beside Fiddy. A fat worm struggled to wriggle free of the hook impaling it.

Fiddy shrieked. "A lady does not gut," she told Mirabella. She kept her back to Mirabella and continued to watch the distant hovering kingdoms. Mirabella slammed a hammer into the picnic table and a spray of fish guts went into the air.

Fiddy turned around, having felt the spray on her back. "What are you doing?" she asked, almost afraid of the answer. She saw Mirabella fishing inside the bucket with her hand, trying to catch another smelt.

"I've got to kill them first," Mirabella said. Panicking smelts splashed in the water and she averted her face. "Aha." She pulled out a fluttering fish and forced the unfortunate creature against the picnic table. It squirmed against her hand, its eyes bulging with the pressure. She lifted the hammer.

Fiddy closed her eyes and screamed as Mirabella slammed the hammer down on the smelt, pulverizing its head. Fish blood, guts and scales sprayed in her face. When she opened her eyes, a lifeless fish lay before her.

"Now, gut," Mirabella ordered.

Fiddy gasped for breath. "Of all the unspeakable things you've done, Mirabella Stuart, this is the most obscene display of cruelty I've ever seen. Upon my soul, the pain I feel is like nothing you've –"

"It's the most humane way to do it." Mirabella fished for another smelt as they tried to escape, darting around the bucket in endless circles. "Letting them suffocate in the sun is cruel."

Fiddy didn't know what to say. She could never, it seems, find a way of countering Mirabella's logic.

"It's better if it's sudden," Mirabella continued. "Trust me." She caught another one and forced it to the table.

Fiddy closed her eyes again and when the hammer came down she winced. *The sound of it,* she thought as it repeated itself over and over again in her mind. *Thump. Squash. Thump*. It was like running over a small animal on the road and hearing the impact over and over again. "You're a monster!" she wailed, covering her ears.

"Shut up and gut." Mirabella tossed her another lifeless smelt with its head mashed.

"I told you," Fiddy said, her eyes filling with tears. "A lady does not gut."

"Gut the fish or I won't take you with me to the mansion." She reached into the bucket, followed the fish around, caught one and forced it to the table.

Fiddy closed her eyes again, kept her ears covered and howled when she still heard the hammer slam against the table. Mirabella suppressed a smile when she saw the blood spraying into Fiddy's hair. "If you gut," she said, when Fiddy had uncovered her ears and was taking deep breaths, "and eat just a little bit of the fish guts . . ." She paused while Fiddy listened. "I'll let you sing a solo."

Fiddy didn't immediately say anything. She considered the offer. "At the Bishop's Mass?" she asked.

"No. Better. The feast day of St Margaret of Scotland in November."

Fiddy considered it carefully while Mirabella fished for another smelt. It was just a small bit of fish guts to eat, she thought. Probably not even an entire mouthful. To gut fish after they were dead was not inflicting torture and if the smelts only knew the joy their sacrifice was bringing to her and the world, surely they would readily agree to her gutting them. "It's a deal," she said and snatched up the knife. Holding it delicately between her multi-coloured nails, she sliced open the pouch of one of the smelts and squeezed out brown, purple and red guts.

"There," Mirabella said, pointing with her hammer to what looked like squashed purple worms. "Eat that."

Fiddy put down the knife and stared, forlorn, at the pieces of flesh. "Please, Mirabella. You can't be serious. I'm helping you gut. Isn't that enough?"

"Eat it or I won't let you sing."

Fiddy's head swam at the thought of placing the pancreas or intestine or lung or whatever part of the fish's innards it was into her mouth and swallowing it. "What if it's poisonous?" she asked. The blood drained from her face.

"It's your choice," Mirabella said.

Fiddy took deep breaths. Her eyes smarted with tears and her stomach churned. She suppressed the urge to vomit and picked up the bits to which Mirabella had pointed. They were cool in her fingers and left a stain of brownish particulate on the table. She looked at Mirabella, then at the fish guts in her fingers, then at the festival of blood and fish pieces around her on the table. She took a breath, closed her eyes, put her fingers in her mouth, swallowed – and fainted.

When Mirabella brought her back to consciousness, she opened her eyes with a start, sat up from the ground and sputtered, "I did it!" She looked around. "Didn't I?" She wasn't sure. Perhaps the fish guts hadn't gone down or perhaps they had come back up and Mirabella had disqualified her.

Mirabella shrugged. "I guess you did it."

"I did it!" she concluded. "I did it! Thank-you, Mirabella. You won't regret this." She pulled her dress above her knees so that she could turn over and scramble to her feet from the ground. "I've already got my piece picked out: *Morning Has Broken.*" She pushed Mirabella aside and struggled to get up to the seat of the picnic table. She turned to face the brook, opened wide her mouth and sang:

Morning has broken,
like the first morning,

Black bird has spoken,
like the first bird!

The brook continued to chuckle and cluck its applause. She bowed to the Northumberland where the islands were still rising for her. She hopped down and resumed her gutting, enthusiastically slicing and scraping scales and skin. She didn't even flinch when Mirabella brought the hammer down to smash the head of another wriggling fish.

MIRABELLA SMILED INWARDLY. Fiddy would have allowed *herself* to be gutted if it meant an opportunity to perform. What she didn't know, however, was that the feast day of St Margaret of Scotland fell on a Thursday which meant there would be four or five people at the Mass at the most. And probably all of them would be deaf. Mirabella couldn't wait to see Fiddy's face. Serves her right, she thought, for not doing her homework. The devil was in the details.

Mirabella managed, after some struggle, to capture the last smelt and hold it to the table. It squirmed uselessly under her hand, almost tickling her as it continued to do the only thing instinct allowed it to do: swim. Even in the air. Its tiny lips gasped for empty breath and its black-green translucent eyes bulged with the pressure of her hand.

For a fleeting moment, it occurred to Mirabella that she should let this one go. She could set it free in the brook gurgling its invitation only a few feet away. The smelt could probably hear it, or at least sense the brook's calling. What would it feel like to be in the brook again, with its clapping rocks, swishing currents, playful eddies and crystal pools catching the shimmering sun on its surface? Would the smelt make it back to the warm strait through the network of creeks in the hills of Wintry Hope, around the swamp, through the frothy gorge and over the falls to the beach? Even if it made it that far, would it make it under the sand and rocks piled high on the beach through which the brook trickled into the Northumberland at high summer?

Not likely, she concluded. Smelts had never made it up the brook as far as Mirabella's trailer. And now its wriggling diminished perceptibly under her hand. Smelts couldn't swim in the air.

Still she couldn't bring down the hammer. Why should the last smelt be so difficult? It was exactly the same as all the others, just like the thousands of other fish in the waters of Tanderlush Delta, in the brooks all over Nova Scotia and from one end of the Northumberland Strait to the other. Just like the sixty billion other fish in the world, all the same, all average, none any more worthy than the others of greatness. Or mercy.

She glanced at Fiddy, worried that her hesitation had been seen, but Fiddy was too deeply engrossed in her work to notice and was happily humming *Morning Has Broken*. The fish stopped wriggling altogether and merely moved its mouth. Its convulsing inner organs sent a dim, vibrating *hum* through her hand. It was too late for the fish. It wouldn't survive in the brook now. She slammed the hammer down and squashed its head. The convulsing stopped and the fish was still and cool under her bloody hand.

Fiddy stopped humming and looked up at Mirabella. "What's wrong?" she asked, pushing her wig back with her arm and leaving streaks of blood and brown guts on her forehead and in her hair.

"Nothing," Mirabella said. She took another knife and began gutting the fish. She was right about the fish, she told herself. The hammer was a far more humane end to its misery than either suffocation in the sun or the endless challenges of the brook. It was cruel to give it the hope that some day it would return to the warm freedom of the Northumberland.

If only Fiddy could learn that.

THIRTEEN

Good babysitters are safety-conscious and take extra precautions to make sure the children are safe from accidents.

– A Guide to the Business of Babysitting

THE APT AGENT entered the elevator of the APT office building, confident that she'd made a good effort at educating Mirabella Stuart. Although the woman had balked at any interference with her garden, she had listened to the basics of recycling, composting and the use of earth-friendly household products. Mirabella Stuart would be changed. The scorpion would learn not to kill.

The elevator doors opened, she stepped out and met the arresting stare of Jiminy. His eyes were red and swollen, as if he'd been demonstrating outside a petrochemical refinery all day. "What is it?" she asked.

"Awful. It's even worse than the seals."

"What could be worse than the seals?"

Jiminy led the way to the media room, where he turned on a monitor. Mirabella and Fiddy came into view at the picnic table. The sun was shining, the grass was green, the brook twinkled with flashes of light, the leaves of the trees trembled in the light breeze. "What are they doing?" she asked.

Jiminy waited for the video to speak for itself.

Fiddy was talking rapidly. Mirabella raised a hammer and brought it down on the picnic table. Fiddy shrieked. Mirabella fished around in a bucket and water splashed. The women were arguing. The hammer came down again. Fiddy covered her ears and screamed, her eyes clenched shut. Mirabella struck again with the hammer. Fiddy had blood on her forehead. Fragments of bloody matter splattered into the air. Knives. Scales. Eyes. Heads. Severed tails. As Mirabella raised the hammer again, the Agent covered her eyes. "Turn it off!" she screamed. "Turn it off!"

"I'm sorry," Jiminy said. New tears ran down his face. He sat down on the floor.

The Agent was nearly hyperventilating. "I can't believe it. How –" She looked to Jiminy, then at her surroundings in disbelief, wondering if she wasn't somehow trapped in another nightmare. A clock ticked. Computers hummed. Through the glass door she could see colleagues busily answering phones and stapling protest signs to wooden stakes. She wasn't dreaming. "They should be in jail!" she wailed.

"It's not illegal to fish," Jiminy said from deep within his catatonic state. "The law says fish can be tortured and killed on a whim."

"We have to do something," the Agent whimpered. "I can't live like this. I can't live in a world like this!" She looked at him fiercely. "They should be the ones to suffer!"

Jiminy looked at her in surprise.

"I'm sorry," she added quickly. "I didn't mean that."

"You're just being honest. And maybe you're right. Maybe Mirabella Stuart won't be able to change until she understands what it's like to suffer like those she tortures."

"I have to try harder," the Agent resolved.

"Maybe you should change your approach. Education doesn't work for everyone, you know."

She looked at him desperately. "Maybe I should show her some movies of the seal hunt or take her to one of our protests so she can find out what real people believe." She strained to think of other strategies.

"Education might not be the answer," he said again.

"I can teach her."

"And if she doesn't learn? What then?"

"I won't give up, Jiminy. I'll be relentless, until the task is done. I won't let you down."

"I admire your effort, Garden, but you've got to think of things from other perspectives. Some people are beyond being educated, beyond the ability to adapt and change. Education only works for rational people like us, not a wild cave woman like Mirabella Stuart. People like Mirabella Stuart remain who they are regardless of the arguments laid out for them. People like Mirabella Stuart remain the way they are – forever."

The Agent was confused. "You're not making any sense, Jiminy. Education is our *only* tool."

Jiminy waved to the windows beyond which the houses and streets of Tina Shingo gave way to the harbour. "See this?" he asked. The harbour, pushing in at high tide from St George's Bay almost to the centre of town teemed with thousands of happy sea birds – osprey, blue heron, terns, cormorants and even the occasional puffin – feeding in the sun-warmed shallow waters. "Further out in the bay, white belugas are feeding, with the tuna and porpoises. I've sat on the beach and watched them chasing schools of mackerel and herring. Do you know what else is there?"

She nodded. She could list at least three hundred species.

He answered for her. "Lobster, the most exploited creature in the world." His eyes became fierce. "Imagine it, Garden: their abduction from quiet, cool depths, being thrown into trays or packed into crates, pierced on their spines and prickles, jailed in small tanks where they're deprived of oxygen. From there . . ." Jiminy struggled to speak. ". . . boiled alive. Some are chopped up while still alive, soaked in a vinegar marinade and . . ." His voice croaked: "Flambéed"

The Agent knew all this. She looked at her boss with a mixture of confusion and discomfort. "Jiminy, what are you suggesting?"

He turned from the window and fixed a passionate gaze on her. "I didn't come to Nova Scotia just to educate."

The Agent met his gaze. "I did." She picked up her knapsack. "Mirabella Stuart will change. You'll see." She left.

AT THE KITCHEN TABLE in the trailer, Mirabella arranged sliced vegetables on a serving tray in the shape of a bear, with the carved roots of chives for white teeth, baked dasheen skins for brown fur and black olives for eyes. The bear grazed, with teeth bared, in a field of salsify, witloof, fetticus and golden cress. Last year's dried dixie butterpeas formed a path and dates formed a thick border. She added the last piece of dasheen and stood back to admire her work. A masterpiece, she concluded. And at the same time a healthy snack.

The children would love it.

She scraped the leftover pieces into zipper bags and put them in the freezer for future casseroles. She looped her purse over her arm, balanced the tray in one hand and lifted two casseroles with the other. The bag of smelts she grasped with two fingers under the tray. She pushed the door open with her back and went out.

Fiddy was strolling alongside the brook near the picnic table while watching the hovering islands of the Northumberland. She had changed her clothes and was wearing her fiery red wig into which she'd arranged large dandelions. With the umbrella as her walking stick, she practiced a random trilling voice, accompanied by the chuckling brook. "I'll be with you in a minute," she called to Mirabella and resumed her vocal exercises.

Fully loaded, Mirabella stood beside the car, stabbing at Fiddy with her most vicious, penetrating stare. It didn't work. She tried opening the door of the car with her foot and surprised even herself when she succeeded. She placed the tray, casseroles, purse and smelts on the back seat and returned to the trailer for her and Fiddy's overnight bags. When she arrived back at the car with their luggage, Fiddy was waiting for her.

"You should have let me help," she said, getting into the front seat.

"I don't need your help," Mirabella snapped. She opened the trunk, tossed in the suitcases and was getting into her seat when a cloud of dust on the driveway indicated a visitor. The Agent arrived, her hybrid-electric jeep giving a soft, friendly hum. "What are you doing here?" Mirabella barked when the Agent stepped out of her jeep.

"Surprise inspection."

"You were here only a few hours ago!"

"Inspections may occur at any time."

"I don't have time," Mirabella said. "I'm supposed to be babysitting my grandnieces and grandnephew. Their parents are leaving to catch a plane."

"This won't take long."

"I have to –"

"This won't take long!" the Agent shouted, the heads and guts of the fish still fresh in her memory. Then she remembered that she was to show Mirabella how to love her fellow creatures, not resent them. "I promise," she said softer. "I won't take too much of your time."

Mirabella groaned but followed the Agent to the back of the trailer.

"What about me?" Fiddy called after them. "Am I supposed to just stay here?" No one answered.

AT APPLEFERN MANSION, Johnny Stuart came down the staircase into the foyer and set down the last of his wife's suitcases. He looked at his watch, tapped it and listened to see if it was still working. "Mirabella is two minutes late," he said with alarm.

"Maybe one of them is dead." Martha didn't look up from the magazine she was reading.

"No," Johnny said decisively, "Mirabella still wouldn't be late. She'd have buried Fiddy's body deep in the Sgairian mountains and been ten minutes early." The telephone rang. "Perhaps there's our answer." Johnny picked it up. "Applefern."

"This is Desdemona Pacifico-Rossini," came Fiddy's most pompous voice. "I would please like to speak with the president of SFP International."

"It's me, Fiddy. What's the problem?"

"Johnny? This doesn't sound like you. Are you sure?"

"Absolutely."

"How do I know this isn't an imposter and you haven't all been murdered? How do I know you haven't been killed by your butler?"

"We have no butler."

"He isn't dead, is he?"

Johnny sighed. "We've never had a butler, Fiddy. What's going on? Why aren't you and Mirabella here yet? We have a plane to catch."

"Mirabella has necessarily been delayed. Her probation officer has just stopped by for a surprise inspection."

"Her *what*?"

"Probation officer. Mirabella's not the person you thought she was, Johnny. She's got a rap sheet longer than a country mile. The officer is inspecting Shaemis's accommodations."

"Who's Shaemis?"

"Our pet lamb."

A pause.

"In any case," Fiddy continued. "The more pressing concern is that I am bored. If you can send a driver for me I can look after the children until Mirabella is free." She held her breath, clung to the phone and desperately hoped they'd go for it.

Johnny covered the mouthpiece with his hand and looked to Martha. "You were right," he said. "Mirabella's dead. Fiddy's on the phone with a story about a probation officer, a lamb and Mirabella being too busy to come right away."

"So we need another babysitter?"

"It appears so. Fiddy's offering."

"No," said Martha without hesitation. "No way. Absolutely not. That woman is not looking after our children."

"We don't have time to get another one," Johnny pleaded. "And we're already late."

"We're better off leaving them by themselves, Johnny. That woman is crazy."

"She's not crazy, just a bit eccentric. She would never harm the children. It wouldn't be for long."

"*How long?*"

Johnny uncovered the mouthpiece. "Fiddy, how long will Mirabella be?"

"A half hour at the most." From Shaemis's barn, Fiddy heard a vacuum cleaner start up. "They're just finishing," she added, hoping Johnny couldn't hear the noise.

"A half hour," Johnny reported.

"I don't feel right about it," said Martha. "I just don't feel right. The last time Fiddy stayed here she deep-fried french fries over the open flames of the fireplace in the Great Room. Your father's portrait caught fire and it cost us twenty thousand dollars in water damage. It isn't worth the risk."

"The fire was years ago," Johnny said. "The children are older now. They won't let her do anything risky."

"I don't feel right about it."

"We're going to miss our flight," he warned. He pointed to his watch: "Saks closes in five hours."

Martha looked at her watch and sighed. "You're right."

Minutes later, Johnny drove into Mirabella's driveway, where Fiddy was waiting, both arms holding Mirabella's vegetable tray. She motioned for Johnny to open the door – the back door, she insisted – and slid in.

"Mirabella knows you're coming?" asked Johnny pulling out of the driveway.

"But of course she knows," Fiddy said with the tone of an aristocrat. "She surely won't be long. The probation officer found maggots in the sheep manure. They need to be removed to a safe location. I love this car. What is it called?"

"Mercedes."

"I should buy one. I don't drive though. A lady is always *driven*. Driving is for the lower classes." She caught his eye in the mirror. "Oh, I don't mean you, Johnny. You're family. You're in the same class as me by virtue of your birth."

He nodded. "No french fries this time, Fiddy."

"I'm so sorry about that, Johnny. You know, it could have happened to anybody. I should never have attempted cooking. It's not for people like me. Someone of my stature really shouldn't do such things. Will your cook be available throughout?"

"Yes. She's cleaning out maggots right now, but she should be available soon."

"Why, that's what Mirabella is doing! I wonder if she's related to your cook?"

"Mirabella *is* our cook."

"For heaven's sake, I didn't know that! I thought you just paid her because you felt sorry for her. I didn't realize she actually *did* anything. Well, that makes it much worse. I do say, you should consider having someone else do the job for you. Mirabella really does lack class. A common household servant? I had no idea. And I allowed her to stay with me. Not enough ambition on her part, I say. She's capable of so much more. She could find herself a husband at least, although she's probably too old and skinny for that now. Men prefer women a bit rounder these days, don't you agree? I suppose I could use to put on a few pounds myself, so I shouldn't criticize poor deprived Mirabella. I shouldn't really criticize at all."

She leaned ahead to whisper. "But if the truth be told, Johnny, she has the personality of snake bite. That, more than anything, is probably what prevents her from landing a husband. Men want women with personalities. They want to be entertained with wit and sophistication, and Mirabella simply doesn't have it, does she?"

"I think Mirabella is quite smart."

"Smarts have nothing to do with it, my dear fellow. Smarts may be useful in figuring out whether to clean the inside or the outside of a window, or whether to polish hardwood in the morning or afternoon, but when it comes to conversation, it's far better not to know anything at all. That's why I do so famously at it. I know nothing about anything except how to perform and that's what people want. A performance. You should think about that the next time you have one of those perennial meetings of yours."

"You mean annual meetings?"

"I'm not sure. Don't they occur every year?"

"Yes."

"I'm sure they're supposed to be called perennial meetings then. I have it on good authority that annuals bloom but once a year and then that's it. Perennials spring up every year. You should change your custom accordingly. And another thing, you should have a Shakespeare reading at your meetings. You could call me and I'd gladly do it. For a fee, of course, and I don't come cheap. Perhaps the *Merchant of Venice* would be an appropriate preamble to your discussions on – what is it you discuss at these meetings? I suppose you have to decide on the colours of your packages. I do think you should change them to gold and burgundy. Maybe some daisy designs instead of a lobster. Have you ever thought of getting into the movie business? I have connections and, of course, I'd be willing to act if

I approved the screenplay. There's oodles of money in it, you know. That's where I made my fortune. It wasn't easy at first but talent speaks for itself. New York, in fact, was very good to me but the weather is better in Hollywood. Sorry to prattle on so. I have no one to talk to all day. Mirabella sucks the life right out of me. What will you be doing in New York?"

She stopped and gasped for breath, indicating to Johnny that it was a question she would not be answering herself.

"I'm meeting with clients, Martha's going to do some shopping and then maybe we'll see something at the Met."

"The Met!?" Fiddy shrieked. "Oh, how they worshiped me there! I remember being virtually suffocated with the flowers they threw on the stage at the end of my performances."

"I didn't realize you were there."

"That's where I got my start. I performed dozens of times up and down Broadway too. I was magnificent." She closed her eyes and was lost in dreams of glories past. She smiled and her lips moved silently to a remembered song.

"Fiddy?" Johnny asked.

She opened her eyes. "Yes, Johnny?"

"You're still magnificent."

AFTER REMOVING THE MAGGOTS to a location where they wouldn't be trampled by the lamb, Mirabella vacuumed the floor of Shaemis's barn. She scrubbed the floor with vegetable based cleaner. She washed the windows with vinegar. And just when she thought she was finished, the Agent handed her a brush. "I want to show you something Shaemis will really enjoy." She put an arm around the lamb, it nuzzled up to her affectionately and the Agent smiled at his response. "See how much he loves this? He's just like a human. They want to be loved."

Mirabella didn't look convinced.

"You should hug him every chance you get." The Agent gave the lamb a hug around the neck, he licked her cheek and she laughed. "See?" The lamb licked her again.

Mirabella didn't like hugging, and she thought the Agent's

behaviour was disgusting. "Do you have some kind of sheep fetish or what? What's wrong with you people?"

The Agent's face went scarlet. She stared at Mirabella, stunned by the vulgar accusation. She stood up. "He needs to have his fleece brushed."

"Fine," said Mirabella. She pushed the Agent aside and began brushing Shaemis so harshly that he squirmed and struggled to get away. Combing through a particularly tough knot, the lamb bleated softly and bolted from her. "Stop!" Mirabella yelled and raised the brush as if to strike him. "Stay!" she ordered, and resumed the battering while holding the collar firmly with her other hand. The lamb squealed but each time he tried to escape, she tugged him back hard by the neck.

Finally the Agent put out her hand for the brush. "Give it to me," she said, her voice a husky whisper. "And go. I'll finish."

Mirabella stopped brushing and stood up, surprised by her sudden victory. "Are you sure?" she asked. She didn't want to sidestep an important chore but if the Agent insisted . . .

The Agent nodded. Mirabella gave her the brush and stood out of the way while the Agent crouched beside Shaemis, pulled him gently toward her, and carefully brushed. The lamb responded to the tender touch, relaxed and nuzzled the Agent's hand. She massaged his throat, gave him a warm hug and then, feeling Mirabella's intruding stare, barked at her to leave.

Mirabella hadn't realized she'd been staring. Now she felt both the Agent and Shaemis staring back at her as though she were an imposter. "Are you sure there's nothing else for me to do?" she asked.

"Go!"

IN THE CAR, Mirabella's hands were shaking. She held them in front of her and wondered what was wrong with them. Her mind flashed with worry: was she taking a stroke? A seizure? She felt no numbness and was able to hold her hands steady when she clenched the steering wheel. She sped down the driveway. To her surprise, she felt something wet on her blouse, looked down and saw drops of sparkling liquid fall from her face. She put a hand to her eyes. Tears? But she wasn't sad, she thought. She wiped them away. If anyone saw them, they'd think she was crying.

When Applefern Mansion came into view, any unnatural or unexplained emotion was decisively driven away. The driveway was packed with police cars, fire trucks, two ambulances and other miscellaneous vehicles belonging to emergency response volunteers. Mirabella cursed Fiddy under her breath and let the comforting emotion of anger take root. What had the twit done now? In firm control again, she came to a screeching stop and ran for the front door of the mansion where a group of firefighters was about to bash through the door with a battering ram.

"Stop!" Mirabella called and they stopped. "I've got keys." They stood out of the way while she fumbled with them. "Who called you and what's happening?" Mirabella had to shout to be heard over the music blaring from inside the mansion.

"We had an undecipherable 9-1-1 call," the burly fire chief answered.

"Dear God."

She turned the key and the door swung open. She gasped. Beside the telephone table in the foyer, Tara was sitting in Mirabella's platter of uneaten vegetables with the telephone cord entwined around her neck. "Tara!" shouted Mirabella and she rushed over. She unwrapped the cord while Tara kept wide eyes on the darkly-caped firefighters entering the mansion. Tara took a deep breath, filled both lungs and shrieked.

Mirabella picked her up and rocked her. "She must have been playing with the telephone and pressed the speed dial by mistake," she told the fire chief.

"She should be checked out by a paramedic just in case." A medic came over and took a screaming, fighting Tara for an examination.

Mirabella headed like a bull moose in the direction of the music.

In the basement recreation room, Fiddy and the children waved white wands with long, rainbow ribbons attached at their ends. Fiddy was dressed as an Arabian Queen, with flowing purple robes, sandals, dozens of clanging bangles on her arms, thick rouge, silver-blue eye shadow and her Miss Wintry Hope tiara on top of her red hair. She bellowed out words she'd made up to go with the *Lawrence of Arabia* soundtrack blaring from the stereo.

Robert was dressed as an Arabian knight and Connie, a princess. All three spun haphazardly around the room like crashing go-carts, knocking into each other and the furniture in a sugar-induced reckless laughing frenzy, their ribbons following in carefree swirls behind them.

The music stopped. Mirabella stood beside the stereo with the electric plug in her hand. The children stopped spinning and when their eyes were able to focus on Mirabella, they groaned. Fiddy's ribbons went limp on the carpet next to her feet. "What did you do that for?" she whined.

"Children, you can go upstairs and start cleaning the mess in the foyer. I'd like to talk to Fiddy alone." The children moved by her like sullen gnomes.

"You've just spoiled a perfectly good time," said Fiddy with majestic indignation. She pulled her robes around her and adjusted her tiara. "You've disappointed those poor children."

Mirabella didn't answer. She waited for the magma in her stomach to gain another few thousand degrees before casting it upon Fiddy.

"What are you looking at?" asked Fiddy, looking around herself, paranoid. "Does my hair look okay?"

"Do you know what you've done!"

"Of course I do. I've given the children memories to last a lifetime. They'll never forget the fun we've had. And they'll never forget you ruining it for them. I do say, Mirabella, you really know how to make everyone miserable."

Mirabella crossed her arms. "Where's Tara, Fiddy?"

"Tara?"

"Yes, the baby."

Fiddy looked around the room. "She must have gone up with Robert and Connie," she said.

Mirabella shook her head. "She's eight months old, you moron. She can't walk."

"She's sleeping then. In her bedroom."

"She was in the foyer when I arrived just a minute ago."

"Then why on earth do you keep asking me where she is?"

"She was choking, you imbecile!"

"Mirabella, you shouldn't be such a pessimist. She couldn't have been choking. I find pessimists such boring people."

"She was choking, you brainless bimbo! She had the telephone cord wrapped around her neck. If I was even three minutes later, she'd have been dead."

"You're lying. I don't believe you. You're just saying that to ruin my fun."

"I'm not lying. While you were down here dancing and playing like a five-year-old, Tara was upstairs gasping for her last breaths. How would you have explained that to Johnny and Martha?"

"I won't feel guilty. Nothing's happened. We were having a delightful time. Tara was sitting right where you're standing, watching us." She gave a small, strained laugh. "We were making her laugh so hard! She had the prettiest smile on her face. Yes, that's it. You must have sneaked her away before we could notice. You're just trying to spoil our fun and make me feel old."

"Fiddy, I wouldn't lie about something so serious. Tara was choking with the telephone cord wrapped around her neck while you were playing foolish games like a juvenile delinquent. Right now, she's outside with the paramedics in an ambulance to make sure she hasn't been injured. You almost killed her. You almost killed Johnny and Martha's baby. How do you think they would feel if they were to lose her?"

Fiddy's bottom lip trembled. "You're just trying to make me feel guilty."

Mirabella snapped off the lights and the red flashes of the ambulance danced across the walls. "See?" she said. "Ambulance lights." When she flipped the switch back on again, a very different Fiddy stood in the middle of the recreation room. Tears tumbled from her small eyes and left black streaks in her powdered cheeks.

"I'm so sorry, Mirabella. I'm so sorry! I didn't mean to forget about her but there's so much to distract me here and I knew you were coming soon so I wanted to have as much fun as possible before you arrived and ruined everything. I'm sorry!"

"I can forgive anything, Fiddy. But not this. You crossed the line this time. You're a danger to the children, to me and to yourself. You absolutely must go to a nursing home."

"I didn't do it on purpose!"

"It doesn't matter. Sooner or later you will hurt someone. Maybe even yourself. You're too old to be on your own. You need help and supervision. You forget things and then make them up. You're old. You need to go to a nursing home."

"I'd rather die a thousand deaths!"

"Nursing homes aren't the way they used to be, Fiddy. They're better now."

"I can't. I won't. And besides, who would help you? How would you live? You'd die too!"

Mirabella laughed. "I'm counting the minutes until I can get rid of you!"

Fiddy looked at her, head cocked in astonishment. "I thought you enjoyed my company."

"I can't stand you!"

Fiddy appeared genuinely surprised by the revelation.

Mirabella continued. "I've never liked you. It's nothing personal, I just can't stand you. I've never been able to stand you. You're impossibly stupid, annoying, overbearing, self-important, narcissistic and irresponsible. Your delusions of grandeur are embarrassing. You think you're some kind of star and you're nothing but a washed up old bag."

Fiddy raised her chin. "Don't you know to whom you are addressing? I am a star. You should be begging me to stay with you, not trying to kick me out. Besides, I've got one of the best attorneys in the country. You simply must let me live with you. It's in the court order."

"Surely you wouldn't insist on staying where you weren't

welcome."

"When, my dear woman, have I been welcome?"

"Now you question my charity?"

"Is that what you call it? I know trolls with softer hearts than yours!"

"You ungrateful wretch," Mirabella spat. "You're nothing but a freeloader."

"I do all sorts of things for you."

"Like what?"

Fiddy stammered out something about the value of the arts.

"Your days of sponging off me are over," Mirabella interrupted. "I don't care what it takes. Court order or no court order, I will get rid of you." She stepped closer to Fiddy so she only had to whisper. "I'm stronger, Fiddy, and you're weaker. I will win and you will lose. It's the way it's always been. You know it. I know it." She paused and could see Fiddy trembling beneath her stare. "You needn't bother fighting me. You will only destroy yourself."

Fiddy raised her small fist. "We will never surrender!" she declared with a Churchillian voice. She added, with flair, "thou cream-faced loon!"

Mirabella shook her head and looked over the strange creature standing before her. "You don't even know who you are." She left.

Fiddy went to the door and yelled up the stairs after her. "I feel sorry for you!"

There was no answer.

"You rampallian!"

No answer.

"Do you hear me?"

Nothing. Frustrated, she returned to where her ribbons lay lifeless on the floor. She picked them up and swung them but they only seemed to languish. She let them down and they died at her feet.

The night was ruined now, Fiddy thought. Ruined by Mirabella. The children would be so disappointed. How dare she! Why couldn't she let them enjoy themselves? Entirely too grown up, too old. Mirabella had always been too old. Always thinking she was better than everyone else. And the nerve! Did she have no marrow in those skinny bones of hers? She'd deliberately tried to make her feel old and Fiddy Washburn was not old. Neither was Desdemona Pacifico-Rossini.

But she shivered, suddenly, with dread. Who was she kidding? She didn't know how to fight anyone, let alone a dragon like Mirabella Stuart. Fiddy was only an artist. A brilliant artist, of course, but artists didn't – couldn't – fight real battles, only those that appeared on stage for them to act out. If someone else would write the lines for her, perhaps she could deliver them convincingly enough in a fight against Mirabella.

Or perhaps it would be better if she sang the lines. Music had a way of reaching souls, even the small piece of cold, twisted, rusty iron that was Mirabella's soul. She could do a little dance with it too. Maybe that would get through Mirabella's rough exterior. Maybe then Mirabella wouldn't send her to a nursing home. Maybe then she'd see who Fiddy really was and ask her to stay. Mirabella was wrong. Fiddy knew who she was. She was an artist, a performer, an entertainer, star of the stage, adored by millions.

She was Desdemona Pacifico-Rossini, wasn't she?

[FOURTEEN]

Ostinato – 'obstinate': a figure or pattern repeated over and over.

– The Penguin Opera Guide

THE NEXT MORNING, after Mirabella set out a lunch for Fiddy, she drove home to her trailer to check that it hadn't been destroyed by a typhoon during the night. She also needed to feed and water the lamb and do some other chores, the number one item being: *Get Rid of Fidd*y. Despite her constant thoughts on the matter, no realistic solution had yet come to her. A verbal demand had been pointless. Ensuring the hot water taps were too tight, and similar tactics, hadn't worked either and probably wouldn't. Fiddy was too stupid to view adverse circumstances as a reason to give up. Neither did Mirabella have the money to fight the court order. Having Arthur's *pro bon*o representation gave Fiddy a decided advantage on that front.

The solution would come to her, she told herself. She would prevail over Fiddy even if she had to chase her to the top of Black Mountain and pound her head against a rock until her neck snapped.

She got out of the car, still thinking. Perhaps she could bribe Fiddy with the promise of solo performances in the choir. It would take quite a few performances, she supposed. And the thought of that greedy songbird spreading herself throughout the church made her feel sick. Perhaps she could lure Fiddy with the promise of clothes or jewelry. Large hats? A fake fur coat? She made her way up the steps of her trailer deep in thought.

At the door she took out her key but suddenly, inexplicably, she had the sense that something was wrong. She looked toward the brook and listened but heard nothing except the summer sounds of locusts and squirrels. There was no wind. She glanced at the Northumberland and it was a silvery, silky stream reflecting a few benign clouds. On the motionless air, however, she detected a bitter and pungent scent. It wasn't a household cleaner like ammonia but it was strong, like fermented onions.

Chives. Mixed weeds. Beet greens. Freshly ground leaves. Slowly, she looked toward the garden.

It was gone. She stumbled down the steps and across the lawn to what was left of it, feeling dizzy with the noxious scents and nauseous with dread. Neat rows of her exotic fruits, vegetables, leafy greens and tubers, some of which she'd been breeding for decades, were now nothing but short-cropped sprigs and bristles drying in the sun. Her tender delicate plants were all just prickly rows of wet necks sucking at the air, dripping with the last of the juices their roots had drawn from the soil. No more gentle waving in the warm western breeze. Just the dismembered feet of her ballet dancers, slashed away from their ankles by the barbarian's blade.

She found a note nailed to a stake, written in charcoal pencil:

> *Dear Ms Stuart:*
>
> *I regret to inform that your garden is comprised entirely of plants and vegetables foreign to Nova Scotia. Their continued growth, while contributing somewhat to the rebalancing of this planet's proper gas levels, poses an immediate risk to the Nova Scotia plant and insect worlds and contravenes section 231 of the court order. I have therefore taken the liberty of mowing it down.*
>
> *Sincerely,*
> *Garden Twinkle,*
> *APT Agent.*

Mirabella crumpled up the note and threw it into the middle of her lawn. Then she filled both lungs with air and screamed, from a rage she summoned from every cell of her body. She screamed at the sky, the trees, the Northumberland, all of Wintry Hope. She cursed the Agent. She cursed the day she'd first met her. She cursed Fiddy. She cursed the world. She damned them all to the fires of hell.

She went to the picnic table beside the brook and tried to compose herself. She couldn't live like this anymore, she thought in despair. Whatever it took, she needed to rid herself of these fiends. She wanted her life back, the way it used to be: austere and difficult, but at least predictably so.

She was sitting at the picnic table, head in her hands for she knew not how long when she looked up and caught, ever so briefly, a sparkle from within the trees at the edge of her lawn. She dismissed it at first, thinking perhaps it was just the sun catching a piece of glass from one of the broken bottles she'd thrown there in years past. She closed her eyes again and went back to the thoughts that flailed in all directions for the vengeance she sought. But when the sparkling caught her eye a second time, she wondered if perhaps there was a bottle in the woods she could locate, clean and claim a deposit for. She moved closer and realized that the bottle, or whatever it was, was higher up in the trunks of the trees, not on the ground. She kept her eyes on the reflection and stepped into the woods toward it. When she reached the approximate spot, she looked up. It wasn't a bottle. It wasn't a broken piece of glass or mirror. It was something attached to the trunk of the tree and aimed in the direction of her trailer. It was the lens of a video camera. The Agent, Mirabella now knew, had been watching her.

Mirabella picked up a rock from the forest floor and was about to smash the camera into a thousand pieces when she hesitated. She let down her arm and allowed the rock to slip from her fingers. She walked out of the woods to the picnic table and panned the trees carefully with her eagle eyes. There were other cameras, she noticed, at least three. And there were probably more on the other side of the trailer to capture her activities from every angle.

Surely it was illegal. Would it mean jail time? Probably not. Even murder didn't mean jail time in today's spineless justice system. Threatening the Agent with exposure to police authorities would probably do no good, and in any case, the fine print of the court order probably allowed for it.

Perhaps there was something else she could do, however. Her thoughts buzzed at the problem like a legion of attacking wasps. A plan began to form, a plan that could potentially take care of all of her problems at once – the Agent, the court order and Fiddy.

The plan was simple. She needed only a shovel, a burlap bag and the determination of a military tank.

"I SAW WHAT YOU DID to the garden," Jiminy said when the Agent had returned to the office. "That's some intense education."

She couldn't tell if he was expressing disappointment or approval of her actions. "I can explain," she said. Then, after thinking about it, she found she could come up with nothing. "Maybe you were right," she said sighing. "She won't ever change."

"She won't. I know her type." He led her by the arm toward the boardroom. "It was a difficult way to learn, Garden, but Mirabella Stuart is not the only one beyond any form of redemption. I think you're ready to take it to the next level."

"What do you mean?" she asked, confused. She followed him into the boardroom.

"This is Garden Twinkle," Jiminy said, introducing her to two long rows of APT Agents on either side of a long table. The Agent took a seat and nodded greetings to her fellow agents, most of whom she already knew. She was still unsure of what was happening.

"I am convinced," Jiminy continued, "that she is the best candidate to replace Fawny. Her commitment to the cause is not limited by conventionally narrow views of morality."

The Agent felt as though she'd entered a dream world. What had happened? While Jiminy spoke, and the agents listened, she tried to sort herself out. Conflicting emotions fought for control of her mind. She saw the encroaching darkness, the darkness of her mind in striking out at Mirabella and the darkness rising from within the APT Society to surround her. But she also saw the lamb, wincing with pain as Mirabella chopped at him with an axe. She saw fish sucking the air in the sun on the picnic table. She saw the carnage she'd made of the garden.

She felt like leaping from her seat and running for the safety of the swamp. What was happening to her? Mirabella couldn't be changed – but what about her?

Jiminy pulled down a map on the wall behind him. "This is the company. The areas marked in red show where the explosives are to be placed." He explained how they would be freeing more than a hundred thousand lobsters from captivity and leaving SFP International bankrupt.

DEEP IN THE SGAIRIAN MOUNTAINS, miles south of her trailer, among the silent trunks of ancient oaks, pines and maples, Mirabella slid the sharp edge of her polished shovel into the soft soil around an infant maple tree. The little tree had a trunk like a long needle upon which it offered three disproportionately large, precariously balanced leaves. She cut through the fibrous arteries meshed just beneath the surface and dislodged the sapling from its loamy pocket. Very carefully she opened the burlap sack and shoved it inside before quickly closing it again.

That was it. That was the last item for completing her list. She hoisted the sack to her back and nearly collapsed under its immense weight. She made some painful progress toward a nearby stream but when she stepped into it, the weight of the sack drove her boots so deep into the muck that she got stuck solid. She let the sack down, cursed the mud for being so weak, and wondered how she would get her cargo home.

She couldn't lighten the load. She needed everything in the sack. But she'd never get down the creek with that much weight on her back. She didn't know the forest well enough to try wandering her way through the mountains to arrive back at her trailer from the east. On her left, a mucky embankment rose at a nearly ninety-degree angle. It led to a meadow at the top which she'd gone through before to find her way home, but that time she'd barely been able to climb the embankment empty-handed. Now she had a burlap bag on her back as heavy as a small automobile. Impossible.

She considered her options again. The creek: impossible. The tortuous wood: impossible. The embankment? She looked up at it again, surmising its height, the softness of the mud, its length. Impossible or not, it was the least impossible of the three. She tightened her grip on the sack, heaved it to her back and struck out of the streambed. Her rubber boots, however, were so old and lacking in grip that she slipped and fell head first into the mud, her face making a loud slapping sound against the firm cake. The sack landed on top of her, its great weight pushing her deeper into the mud and suffocating her. She wriggled it off her back, freed her face from the muck and gasped for breath. When she cleaned enough from her eyes to see, she saw only the embankment mocking her.

Two hundred feet of mountain mud. She ground her teeth together, pulled herself free, took a firm hold of the sack and attacked. She pushed the sack ahead of her and pulled and scraped her way up behind it, hands and knees pulling and pushing at the mud, teeth grinding. She managed to scale five feet where she reached a small bush failing to prosper on the steep incline. She grabbed it, used it to pull herself up a few more feet, and left it behind her twisted and broken. She clenched anything within reach: rocks, small ridges, harder soil that had dried in patches where the sun struck it through the canopy, the occasional trunk of a small tree in decline. She was soon covered in spruce sap, pine needles, leaves and splinters. She scaled another five feet where she cut her arm on a dead spruce branch. Dark blood oozed from her shoulder but the flashes of pain gave her a surge of anger that only increased her motivation. She threw the sack ahead of her and slashed at the embankment with both hands and feet, grinding her teeth together so fiercely they nearly shattered in a chalky dust. Another five feet.

With feet pushing and hands pulling and scraping, in a half hour she managed to inch her way up to just below what she thought must be the halfway mark. Then she was three-quarters of the way up. With tears and a deep groan that could be heard for miles, she reached a dead gnarled tree that was only twenty or so feet from the top, albeit where the embankment seemed to curl even steeper toward the sky.

Heaving and panting, she remained a moment at the dead tree, resting. Keeping the sack securely in the grip of her left hand, she balanced herself on the tree and held to its spindly trunk with her right hand. She wiped her brow on her shoulder, and, very carefully, looked down. She saw the forward print of her body in the muck of the streambed far below, the blind mask of her face imprinted at the head of her torso, and the tracks to her present position looking very much like the mad ravings of a lunatic animal. She smiled at the distance she'd covered – and perhaps it was that extra effort that shifted, ever so slightly, her balance and angle on the tree because suddenly the trunk, dry with rot, snapped away.

Down the mountain she slid like a runaway caboose, shrieking as she plummeted. The burlap sack, heavier than she was, fled before her like a wild dog at the end of its leash. In her other hand she brandished the trunk of the broken tree, using it to defend against the bushes that came flying at her like clouds of wasps. She frantically tried to steer herself with her boots to dodge a slalom of bushes and rocks. Blinded with the spraying mud, she found herself steering directly for the immovable trunk of an ancient ash. Her screams ended with a *wump*. The tree trembled to the tips of its uppermost leaves.

Her breath was knocked out of both lungs. She couldn't even moan. Every rib was on fire. Blood seeped through her blouse in several places. Her slacks were shredded from her ankles to her thighs and each tear showed a flash of scarlet. She had descended almost half way down the embankment. Her clothes were ruined and she was suffering a multitude of injuries. But it could have been worse, she thought. She could have cut an artery, been knocked out – or she may have let go of the sack.

She tossed away the broken tree, extricated her arms and legs from around the ash, secured herself against its trunk and looked up at the embankment with hatred. It wouldn't win, she told herself. She had suffered too much to give up now. Mirabella Stuart would not be beaten, not by a mountain, not by an APT Agent, not by the court system, not by Fiddy – not by anybody.

With a tribal war cry, she attacked the mountain again, this time going ahead of the burlap sack. She threw herself against the mountain and dragged the sack up behind her in quick, violent jerks. Her eyes watered. She grunted, screamed, growled, yelped, squealed and groaned, inch after inch, step after step. She fought the mountain. She fought the mud. She fought the thorns in her hands. She fought the blood on her blouse. She fought her scratches, she fought her pain. She fought all of them, all of her enemies, kicking and stabbing at them inch by inch up the embankment. She punched at Fiddy's stupid face. She clawed at the eyes of the APT Agent. She scratched at the judge and Arthur and all of her enemies until with the last bit of her strength she heaved herself over the top of the embankment to the meadow and pulled the burlap sack up behind her.

She collapsed on the grass and smiled. Every drop of blood, every welt, every scrape, every bruise, every flash of pain told her: she had won. She had beaten them all.

MIRABELLA WAS LATE WITH HER CALL and the Agent was mentally calculating what the penalty should be. She sat at her desk waiting impatiently. Twig snored softly from her basket at the edge of the desk and the Agent wished she could take a trip to the napping room herself for a snooze. Finally, the phone rang. "Animals Are People Too" she answered, her voice tired. "Agent Garden Twinkle speaking."

"It's Mirabella Stuart."

"You're late with your call. Report on your activities."

"Turn on your television for a special live broadcast."

The Agent stiffened, fully awake all of a sudden. "What do you mean?"

"You know damn well what I mean!"

The Agent put the telephone on hold, ran to the media room and flicked on a monitor. Jiminy was checking video footage of another matter he was working on. "What's going on?" he asked when she rushed in.

"My client may have discovered our surveillance system." When the monitor came on, she shook her head in frustration. Mirabella's unmistakable string-bean outline stood next to the picnic table. Jiminy came over and watched as the Agent zoomed in closer.

Mirabella was looking directly into camera three. She had a few scratches on her face but was otherwise neatly attired in a clean pinstripe blouse and slacks. Beside her on the picnic table in a neat line were the three trees she'd appropriated from the forest, transplanted into red clay pots. Their large leaves waved in the gentle breeze. Next to them, a wire cage held three nervous bandit-eyed raccoon kittens, two of which were limping on tender feet they'd injured when Mirabella had crashed into the tree.

The Agent picked up the nearest phone extension. "The court order expressly prohibits the domestication of wild trees and animals.

Cease at once or I'll have you thrown in jail." She was glad Mirabella couldn't see her through the camera as the telephone was shaking uncontrollably in her hand.

Mirabella smiled on the monitor. "I'll not bother explaining this to you." She lifted a bottle of lighter fluid so that the Agent could see it clearly and sprayed the first tree.

The Agent and Jiminy were both so stunned they neither breathed nor blinked. They could only watch helplessly as Mirabella took out a match.

"She wouldn't," the Agent croaked in disbelief, her voice barely audible.

"She couldn't," Jiminy agreed. "No human being could possibly . . ."

"Just watch me," said Mirabella. She lit the match, threw it on the tree and its three green leaves exploded in flames.

Jiminy and the Agent wailed – as if *they'd* been the ones set on fire. In a few seconds, the fire was out, and all that was left of the tiny tree was a single burnt stick protruding from the pot. The ashes of the leaves faded into the hot wind.

Mirabella, who could hear Jiminy and the Agent sobbing from the other end of the telephone, laughed. "What's your answer?" she demanded. "Am I free of the court order or do I burn another?" She dangled the bottle of lighter fluid in front of the camera. "Or how about roasted raccoon?" She laughed again, a harsh throaty smoker's laugh.

Jiminy floundered on the floor like a wounded fawn. "They're only saplings," he moaned. "Saplings!"

The Agent recovered enough to shake her fist at the monitor. "You witch!" she sobbed into the phone. "You horrible witch!"

Mirabella waited. "Do we have a deal or not?" She shook the bottle of lighter fluid threateningly, waited for another moment, and when she heard no response, sprayed the second tree and set it on fire.

The Agent wept as she watched the life of the tree vanish forever into the wind.

"I want my answer," said Mirabella even before the flames

went out.

"We can't revoke the order!" the Agent cried. "It can't be done!"

"They're only saplings!" Jiminy groaned.

Mirabella aimed the lighter fluid toward the third tree. The raccoons clamored to the other side of their cage, as far as they could from the smoke and sparks blowing in on them. Through the telephone, the Agent could hear their panicked whimpering. As Mirabella stepped toward them she heard their whining grow to high pitched yelps.

The Agent closed her eyes against the monstrosity that was about to occur but she saw the raccoons flailing in a bonfire, their soft grey-flecked fur a mess of raw blistered flesh. She opened her eyes and saw their bandit's eyes imploring her for help. She heard them bawl as they clawed and bit at each other, inflicting senseless wounds in a blind and confused attempt to get out of the cage. One of them had a torn and bleeding ear. She sobbed in utter defeat. "Please, Mirabella. You can't do this."

"I can," Mirabella answered, her voice cold. "And I assure you, it will only get worse." She paused and a malicious smile came to her face. "Have you forgotten? I've also got a lamb. Have you seen how fast they can run when set on fire?"

Tears spilled down the Agent's cheeks. She looked to Jiminy for help but he was still writhing uselessly on the floor, moaning incoherently.

"Find a way to revoke the court order," Mirabella said. "Have it removed and I'll plant this tree beside the brook. It'll grow so high it'll be able to see all of Wintry Hope. It'll sway gently in the wind and in autumn, pass over its leaves and seed to the brook, which will carry them to the Northumberland and from there to the world. Everything will be changed because of this tree. I'll let the raccoons go free and Shaemis will lead a long comfortable life. I won't hurt him, I give you my word. But if you don't have the order revoked, you will witness unimaginable horrors that will haunt you for the rest of your life. Make your choice. You have five seconds."

"Okay," the Agent said immediately in case she fainted and

lost the five seconds. "You win. We'll have our lawyers take care of it."

Jiminy looked up from the floor. "Only the court can revoke its own order."

"It will revoke it," the Agent said, "when I inform it that I lied about the evidence. I'll just tell them I made a mistake."

"Finally the truth comes out," said Mirabella from the other end of the telephone. "I won't pursue charges of perjury against you, but if you ever interfere in my life again, I'll send you a lamb's burnt carcass in the mail." The telephone clicked.

The Agent put down the phone and watched the monitor as Mirabella planted the tree next to the brook and released the racoons. When she saw them scurry to safety, she turned off the monitor and faced Jiminy, who had found the strength to sit up. His face was a white blank. They remained together in silence for a long time. Their tears dried and left salty stains on their faces.

"I've got to take some time off," the Agent finally said, her voice hoarse.

Jiminy nodded.

"They're just too strong. I don't know how I can be who I am anymore." She ran from the room.

[FIFTEEN]

What should you do if you are suddenly confronted by a bear? Whatever you do, try to remain calm. Don't run. This may excite the bear into pursuit.

– Joel F Meier: *Backpacking*

THE AGENT FLED to the marsh to roam the unthreatening puddles, ponds, fens and grasses. She needed to share her wound with the marsh's great black wound. She found it, still wet and throbbing, where the bulldozer had cut it.

She wanted freedom from herself. It was too difficult caring so deeply for the earth. It was too difficult always fighting the enemies of the earth, enemies with a power she couldn't even begin to comprehend, let alone conquer. She trembled in fear merely thinking of Mirabella Stuart. Where did that strength come from? Why couldn't the Agent find that kind of strength? Why was it that she could find no weakness in Mirabella Stuart as Mirabella had in her?

Mirabella Stuart had no weakness. None. How could there be weakness in one who had no heart? Love had been the Agent's weakness. She couldn't stand by to watch defenceless frightened creatures tortured, set on fire and killed. What did Mirabella Stuart love? Her garden. That was it. And striking at that had turned her into a rampaging gorilla.

The Agent, she concluded to herself, needed to become a person of diminished loves. She had to find a way of caring less so that she could fight more. She sighed. What kind of paradox was that? Impossible. She wanted to give it all up. She wanted to *give* up. Why not move to the city, pollute herself with smog and live like the rest of the robotic human race, eating and drinking her fill, driving a Volvo and consuming rapaciously everything the hinterlands could produce for her? She could work in a sterile, air-conditioned building doing pointless research while wearing a white polyester lab coat. She could produce garbage that wouldn't necessarily be recycled. She wouldn't care that her trickling brook, her marsh, her birds and the strait were all left defenceless to their predators. It all hurt too much. She needed to be free of the pain. She needed to be free of herself.

But most of all, she needed to find a white iris.

As usual she avoided the rusting culvert near the edge of the pond, unable to stand the blight of it, and stopped in a grove of healthy blue irises. She begged to find one. Just one. She wouldn't tell anyone. No one else would have to come and look at it, to rejoice over what was thought to be extinct and now found alive. Alive! With its genetic existence standing starkly against an empty universe, defiant, triumphant. What a victory that would be! Then she would know for sure that she was the person she was supposed to be. She would know that she had a purpose, that she was meant to succeed, that she could conquer, that good would prevail. If the white iris could conquer extinction, perhaps she could too.

There were no white irises in the grove. She wandered throughout the marsh, from bush to bush and flower to flower, examining each in a kind of daze, hoping, pleading for a white iris. There were none. She met the road leading from the main highway to the SFP International lobster plant and crossed it into the plain.

At the western side of the plain she found her brook and followed it into the hills. She went all the way to the source of the brook, a collection of springs and tiny creeks tumbling down Black Mountain throughout the trunks of hardwoods and mossy rocks. She sat down on a rock and allowed Twig to drink from a spring. Around her, nothing moved. The trees were silent. She put her head in her hands and sobbed.

She didn't stop for a long time. Not until she felt the warm tickle of Twig's pink tongue licking her face through her fingers. The Agent uncovered her face and smiled in spite of herself. "I know," she said. "I have to pull myself together." She bent down to pick up her pet but Twig pulled away and gave a sharp bark.

"It's not play time," the Agent said.

Twig growled and ran in a circle.

"What is it?" she asked. Slowly, she looked behind her.

Coming toward her, slowly, heavily, on all fours, sniffing the ground while scanning – was an Eastern Black Bear. At least as big as a station wagon. The Agent knew it wasn't what she was supposed to do, but she couldn't help it: she screamed. Then, when the startled bear bounded toward her, she grabbed Twig and ran shrieking into the woods.

HOURS LATER, when night was filtering its way into Wintry Hope, a squall of northeast wind and drizzle made its move across the strait against Wintry Hope. In the swaying upper limbs of a pine tree, beyond the bear's reach, the Agent clutched Twig in her arms and tried to stop her teeth from chattering. The tree swayed in the wind like the mast of a floundering ship and drizzle gusted into her face. The swaying made her nauseous and the cold caused every tendon in her body to cramp.

She sobbed. All she had ever wanted was to love the earth and be loved by the earth. Now she felt as though she didn't even know the earth. The organisms around her, formerly her familiar friends, were like foreign invaders. The bark and needles of the pine tree scraped and pinched her. The insects, despite the rain, crawled over her and helped themselves to her blood. And far below was the creature that had hunted her for miles through bushes, over creeks and up and down mountains. She couldn't see it in the darkness but between gusts of wind she could hear its snoring. Under a thick blanket of fur, it would be warm and dry. "Go away!" she suddenly screamed but her voice came out in a dismal croak.

Eventually, with Twig in her arms cuddling for elusive warmth, she fell into a distorted sleep in which she was neither free of her wretched reality, nor fully in the comforts of the dream world. In this in-between state the demons of each realm warred for her. Hunger and pain drove their nails into her stomach, feet and spine while Mirabella, in the form of a bear, hunted her in the marsh with a flame thrower. She awoke croaking out a scream and nearly fell out of the tree. She tried to get back to sleep but it was no use. Whatever terrors she had to endure in this world were nothing by comparison to the terrors of Mirabella Stuart. She stared into the darkness below where the bear snored comfortably.

MIRABELLA RETURNED TO THE MANSION, barely able to contain the joy of her victory. She arrived at the mansion just as the squall struck from the northeast. She quickly closed all the windows and made her way to the kitchen to make supper for Fiddy and the children. Fiddy's usually ubiquitous presence was strangely absent until she arrived for supper dressed in a flowered bedspread tied in places to appear as a rough kimono. When she started to sing an aria from *Madama Butterfly,* Connie and Robert threw spoonfuls of green-gourd-marmalade-sauce. Although it was a waste of perfectly good green-gourd-marmalade-sauce, Mirabella couldn't resist allowing it, until in their enthusiasm Connie and Robert began taking the sauce directly from the jar by the handful to splatter it at Fiddy and the wall above her head. Mirabella put a stop to the rebellion but a shrieking Fiddy fled.

After supper Mirabella supervised Robert and Connie's homework, tested them on it and when they passed, sent them to bed. With the children all sleeping, she went in search of Fiddy, at last able to tell her the news of her victory. Fiddy's free-loading, she would announce, was now at an end. Off to an institution she would go, along with all of the other people who were too old to be of any use.

The northeast squall had whipped up the Northumberland at the edge of Wintry Hope and lashed sea froth against the windows of the sunroom. Draped across a wicker couch where she could gaze out on the dark Northumberland, Fiddy sat on the safe side of the windows. Waves with snarling teeth and lips of froth dashed themselves on the rocks and the parts flew into the air. Mirabella entered silently and stood at the door.

She watched Fiddy for a moment, examining her through shrewd eyes, looking for what was left of the façade. Mirabella almost felt sorry for her. Almost. If she hadn't endured so many years of Fiddy's insufferable hope, she'd have been able to offer more pity. The gown improvised from the bedspread made her look even rounder and more disproportionate than she already was and now the ensemble was blotted with green-gourd-marmalade-sauce. Mirabella refused to pity her. If there was anything sad about the situation it was the vivid proof of what happens when people's dreams don't die when they should.

Dreams, Mirabella knew, were an evil that lingered just above the waters only to tantalize and deceive those whose lives were destined to be lived beneath. Allowed to live, dreams distorted the lives of their victims, pushing them in directions that defied practicality, leading them with promises of flickering candlelight into corners of darkness that should never be explored. The lightness of air could never penetrate the depths of the sea and neither could the sea aspire to be sky. No amount of hope, no depth of conviction, no dream could change one into the other.

That's why they had to be killed stone dead the first time. *Kill the dream, save the soul*. Poor Fiddy had been encouraged too much as a child, and even as an adult her hopes and dreams had never been allowed to die – despite Mirabella's best efforts. Now, at the end of her life, those dreams were still afflicting her, separating her from the reality of her lacklustre talents, her fat homely face, her short round body, her shrill unrefined voice, her exaggerated performances.

"You're watching the waves," said Mirabella, her voice containing no comfort.

The waves crashed on the rocks outside and sprawled, their white guts spilling across the pebble beach. Their comrades foolishly followed, tripping over them to die like soldiers under heavy fire.

"Yes."

"The rocks, the beach, the sand – will always stop them."

Fiddy didn't say anything.

"The waves give up, Fiddy. They always give up. Hasn't it ever occurred to you to wonder why?"

Fiddy shook her head.

"Somewhere," Mirabella continued, "far out in the Northumberland, they rise from their depths, arrive at the surface, unfurl themselves and begin. They come, never knowing exactly why. When they hit the shallow waters they rise up and see the land come into view. For the first time they see perhaps what they only ever dreamed about and they have hope. But just when they think they are to be transformed into something new, the rocks and pebbles gouge out their bellies, they slide against the beach and die. They die, Fiddy. They don't rush up the banks to start new lives. They give up. Haven't you ever wondered why?"

"I want to know why they never give up."

Mirabella sighed. "They give up because they have no feet or arms or knees. They can't walk. They keep coming even though they will all die. It's the same for all of us."

"I should have stayed in New York," Fiddy said. "I should never have come home to Wintry Hope."

"You were there for two weeks and it was decades ago. You tried, you failed and that's the end of it. You can't start bringing up stuff like that now."

"I should have tried harder."

"No one tries harder than you, Fiddy. That's what's so irritating. You've got to face the fact that you're just like everyone else. You're just a wave, coming to your end."

Fiddy watched the Northumberland, boiling with a thousand white waves. Now that Mirabella had mentioned it, why did they give up? Perhaps they should be heading in the opposite direction, toward the midst of the Northumberland so that they could become part of the sky. That's where Fiddy would go if she were a wave.

Mirabella decided: it was time to tell her. She made her voice harsh again so that it wouldn't be mistaken for sympathy. "Fiddy, you need to move out of my trailer. You have no right to impose yourself on me. You're old. You can't look after yourself. You've got to go to a nursing home."

"Why can't I stay with you?"

"I don't want you."

"You need me. The judge said so."

"The court order is no longer effective. Garden Twinkle agreed to remove it, including the provision forcing me to take you in. Besides, you know as well as I do that we can't live together."

Fiddy faced the storm. Rain and ocean froth slapped against the glass inches away from her face. She reached a hand out and touched it.

Mirabella saw the plump, wrinkled hand on the glass and

made a mental note to wipe away the smear when she next had the chance.

"I don't want to die," Fiddy said. "Not with all those other people. I'm not the same as them."

"Don't be so arrogant. There's nothing wrong with being like everybody else, so long as you don't find yourself in hell with them. You are the same, Fiddy."

"Please, Mirabella, I don't want to die!"

"You aren't dying."

"But I will! I will! I can't leave Wintry Hope or I'll die!"

"Don't be ridiculous. Lightning won't strike you at the borders."

"There's no air out there! I'll suffocate!"

"Stop talking foolish. Of course there's air out there."

"It doesn't feel the same. It burns me. My voice can't go high. My spirit becomes cold. I'll die. I'll die just like the waves."

Mirabella was unmoved. In her view, Fiddy was far more endurable in this defeated state than when she was soaring across the sky in the general direction of the moon. A flash of light with a distant source, somewhere up the driveway, struck the windows and for the first time since entering the room, Mirabella could see tears streaming down Fiddy's cheeks. The light grew brighter and a car entered the garage. "Johnny and Martha are home," Mirabella said. "We have to leave now." She went out.

Alone, Fiddy turned back to her reflection in the window and watched the storm whipping within. Waves continued to give up, from one end of the pebble beach to the other.

JUST BEFORE DAWN the Agent opened her eyes. The tree had stopped swaying and the light wind was on a warm advance from the southwest. The squall had fled, perhaps in anticipation of the sunrise. Feeling a sting on her cheek, she slapped at a mosquito. It left splattered legs, guts and the blood it had gathered from her during the night. She flicked away the remains into the chasm below. Twig whimpered. "It's just a mosquito," the Agent said huskily.

A glimmer of light from the east warned of the rising sun

and the Agent suddenly became aware of herself. She resented it. She had cramps in her legs, spasms in her back, sores on her hands and a sprain in her neck that felt like a festering tumour. She looked over the edge of her perch hoping the bear had given up and gone away in the middle of the night. It hadn't. "Get away from me you smelly bag of guts!" she screamed. The bear answered with a low growl, sniffed at the air by raising its nostrils but otherwise didn't budge.

The Agent sat back against the trunk of the tree and wondered how much misery one human being could withstand. The tragic irony of it all was that she had likely saved the bear's life. She had marched against Japanese corporations guilty of harvesting and selling their dried gall bladders. "And this is how you thank me!" she bawled. The bear continued to watch, presumably unmoved by the little tree woman's past acts of charity.

Fear. Hunger. Cold. Discomfort. Was this the natural universe the Agent loved, that inflicted these tortures? The splinters of a tree for which she had been willing to give her life were driving their way into her back and bottom. Sap ran into her hair and seized clumps of it in gummy masses that tightened as they dried and pulled her hair out of her scalp. She was soaked by rain. The cold forced icy daggers into every artery, making them feel like cold quivering worms in her arms and legs. The insects she had defended from pesticides and spraying programs chewed away at her, fed on her blood and crawled under her shirt and up her legs. She felt the besieging armies of the natural world from every direction.

It dawned on her: she was how they survived. She was their food. They would die without her. And she would die if she didn't start fighting back. She held Twig tightly and leaned over to get a better look at the bear. It met her gaze and she was paralyzed by what she saw: centuries of darkness; blood on black lips; fear. And she saw what had survived hundreds of generations: a malicious, almost omniscient confidence. The bear knew how to kill. It knew how to survive.

Did she? She had to. She thought of the possibilities. She couldn't outrun it. She had no weapons to fight it. She couldn't fly. But one plan, one possibility came to her – with a giant ethical dilemna at its centre. At this point, however, she couldn't consult her APT manual's chapters on ethics. She couldn't turn her mind to all the considerations. She had to survive. She had to do what she had to do. It was the only plan to offer any hope. It called for pain. It called for a sacrifice of principle, but it was her only chance.

She held Twig close to her chest. "We have to try this," she whispered, and Twig affectionately licked at the tears running down her master's face. "It's the only way." The Agent gave her pet a hug and held her away from her. Twig looked only to her friend, not to the bear directly below. Her eyes held only pure trust for her master. "It's the only way," the Agent wept. Then she dropped Twig.

[SIXTEEN]

In addition to their harsh calls and occasional jaded shrieks, most corvids have a repertoire of chirps, rattles, and other odd noises ...

– Raven J. Brown, *Corvidae Calls*

ON SATURDAY MORNING Mirabella pulled Fiddy out of her bed at seven o'clock so that they could be at the church an hour early for their second choir practice of the week. The choir performed acceptably well, by Mirabella's standards, except in the Gloria Fiddy rose out above the rest with a screeching descant that didn't halt until Mirabella threw a hymnal at her.

Despite her victories, Mirabella was in a black mood, made worse when she spotted a crow on her doorstep on returning home from choir practice. As they pulled into the drive the crow leapt from the railing, swooped down so close to the ground that it scraped its tail-feathers on the grass, and then, by rapid pumping, tried to climb the air and avoid Mirabella's car. Mirabella and Fiddy both involuntarily ducked as it soared directly toward them but the unwieldy crow made it over the hood of the car, clumsily turned, and coasted into the woods where it disappeared in the shadows of the hardwoods. Mirabella honked the horn and hollered an insult at it. She turned to Fiddy. "You've been feeding that crow, haven't you?"

"I did no such thing," Fiddy lied.

Mirabella turned off the car. "If I see it on my doorstep again," she warned, "it's going to be a dead crow. Dead."

Fiddy shrugged. Mirabella got out of the car and scanned the woods for the crow. She hated crows. She hated everything about them: their flea and lice infested feathers, their incessant morning squawking, their petty and vindictive rivalries, their snoopiness, the speck of shimmering oil in their eyes, their consumption of the rotting dead, their general filthiness. No crow on Mirabella Stuart's property could be allowed to live.

In fact, Mirabella devoted her spare time to hunting down

their nests and killing them. Crow's nests were notoriously difficult to find. Some of the older people in Wintry Hope even hypothesized that they had no nests at all and brought up their young in the long grasses of the plain. After years of searching, however, Mirabella had found that they did indeed have nests. She found them in a grove of dead pines on the southern edge of Black Mountain. It was in the spring and Mirabella had been overjoyed with the discovery: nine nests. All but two had throbbed with black puffs of open-throated young.

She destroyed every one of them. She knocked the nests out of the trees with a long pole and trampled the black, peeping puffs under foot, surprised at how easy it was to break their necks. Baby crows had no claim to innocence, she had argued to herself. They were guilty of natures beyond any form of redemption. They were guilty of future indecency and could never change.

Crows in Wintry Hope were rare ever since and it was only the occasional one that would wander through, until Mirabella spotted it and took the necessary measures. This imposter, however, continued to evade her eyes. She growled a warning and returned to the trailer where, to improve her disgust, she noticed a white stream running down the siding and across her box of geranium leaves. It gleamed creamy in the sun.

"What's wrong?" said Fiddy huffing as she came up the steps behind her.

Mirabella pointed to the crow's signature.

"Poor thing," said Fiddy. "It couldn't hold it in any longer."

Mirabella glared. "That 'poor thing' is going to get shot in the head, that's what." And then she would drape its carcass across the driveway as a warning to other crows who might be considering a move to Wintry Hope.

They went inside and Fiddy went to her bedroom for a nap. Mirabella put her purse in the closet, checked that the refrigerator and freezer were still running, made a cursory inspection of the rest of the premises and went back outside with a mop and bucket to clean up the crow's mess. She wiped the siding down and then used a rag to clean each affected geranium leaf. She watered the geraniums, plucked a few suspect buds, and, after peering into the woods once more in the hopes of finding the crow, left for the mansion.

FIDDY SLEPT PEACEFULLY for two hours. She didn't wake up until the heat of the mid-afternoon sun was searing through the roof of the trailer, making her otherwise contented sleep uncomfortably wet. She got up and stumbled to the kitchen, hoping Mirabella had left her a lunch. Maybe, she hoped, a cold plate with pastrami and potato salad and some salsa and freshly baked tortillas.

There was no lunch. Fiddy put the kettle on the stove and took four slices of bread from the bread box. She put two in the toaster and crumbled up the others on a plate, covered the crumbs with molasses, scraped out a can of tuna on top and took it outside. She stood on the step with plate in hand and watched the woods for signs of the crow. "Here crow!" she yelled in a high-pitched voice.

Squawk, answered the crow from the shade of the trees. She put the plate down and quickly returned inside where she stood on tiptoes at the window to watch. The crow soared in and alighted on the railing. It peered with its tiny, flickering eyes at the window and, failing to see Fiddy, hopped down to the step to feed. Fiddy sang in a whisper:

One crow, sorrow,
Two crows, joy.
Three crows, a girl.
Four crows, a boy.
Five crows, silver.
Six crows, gold.
Seven crows, a secret
that never should be told.

As she sang, she scanned the woods and lawn for more crows. She needed six in total for gold. Just six. She pleaded for them to come but the sky remained empty. Just the one remained.

Up close, Fiddy could see why the crow didn't have any company: it was old. Younger crows had shiny, black feathers that glistened like oil in the sun. Up close, this crow's feathers were dull and dusty, as though the crow were too lazy or perhaps too tired or arthritic to clean itself. Underneath its wings, feathers were missing in blotches and Fiddy could see wrinkled, leathery, black skin. A few of the larger feathers in its wings were tattered or broken.

Despite its appearance, however, the crow strutted around the doorstep in the proud, haughty way crows did regardless of their status. Having finished feeding, it surveyed its territory possessively. With head high and smart, it swaggered around the step disdainful of its domain. One of its wings refused to pull tight to its body and there were small white bugs in the feathers on its head, looking like dandruff. How did the crow not know it was so ugly, thought Fiddy? How did it not know it was ugly even for a crow?

It hopped up to the railing and squawked at a distant seagull. The gull took no notice and kept by, riding the summer westerlies high above the Wintry Hope coastline where a crow couldn't even dream of flying, especially not a crow with lopsided wings. *Squawk*, the crow called again as the gull disappeared up the coast.

Poor crow, thought Fiddy. To be so proud and yet to have nothing of which to be proud. Born a scavenger, now it was old, diseased and alone and would never become anything besides a scavenger. And as the crow squawked again, this time apparently for no reason at all, she realized, with dismay, that crows couldn't sing. A squawk or a *caw! caw! caw!* was all she'd ever heard from them. Never to sing – what unendurable punishment! And how much worse for a bird? All birds were supposed to sing. It was ingrained in their natures. Not to sing would be like constant suffocation, a denial of its purpose, a denial of its very self.

Suddenly, Fiddy could think of nothing else but that she should help the crow to sing. She searched her mind for the proper song, something easy but which would point to the divine possibilities of music. She decided on the aria *Dove sono* and stepped up closer to the window. The crow gave her its piercing, black look but didn't fly away as it continued to measure the threat of Fiddy against the effort of departing. Fiddy smiled wide, gave a polite nod and began to sing. Just as she let out the first note, however, her dentures came loose and she partly choked, partly coughed. All that came out was a squawk of her own, not unlike the crow's, followed by snorting and gulping. Frightened by the sounds, the crow flew away. She sucked her teeth back into place but it was too late. The crow had flown away. She called after it but it would not come out of the woods again. She sighed. Poor crow. Poor Sorrow. It would never sing now and would die without ever discovering its purpose.

AT FOUR THIRTY-TWO Mirabella arrived home with a casserole in hand: a quarter pound of deer burger and one diced tomato mixed together with eight cups of grated girasole tubers. Less than one milligram of cholesterol per serving. "I'm home," she announced without enthusiasm.

Fiddy, wearing a one-piece robe that was a bed of daisies and zinnias, was crouched in the middle of the kitchen floor with her head stuck inside the oven.

Mirabella sighed, put the casserole on the table and removed her coat. "It's an electric stove, Fiddy. Not gas. You'd have to turn it on and bake yourself to death." She went to the freezer and found a cigarette. "You can threaten to kill yourself all you like. You're still going to the nursing home on Monday."

"I'd rather die a thousand deaths!" Fiddy wailed from inside the oven. The steel container of the oven added a hollow woefulness to her voice.

Mirabella felt like putting her cigarette out in the middle of Fiddy's behind. She blew out smoke, let herself enjoy a few more wicked thoughts, and turned on the oven. The elements brightened into red bars and heat vibrated from the door. Fiddy groaned, then yelped and pulled her head out to take a few quick breaths. After panting for a few moments she stuck her head back inside. A few moments later, she had to come out again, giving Mirabella the impression she was bobbing for apples. Fiddy's face was the colour of a hotdog and the silver wig was glossy where the heat had melted it. As Fiddy was making a third attempt, Mirabella, strengthened by her cigarette, managed to toss the casserole in ahead of the silver head and slammed the door shut. She stood in front of the oven and faced Fiddy.

"Let me die!" wailed Fiddy when Mirabella refused her entry

into the oven. "Let me die!"

"It's taking too long," said Mirabella. "And you're not the one who pays the electric bill." She looked down at Fiddy and met her pouting face. Fiddy averted her eyes and looked down at the floor, unable to meet the disdain. She sat, weeping softly, while tracing the outline of the beige and green flowers on the worn oilcloth of Mirabella's kitchen floor. The silver hair was a tight, melted mound around her head.

"You have no one to blame but yourself, Fiddy." Mirabella's voice was even and cold. "This isn't my fault."

"This oilcloth is not very nice," Fiddy said. "I'm more beautiful by far."

"You know I didn't want to do this. I have no choice."

Fiddy looked up. "You're enjoying every bit of this. It makes you feel as if you've been right all along."

"I have been right. And you need a good dose of reality."

"Reality is a word that doesn't exist in my dictionary."

"You mean vocabulary."

"I mean dictionary!"

Mirabella sighed. "It exists whether it's in your *vocabulary* or not. Now get up before someone sees you like that." By anchoring herself to the kitchen sink Mirabella pulled Fiddy to her feet. The abrupt change in altitude, however, made Fiddy dizzy so Mirabella walked her to the corner of the livingroom and sat her down. "I'm not going through with you what I went through with Mama," she said.

Fiddy settled into the seat and Mirabella put a stool under her swollen feet. "Your mother was such a saint," Fiddy said. "I can't imagine that she was any trouble at all."

Mirabella bristled. "She needed twenty-four hour care and I still had to work at the factory. No one helped me." She went to check on the casserole.

"You're strong," said Fiddy. "You can do anything."

The blue flames appeared in Mirabella's eyes. "So I'm supposed to take care of everyone?"

Fiddy shrugged. "You have no idea how difficult it is being an artist. Everyone expects so much of me. It's much easier being you. Your life is predictable."

Mirabella forced herself to take deep breaths but she couldn't unclench the spoon in her hand. She could easily kill Fiddy with it, she thought. Or slam the refrigerator door on her head a few times. Bash in her skull with one of the detachable legs of the coffee table. Knock her out with the clothes iron and drown her in the brook. Bury her somewhere on Black Mountain. After disposing of the body, she could tell everyone that Fiddy had simply left for Broadway. No one would question her further.

Thinking about killing Fiddy helped release some of the pressure. "On Monday morning I'm dumping you off at the nursing home. What you do with the rest of your life after that is your own business."

She paced in front of the oven until the casserole was done, whipped it out and slapped it down on the table.

FIDDY SAID NO MORE. She sensed that it wasn't a good time to talk about it. It didn't matter what Mirabella said. Fiddy Washburn would not be going to a nursing home. She very well couldn't, could she? It wouldn't be proper for a lady of her standing. Besides, poor Mirabella needed her. Fiddy was her best friend and if Fiddy couldn't stay to help her, who would?

Yes, Fiddy would stay with her good friend. She would stay and help Mirabella through this tough period in her life, regardless of the cost. That was her plan and she intended to stick to it.

[SEVENTEEN]

> Chickens love to take dust baths, sit in the sun, and cuddle up to each other. They cry out when someone hurts them, and they get excited and happy when they are free to scratch at the ground andexplore. But chickens are in trouble. Every year, more than 8 billionof them are killed and cut up for restaurants . . . or sold in grocery stores.
>
> – PETA: *Animal Companions*

TWIG SQUEALED AS SHE plummeted with flailing legs from near the top of the pine tree toward the ground. She landed on the bear's snout where she held on with legs locked in terror. The bear scrambled to its feet and tried to shake off the dog by whipping its head in all directions, snapping at her, then trying to scrape her off against the tree, all of which caused the Agent deep suffering. When a branch lodged itself in the bear's ear, it yelped and bolted into the woods with Twig still holding to the bear's great head.

The Agent listened until she heard the thrashing move far away into the forest. Then she climbed down the tree and ran in the opposite direction as fast as her cramped legs would carry her. She couldn't help but think of the last ignoble moments of Twig's life, the humiliation of blood and soiled fur and wailing and death. She pushed the painful thoughts from her mind and concentrated on her own escape. She had made her choice. She needed to use her choice to survive.

She splashed down a creek and nearly slipped on the slimy rocks. She fled across a meadow and tumbled down an embankment like a blind bull. Bears, she'd learned, were faster going uphill than down. She couldn't get her lungs to work hard enough – the air felt like razors clawing at the inside of her chest. She fell down a ravine and climbed up the other side. Her legs burned but the pain told her that she was still alive and about to be free.

Hours later, with night falling, she found herself free of the bear but hopelessly lost and exhausted. She fell into furtive sleep on some gravel in a dry stream bed and awoke the next morning in breathless panic, having dreamed of the bear. Fleeing in confusion, she stumbled like a sick horse into a mass of prickly trees that clawed at her eyes and face. Her arms were so heavy they felt like dead meat hanging from her torso.

She made it through the trees, headed for a hill and found herself climbing a dry, dusty cliff. She found a group of caves with mouths gaping open like creatures who had died together in the midst of a yawn. She stayed in one and rested for the remainder of the day in the hopes someone would find her, always keeping a careful watch for the bear. When night came she slept uncomfortably on the rock, trembling with cold. Each gust of wind across the mouth of the cave made a hollow moan which she mistook for the bear's low growl, invading her sleep. She screamed in fright and scrambled blindly in the darkness against the wall of the cave, cutting her hands on the sharp rocks.

The next morning she gave up any hope of being found and decided to set out through the dense virgin forest. As she fought with the wretched claws of the undergrowth, she couldn't help but wonder: virgin forest? The word denoted purity, chastity and devotion to an elevated cause greater than simple animal lust. Clever marketing, the Agent now concluded, and entirely false. The trees had a lust all their own. They lusted for her eyes, her arms, for any exposed skin. And she began to think they were capable of deception. She saw a branch move and it startled her into thinking the bear was coming after her again. She ran blindly into the brambles and was abruptly caught in their claws. She could hear them laughing with their high pitched hyena screams while tearing her apart. By the time she extricated herself, her neck, face, temples, even her eyelids, were scratched and bleeding, and there had been no bear.

She managed to survive another night, this time on some moss, and found some berries to eat the next morning. She dug up some cattail roots and gnawed on them hungrily. *Murderer!* she heard in her thoughts but she ignored the voice. The food was enough to keep her alive, or at least give her the semblance of being alive, but it wasn't enough to nourish her. She went through so many degrees of hunger and thirst that all of her needs seemed to meld into one great insatiable desire for the safety and comfort of home.

To free herself from the wooded maze, she tried following the shadows of the sun but for long distances it was too dark in the undergrowth to see shadows and so she arrived back at her point of origin. She tried going toward a distant hill but once again, the trees concealed the direction and she ended back at the same place, hours later and even more exhausted. She found herself at the same place a fourth time, near the bottom of a wooded mountain next to a white-grey rock that looked like the top of a troll's bald head. Beyond hope, she stood beside the rock and felt like falling where she stood.

She couldn't continue, she told herself. She had to make a decision. She looked up at the slope, rising gently from the troll's head. It became steeper higher up and peaked at the top of the mountain. Downhill was a tea-coloured stream she'd already tried to follow but it had somehow tricked her into returning to the same place. She'd tried every direction. She was stuck. With her energy waning there was only one thing left for her to do.

She started running. She dashed into the tea-coloured brook and up the other side. She went between trees and when they came for her eyes she screamed at them. Seized by madness, she ran without any plan or purpose, leaving her thoughts with the skull of the troll and abandoning herself to the wild. She used a stick to protect herself from the trees and swung it at anything that threatened her. She swung at rocks, brambles and even saplings whose leaves she whipped off easily. Groaning, then growling, she plodded through the woods like an animal, daring any creature to show itself. She was the predator now. She was monarch of this forest. She was the bear.

She crossed hills and valleys, went around ravines and scraped her way up muddy embankments. In a few hours, the bear's feet were too heavy to carry her. She trudged among some hardwoods. All was a blur around her. The trees were swaying and dancing. She dropped her stick. A few feet later, she fell to her knees. On some moss, she let her head fall, gasped for breath. She would rest awhile, then resume the hunt. She closed her eyes. She could hear the leaves of the canopy far above her, chirping like birds. The trunks of the trees croaked and groaned. Wind. Singing. Soft, sweet singing, an aria of love, an aria of hope. "Wintry Hope," sighed the Agent.

The singing continued. Whatever illusion her mind was conceiving for her, she didn't care to analyze it. Her mind was preparing for a good death, a form of biological palliative care. But when the singing continued with vivid, audible clarity, she opened her eyes. "Wintry Hope?" she called. She listened and could almost swear she was hearing it with her ears: singing. High notes, coming down from the top of the trees and falling upon her like sweet nourishment. The Agent looked into the canopy for the source of the song but saw no angel, no phantom to which she could attribute the music. She pushed herself up to a sitting position on the moss and listened.

It was a woman's voice, unmistakably, blended with the sounds of the forest. Had she died at last? Was she being summoned to the land of perfect harmony? Dead or not, the song was real. She struggled to her feet and followed it. Through the trees she stumbled and scanned. When the song paused, she stopped and waited. It resumed again and she continued toward it. A clearing opened up between the trees and she stepped into it.

She found herself standing at the edge of Mirabella Stuart's lawn gazing incredulously at Fiddy. Gowned in zinnias and daisies and with silver hair, Fiddy greeted her with a smile and bowed. The Agent collapsed to the grass.

THE AGENT AWOKE as her stretcher dropped from the ambulance and she was wheeled into the emergency department of Tina Shingo General. "I'm hungry," she told the first nurse she saw. Her stomach tugged in spasms at the bottom of her throat.

"We'll send the requisition right away," said the nurse. The Agent explained that she was a fruitarian and therefore did not eat any substance derived from animals or plants which would cause them pain. No lettuce, no spinach, no roots, tubers or beans. She could eat fruits bearing seeds, she told the nurse, such as apples, oranges, tomatoes and most melons because those fruits were devices for the effective dispersal of seeds. But lima beans, potatoes, carrots, soy-based products and rice were out of the question. Meat, milk and egg products were unthinkable, she told the nurse. The nurse looked back at her skeptically but copied down the information and sent in the request.

Twenty minutes later, no food had arrived. "I'm hungry," the Agent told the physician examining her.

"The nurses are taking care of it," he said.

"I'm hungry," she told the student nurse who cleaned her wounds with alcohol, an hour later.

The student nurse shrugged.

"I said I'm hungry!" the bear roared and the student nurse screamed and ran out.

The Agent slid out of bed and, with a growl in her throat, went to the nurse's station to demand food. They told her the food service department had consulted with the dietician, that they were coming up with a list of recommendations, that they were planning a meeting to discuss her request and that special arrangements would have to be made with a supplier. The Agent checked herself out of the hospital.

She entered her apartment and stumbled to the kitchen. She opened the refrigerator to see shelves loaded with precious food: bottled water, vitamin B6, vitamin B12, vitamin C, vitamin D, vitamin E, iron supplements, riboflavin, thiamine, a multivitamin and two drawers filled with weary seeded fruits. She launched into a meal of apples, grapes and sliced oranges and a glass of water with a slice of lemon. She gulped two pills of each vitamin. She ate while sitting on a cushion in the middle of her livingroom floor.

When she was finished she was still hungry and went back to the refrigerator for more. All that remained were the sterile bottles of vitamin pills and she didn't want to risk an overdose. She decided to take a bath but as she lathered her blistered feet and other wounds, she could think of nothing except how hungry she remained.

After her bath, she went to bed and it welcomed her in a soft embrace. She squealed with pleasure. But as her stomach resumed its tugging and lurching, she was unable to sleep. She got up and paced her bedroom. She moved to the livingroom. She could think of nothing but food.

It would be another seven hours before grocery stores would

be open in Tina Shingo. She'd gone to local restaurants in the past but none had been able to accommodate her diet. Perhaps, she considered, she could try a few steamed vegetables. French fries? Perhaps even a spear of broccoli. Cheese. Would it kill anybody to have just a bite of cabbage? Her mouth watered.

No, that would be wrong. That wasn't who she was. She sat down on the cushion in her livingroom and concentrated against her hunger. She could wait. She could wait. She kept one hand on the telephone. Saliva dripped from her mouth. Surely some takeout salad wouldn't be entirely wrong? Some lettuce and tomato with a bit of vinaigrette? One fresh, warm roll with a dab of melted butter. Mashed potatoes with gravy.

Onion soup.

Beef stew!

Her eyes rolled back into her head as her body quaked with desire. The phone was in her hand. She saw her other hand dialing. It was ringing. She heard her voice blurt out the order: "A bucket of chicken, now!"

"I'll connect you with the Chicken House," the operator said.

After she placed the order, she resumed pacing. She told herself she wouldn't eat the chicken once it arrived. She hadn't violated her code yet. She could still resist. This was just a test to see if she was who she thought she was. She wouldn't eat chicken. She hadn't even ordered it. The bear had.

No, an APT Agent would never eat *chicken*. And certainly not her. She would simply research it, in a study of the eating habits of human beings which she would later publish in *Planet Earth*. She laughed. How could she possibly eat chicken? She wouldn't eat one of those poor wretched birds forced to live ten thousand at a time in separated wire cages, never to see natural sunlight. Forced to eat, forced to excrete, no room to move so that their muscles remained tender, never to see blue sky, never building a nest, never bringing up young, never scurrying among bushes to gather up seeds, never breathing natural air. A life of misery followed by death in a deep fryer. Then incisors biting into the atrophied muscles and someone having the nerve to complain that it was *dry*.

She wouldn't eat chicken. She had no intention of eating chicken. She would only perform her research. She would smell it perhaps, but that would be all. Surely that would satisfy her hunger. When the chicken arrived, however, the powerful scents unexpectedly swamped her, overloading her senses completely. The Agent could only watch while the bear attacked the chicken pieces with frightening violence. She heard herself laughing with pleasure. The broiled skin, crisp and crackling on her tongue, sent a wet saltiness throughout her mouth and made her entire body tingle. She gulped the pieces. She ripped the tiny atrophied muscles, veins and tendons from their bones with bared animal teeth and swallowed large chunks whole. Skin! You're eating the broiled skin of a fellow earth companion! Her conscience wailed at her but the inner animal prevailed until she had chewed away the flesh from every piece of chicken in the bucket and spat the bones out in a neat pile.

When she finished, the delivery boy was still standing at the door, looking at her with revulsion. He asked for the money. Embarrassed, she paid him. She closed the door, lay down on a cushion in the middle of her livingroom and sobbed herself to sleep.

SHE SLEPT LIKE THE DEAD for days, during which her body knitted itself back together again with the protein and nutrients of the chicken. Her sores and scratches were sealed up with new skin and the rashes were coaxed away. Three days later she opened her eyes, stretched out new arms and with a yawn welcomed the morning.

She was hungry again and after tasting the heavenly nourishment of the meat, decided that she couldn't endure her former diet. She donned a disguise of hat, gloves, sunglasses and polyester sweater, a gift from her mother she was now glad she hadn't thrown out, and walked to a nearby fast food restaurant where she ordered scrambled eggs, sausage, coffee with cream and a deep-fried potato product. She loved the feel of the eggs in her mouth and as they slid down her throat. They had a moist, comforting slipperiness that no pill had. She hardly had to chew at all, shoveling great gulps of them into her mouth, followed by chunks of glistening sausages. She moaned with pleasure and an elderly couple sitting nearby looked at her as though she were a pervert.

She returned home, replaced her disguise with her earth-friendly hemp clothes and went to the APT offices. In the foyer, in the elevator and as she walked down the hallways, she couldn't help but wonder if her colleagues noticed the difference in her. Did she glow with the guilt of her crimes? She felt their overly inquisitive eyes. Had someone seen her enter or leave the restaurant? Were her sins evident in her blushing cheeks and alert eyes? What if the pets of her colleagues sensed it and managed to pass it on to their human companions?

She shrieked when Jiminy tapped her on the shoulder. "Garden, you're alive!" he shouted and embraced her.

The Agent pushed herself away from him as discretely as she could and stood at a safe distance lest he detect her crimes. "I was in the marsh and got lost." She wondered why no one had come searching for her. "I'm fine," she said.

"Where's Twig?"

Twig. The Agent had been so preoccupied with her cannibalistic behaviour that she'd almost forgotten. Now, the memories of her betrayal of Twig came flooding back. "Twig," she said with some effort, "didn't make it." She felt guilt twist like a knife in her chest. "We were chased by a bear," she choked.

Jiminy was looking her over. "You look well for someone who's been through all that," he said.

She shifted uncomfortably under his gaze.

"Are you sure you're able to work?"

She nodded.

"Good. We're moving ahead with our operations against SFP International tonight. We can't do it without you."

Her heart sank. She didn't know if she was up to such a job so soon after her experiences of the past few days. She gave him a noncommittal nod and went to her office where she slumped down at her desk. Someone had left her a stack of protest posters to work on: *Seals Are People Too*. She dipped a hand into a bottle of liquid red and splattered the top poster. Adorable seal pups, as they lounged comfortably on ice floes, couldn't be seen for blood-smeared miles of sea scape. The poster itself looked as if it had been used for clubbing seals. She wiped some of the blood off and took her time on the next one. She used a paintbrush to add slashed throats, crushed heads and bellies with guts protruding. Her hands were good at their job. She had elegant hands, capable of fine detail. She watched them paint and was amazed by not only how well they did it, but that they did it without her thinking about it. Hands, it seemed, had a mind and memory of their own. It was true, they took a long time to learn, to remember, but once they did, it seemed they couldn't forget.

And so the Agent couldn't stop them now. Her hands had learned who they were over a longer period of time than that in which her mind operated. Her mind was still trying to recover from the experiences of the past week in the forest. She couldn't interfere with what her hands were doing, carving neat lines of blood in snow and fur. She couldn't interfere with the extensive plans her colleagues had made to attack a corporate enemy, plans she'd helped design. Her hands were much older than the experiences of the past few days. She was in the first order of environmentalists. She was a centurion in their army. She was a defender of the rights of animal people, including lobsters. Whatever it took to make the human race live in harmony with the kingdom of the animals, she had to be willing to do it. Or at least her hands would do it and the rest of her would follow. They remembered who she was. She would have to trust them.

But could they trust her? At lunch time she still felt unsettled in herself. The excitement of her colleagues, their bubbling cheer, their quick chatter, made her hate them. What they were doing was serious. And dangerous. Human life walked on a tiny thread, stretched taut across a giant chasm from where the jaws of bears snapped for their lives. It wasn't the same as a marketing campaign to get people to stop eating meat.

She left the office and went for a long walk along the streets of Tina Shingo, eventually climbing Mount Mercona at the edge of town. It overlooked Tina Shingo harbour with its thousands of feeding gulls and sea birds. She wondered how she would be able to return to the office and join the assault on SFP International. She looked to her hands for the answers but they told her nothing. Hand memories didn't speak. They only acted. That's why they couldn't be trusted. On her way back to the office, she walked past window displays in the downtown shops of Tina Shingo. She stepped inside a toy store and browsed the happy rows. She picked up a doll. As a little girl, she hadn't been permitted dolls. Only "play-gurines," gender-neutral creatures with large, demon-possessed eyes. She decided it was time she had the toys she was never allowed as a child. She filled a basket with play dough and went to the checkout.

HOURS LATER, as the sun was setting, the Agent climbed into the back of a black van with six other members of the attack team. They loaded the equipment for the operation and pulled out of Tina Shingo toward Wintry Hope. The Agent sat with her hands under her legs while the other agents chattered among themselves. They were excited and nervous about taking action after long months of preparation. None of them had ever been part of such a daring operation, she knew. In their eyes she saw the foolish idealism she'd had prior to her encounters in the Sgairian highlands, its fauna and the vicious trees. She knew by their awkward fleeting glances that they sensed in her a distance and coldness. Perhaps they thought she was just nervous like them. Only she knew what it really was: the pessimistic wisdom borne of experience. She avoided looking at them and watched the landscape pass until they reached Wintry Hope.

Jiminy slowed down and the chattering agents went quiet. Wide eyes took in the landmarks Jiminy pointed out which, except for the Agent, the others had only ever seen on maps. He pointed out the driveway to Applefern Mansion with its enormous stone gates and gleaming white-blue cement driveway. "A *heated* driveway," he told them. "Can you imagine the waste?" They went past a large church and a mile or so later turned into a provincial park. They drove to the north side of the park to a cleared area overlooking the Northumberland Strait from where they could see all of Black Point with its sandy beach on the inside arc, the buildings of SFP International across the centre, and a ridge of black volcanic rocks on its northeast side. The agents sat in silence, all eyes on SFP International and the buildings containing millions of defenceless lobsters. One agent, with a nervous, quivering voice, said the buildings looked like the barracks of a concentration camp.

When it was dark, they slipped out of the van, struggled with their heavy packs and followed a path through the trees toward their target. At the beach, on the western side of the point and within a hundred feet of the buildings, they divided into three teams: one to form the base camp and two to fix the explosives to the buildings. The Agent led an explosives team to start at the southeast end of the complex. She divided up roles and they hiked to their starting point. She pulled apart bits of the putty and carelessly slapped it against the foundation of the tank house. When her assistants, laden with wires and fuses, stepped back in horror at her rough use of the explosive, she felt their glances and stopped. "It needs a spark," she explained. "Otherwise it's inert."

She continued into a narrow alley between two tank houses, attaching the explosive to the foundation in four foot intervals. After the tank houses were wired to go, she moved to the cold storage building, the largest building in the complex. As long as a football field, three stories tall and humming with dozens of straining compressors, the cold storage facilities and the products they contained were kept at a constant temperature of minus twenty-six degrees. She'd seen the inside of such a building while scouting a similar operation in Prince Edward Island. The meat of tens of millions of lobsters, once extracted from the shells, was frozen in tins, packaged in clean, white boxes and then stacked, one hundred and twenty-eight boxes to a pallet, in the shape of a white cube. The cubes were then placed ten high in the freezer. The sharp and prickly lobsters were made to comply with human-imposed order. Just like the trees used to make paper and the rocks pulverized and used to make the steel on the SFP International buildings now standing with brutal silent strength against the Northumberland quaking only feet away.

They finished wiring the cold storage building and moved to the office building at the centre of the complex. Well lit by towering lights, it was difficult to scout around without being seen. They wired it as quickly as they could, sprinting down one side and up the other.

As they crossed the main entrance, the Agent noticed a light inside one of the offices, behind drawn shades. There were no cars in the driveway, however, and she didn't see any motion inside.

They finished wiring the office building. At the same time, the second team was finishing the rest of the facility. They met near the ice production plant, pulled all of the wires together in one great mass and drew it along behind them to the base camp at the beach. There, Jiminy slid each wire through a slot in a large electrical board attached to a single ignition charge. He screwed the wires into place. The agents held their breath.

"That's it," Jiminy said. He stood up with the ignition switch in his hand and surveyed the buildings of SFP International. From the beach, they looked ominously silent and dark.

A westerly wind made short, choppy waves against the beach and above their heads it moaned through the power lines. Eel grass fled across the dunes with the strong breeze. The boats moored at the wharf pulled at their ropes like nervous horses and their buoys squeaked when pinched against the pilings of the wharf. Sand circled in small eddies at their feet.

The agents watched wide-eyed as Jiminy activated the switch and the timer began counting down. Two minutes . . . one minute fifty-nine seconds . . . one minute fifty-eight . . . "This is it," he said softly. "This is what we've worked for. This is justice."

Thirty seconds. Twenty. Fifteen. The agents crouched down on the sand. Jiminy held the timer where everyone could see it. Five seconds. They covered their heads and went flat against the beach.

THE POLICE CAUGHT the APT agents as they were pulling out of the provincial park and quickly surrounded them. Officers with handguns drawn and aimed on them formed walls on each side. The agents debated briefly whether they would martyr themselves. Jiminy was the only one who thought they should but he was easily outnumbered. He shook his head, disappointed at their lack of commitment and called Mr Trotatuch on his cell phone. They surrendered and the police cuffed and loaded them into a police van.

The Agent sat with her hands behind her back, beside Jiminy, on the floor of the police van. “I don’t understand,” Jiminy whispered into her ear, under the roar of the vehicle. “It should have blown. Everything was set perfectly. It makes no sense.”

“Maybe it wasn’t meant to be,” she said, shrugging.

At the jailhouse in Tina Shingo, the agents were marched from the van to an interrogation room where Mr Trotatuch was waiting for them. The room was brightly lit with long rails of buzzing fluorescent lights, meant, no doubt, to expose every blemish to prosecutorial scrutiny. They were seated along a wall and warned by Trotatuch not to say anything without his permission.

The Crown Attorney entered, slammed the door and caused five of the agents to flinch. The Crown Attorney, except for his business suit, looked more like a street fighter than a defender of the law. He paced up and down the line of agents to examine each one, lingering for a long time on the Agent. She shivered and avoided his eye. He went to a small table, opened a file, took out a piece of paper and began reading aloud. “Mischief, property destruction, weapons violations, unauthorized use of explosives, theft of explosives, terrorist activities, attempted murder, half a dozen other serious attempts and criminal negligence, all of which are indictable. You are each looking at extended prison terms.” He put down the paper. “I’ll make you a deal. The first to tell me all about your plans and intentions, including who else was involved, gets a year off his sentence. Who’s first?”

“No one is saying anything,” said Mr Trotatuch. “You can give us a better deal than that.”

“A better deal? You were caught red handed! You’re looking at fifteen years each unless they can give me some useful information. For example who’s the leader? Is the –” He looked through his file momentarily until he found another paper from which he read. “Is the APT Society involved in this? Are there ringleaders above you who are directing or funding criminal activities? Give me bigger fish and we’ll talk bigger deals.”

No one said anything. The Agent slowly leaned forward so she could see Jiminy. He had his head down. She wondered if he was willing to sacrifice himself and them to save the leadership at the APT Society. “I can provide some information,” she said, surprising herself more than anyone.

"Quiet, Ms Twinkle," warned Mr Trotatuch. Jiminy kept his head down.

"I'm the leader," she continued. "But if I provide information, I want us all to benefit from it."

"It's worth up to one-third off everyone's sentence," offered the Crown Attorney. "If it's really good."

"It's worth more than that," she said defiantly.

"Please, Ms Twinkle," said Mr Trotatuch again. "I'm your legal counsel and I'm advising you to remain silent."

"There's been no crime," said the Agent, ignoring him.

"You nearly blew up half of Wintry Hope!"

She looked directly at the Crown Attorney. "It was just a stunt. We only wanted to make a political point. We wouldn't harm anyone or destroy property."

"A young girl was working in the office who could have been killed. If the explosion went off four hundred employees would have lost their jobs at the distribution centre alone, not to mention the five thousand other employees of SFP International."

"No one would have lost anything," retorted the Agent. "Except those who make their blood money by torturing defenceless animals to death and eating their corpses."

The Crown Attorney rolled his eyes. "Listen," he said exasperated. "I don't need a lecture on animal rights. We're talking about property damage and killing people. If you have no useful information for me, you can save it all for the judge." He crossed his legs, looked at an empty corner of the room and waited in silence.

One of the younger agents started to cry but no one attempted to comfort her. They sat in silent stalemate until the Agent took another deep breath and spoke. "They weren't real explosives," she admitted.

Jiminy and the other agents stared at her in disbelief.

"The blue putty was just play dough," she continued. "I bought it myself this afternoon in a toy store in Tina Shingo. I have the receipt. It was just a stunt. We didn't intend to do anything wrong." She turned and looked deep into Jiminy's eyes. They blazed.

The Crown Attorney had noticed their reaction, observing genuine surprise, as well as some visibly hostile body language aimed at their confessing colleague. "We only wanted to make a point," she concluded. "We would never risk harming anyone."

"It's still a criminal attempt," said the Crown Attorney.

"I disagree," said Mr Trotatuch, who had apparently decided the Agent's information was helpful after all. "There's no *actus reus.* If there was no possibility of them ever committing a crime, then there can't be any possibility of them attempting a crime. There's nothing illegal about putting blobs of play dough around a few buildings as part of a demonstration." He was beginning to look triumphant. "Nothing except for trespass and I noticed you aren't planning to charge them with that one."

The Crown Attorney's face remained emotionless. He looked at the Agent and wondered if perhaps she was the anonymous informant who had reported the incident. He had heard the tapes and it sounded like her but he couldn't be sure without an expert's opinion. She nodded to him, almost reading his thoughts. "The rain in Spain falls mainly on the plain," she said, clearly enunciating every word.

Jiminy slowly shook his head.

The Crown Attorney stood up from the table. "You'll be held until we've examined the blue substance. Then we'll decide what to do." He went to the door, knocked on it and when it opened, he left.

[EIGHTEEN]

> The birds flew down from branches
> towards this sweet singing
> and her eyes wept so much
> that the rocks pitied her.
>
> – Verdi: Desdemona, *Otello*

EARLY SUNDAY MORNING, the Northumberland's angry, jagged waves returned to the stillness of the deep and left only smooth curvaceous swells in their place. The summer heat struck with the rising sun and by mid-afternoon, the sun was pouring out its full measure. The islands on the strait's horizon grew thick and began to flicker like flames in the hazy air. In a sudden, silent swell they escaped their sea moorings to rise above the water and levitate in the air: the *Fata Morgana*. Small sailboats in the midst of the Northumberland moved among the wavering islands like floating cathedrals, disappeared, and appeared again further up the strait. Even a whisper could be heard as loud as a shout on the banks of Wintry Hope.

At low tide, the pebble beach was as wide as a superhighway with lanes of sand, pebbles and cobbles running from Black Point to the beach below Applefern Mansion. Reddish, pink and black pebbles comprised the lane closest to the water. Weak waves sighed gently upon it and the pebbles shook together, no louder than the rattle in a hand of a sleeping child. Next to the pebbles was a lane of larger stones the size of loaves of bread, knitted firmly into place in the middle of the beach, as solid as a cobbled street. Then, two lanes, one a path of dark volcanic sand baking in the piercing scream of the sun and the other a strip of light silica. Both were clean and smooth with no tracks, the breezy night having coaxed into the air the day's stampede of footprints. Heat vibrated above the beach like gas fumes about to explode.

After Mass, in which the choir had done acceptably well, although not well enough to attempt No. 51, Mirabella had, as an act of charity, agreed to take Fiddy to the pebble beach. Fiddy had driven her nearly mad with incessant demands for attention. Before Mass, Fiddy had needed help picking out outfits and tried for more than an hour to secure a compliment from Mirabella's tight mouth – to no avail. On the way to the church she chatted without cease in an attempt to convince Mirabella to try the No. 51 chorus. Mass provided some reprieve but the annoyances resumed soon after with pleas for practicing her solos. Even reminding Fiddy, five times, that she was going to the nursing home the next day, did not succeed in deflating her in the least. Finally, Mirabella had suggested they go to the beach, hoping a few hours of sweltering heat would kill the bubble.

Mirabella parked the car at SFP International. The parking lot was empty except for Johnny's black Mercedes, a police car and a bomb squad van. Johnny had called and told her about the attack the night before, in case she'd heard rumours and was worried. She told him it was his own fault for flaunting his wealth and that if he would only stop to think of all the starving children in the world such things wouldn't happen.

She took the beach gear out of the trunk and loaded herself up with it. On her right arm she hooked two umbrellas and in her hand grasped two lawn chairs. Around her neck she looped the beach bag, containing two towels, sun block, aspirin and three large reference books. In her free hand she picked up the cooler which contained sliced girasole sandwiches, bottled juices, fruit, digestive cookies, water bottles, a small jar of green-gourd-marmalade-sauce and ten ice packs – at least seventy pounds in all.

She struggled under the weight of the load, keeping to the firmer footing of cobbles in the middle of the beach. Her feet plodded along on the cobbles until one of the rocks sank beneath her and, like an ox whose partner at the other end of the yoke had collapsed, she nearly lost the toppling load. She paused, as though waiting for the partner to come back to his feet, recaptured her balance, and continued.

Fiddy followed happily, dancing, prancing and skipping gaily like a water sprite, on the ridge of loose pebbles near the water. When she came too close to the water and got her plastic sandals wet, she yelped like a puppy and bounded off across the lane of cobbles to the streams of sand. She twisted her feet and kicked up the sand like a playful pony. She threw herself on her back on the sand and flapped arms and legs to make sand angels. She wrote out *Desdemona Pacifico-Rossini* with a piece of driftwood in long baroque curves. She serenaded ships in the midst of the Northumberland and the sailors waved to her.

By the time she caught up to Mirabella at the other end of the beach, camp had been set. The two umbrellas had their posts anchored into deep holes in the sand with large rocks piled around them. A lawn chair was set up under each umbrella with towels in the hot sand for their feet. The cooler sat in the shade between the umbrellas and Mirabella sat in her shaded chair with her feet wrapped in a towel, the rim of a large straw hat hiding her eyes. She was scribbling in her notebook. "Look at the mess you made," she said without looking up.

"What mess?"

Mirabella pointed with her pencil at Fiddy's tracks, the sand angels and the signature. "There. The sand was clean and smooth and now look at it. It looks like strewn worms."

Fiddy looked back at the beach. "The wind will sort it all out anyways." She strained her eyes, as if looking for something and gave a small gasp. "Mirabella – where are your tracks?"

Mirabella gave her a sharp look. "What do you mean, 'where are my tracks?' Stop talking like a –"

"You're a vampire!"

"I walked on the rocks in the middle of the beach like a normal person, you idiot. Now, shut up and sit down." She nudged the cooler closer to Fiddy. "And have something to drink before you collapse. I won't be able to carry you back to the car along with all this other stuff."

Fiddy ignored the cooler and stepped in under the umbrella where, to Mirabella's annoyance, she pushed the chair out of the way and flopped on the sand. Her freckled chest heaved and she was as wet with perspiration as if she had just come out of the water. She scratched her wig and it shifted back and forth on her scalp. She still made no effort to get a drink from the cooler. Unable to bear it any longer, Mirabella opened it herself and offered Fiddy a drink of red juice.

"Aren't you going for a swim?" Fiddy asked after she'd taken a deep draught.

"I haven't swum in fifty years."

Fiddy downed the rest of her drink and tossed the glass on the sand beside the rejected chair. Then she belched and scrambled to her feet as if the drink had instantly renewed her energy. "I'll race you!" she shrieked.

She pulled off her flowered sun dress and headed for the water, spraying Mirabella with the pebbles and sand she kicked up. Her straw hat, sunglasses and sandals went flying from her and she tumbled into the water, holding to her wig with one hand. She came up splashing, thrashing and squealing like an adolescent porpoise. She dog-paddled in circles. She tried to splash Mirabella but couldn't reach her. She kicked like a dolphin and did everything she could to get Mirabella's attention, short of drowning. Attempting a backwards somersault, she slipped, went under the surface unexpectedly and came up gulping, choking, sputtering and laughing.

"You're going to the nursing home tomorrow, don't forget," said Mirabella who was sick of the performance.

"Tomorrow, I will be in the sky!" sang Fiddy. "With the islands of my desire!"

Mirabella shook her head in frustration.

While Fiddy swam in circles, Mirabella left the shade of her umbrella to gather up Fiddy's discarded clothing. She folded the dress and put the rest of the clothes and accessories next to her chair, which she put back into place under the umbrella. She found Fiddy's cup in the sand, cleaned it, dried it with a towel and placed it on top of the cooler which she also brushed free of sand. She straightened out the towels. She made sure the umbrellas were still anchored properly. She spread the sand out evenly around the perimeter of the camp and wished she'd brought a rake to clean up Fiddy's footprints and the extravagant *Desdemona Pacifico-Rossini*. Unable to fix it, she sat down and resumed her writing. *Witchcraft is witch crap*, she began and scribbled furiously until Fiddy came out of the water, pushed the chair out of the way and flopped on the warm sand like a beached whale. “The water’s gorgeous,” she said. She wriggled in the sand, soaking up the heat. “I could have stayed in all day,” she added. “What are you writing on?”

“Witchcraft.”

“Could I have another drink? You can’t burn them anymore, you know.”

“It’s in the cooler. I know we can’t burn them anymore.”

Fiddy straightened her wig. “In the cooler?”

“Yes. In the cooler.” And she wasn’t getting it for her this time.

Fiddy waited. When Mirabella didn’t get it for her quickly enough, she sighed and with mammoth effort, opened the cooler and began digging among the ice packs. “Ouch,” she said, gingerly moving sandwiches and jars out of the way in search of the bottle of red juice. She noticed, with alarm, that Mirabella had seen fit to take a full jar of green-gourd-marmalade-sauce.

Mirabella watched in agony as grains of sand fell inside the cooler, along with drops of water from Fiddy’s wig. She chewed the end of her pencil so that she wouldn’t use it to stab Fiddy’s pasty skin. The deep folds of pale flesh reminded Mirabella of the fatty whitish blubber of an arctic seal. It repulsed her. She tried to keep her mind on her article, not on Fiddy’s imperfections or the fact that she should be at home watering her lawn. She had other chores to do too and if she didn’t have enough to do she could get a start on her Christmas fruitcakes.

Fiddy found the juice and pulled it from the cooler. She gulped directly from the bottle and sat back on the sand. “Why don’t you go for a swim?” she asked, juice dribbling down her chin and into her bathing suit.

“I told you, I don’t like the water.”

“You did when you were a kid.”

“That was a long time ago.”

“It’s so warm, I think there might be hot springs underneath.”

"I didn't bring my bathing suit."

"You don't need one. You could go in the nude or you could borrow my bathing suit and I could go *au natural*."

Mirabella sent a sour glance to the pink frills hugging the ripples and folds of Fiddy's body. "Immodesty is a mortal sin," she said.

"Nudity isn't immodesty."

"It most certainly is."

The sun emptied a full cauldron of heat upon them while the Northumberland sealed up its surface from Fiddy's intrusive splashing. In a moment, all memory of Fiddy's movement was gone. From the edge of the pebbles all the way to the sky, the water was like highly polished blue ivory with a whisper of silver trapped within it.

"I simply detest the prospect of getting old," Fiddy said suddenly. Mirabella stared at her, surprised by the admission. "I'm not sure how much longer I'll be able to hold it off," she added.

"I have news for you," Mirabella said. "You're already old."

"At least I wasn't born old." Fiddy picked up some pebbles and sifted through them. "It's never too late to start looking, you know." She picked up another handful and sifted through them.

"For what?"

"Diamonds."

Mirabella sighed. "It is geologically impossible for there to be diamonds on this beach."

"This is where I found my first diamond. I was sixteen. It was gorgeous. I held it up and it sparkled like the drops of a sun shower. I danced in the light. I heard flutes, bells and trumpets. I sang to the sea and he sang back to me." She sang her highest, sweetest note. "That's when I decided to become a star. And so I did."

"When I was sixteen," said Mirabella, "I started working at the factory for three dollars a week. I scrubbed the floor and made sure the drains were clear of fish guts."

Fiddy looked at her, horrified. "No wonder you're so bitter."

"I'm not bitter!" Mirabella shouted and Fiddy's handful of

pebbles went into the air.

"Okay, okay, you're not bitter." Fiddy picked up another handful and searched through them.

"I had no choice. It was either work or starve."

"I'd rather have starved," Fiddy declared. Then she looked up from her pebbles to Mirabella's face, pensively. "Your father owned the factory. You could have gone on vacation or to the theatre or at least gotten a better job. Why on earth would you work in the gutters?"

"I never got a thing from my father."

"Maybe you should have been nicer to him."

Mirabella's eyes flashed. "Just because I was related to the owner of the factory didn't mean I should receive preferential treatment."

"No one was offering to worship you, Mirabella."

"Who was asking to be worshiped? Who was asking for anything?"

Fiddy looked up at her as if deeply confused. "I thought we were talking about you getting a better job?"

"Oh, shut up." Mirabella didn't know why she even bothered to talk to Fiddy. Fiddy would never understand what it meant to *earn* something. Work? That was something other people did. Other people cleaned up the messes of Fiddy's life, her juice bottles, her discarded clothes, her dishes, her plugged gutters. It was ludicrous. Fiddy's whole life was one freeloading trip after another at the expense of other people. Mirabella went back to writing her column.

Fiddy continued sifting through her pebbles, tossing them to the edge of the water where they struck like discordant notes playing against each other. She thought she saw a sparkle and gasped. "I think I found one, Mirabella. A diamond!"

"You did not."

"I did," she cried. "I found another one!"

"Let me see." Mirabella held out her hand for the stone.

"It's mine," Fiddy said, holding it behind her back and as far away from Mirabella as she could.

"I just want to see it for a second. I'll give it right back."

Fiddy didn't budge. "You wouldn't know what to do with it, Mirabella. It's a thing of beauty."

Mirabella leapt from her chair, lunged at Fiddy and had the stone in her hand before Fiddy could even blink. She scrutinized it carefully.

"Be careful," Fiddy pleaded.

Mirabella looked at the stone from all sides, twisted it, turned it, shook it and – as Fiddy gasped – tossed it into the air a short distance to feel its weight. "This isn't a diamond," she said. "It's just common quartz. It's absolutely worthless."

"It's a diamond," Fiddy declared. "Give it back."

"It's quartz, you idiot. A stupid rock. Just like the other rocks in your head."

"This one is real."

"It's not even a pretty piece of quartz," Mirabella continued. "It has brown flecks in it and bits of mud and it's so small you can hardly even see it. It's worthless." She raised her arm as if to throw it away.

"Don't!" Fiddy cried. "It's mine!"

Ignoring her, Mirabella drew back her arm and with a soft grunt, threw the tiny rock as far as she could. It made a fine arc across the hazy sky and landed with a soundless *plop* fifty feet away in the water. One shallow ring rippled away from where it disappeared, then there was nothing. The Northumberland sealed it up with its great weight, hiding it safely among a few reflected clouds.

Fiddy's eyes, filling with tears, lost sight of where it had gone. "You threw away my diamond!" she sobbed. She ran into the water, her eyes searching for it. "That was mine!"

"It was just a rock," Mirabella seethed. "Worthless, just like all your other rocks."

In the water, Fiddy stumbled precariously on her feet, trying to maintain her balance in the pebbles and rocks beneath the surface. "It's taken me years to find that diamond."

"It's time to face reality," Mirabella said. "Maybe if you'd done that a long time ago, you wouldn't be in the mess you're in now."

Fiddy wasn't listening.

"Don't you think," Mirabella continued, "that if they were real diamonds other people would be here looking for them too? Do you actually think diamonds lie around here on the beach all day, here in Wintry Hope of all places, just waiting for a lazy old cow like you to stumble along and pick one up? What makes you think *you* can find a diamond? Have some common sense."

"They are diamonds," Fiddy stuttered. "You're just jealous."

"How could anyone be jealous of you?"

"You are!" Fiddy wailed.

Mirabella glared. Fiddy glared back. Shaking her head, Mirabella snatched a towel and headed across the beach. As Fiddy watched, Mirabella trudged through the sand to the place of Fiddy's revelry and dropped to her knees. With long swipes of the towel she started to clean the mess in the sand. Gentle swoops of the towel smoothed out the tracks. The angel fled and the strewn worms vanished, along with *Desdemona Pacifico-Rossini.*

FIDDY WIPED AWAY TEARS and tried to look for the diamond in the clear water. Of course Mirabella didn't think it was a diamond. Staring at anything that hard, for that long, would make it look common and ugly. Or staring at *anyone*, for that matter. She suddenly felt very hot and ill. Her stomach churned and she crouched over to quell the nausea. She came face to face with her trembling reflection in the water between her feet. She had to admit: she wasn't looking her best. Her eyes looked like bleeding raisins crushed into puffy pockets of wrinkled skin. Her face was as colourless as a corpse's. Her lips were tight and purple. She could see her scalp beneath the wig. And in the middle of it all, her wide forehead wobbling in the rippling water, huge. Monstrously huge.

This wasn't her, she told herself. It was someone else peering up from the water. She smiled at the woman to cheer her up.

The woman smiled back. Her teeth were too big for her mouth which seemed to have shrunk back from her dentures. Wrinkled skin, wrinkles on the wrinkles, like a dried up apple core. Folds of fat, arms that flopped and sagged. This wasn't *Desdemona Pacifico-Rossini,* she told herself. This woman's forehead was far too wide. Fiddy clenched her eyes shut and the tears fell into her reflection. A long sob escaped and sounded across the waveless strait like a foghorn.

It was time, she told herself. She looked up from her reflection. It was time for her to rise and join the other islands hovering in the sky.

[NINETEEN]

Pure stream, in whose transparent wave
My youthful limbs I wont to wave;

– Tobias Smollett, *To Levin Water*

THE APT AGENT SPENT the night in jail with her comrades. The next morning they were released when the crime laboratory reported that the blue substance was indeed the children's dough the Agent had exchanged for the real explosive.

But now, having betrayed her friends and herself, she was afraid of the consequences. She spent the day moping around her apartment, trying to convince herself that it would be okay to go to the office. The usual procedure after an operation, whether successful or not, was to meet in the APT offices for debriefing immediately afterwards. But Jiminy hadn't called her in the morning or that afternoon. Neither did his secretary or any other member of the team.

She read a fantasy novel and found escape for a few hours but the dread of facing Jiminy made every task feel heavy. She did housework for a while and read a magazine, *Planet of Life*. She went for groceries and didn't buy any meat, although she did buy cheese and eggs along with her fruits and vitamin supplements. She felt that was a good compromise between the old and new selves. In the evening she rented *Gorillas in the Mist* and watched it three times back to back. She fell asleep on her cushions some time through the night and dreamed of Twig whining helplessly while the bear pulled red-brown viscera from her abdomen. She cried. She dreamed of woods and bears and hunger. She ran from hoards of screeching trees. She dreamed of Jiminy's hurt, disappointed eyes. She dreamed of explosions and heard sirens and saw red lights.

The nightmare dissipated with the morning breeze wafting in through the window carrying scents of fresh lupin shoots and cherry blossoms. Still in her dream state, she left her bed with the lightness of air and followed the streams of scent out the window, above Tina

Shingo's maples and elms, and over the hills and highlands to the coast of Wintry Hope. Then she was standing in the marsh under a rising sun turning the breath of dew on every blade and petal to gold. Directly in front of her, in splendid white robes, was a white iris. She slowly approached. When she reached out a hand to touch it, she woke up.

She opened her eyes and stared at the window for a long time. The white iris lived. She knew it. She would find it. And in the meantime, it would continue to call to her. She got out of bed. It was time to go to the APT Offices and face whatever she had coming to her.

She walked through the streets of Tina Shingo, empty of cars but full of families with joyous faces, on their way to the cathedral at the centre of town. She hurried along, finding the sun hot on the cement sidewalk. She reached the doors of the office building and pushed in her key, hoping it still worked. It did. She breathed a sigh of relief. At least the locks hadn't been changed.

The lobby was submerged in the soft dusk of inactive weekend hours. It was empty, quiet and free of unfriendly fluorescent light or busy officious workers. She walked by the reception desk to the elevator and pressed the button. She could see that it was on the sixth floor, which meant that someone else had either just arrived or was just leaving. She held her breath as the elevator descended, floor by floor, until the bell above the elevator sounded politely and the doors opened.

It was Jiminy. "Garden." His voice was cold and he was holding a file box.

She searched his eyes. She saw nothing but anger. "Hello," she croaked.

"I thought you'd have stopped by yesterday. You didn't show up for the debriefing."

"No one called me."

"I thought you'd show up just the same."

The Agent squirmed. "What's going on, Jiminy?"

He put the box under one arm and held out his free hand. "I need your key back."

"No!" she shouted. "Someone could have been killed. I saved them!"

"You disobeyed orders. You compromised an operation."

"I kept you and the others out of jail. I saved the APT Society!"

"They wouldn't have caught us if you hadn't made the call. They're the murderers, not us."

She still didn't hand over her key. He pushed her toward the main entrance with the file box between them. "Give me your key and get out."

"Don't do this," she pleaded, stumbling before him.

He continued to push her toward the doors. "Get out!" he shouted.

He pushed her through the doors, she tripped over the girder and fell into the street. She covered her head with her hands when he tossed the box on top of her. "You don't have to do this," she wailed.

Jiminy pulled the key from her hand and stood over her. He said nothing but there were tears in his eyes. He opened his mouth to say something but couldn't get it out. He tried again and his voice came out in a croak. "We could have –" He was unable to say it.

The APT Agent, looking up from the ground, met his eyes. Suddenly she knew what he was unable to say. "Jiminy," she said softly. "Oh, Jiminy, I had no idea."

He shook his head and went back inside the building.

It was some time before Garden Twinkle was able to gather up her belongings with her trembling hands. She hugged a broken picture of Twig in her arms and shuffled away with the box. People on their way to the cathedral stared at her as she limped along on the sidewalk. She felt like an outcast, the old lone grey wolf whose thin arthritic body had been spent for her suckling young only to have them turn on her with their new sharp teeth. She made it to her apartment, fell on the cushions and sobbed for a long time, wondering, sometimes with thoughts that screamed, who she would be this time when she woke up.

IT WAS DARK by the time Mirabella finished cleaning the beach. She called out to Fiddy, who was swimming a short distance from the shore, but in the darkness, could easily disappear from view. "It's time to go, Fiddy. It's not safe to swim in the dark."

"I found something," Fiddy said. She waved her hands through the water. "See?" She beckoned to Mirabella. "Water diamonds!"

Mirabella came to look. Fiddy waved her hands in the water and created small flashes of light, like underwater fireflies, scattering in eddies. Fiddy laughed.

"They're called dinoflagellates," said Mirabella, pronouncing her definitive judgement. "There's no mystery in them at all. Bioluminescence is just a defence mechanism. It's time to get out of the water. We have to go home." She needed to get back to the trailer to feed the lamb and review her checklists for putting Fiddy in the nursing home. She planned to pack up Fiddy's belongings so that when they visited the nursing home the next day she could dump her there for good.

Fiddy was trying to capture the flashes of light flowing through her hands. "They're diamonds, Mirabella. We could make a fortune."

Mirabella sighed and cast a glance up the beach toward the lights of SFP International. The beach was a dark shadow and the water shimmered silvery black under the sky. The moon was yet to rise. "I'm taking this stuff to the car and when I get back, I want you to be ready to go. Hear me?"

No response from Fiddy, who had given up trying to capture the dinoflagellates and was flailing both arms and legs in the water in an attempt to light up as many as possible. "Star dust!" she exclaimed as it glittered all around her, together with the reflected stars of the northern horizon.

"Do you hear me?!"

"Of course I hear you, Mirabella. The monks at Monk's Head can hear you." She pushed herself into deeper water, beyond Mirabella's considerable reach.

"Don't go out further. You'll get disorientated and we'll

never find you."

"You'll find me in the sky," said Fiddy.

Mirabella gathered up the beach bag, cooler, umbrellas and lawn chairs and started across the beach to the parking lot, leaving Fiddy's packed beach bag behind. "Good-bye, Mirabella!" Fiddy shouted. "See you in the sky!"

Mirabella grumbled and kept going, finding the way difficult as she couldn't quite make out the uneven cobbles under foot. She grunted her way across the beach and loaded the trunk with the beach gear. She found her flashlight in the glove compartment and headed back across the beach, carefully keeping to the firmer parts. Only one more night, she told herself, and the useless twit would be gone.

Night had taken complete possession of the land. The lapping Northumberland blended sleepily with the chorus of peepers in the swamp just above the slumping banks of Wintry Hope. At the other end of the beach, the illuminated walls of Applefern Mansion glowed like a medieval castle, with the beach a dark void below. Mirabella's flashlight caught Fiddy's beach bag.

She picked it up. "Fiddy, I told you we're going. I'm not going to warn you again." She aimed the flashlight at the water. "Fiddy?"

No answer. The flashlight threw a quivering silver dollar on the black surface. She followed the water's edge with the light, from the dragon rocks near the mansion to the open water of the Northumberland, toward the rocks at Black Point and SFP International. No Fiddy. No breaking water to indicate a floundering swimmer. Nothing but the continuous cadence of little waves, reaching up with white pleading fingers to grasp at the edge of Wintry Hope, sighing and dying, sighing and dying.

IT WAS AFTER MIDNIGHT when Mirabella saw the lights of a van coming up her driveway. She met the Fire Chief and a white-faced Johnny at her door.

"Well?" she barked. "Did you find her or what?"

Neither one spoke.

"Spit it out. I haven't got all night."

"This is all we found," Johnny said. He held up Fiddy's frilly bathing suit, dripping with Northumberland brine.

"That's the one she was wearing. No corpse?"

The Fire Chief shook his head.

"How long does it take before . . . the body rises to the surface?" Mirabella kept her voice firm.

"Two, sometimes three days," the Fire Chief answered.

"I told her to get out of the water," Mirabella snipped. "She wouldn't listen to me. She never did. Sooner or later I knew she'd get exactly what –"

A sharp glance from Johnny cut her off. "We'll let you know when we find her," he said and they left.

From behind the curtain in the livingroom she watched them get into the van and drive away. She went back to the kitchen, noticing how blessedly silent it was. Nothing but the sounds of the wheezing refrigerator and the air exchanger humming from the hall. Her home was free. She was free! Peace and quiet, the way her life used to be before Fiddy had so rudely interrupted it. At long last the hurricane had passed and Mirabella had her life back. Perfect peace with no one to bother her. A perfectly empty trailer.

Now, she could bake cookies if she wanted and she didn't have to worry about Fiddy eating them all. She could smoke five cigarettes in a row if she wanted. She could get into the bathroom when she wanted. She could do anything. She could even make her fruitcakes.

She turned on the television, for which she'd paid two dollars at a flea market twenty years ago. The tube was busted and it had never produced a picture so Mirabella used it simply for listening. The sound was full of static. She listened carefully to determine what program was running. Someone was walking on gravel. A car drove by on a road. Steps, perhaps high heels on pavement, then on gravel. The car stopped. Someone laughed, someone screamed and six gun shots went off.

She turned it off. Silence again. Blessed silence, with no one to disturb it. Fiddy's chair sat in the corner quietly like a loyal dog waiting for its owner. The plastic mat in front of it was crooked.

Mirabella straightened it. She readjusted the protective arm rests and wondered if she should vacuum the chair in case Fiddy had soiled it with crumbs or left hairs on it. She could vacuum the carpet too to remove the tracks left by Fiddy. Maybe later.

She corrected the plastic mats near the couch. She straightened the telephone on the telephone table and readjusted the phone cord which was as twisted up as a mortally injured snake. Perhaps Johnny would call her later to let her know about the body. She looked at her watch. Twelve thirty-five.

Peace and quiet. Thank goodness she had some peace and quiet at long last. She paced the kitchen, enjoying it all. She looked out the window. She rearranged the curtain. She straightened the mat for her shoes near the door. She paced again. She looked at her watch again. She could go to bed, she supposed, except she wasn't tired. Not in the least. Tonight, of course, she could go to bed at whatever time she pleased. She could do anything. She could clean the toilet. She could start another crewel work. She could pick out new music for the choir, something perhaps to replace the failed No. 51 chorus. Or she could make fruitcakes.

She went to the freezer for a cigarette. She smoked half of it while sitting at the edge of the couch. At long last, she could enjoy a cigarette in the peace and quiet of her own home without Fiddy asking stupid questions or making ridiculous observations about irrelevant nonsense. She could enjoy the tar and nicotine and two thousand other toxic substances without having to correct Fiddy's vocabulary and grammar. She crushed the cigarette in the ashtray and blew her last breath of smoke over Fiddy's empty chair. Finally, she thought to herself, she could blow smoke wherever she pleased.

Peace and quiet at last. She turned on the radio in the kitchen. Fiddle music. A good jig: *The Long Necked Fiddle*. That's more like it. She turned the volume up loud, went to the stove and put the kettle on to boil for some decaffeinated tea. Perhaps she could make some cookies before going to bed. Not fruitcakes. Cookies.

She went to the cupboard and assembled the ingredients for molasses cookies. She put shortening, sugar, molasses and eggs into a large mixing bowl and beat it with the electric mixer. The radio changed to loud static under the industrious drilling sounds. She swung it around the glass bowl and the steel beaters clanged like a broken fire alarm bell. As the mixture blended she moved up the scale of speeds until bits of sugary batter flew around the bowl like scattering ghosts. The radio blared its static, the beaters clanked, the mixer wheezed. Finally, peace and quiet in which Mirabella could do whatever she pleased.

She added the other ingredients and when the batter was mixed she yanked the plug out of the wall. The beaters ground to a halt, the radio cleared and she suddenly heard the kettle's furious whistling. She ejected the beaters by shooting them into the steel sink where they bounced and clanged. She rescued the uproarious kettle from the stove and it let out one final injured scream. She poured the tea while the radio blared *Paddy on the Turnpike*. She loaded the first sheet of cookies into the oven.

She went to the television set and turned it on again in case something better had come on at the top of the hour. She could listen to two things at once. She could do anything now that Fiddy was gone and she finally had some peace and quiet. Race cars going around a circuit. *Vroom, vroom, vroom*. A most satisfying sound that sometimes could be punctuated by crashes, accidents and explosions. She left the television on along with the fiddle music from the radio. They nicely matched the peace and quiet of the trailer. She washed her dishes, cleaned the counters and put the remaining cookie dough in the freezer.

When the cookies were finished she took them out of the oven and turned it off. The trailer was filled with their sugary scent. She didn't bother to taste them, even one. She hated molasses cookies.

Fruitcakes, however, she loved. But she could wait a little while longer before starting them. Just a little longer.

[TWENTY]

For an even moister fruitcake, soak the fruit pieces in liquor before adding them to the batter, or puncture and douse the cakes in liquor afterward and wrap them in liquor-soaked linens to age.

– Cooking with Mrs Carlyle

MIRABELLA HAD WORKED at the mansion on Saturday so that on Monday she would be free to take Fiddy to the nursing home. Now, she regretted it. She didn't need a day off. Her house was spotless. Not even a dandelion had dared to creep out on her lawn.

She decided perhaps God's house was in need of a cleaning and set out to the church with mop, pail, cloths, vacuum and disinfectant. She started with the pews, wiping seats and handrails clean. She vacuumed the aisles, cleaned out the holy water fonts, threw out old flowers, replaced votive candles and sorted Bible literature at the back. She polished the bronze candlesticks at the altar and washed the linens by hand in her bucket. She washed the windows as high as she could reach, both inside and out, and replaced two burnt out light bulbs in the sanctuary. She dusted off the tabernacle and vacuumed out the confessionals.

She climbed the steps to the choir loft, swept the dust, dirt and flies down the stairs and went back up to dust off the organ and rearrange the hymnals. When she was finished everything she could think of she stood at the edge of the choir loft and looked to the silent church below. All was ready for the funeral.

On returning home, she pulled her *Park Lane* into the driveway and slammed on the brakes in a pile of refuse. When the dust coasted away with the soft breeze she could see: her garbage can had been upturned and the contents dumped across her driveway. "Damn crows," she muttered. She got out and scanned the sky for the likely perpetrator. She could see nothing and when she listened, heard only a soft rustling among the hardwoods. She'd get that crow, she promised, even though the APT Agent had confiscated her gun and not yet returned it. She'd have to poison it, she supposed, with antifreeze. Or, less cruelly, she could trap it with a net and dispatch it with a whack of the shovel. She'd drape its carcass over the garbage can as a sign for the other crows to stay away. And they would. Everyone would stay away.

She set about gathering up the garbage and couldn't help thinking of the great value garbage was to archeologists. Pieces of aluminum foil, those that couldn't be cleaned and reused anymore because they were threadbare. Bottle caps, low-acid juice cans, empty low-grade plastic bags that couldn't be recycled, food packages. The crow certainly hadn't discovered a feast in Mirabella's garbage. She also discovered in her garbage the things Fiddy had discarded: a perfectly good zipper bag that could have been cleaned and reused, a soiled piece of paper towel that could have been composted and a tuna tin that could have been recycled but which was now scrunched up underneath Mirabella's front tire. She tugged at the tin in an effort to dislodge it, careful not to cut her fingers on the sharp edge. She rocked the car with her shoulder, pulled, tugged, pulled and tugged until with a loud hiss the tire deflated and covered the tin completely. Mirabella screamed. The tin had cut through her bald tire. She cursed and screamed again.

She had no spare tire, as second-hand tires for a car as old as hers were almost impossible to buy. She'd have to call *Trading Spot* every day until she got one, and that would take weeks. She shook her head miserably. Her *Park Lane,* her great pride, in its injured state, looked like an abandoned mule with a broken leg. She felt like kicking it to get it to move, but she knew that wouldn't help. She considered spraying gasoline across the whole mess and setting it all on fire. Instead, she finished cleaning up the garbage and walked the rest of the way up the driveway.

Her trailer was a mess. She'd left it spotless before going to the church but now she noticed things she hadn't noticed before. Standing at the door, she saw that a layer of dust and germs had settled on everything. Was that a fly on the window? She was shocked. Everything was dirty. The windows showed smudges. The carpets, the floors, the walls and the ceiling seemed yellowed by a film of grime. When she strained her eyes she could see it clearly: brownish grime spreading from one item to another, from the table and chairs to the floor and walls, from the walls to her crewel pictures, to the refrigerator. She covered her mouth and gagged. How could she live in such filth?

She started with the livingroom. She removed the plastic mats from the floor and vacuumed the carpets. She washed the plastic mats and put them back in place, rotating them from their original positions so that they would wear evenly. She vacuumed the furniture and the curtains. She dusted her pictures and scrubbed the walls and ceiling with a diluted bleach solution. She cleaned the coffee table beside the window and washed the last three remaining leaves clinging to her plant, one of which fell off in her hand. She watched to see if the remaining two would surrender. Unable to bear her scrutiny, the last two leaves fell. Mirabella threw pot and all into the composter.

Which gave her an opportunity to notice that the garbage cans next to the composter were in need of cleaning. She washed them in the sink with steel wool and bleach. She scrubbed the sink, the counters, the walls, the kitchen floor and gave the ruffian mop a haircut. She changed her clothes and wheeled the mobile washer into her kitchen and loaded it with her dirty laundry. After it finished munching and gnawing she went outside and hung the wet clothes on the clothesline in the setting sun.

While she was outside, she fed and watered the lamb, shoveled the manure out of the barn, vacuumed the floor and put down fresh straw. By this time it was dark. Pulling hard on his chain, she dragged a reluctant Shaemis into the barn from the spot he'd stood all day watching the corner of the trailer, apparently waiting for Fiddy's return. "She's not coming home," Mirabella told him. She was dead, drowned by foolish dreams. They were still looking for the body, although they might have found it, thought Mirabella, and not bothered to call her. Perhaps Johnny was too busy making all of the funeral arrangements without consulting her. With a kick, she forced the lamb into a corner of the barn and wrapped the chain around a joist nine times, leaving Shaemis just enough room to rest his head on the floor. With a sigh, the lamb closed its drooping eyelids and went to sleep. She resented anyone or anything that could sleep so easily so when she closed the barn doors, she slammed them. She wedged a two by four against the doors so that, in the event the lamb managed to untie the chain and unlatch the door, it still wouldn't be able to escape.

She came around to the front of the trailer to take in the dark night over the Northumberland. The strait was motionless. Not a ripple marred its surface. It lay silent over its secrets like a heavy black stone. The air was humid and the thick manes of grass lining her driveway had gone limp with the heat. The brook, a withered black vein, grumbled as it left Mirabella's property among the gnarled roots of the hardwoods. The air over Wintry Hope was like smoke. Everything seeming to be waiting, and while it waited, wilted.

What a long, hot, night this would be, Mirabella thought. Even the vast sky felt heavy upon her.

She shook the irritation from her head. What was she worrying for? Worry was a form of atheism, she told herself. Death was a fact of life and it would happen to everyone, including her. Her turn to drown would come. She didn't expect anyone to mourn over her when she was gone. No one would be holding her hand while she stepped out of this life and into God's judgement. There wasn't any point in dwelling on it, even for one second.

She hadn't eaten anything for supper, which would have been five hours ago, and she was getting hungry. But as she glanced across her front lawn at the decapitated stalks of her ruined garden, she decided she could ignore that chore no longer. She found her implements, set up flashlights around the perimeter of the garden and started to prepare the soil. Mechanized tillers killed too many of the worms responsible for aerating the soil so she always prepared it by hand. She dug deep and hard with her hoe to remove the stringy roots and scrape away the headless stalks which had long since ceased their useless sucking at the air. She grunted with the effort of removing some of the root systems, pulling apart the dry compacted soil, ignoring the blisters that formed on the balls of her hands even when they split open and bled into the dry wood of the handle. With every stroke, she felt like she was clutching the sharp edge of a sword. It felt good, sending a thrill through her that spurred a fury against the soil. Pain was good that way, in getting her to work, in getting her to fight. Far more practical than pleasure.

She mixed and kneaded the soil hour after hour, losing all sense of time as she became lost in her work. The flashlights grew dimmer until they completely closed their eyes. When she finished she rested against her hoe. The sky had changed. It was closer now, a black velvet curtain studded with stars of different sizes. The larger ones were so vivid they appeared to hang like bulbs, so pregnant they threatened to fall. The silver dust of the smaller stars was a careless spray, like an hourglass smashed across the sky. It was all too close for Mirabella, the walls of a cave falling in. Finding it hard to breathe, she left the hoe beside the garden and went inside.

She drank a glass of cold water and that seemed to help. She wasn't hungry any more, the work having eaten it. Nor was she tired. It was time to organize her thoughts, maybe even write some letters to newspaper editors or another column. She sat down at the kitchen table with her typewriter, finished another glass of water and after a moment of thought began to type.

She decided to attack historians in one letter, their secular humanism and revisionism. In a brief note to the editor of the *New York Time*s she identified seven incorrect uses of the apostrophe. A post script urged the editorial board to take sensitivity training so as to cease publishing anti-Catholic bigotry. She issued letters of warning and outright threats to the world's major papers and the evil tycoons who controlled them, pulverizing page after page with words and facts, snapping out phrases like a lashing whip. In an hour she wrote seven letters and, while her mind was rolling along victoriously like lightning across the sky, she wrote another *After the Fall* column for *The Northumberland Catholic.* She checked her files for a topic and quickly chose one: a commentary on an ignoramus journalist who had referred to the summer solstice as an 'equinox.' It gave her a migraine just thinking about it.

When she finished her column she still wasn't tired. If anything, she'd gained momentum. She was all iron now. Perhaps she would never need to stop, her body having become inexhaustible and her mind even more so. Her thoughts were relentless. They would never stop. They would never cease their attack on injustice or incompetence. They would search out everything, find every particle of dirt and clean it. Nothing would tame her power, nothing would withstand the hegemony of even one of her thoughts. Not even her.

She looked at her watch. Three-thirty. And still no news from Johnny. How could Fiddy's body have stayed down so long?

She took another glass of water and while she drank, thought, with a shrug, that she might as well stay up the whole night. She'd done it before, many times. A night was just a multitude of seconds, after all. Survive one second and she could survive another and another until she had conquered the whole thing. She would conquer the night like she conquered all her enemies: with persistent strength. She'd conquered the Agent, the justice system, the forest, the mountain, the garden and of course, she'd conquered Fiddy. What was it to conquer the night?

She shook her head and pulled the steel cables tighter. There was nothing to conquer, she told herself. She had no reason to be waiting in agony for the telephone to ring. Fiddy was dead. So what? What was the big deal about death, anyway? It happened all the time. It was happening now all over the world, at least three hundred thousand every day. Most people would gasp for their last breath as old age conquered their organs, shut down their kidneys or inflicted cancerous tumours on their brain. People everywhere were being murdered, hacked to death, strangled, shot, stabbed, poisoned, crushed, hanged, gassed, starved, burned, frozen to death – or drowned. Three hundred thousand people every day stood alone in judgement before God, none any better than the others and almost all of them carried off into hell with a demon at each arm, surprised beyond belief that God didn't conform to their self-serving ethical standards. Death was merely a formality through which one passed on the way to judgement. It was unnecessary, if not impractical, to dwell on it. Death was simply a question of spiritual geography.

Perhaps, she thought, before her thoughts became too dark, she should just give in and make the fruitcakes. Otherwise she would never have peace from the power of her relentless thoughts.

"No!" she shouted, startling herself. "No," she repeated softly. She could wait. She could endure a while longer. She could pull the cables tighter. Just a while longer. The night was only one second long, together with another second, one ordered unit of time after another until the sun would come up and the day's work would begin again. The fruitcakes could wait. She'd make them some other night. She looked at her watch. Five minutes to four. She had four hours before she had to leave for work at the mansion. Four hours before she'd have to pretend that everything was okay with her, that she'd slept peacefully all night and had awoken in the sun like a morning glory. On arrival at work she'd be told that Fiddy's body had been found and that all the funeral arrangements had been made. She'd be fine. What time was the body found, she'd ask? *Around four o'clock.* Then Johnny would correct himself. *No, actually, it was five minutes to four.*

Or would it be four minutes to four? No, it would be one second after that. Or would it be one second after that? She put her head in her hands and groaned. How could one second, or one thought for that matter, inflict such torment?

There was nothing left for her to do. Her lists were completed. Every last item. Everything except the fruitcakes. She had to make her fruitcakes. She could not live otherwise. The chore was like a guillotine over her head. She had to pull the lever and finish the job or else she'd explode. She knew the phone number to call. She couldn't forget it, even after all these years of not using it. One doesn't forget the most important things in life. The flesh won't let you. The memory of the hands, the eyes, the heart, the flesh is far superior to any other type of memory.

A man's sleepy, gruff voice answered on the fourth ring. "Gorble Gote?" she asked in her most stately voice, the measured dignity of a Stuart.

"Ya, it's me, whadya want?" His speech was slurred and he hadn't recognized the voice yet.

"This is Mirabella Stuart."

A pause. He laughed. "I knew you'd call."

"I hate to dash your hopes, Gorble. It's not what you think. All I need is a bit of brandy for my fruitcakes."

"Ya right, at four in the morning."

"It's only three minutes to four. Can you deliver it?"

"You got the money?"

"Of course."

"I'll come quicker than a pig in heat."

She hung up the phone wincing. Already she felt dirty. She washed her hands at the sink. She wasn't doing anything wrong, she told herself. She went to her bedroom and opened the steel strong box holding her savings. Clean, crisp, hundred dollar bills, twenty-six of them. Using just one wouldn't hurt. It'd been ages since she'd enjoyed a luxury of any kind. She deserved to splurge. And if she gave the fruitcakes away, it was the same as charity, which was a virtue. She went to the livingroom and watched the driveway from behind the curtain.

It seemed to take a long time. He lived only eight minutes away, she knew. She looked at her watch. Two minutes after four. Why couldn't he hurry? She grew excited in anticipation even though she was only making fruitcakes and there wasn't anything wrong with that. Fruitcakes were a Stuart tradition. Even if she added a bit of brandy for flavour and moisture, that wasn't a sin. The alcohol would evaporate in the oven. She breathed deeply. She could already smell it baking. She could already taste it.

And even if she were to take a small drink herself, that would be okay. Just a little something to settle her down so she could sleep for a few hours before going to work. Surely, that wouldn't be setting a bad example? It was for medicinal purposes. Nobody would even know. Just one little drink. She wouldn't even take a full ounce. And then maybe she'd be able to get through this night. It wasn't like she needed the drink. She wasn't depending on it but merely using it for assistance. She continued to watch the driveway with her eyes unwavering. Her mouth watered. The lights of Gorble Gote's truck suddenly lurched through every window of her livingroom and she was at the door waiting with the money. He sauntered up the steps wearing unbuckled trousers, a stained undershirt and a greasy SFP

International cap that Mirabella felt like ripping from his head.

"This is the smallest one I have," he grunted through a chewed cigar and forced a forty-ounce bottle into her hand. She passed him the money without saying anything, only wanting the short stinking whiskered man to be gone. There was no change from the hundred. Delivery, especially at this hour, was extra. He winked at her. "Any time, sweetheart, day or night. Y'know who to call." He paused and seemed to be looking her up and down. "For anything," he added.

Mirabella slammed the door in his face. From behind the door, she heard him chuckling as he went. His steps crunched on the gravel, the door of his truck slammed shut and the truck rumbled away down the driveway. She stood with her back against the door until her silence and privacy were restored. The thick glass of the bottle was cool to the touch, a fact that amazed her because the liquid inside had always tasted so hot.

She put the bottle on the table and moved a chair to the counter so that she could reach up into the highest shelves of the cupboard for the large bowl she used for making fruitcakes. She found it and brought it down. She arranged what ingredients she had: flour, baking powder, baking soda, salt, nutmeg, sugar, mace, cloves, molasses. She even took two blocks of butter from the refrigerator to thaw on the counter. That's all she had. She had no candied fruit but she'd known that before she started. She sat down at the kitchen table with the bottle of brandy in front of her.

She had an old tumbler in her hand, which she'd retrieved when bringing down the bowl. And, as it happened, the tumbler had five ice cubes in it, melting and steaming in the warm glass. The first few drops of brandy brushed away their jagged edges and transformed them into beautifully polished amber jewels. To Mirabella's eyes, they were diamonds. These ones, however, unlike Fiddy's, were real. They tinkled in the glass and she swished them around to hear them again. *Tinkle, clink, tinkle*. They gave the same notes as the brook in spring. She brought the drink closer so she could smell it.

But she dared not drink it. Not yet. The expectation of the pleasure was half the fun, for she knew from experience that the reality never satisfied the dream. She needed to push the *crescendo* of the pleasure as far into the future as possible in order to maximize it. Like her carefully pruned geraniums. She cursed the years for which she'd foregone this innocent pleasure. It was so small. So beautiful. Amber jewels. There was nothing dangerous or cunning in it. Surely God approved of an innocent drink of brandy. Surely God had invented it.

And then the wave of pleasure threatened to pass and the corners of her conscience began to tell her that perhaps there was nothing but a cool liquid in her hand. The mystery threatened to materialize into something she could see for what it really was. The human condition dictated that all carnal pleasures were eventually reduced to boredom unless new aspects were continuously discovered and explored. She couldn't let the mystique fade. She couldn't let this pleasure slip away. She had to move forward to explore, to extend the pleasure, to shorten the delay of promised gratification. She lifted the tumbler with both hands to her face, closed her eyes and breathed in the sweetness. It filled her completely, satisfying all the longing of the endless night. She knew now that Fiddy was fine, wherever she was, and if she wasn't fine she was in hell and there wasn't anything anyone could do about that.

Before she lifted it to her lips, a clean thought forced itself through to the front of her mind: she'd had enough pleasure. To hold it, to smell it – that much had satisfied her. She was fine now. She didn't need to go further. Further? She'd never intended to go further. Drink liquor? Never! What kind of example would that have been? She put the tumbler down and pushed her chair away from the table. That's all she'd needed. One good breath of it. It had filled her up and now she could leave it alone. Brandy? How could she even think about such a thing? What was she, some kind of drunk? Of course she could leave it alone. She'd never intended to drink it.

Then, suddenly, as the pleasure threatened to leave her, she snatched up the tumbler and in one quick flash took in a mouthful. She closed her eyes and smiled, keeping it in her mouth without swallowing it. She felt the hot poison loving her mouth, ravishing her and she held it there, at its current peak. She wouldn't swallow it. She had never intended to swallow it! No, she was just tasting it.

She wasn't drinking it. She'd never intended to drink it. What kind of example would that have been? But now that it was in her mouth, she thought, before it would become warm and watery, she might as well swallow. It coursed down her throat like a hot sword. Eyes closed, she placed the empty glass with trembling hands on the table.

She'd seen, once, on Johnny's television, a documentary on water. It had shown, in slow motion, the instant in time in which water froze. Crystals suddenly erupted from nothingness to form dazzling cathedrals with white spiral staircases, framed by finely etched forests of delicate lace. She saw it now, in colour, with her eyes closed, and she felt what it was like to move from one impossible state to another. The cool poison burned and healed and ravished and hated and completed and destroyed and loved her. All the lost emotions of her life came alive in an unwavering, vibrant form.

She opened her eyes. The glass was empty. Already the crescendo of pleasure was a disappearing wave behind her. There would be new waves, though. The nearly full bottle of golden sunshine on the table before her promised it. And if one small drink wasn't a sin, one more wasn't either. She hadn't had a drink in ten years, eight months and eleven days. The number at the top of every day's list testified of how good she'd been. Surely she could have another. She poured it out on the shrunken ice cubes and sipped it slowly in case this one was her last.

Was one more after that a sin? A venial sin, perhaps, she had to admit. Nothing serious. Just the near occasion of sin. When would it become mortal? "There's only one way to find out," she said giddily and she finished the drink with a gulp and a laugh. The rebellion was gaining momentum. The pleasure was growing anew. She laughed again. How long had it been since she'd laughed? A year? Two years? Five years? Ten years, eight months, eleven days.

She had nothing to feel guilty about, she told herself, feeling the pleasure begin to pass again. She had done nothing wrong. Three small drinks, although perhaps a venial sin for her, did not comprise a mortal one. And Fiddy was to blame for her own demise. There wasn't anything Mirabella could have done about her. She wouldn't feel guilty. She refused to feel guilty. But the fourth drink made her cry. Damn tears. They had lives of their own to lead, it seemed, spurred on by their pointless hopes. They didn't know that their hidden place was safe and that when they left it to shimmer in the eyes and run down the cheeks they were meant to die. Like the waves sliding against the beaches of Wintry Hope with Fiddy's blubbery body, sighing and dying, sighing and dying.

[TWENTY-ONE]

> Bladderwort includes 100 species, cosmopolitan in distribution. They are all herbs of aquatic habitats or wet soils, equipped with bladders that trap small animals.
>
> – A.E. Roland: *Flora of Nova Scotia*

THE NEXT MORNING, a truck came to a stop at the side of a logging road on the east side of Wintry Hope. Garden Twinkle, minus her APT Society credentials, slid out the door, retrieved her equipment from the back, thanked the driver and watched as the truck slowly pulled away. She sighed and looked at her feet where all of her worldly possessions lay, contained in one knapsack with a rolled up tent and sleeping bag. Her apartment and most of its contents had been owned by the APT Society and Jiminy had persuaded them to evict her and repossess it all, including her jeep.

Now, her options were few. She'd called the earth sciences faculty at a university in the city and been immediately offered a lucrative fellowship to complete her doctoral thesis. Although surprised and flattered by the offer, she'd resisted. She needed time to think about it. She needed to consult. She needed to go into the great marsh of Wintry Hope to see if the option met with approval. They gave her twenty-four hours.

She picked up her knapsack, containing a new sketch pad, charcoal pencils, recording device, map, matches and compass and latched a canvass tent to the sack with her sleeping bag. She headed into the marsh, bear whistle in one hand, pepper spray in the other, just in case.

She was wandering down a wide path through the marsh when, sensing the familiar, she realized where she was: on the bulldozer tracks. The growth, in only a few weeks, had done much to heal the wound. Green tendrils, as straight as pencils, were scattered in the caked mud like whiskers. The footprints of animals hopped back and forth across the trenches. Puddles flickered with flies, bugs and larvae. Blue irises, dwindling as the summer gained momentum, leaned out across the tracks to gather up the sun. She lingered on the irises, allowing herself to hope for a moment that the bulldozer had shaken a white one into life. It was silly to hope for such things, she knew, but she couldn't help it. She would cling to her foolish hope on what might be her last day in the marsh and let it die some other day – perhaps when she arrived on the outskirts of the city. Hope was of no use in a city.

Hope was no use anywhere. With hope, she now believed, came a certain kind of starvation. It was the expectation of things to come – that never came. It was the dwindling of life. It was a constant, unquenchable thirst. It was desire. It was illusion. It was begging and pleading unto blood. The thirst never ended. Did no one else know this thirst? Hope and despair, she was beginning to believe, were exactly the same.

She needed to find a white iris. She needed to be filled. She needed to be completed. She held her breath as she walked among the scattered blue irises, examining each one carefully, even the unopened buds, for a hint of white. There were none. All blue.

She chastised herself for being so ridiculous as to hope for a white iris. It was extinct. No one had seen one since 1922 and that was at a location over a hundred miles away. The white iris was gone and would not be springing back into existence again. What a foolish creature she was to have hoped for it.

She left the bulldozer tracks and stepped into the rushes and cattail leaves which were now a foot higher and beginning to turn from spring green to summer gold. In the sky above, a stray osprey swept in from the Northumberland, circled, and headed back to the strait. She could hear a marsh wren fussing in her nest, somewhere deep within a pocket of sedges. She caught sight of a shy whistling swan that put its head down and closed its eyes. When she waited, however, without moving for a few minutes, she heard its gentle trilling which she captured on her recording device. She found small orange asters in full bloom and swamp roses framed by pink tickseed. Blades of blue-eyed grass winked at her with reflected light in the breeze. Water pennyworts waved at her with their single brave green medallions atop thin weary arms. She found a single plymouth gentian in some gravel and sand at the edge of the pond, nine pink petals surrounding a yellow disc, a sun with flamed edges. On her haunches, she looked past her reflection into the tea-coloured water. Water fleas danced around some sedentary freshwater snails and, in a silver flash, a mummichog fled beneath a group of water lilies gliding among reflected clouds.

She spotted the carnivorous bladderwort, its green bladders and pouches looking like knobs on tentacles reaching blindly throughout the pond. The bladders were, Garden knew, sophisticated trapping mechanisms that caught unsuspecting water insects attracted to a mucus secreted near four hairs. When touched, the hairs triggered the bladder to open suddenly, sucking in larvae, water fleas, microbes and water climbers. An enzyme and bacterial soup would seep into the pouch and slowly suffocate, dissolve, and absorb the nutrients from the insects until all that remained were their tiny exoskeletons. Garden had seen and studied every stage of the bladderwort's life which culminated in late summer when a thin bony finger, like the claw of something dead, would leave the water to rise two feet above the level of the pond and sprout three pale petals.

There was little conventional beauty in it, Garden had to admit. Insect sarcophagi. It was a plant that drew its life from death. Not exactly the white iris, but somehow, its struggle to exist was admirable.

She stood up and shielded her eyes against the sun soaring down on the earth's northwest curvature. She could hear the waves of the Northumberland washing the sand of Wintry Hope's shores. Screeching gulls. The playful brook tossing its stones together. The leaves of the rushes. Her own breathing.

All things were working according to their purpose, whether by living or by dying. How could she go to the city and leave it all? How could she abandon her search for the white iris, just as she was about to find it? She opened her map. The white iris was here, in her marsh. She knew it. If the ugly bladderwort could survive the pollution of humanity, her white iris could. It was like a rule, a law. In the end, good, purity and innocence *had* to prevail. In the end, life would win, death would die.

[TWENTY-TWO]

O thou invisible spirit of wine, if thou hast no name to be known by, let us call thee devil!

– Shakespeare: Cassio, *Othello*

MIRABELLA OPENED AND QUICKLY closed her eyes, feeling as though the back of her skull was being stabbed by a thousand knives from the sun. She was facing direct sunlight on what felt like the ribbed plastic mats of her livingroom floor. She was hot. Her cheek was pasted to the mat with a sticky fluid and her arm was soggy and lifeless underneath her. Keeping her eyes closed, she groaned in pain, pushed herself up on all fours and rolled away into the shadows like a witless salamander afraid of light. She took deep breaths to quash the nausea and tried to sleep.

Some time later she heard a distant bell ringing. The sun had found her again so she kept her eyes closed, pushed herself up from the floor and toppled over into another shadow area. The ringing continued and she suddenly recognized it. "Mama?" she called, eyes still closed against the disorientation swimming around her. Her mother's bell continued to ring. Perhaps her mother had fallen out of bed again. "I'll be right there, Mama!" She broke through the crust, opened her eyes and looked around. The ceiling was a wavering pond of yellow and brown lines. She held her stomach and took deep breaths lest she be sick. Then she heard it again, the impatient bell. She rolled to her side, pushed herself to her knees and sat up, panting and sweating. "I'll get your breakfast in a minute," she said with a voice she hoped wasn't quivering as badly as was her body. She just needed a few minutes to get herself organized. Where was her list? She tried to remember Mama's breakfast: two pieces of wholewheat toast, a light spread of margarine, stewed prunes with just enough juice to cover them, a cup of tea, not too hot, with two tablespoons of milk, not skim milk, whole milk. Mama needed her breakfast and medication. More ringing. Mirabella was suddenly angry. "I told you, Mama, I'd –"

She stopped and listened. It wasn't her mother's bell at all. Mama was dead. It was the telephone.

The call. Finally, they'd found her.

Mirabella was ready for it. She'd been expecting it. Johnny was making the funeral arrangements and wanted her opinion as to what the choir should sing. Mirabella knew exactly what to suggest. She could already hear the hymn echoing throughout the church:

Morning has broken
Like the first morning.
Black bird has spoken
Like the first bird . . .

She was surprised to hear herself half humming, half moaning the melody. A solo, for Mirabella to sing at Fiddy's funeral. She laughed at the morbidity and picked up the phone on the fifth ring.

"Yes?" she answered in her firmest voice. They were wrong if they thought she'd be upset. She'd be detached and respectable throughout the whole thing and they would wonder at her strength. Her head wavered like the flame of a candle and she rested it against the faux paneling of the wall. "Yes?" she said again, this time impatiently.

"Mirabella? Are you okay?" It was Johnny.

"I'm fine," she snapped, her voice a razor. "Why?"

"I thought you were coming to work today. At least since you didn't call. But it's okay if you don't. If you want some time off, that's fine."

"Time off? For what?"

"To mourn."

"Mourn?" Mirabella suddenly felt well enough to fight. She laughed. "Mourn what? A wasted life?"

Johnny didn't respond.

It suddenly angered her that he wouldn't discuss the issue. He wouldn't fight about it because he knew she was right. She was right. She'd always been right about Fiddy.

She had seen through Fiddy. She knew Fiddy had been on a path to self-destruction. She'd always known how Fiddy's life would end: alone in bleak poverty. All because no one but Mirabella had summoned the guts to tell her she was homely, that she had a disproportionately fat forehead, that she had no talent and no possibility of success. If only they had followed her lead and done as she'd done, Fiddy's life could have been more productive. The dreams and delusions could have had a chance to die, giving way to a more prudent, sensible and economically productive Fiddy.

Since Johnny wouldn't take the bait, she decided to punish him. "To tell you the truth," she said, ensuring her voice didn't wobble. "I think maybe I'd like to go back to work at the factory."

Johnny gasped. "What? Why on earth would you want to go back there?" Not that it was such an awful place for his employees to work. "You earned your way out years ago."

"No reason," she said simply. She wouldn't dignify him with an explanation.

"You can't be serious." He sighed, the days of searching for Fiddy's body weighing on him. "Tell me what's wrong, Mirabella. Did we do something? Is it a raise you want? We can work something out. Maybe you're just upset over Fiddy. This isn't the time to be making major decisions. You'd be surprised how things can work out for the better. Take some time off. I'll continue your pay of course."

"You'll not pay me for doing nothing."

"It isn't nothing. It's an investment to make sure you come back. We need you here."

"Don't be insane. Housekeepers are a dime a dozen."

"Mirabella, you haven't had a vacation or a raise in twenty years. I think you can take some time off with pay."

"You can't treat me any differently than your other employees."

"Would you stop?!" he finally shouted. "You're my aunt, not an employee. Why are you doing this to yourself? Why do you always refuse my help? Why is it that you deserve less than everybody else?"

"I won't take what I don't deserve. Just because other people will, doesn't mean I should."

He sighed. "What are you going to do with yourself?"

"I just want to go back to the factory," she croaked, barely above a whisper. She bit her lower lip and tears streamed down her face. Thankfully, Johnny wouldn't see them and think she was crying.

"I don't believe this," Johnny said with another deep sigh. "Maybe you should wait until we find the body and you've had a chance to –"

"I'm not going to beg, Johnny. Are you going to let me transfer to the factory or not?"

A long pause as Johnny, Mirabella could tell, was shaking his head. "Fine," he said at last, his voice hoarse. "I'll let the personnel manager know you're coming. They'll be expecting you whenever you get there." He hung up.

Mirabella hung up and managed to pull herself up to the couch from the plastic mat. She sat and waited for the blood to reorientate her head. Indeed, she would go to the factory. That's where she belonged. Imagine – a drunk like her employed at the mansion! A drunk like her responsible for meals and children and dinner parties with guests who were business associates and millionaires. Who knew what would happen? No, the best place for her was at the factory. Johnny ought to be ashamed of himself, trying to bribe her with paid time off. She didn't deserve it. She hadn't earned it. Where was his pride? Factory workers didn't get time off to laze about, sick and drunk. Why should she? Ridiculous.

She wasn't taking any of his charity. She was only his former housekeeper and now just a common factory worker. And the family drunk. She'd work at the factory for her few pennies, drink herself comatose every night, live like a drunk until she died and either went to hell or scraped her way into the bottom level of purgatory – where Protestants would be the ones to teach *her* the *Baltimore Catechism.* What they couldn't learn they could always teach, she thought uncharitably. It's exactly what she would deserve. She picked up the phone and called Gorble Gote. She wouldn't even bother with the Stuart pride this time.

HUGGING THE SHORE in the shallow water, Fiddy had watched as Mirabella lugged the beach gear into the darkness and, when she faded from view, listened as the crunching of her feet dissipated gradually across the beach.

The beach bag was within Fiddy's reach. She opened it, put on her tiara and took out the pouch of diamonds which she tucked inside her bathing suit. Now she was ready, she thought, and pushed out from the shallows into the deeper waters. A weak vapor of light followed her like a comet's tail as the dinoflagellates lit up. Strong strokes. Kick. Flutter. She could have been an Olympic swimmer with her strong strokes, she thought, at least in the dog paddle competition. She headed toward the guardian rocks dividing the warmer shallow waters and the open strait. The rocks were crowded with the shadows of resting cormorants and as Fiddy moved by they stood like gothic statues watching, but refusing to warn.

She passed the rocks, entered open water and aimed herself toward what she supposed was the direction of the closest island. The glassy surface, without a ripple in any direction, concealed the islands. Even if they should be dotted with street lights, she was too low and heavy in the water to see past the curving world. They were there, she knew, waiting for her to reach them before exercising their muscles and lifting themselves into the sky.

The deeper water was noticeably cooler and she saw that her hands no longer generated flashes of light. She rolled over to her back and pushed with her legs. The great mass of Wintry Hope, a darker darkness against the starry sky, was diminishing as she pulled away. She had to stop and rest. She treaded water while taking in the stars. They were so vivid she could tell which ones were closer and which ones further away. She lifted a hand up to touch a close one but it was just beyond her reach. She watched for a falling star. Just one. She would wait. A vast ocean silence surrounded her. No falling star.

She started out again, keeping to her back. Her legs and arms ached. Her breathing seemed as loud as a thunder clap in the silence and she worried that Mirabella would hear her even as far as the beach. Then, so weak and distant that she almost missed it, she heard Mirabella's shouting voice: *Fiddy! Where are you Fiddy!*

She turned over and paddled faster. Strong strokes, away

from Wintry Hope, away from Mirabella, away from a carnal world with no eye for the transcendent. Soon she would feel herself getting lighter. Soon she would leave the water with airy wings to join all the others who lived in the land of sky. And they would welcome her with applause and wonder why she hadn't come to their realm earlier.

The water, however, only seemed to weigh heavier on her arms and legs. She struggled against it on every stroke. She had to stop again to rest on her back. The stars continued to watch her progress with scientific imperviousness. Fiddy stared back. They almost seemed to circle her while they peered and she thought perhaps the currents of the strait were turning her. It was making her dizzy. She closed her eyes.

Maybe it would be better to wait while the islands came to her. Or maybe the islands only rose from the strait in the daytime and at night the waters regained their strength to pull them back down. She shivered with cold. It's not far, she told herself. She could do it. She couldn't doubt now.

She opened her eyes, started again and stopped. She didn't know which direction she should go in. She tried to get her bearings. The darker looming presence of Wintry Hope was gone. The guardian rocks were gone. There was only darkness in all directions and blurry sky. Which way was it? She continued in what she thought was the direction she had been swimming but now she wasn't sure. She struggled to tread water and at the same time look around. The water, in all directions, simply stared back at her.

She swam blindly. She was close. She knew it. Swim, stroke, flutter, push. The pain in her arms made her wince but when her strokes slowed she began to sink. She couldn't give up now, she thought. Not when she was this close. The water would not win. It wanted her for itself, it wanted her tiara and her diamonds but it would not get her. She was for the air.

Her legs felt like blocks of waterlogged wood. She gasped for breath. Push, push, flutter, flutter. Why did she feel so heavy? Her pouch of diamonds, her store of treasure, was pulling her down. She thought, fleetingly, about dropping them but she couldn't free a hand to do it even if she wanted to. And what point was there in living without her diamonds? Neither would she cry out for help. *I told you so*, Mirabella would say. No, Fiddy would wave to Mirabella from the sky on her way by.

She could feel herself sinking. She choked on some brine and coughed. She struggled to move her arms and legs but invisible belts, threads from the deep, were binding her. She could barely keep her chin above the surface. Mirabella would be pleased. A pain suddenly shot through her chest and down her arm. "Help!" she cried. Panic seized her. She moved to her back, unable to use her arms, and tried using her legs to stay afloat. She was sinking. The pain was too much. The stars, the sky, the universe – it was too heavy for her to keep holding it all up. A furtive breath. A small cry. She could feel herself falling. She went under and she felt her wig float away. She climbed for the surface but her world had suddenly become slow. With odd detachment she saw herself fighting, she saw her hands clawing at the water in an effort to climb. And she saw flashes of light, the dinoflagellates, which were like great bursts of spectacular light when seen underwater. She came up sputtering. "Help," she gasped. The pain paralyzed her arms. She couldn't fight anymore. She turned to her back, looked at the sky and sang, "Goodbye!" She relaxed. If the stars above would not have her, the stars below would. She stretched out arms and legs in the snow angel position, gave a final flap to set the waters ablaze, took in a breath and let herself sink. She was so relaxed and at peace that when her rump touched the sand, she didn't realize at first that she was in less than three feet of water. Then her lungs told her she should try to live so she stood up.

She was standing in the middle of the Northumberland Strait, it appeared. The strait, a black mirror, stretched beyond her to infinity and she wondered how such a small plot of sand had formed so far from land, just for her to stand on for a rest. While she caught her breath and pondered, she noticed the strait begin to take on a white luminescence. She turned and saw the source of the light, the moon, rising from Wintry Hope on whose shores she stood. Her wig, with tiara still attached, bobbed at her feet. She shrugged. Perhaps she could try for the islands another day.

She sat down on the beach and rested while trying to determine where she was. The current had apparently taken her east, toward Brocktod's Roo, far from houses, cottages, roads and lights. The moonlight showed silver-tipped grasses typical of Wintry Hope's marsh, perhaps a few more trees and bushes, the slumping banks that would be easy to climb. She picked up her wig, wrung out the brine, put it on and straightened the tiara. Her wet bathing suit was chilling her so she stripped it off and kicked it into the water. She made her way up the strand with her pouch of diamonds, climbed the bank and entered the marsh.

In the morning she awoke in the sunshine on a patch of dry grass, the summer air providing a warm blanket. A moat of sundews and violets surrounded her. She yawned and stretched like a fawn.

She spent the morning wandering through the marsh, heading in no particular direction but noticing with gasps of wonder all the living things in full bloom. There was a glow to creation, as if it had been newly blessed, or newly created with the sun rising on it for the first time. Yellow heath flowers, button bushes and meadow beauties lined her path. A grosbeak with breast of dusty rose peered at her with blinking eyes from a thick arm of choke-cherry blossoms. Why, she wondered, hadn't she seen this before? Somehow she'd missed it on her last trip through the marsh on the bulldozer.

She was so captivated, so awed that she moved through the marsh almost in a trance, not even taking notice when she nearly stepped on a well-concealed Garden Twinkle. In a pocket of blooming marsh marigolds, Garden was sketching a white admiral drying its wings at the edge of a raspberry leaf. When the bare foot was planted beside her, Garden shrieked and the annoyed butterfly danced away to an aspen.

"Good morning," said Fiddy on her way by, as if passing her at the Lieutenant Governor's garden party. Speechless, Garden watched as Fiddy carefully stepped through the spikerush and disappeared behind a bank of pink coreopsis.

Fiddy stumbled upon the bulldozer track and followed it to the community centre where dozens of cars, including emergency response vehicles, were parked. From inside, officious voices competed with two-way radios. Fiddy thought she should investigate what was going on inside but was starting to miss her breakfast so she tiptoed past the centre to Henrietta Gillis's house which had, in the back lawn, a clothesline gloriously filled with nearly dry laundry. She selected some underwear, pulled it on, and searched for suitable outerwear. What she really wanted was a tablecloth but finding none she chose a blue blouse, skirt, some stockings and to pull the ensemble together, a multicoloured afghan she used as a wrap. Henrietta Gillis's car was not in the drive so Fiddy stepped inside the porch and borrowed a pair of green pumps. She thought about making herself some breakfast but was worried about Henrietta coming home and catching her so she left quickly, walked up the driveway to the highway and stuck out a thumb.

Almost immediately, an enormous motor home with California licence plates stopped. The driver lowered the window and asked for directions to Tina Shingo. "I'll take you there myself," Fiddy offered. The door opened and she climbed in. "Do you have anything for breakfast? A zucchini frittata would be nice."

As luck would have it, the motor home had two passengers, a California couple who were both retired chefs. Fiddy sat down on a sofa and kicked off her shoes while the food was being prepared.

She directed them to follow a longer scenic route to Tina Shingo, across Cape Reggeo and the highlands overlooking the Northumberland. While eating their frittata lunch they watched porpoises feeding on the schools of mackerel below.

"Brigitte would be so pleased," said Fiddy and told her California friends of her and Brigitte's efforts to save the planet. "Some people don't understand just how important it is to save the grass." She entertained them with stories of the various charity causes she worked on with other celebrities. "My Hollywood years were cut short," she told them. "Because Andrew needed me in London. I couldn't very well say no to him."

"Andrew?"

"Andrew Lloyd Webber, of course."

They spent the day touring Tina Shingo County and in payment the California couple cooked Fiddy magnificent feasts. The day ended with Fiddy directing them to drop her off at Tina Shingo's best hotel, *The Moreclay,* where they pulled in and waited while she went inside to make her arrangements.

She swept into the lobby and handed her pouch and tiara to the hotelier. "These are my diamonds. Please put them in your safe."

The hotelier's eyes widened as he felt the bulging pouch. Fiddy watched carefully as he opened the safe and put the pouch inside. "You are adequately insured?" she asked.

"Yes."

"Good. Can you tell me, is the Presidential Suite free this evening? I am in dire need of a vacation. I've been cooped up in my motor coach for weeks and I'm not done performing yet. Be a dear and check."

The hotelier looked past her at the waiting motor home. It was as long as a small train, had California licence plates and was towing a small BMW convertible. He checked his manifest. "I do believe it's free," he said and led the way to the Presidential Suite.

[TWENTY-THREE]

Work is the curse of the drinking classes.

– Oscar Wilde

THE MORELIS FACTORY had been rebuilt by Mirabella's father in the nineteen sixties after a hurricane swept away every trace of it except the black concrete floor. Johnny had modernized and refurbished it and made it the hub of what became the largest lobster distribution company in North America: SFP International. Mirabella had worked in it for thirty years, had earned her freedom, had tasted glory as the housekeeper of Applefern Mansion – and was now back where she had started. She arrived on Friday morning at seven-thirty, having caught the factory shuttle at the bottom of her driveway on its way from Tina Shingo.

Already feeling grey and gaunt when she entered the main entrance doors to the factory, she nearly collapsed when she was met by a wall of old familiar fumes from a life she didn't care to remember: steaming lobster, stagnant rubber boots, latex gloves, industrial cleaning chemicals. It hadn't changed. It was the same factory she'd left. She was immediately recognized by a group of factory women standing near the steps. One of them audibly gasped. Mirabella avoided eye contact and with rubber boots in hand walked past them into the office of the personnel manager.

"We'll put you on the packing table," he said. He handed her a hair net, cap, smock, plastic apron and gloves.

"That's a senior position," Mirabella said, her voice even. "I'm just starting."

"You've got experience. We need you on the packing table."

Mirabella shook her head. "I'm not jumping the line just because I'm a Stuart. You can put me on legs or knuckles."

"That's where we put people with no experience," he said. His voice had an air of sincerity, of one experienced in persuasion.

"We need someone on the packing table who knows what they're doing."

"You can put me on legs or knuckles," Mirabella insisted. She'd forfeited her right to a senior position when she'd left the factory. It was only fair. It's what she deserved.

He looked at her with cool, blue eyes, calculating, no doubt, what would work best in persuading the strong, wiry woman in front of him. "Anything you say, Ms Stuart," he said with a sigh that implied she was getting her way simply because she was a Stuart.

An admirable tactic, Mirabella thought. His abilities to manipulate were undoubtedly prized by Johnny, the reigning king of manipulation. She said nothing. The personnel manager waited for a long moment, expecting her to change her mind. She didn't. She gathered up her boots, gloves, hair net, cap, apron and smock and headed out the door.

She went past the gossiping women and up the sandpaper steps to change into her work clothes in the designated area. She smoked a cigarette at a picnic table in the lunch room and ate two soda crackers with a cup of water mixed with pickle juice, her remedy for a hangover. She gulped down two aspirin tablets and went downstairs, stepping through the curtains to the factory floor at a quarter to eight.

Indeed, it was the identical factory. The smells were the same, the sounds were the same, the stainless steel tables gleaming under long tracks of fluorescent lights were the same. The taps and hoses from white-washed walls were the same. The hazy sea of blue aprons, smocks and caps was the same. The mechanical din and hum of sealing machines, rollers, suction devices and the clanging and banging of knives and hammers were all the same.

Perhaps, she wondered, she hadn't even left. Perhaps her life at the mansion, on the periphery of Johnny and Martha's important lives, had been only a dream. Perhaps her years at the mansion had been only a deluded attempt to escape the slavery of the factory. Perhaps she'd just blinked her eyes, lost consciousness for a few seconds, and now was back.

Looking around at the dozens of women standing at the

stainless steel tables confirmed it. She recognized almost all of them. She found herself staring at a young woman with a plump, ruddy face. "Juny?" Mirabella asked in amazement. Surely it couldn't be. Juny had worked with Mirabella thirty years ago and at that time had been nearly seventy. Surely she was retired or dead by now. Surely she hadn't been forced to come back to the factory too?

The woman chuckled and it was Juny's chuckle. "Juny's my grandmother," she said. "And she's as feisty as ever at the nursing home."

"Aren't you –" A woman whose mother had never been able to keep her mouth shut managed to shut hers just before completing her sentence.

"Yes," said Mirabella wearily. "I'm Mirabella Stuart." She continued to her workstation as knowledge spread throughout the factory that the aunt of the owner, no less, was working there with them, on the production line. As the news went from table to table, Mirabella felt consecutive groups of eyes fall on her from across the factory floor. There would be no limit to the speculations. Was she a spy from head office? Had there been a scandal? Was the family experiencing financial trouble? Had there been a falling out? Perhaps Mirabella had been caught stealing. The further the news spread out from the epicenter of Juny's grand-daughter's table, the wilder the explanations grew.

Mirabella pulled on her gloves and stared at the wall where a large clock, unavoidable for anyone who worked in the factory, glowered down on them at a quarter to eight. She noted the slowly ticking second hand and let her eyes drift along the walls to the southwest corner of the factory from where the first batch of cooked lobster would arrive. It came, glistening orange and steaming, a thousand pounds at a time, dumped from a stainless steel cage which came through a plastic curtain on a track attached to the ceiling. Mirabella watched as the break-off workers pounced on lobsters with yellow-gloved hands like starving children reaching for cookies. A quick twist and a lobster would be split in half. Squirts of green tomalley were aimed into small bowls to be bagged for shipping to Asia. Off came the claws, legs and tail into their various piles.

The gib was squeezed out from underneath the carapace and the stripped bodies were cast into a shell crusher for extraction of paste. A conveyer carried the waste shell to a dump truck parked outside. The claws, knuckles and tails went to their respective sectors of the factory.

The legs came to Mirabella. She looked at the clock as the carrier dumped a container of legs in front of her, perhaps five thousand in all. She looked up at the clock. Thirteen minutes to eight. Not bad, she thought. Johnny had bettered his father's time by two minutes. That kind of efficiency, if carried over into all of SFP International's factories, would no doubt mean three or four extra shopping trips for Martha each year.

She fed one leg into the grinding steel rollers in front of her and it was snatched from her fingers in an instant, producing an infinitesimally small filament of meat which was deposited into a stainless steel bowl on the other side. The empty shell fell into a trough of water which would draw it to the conveyer and the dump truck outside. Mirabella peered over her rollers to see how much meat had come out of one lobster leg. It looked like the tongue of a hummingbird. It would take tens of thousands to fill the bowl.

The trick, she knew, was to have a dozen or so legs in one hand ready to force through the rollers continuously one after the other. There could be no period of time in which legs were not entering the rollers and the rollers were not rolling out meat. It was critical, however, not to force in one lobster leg before the other one had shot out because the machine could only handle one leg at a time. Otherwise, she knew, it wouldn't squeeze the meat out, it would become jammed or, if more than three legs entered at the same time, the apparatus would be derailed. It required exceptional coordination, concentration and timing to maximize the rollers' efficiency, always pushing the machine to its maximum capacity without causing a jam or derailment. One after the other. Not two at a time. No space between them. Fast, but not careless. Quick but not impatient. Careful but not overly cautious. It was like having half of one's body tortured with fire and the other half with ice.

She glanced at the clock. Twelve minutes to eight. She'd

wasted an entire minute.

She sighed and began feeding the legs into the hungry rollers, forcing herself to look away from the clock. She recalled from her years past that the clock was nothing more than a merciless tyrant ruling the workers heartlessly from its throne upon the wall. Hopeful faces of factory workers, faces that pleaded for time to have surged ahead toward the close of the day, were drawn by its strange force to take a glance, hoping much time had passed. When they did glance, they were always punished. Never did time pass at the same rate as it felt it was passing in the factory. It was as though Johnny had paid the master of time to make every second last a fraction longer in order to make his factories more efficient.

Mirabella didn't dare look at the clock as she fed her lobster legs into the rollers. She would keep her head down near the piles of amputated legs and focus only on feeding them into the rollers as quickly as she could without jamming the machine. The clock could rule everyone else but her. Later she would take a look when she was sure time had surged ahead. Then she would be astonished at how quickly it had gone by. That was the way to beat the clock – to ignore it. To be independent of it. Not to need it. It was a strategy that worked for most things.

Her hands hadn't forgotten their task but, she noticed in side-long glances at her neighbours, she was much slower than they were. She sped up in an attempt to match their pace. Then, when she was glancing to see if another batch of lobster was coming, her rubber glove got caught in the rollers and, with a *thwack*, was yanked from her hand like a slingshot. It exploded out the other side with a puff of meat and landed in the bowl. She picked the tattered glove out of the bowl and wrung it out, leaving as much of the meat and water as she could. She tossed the frayed glove in with the discarded shells and continued with just one gloved hand. A pair of new gloves would cost eight dollars, an amount she couldn't afford, especially given her current spending priorities. And it had been her own fault, after all. She would suffer it out with one glove even if the skin on her hand wore out. She gathered up a fresh handful of legs and began feeding them in.

A few handfuls later and her coordination seemed to improve. Her hands, somehow, were recovering their memories of years past. She kept her eyes on them, carefully avoiding the clock, and fed legs into the rollers while her mind began to wander.

She couldn't help but wonder what they were doing at the mansion. Had Johnny replaced her yet? Who, from the factory, would he be able to trust? Who would that lucky woman be? Perhaps it was someone on the packing table, the same one the personnel manager had urged Mirabella to fill in for. Whoever it was, she hoped the new housekeeper would have the brains to dust the overhead fan in the foyer.

She wondered who they found to take care of Tara and whether they knew that she wouldn't drink grape juice unless it was in a red cup. She wondered if they would read and follow the directions for cleaning and ironing Johnny's dress shirts which were so sensitive that Mirabella herself had once driven the iron through a shoulder. She'd insisted on paying to replace it, of course, since it had been her fault. It had been a special order item from Turin, Italy and had cost her three weeks of wages. No doubt, a new housekeeper wouldn't have the scruples to do the same.

She wondered if the children would ask about her. Connie would be happy, she supposed. Robert would be pensive and Tara wouldn't know the difference until it came time to drink her grape juice.

She wondered if someone would remember to water the plants hanging beside the Gothic arch in the ballroom. They looked plastic and fake – until they wilted and died. She wondered what the sun looked like on the Northumberland shimmering happily just beyond the lawns of the mansion. She wondered if the mansion would smell the same if she wasn't the one cleaning it. She wondered if someone would remind Martha to pay for Connie's bagpipe lessons.

And she wondered why, for pity's sake, no one had yet called her to update her on the search for Fiddy's body. Perhaps the news had come when Mirabella had been sick in bed. Or perhaps they'd found the body but were struggling to meet some idiotic request Fiddy had included in her Will – to be cremated, perhaps, and her ashes strewn over the streets of Broadway. A fitting tribute, thought Mirabella, the ashes becoming black grime under foot, trampled by the rich and famous and the poor and unknown alike, all of whom would continue to ignore Fiddy in death as they had in life.

Mirabella's legs weren't used to standing on concrete. An ache began near her shins and radiated upwards into her spine. By the end of the day, she supposed, it would reach her neck and she would hardly be able to move. She stepped from one foot to the other and shook each one to keep the circulation going. It was just a little pain, she told herself, nothing to complain about. Pain was good when borne of hard work. Pain told her she was doing something, that she was productive, that she was making a difference, that she wasn't useless like so many other people were. Pain told her in no uncertain terms that she still existed – even though she might resent it.

But she did wish Johnny would call, just to let her know the status of the search. Surely his aunt deserved that much. She might think about going to the funeral if she were feeling well enough. The least Johnny could do was to leave a message on her door if he couldn't get through to her by phone. Or he could come to the factory to tell her.

She grumbled to herself and then chastised herself for grumbling to herself. What did she care about what happened to Fiddy? She would think about it no more.

She continued her work, inserting a thousand, or perhaps ten thousand lobster legs into the rollers. Time moved forward like a slow barge. It wasn't lunchtime yet but Mirabella felt it must be getting on toward mid morning. She'd been good – she hadn't dared to look at the clock since the first batch of lobster arrived. How many batches had it been? She hadn't kept track. She could only remember the first. But her stomach was rumbling hungrily and the pain from her legs had followed her spine to reach her neck, as if a current of electricity were being fed into her from the concrete floor. All of which indicated that several hours had passed. Surely the clock would have a pleasant surprise for her. So she looked.

And she was punished for it. She stood looking at the clock in disbelief, wondering if someone wasn't playing a trick on her. She looked around for the hidden camera. Had the APT Agent set her up again?

There were no cameras. She dropped the legs of lobster and continued to stare at the impossibly cruel clock. Had it stopped? Was it broken? She looked closely at the second hand. It seemed to be moving. Infuriatingly slow. She shook her head, still unable to comprehend the mystery of time's slow ebb. She was only startled back to reality when the rollers somehow caught her remaining glove and pulled it from her hand with another quick *thwack*.

It was twenty minutes after eight.

She left the factory without bothering to get credit for the meat she'd produced. She didn't bother going upstairs to change out of her factory clothes and retrieve her outdoor clothes. She didn't stop at the office of the personnel manager to let him know she was leaving. She kept on past the entrance foyer, out the doors, across the parking lot and up the hill to the main highway where she stuck out her thumb and hoped no one she knew would be going by. She didn't have to wait long. A truck came to a sudden, careening stop beside her, the pleasant sound of chiming bottles accompanying it. Gorble Gote. The back of the truck was filled with crates and boxes.

When they arrived at her trailer, she made her selection, a forty ounce bottle of rum, and paid him.

[TWENTY-FOUR]

> Cabaletta – a quick, often brilliant, final section of an aria, especially in Italian opera.
>
> – *The Penguin Opera Guide*

FIDDY MOVED INTO the Presidential Suite at the Moreclay and the hotel's pedicurist arrived the next morning to work on her toenails. She ordered a champagne cocktail and walnut soufflé for breakfast and told the waiter to scrape off any girasole tubers or green-gourd-marmalade-sauce that might be included with the soufflé. For dessert she requested tiramisù with extra brandy. She ate it all from the comfort of a bed as long and as wide as the *Exxon Valdez.*

"Whoever says money doesn't buy happiness doesn't have enough of it," she told the waiter when he arrived with her second champagne cocktail. Money wasn't the *only* happiness, she explained, but it was a good portion of the happiness currently in existence. "Those who disagree," she told him, "haven't seen enough game shows." Watching a contestant spinning around in circles and screaming hysterically or whooping with glee for an undeserved jackpot was proof enough, she explained. The waiter agreed with everything she said. She switched the channel to *The Price is Right* so she'd have other people with whom to share her happiness.

After the pedicure came a manicure and *Hollywood Squares*. After the manicure came a full body massage and *Family Feud*. After the massage came a facial, *Wheel of Fortune*, and an afternoon snack of *crêpes Suzette* with whipped cream and Cognac. After that, a nap in which she dreamt of the day she lured Clark Gable to her Parisian suite after her performance at *L'Opéra Bastille*. He heard her from his suite at the Four Seasons as she sang from her balcony:

On the rose-scented wings of love,
go, pained sighs:
go to salve the mind
of him that lies imprisoned . . .
Like a breeze of hope

linger in his room:
wake him up to remember
his dreams of love!

After three standing ovations, she awoke and went to browse in the hotel's shops for something to wear. She found the perfect outfit: a silvery-blue gown, a matching gargantuan hat in the shape of a butterfly, laced heels and a pink ostrich-feather boa. She charged it to her room.

The next day she watched more television, ordered more room service and considered having another set of facials and massages but her skin was still raw and sensitive from the last and her hands, nails and toes were already beyond perfection. She was bored. Already. It was shocking that sloth and gluttony could now provide so little pleasure. Perhaps if they hadn't been decommissioned as sins they'd have provided more. She made a mental note to ask Father Francis about changing it back.

For days, it seemed, she slumbered in her bed, watched television and ordered room service, moving occasionally from the parts of her bed that became soggy to the fresher, cooler parts, and back again. She was able to endure another manicure and pedicure but on the morning of the fifth day, she could stand it no longer.

She needed to sing. Like a deep imploding groan within her, it pleaded to be let out. What it was to suffer such craving! Did no one know what it was to desire something so badly? To desire it so madly? To desire it so blindly that she was willing to forgo anything in order to have it? Just one small taste, one tiny morsel, was all she wanted. One little taste would fill her up. She needed to be heard once, only once. Then she would be filled. Then she would have what she was seeking. Then she would never need it again.

She couldn't help herself: she leapt from the bed and sang out her high E, moved to the F, held it for a good minute without taking any more than three breaths, and went higher into what she supposed was the F sharp. Then the G. She held the G, with her eyes closed, and saw the masses of people in her audience, holding their breath, unable to believe the majesty of her voice. She held it longer and went even higher, into a realm unmatched by any other soprano in history – the illusive note of high H. She held it while her audience watched in wonder, a feat beyond the limits of human lung capacity. She was singing with the angels now. She held the note longer than any mere mortal could – until the hotelier, with two security guards, all with ashen faces, broke down her door and tumbled into the suite to save their best customer from what any objective observer would suppose must surely be an awful homicide. Seeing that she was in no danger, they apologized for interrupting and explained that they believed her to be under attack.

She didn't mind. She gave them her wide, superstar smile. "I'm singing." She recited a few measures from *Carmen* before they were able to creep out of the room through the broken door and back to their jobs.

The promise of an audience, then its absence, exhausted her. Who knew how loud to sing when there was no audience? She fell on the bed in despair. Didn't anyone know what it was to want something this badly? So badly she'd trade anything to obtain it? If she were asked for anything, she would give it. Gladly. She'd give everything: her money, her jewels, her clothes, her career, her health, her love, her tiara, everything, even her new butterfly hat, to stand at the edge of the choir loft at St Margaret's in Wintry Hope, listen as the drums and trumpets began, and sing T*he Battle Hymn of the Republic:*

> *Mine eyes have seen the glory of the coming of*
> *the Lord . . .*

She'd invite complete destruction to sing *Jerusalem My Destiny* with Michael Crawford and the London Symphony Orchestra. Or *Panis Angelicus* with the full choir of St Margaret's moving in behind her with their glorious harmonies, along with the Nova Scotia Symphony. Sopranos like towers reaching to the sky, basses like trembling mountains shaken by the earth, altos and tenors weaving in and out of each other like streams of joyous songbirds, violins like lonesome crying – or dying. And Fiddy, a shy innocent voice quivering in blinding unapproachable light above them all.

Did no one know this thirst? Mirabella? The Agent? Johnny? Surely not one of them did. If they knew her thirst they'd have sought her out and allowed her to pour out her libation upon them. No, they knew nothing of this thirst, this craving for which personal destruction was but a small price. Just one taste! That's all she wanted! One small sip would fill her up completely so that she would never need another. It wasn't the taste she wanted. It wasn't the aroma, the glory, or the thunder of the applause.

It was God.

No, Mirabella knew nothing of this thirst. She couldn't possibly. But she would – because Fiddy Washburn was going to tell her. She picked up her telephone, careful of her fingernails, and dialed Mirabella's number. She thumped an elegant foot impatiently as the phone rang. A piece of her mind, that's what Mirabella would be getting. How dare she! How dare she not know the pain she caused by refusing to let her sing. And, Fiddy remembered with a gasp, she'd been promised a solo. She couldn't remember when it was supposed to be, but whenever or whatever it was, she intended to collect on that promise.

The phone continued to ring without anyone answering. Fiddy let it ring another thirty-five times and slammed it down in frustration. "Mirabella Stuart!" she screamed. "Why on earth won't you answer your phone!"

Didn't she know Fiddy's thirst? She managed to calm herself down and called the front desk. "Desdemona Pacifico-Rossini," she said sweetly. "Calling from the Presidential Suite." She paused dramatically before making her announcement: "I am returning to Wintry Hope. I cannot refuse her my song. I will need my diamonds and tiara, please."

The hotelier tactfully informed her she had not yet made payment arrangements and that payment was required in full before releasing the diamonds and tiara.

"You didn't say anything about a payment!" Fiddy cried. "You said this suite was free!"

ONE CALL TO HER SOLICITOR would straighten out the misunderstanding, thought Fiddy. Oddly, however, Arthur wept when he heard her voice, causing her great confusion. "Pull yourself together, Arthur. It's not like I've been charged with crimes against the grass."

Arthur sniffled. "I might not have a heart," he said. "But I'm still a lawyer."

She relayed her troubles and, composing himself, he agreed to take care of it.

A few minutes later a chastened hotelier came to her room with her diamonds and tiara and apologized for his earlier false advertisement of a free room. She demanded a limousine for her trouble. This time, however, he informed her that the limo was not free.

On the outskirts of Tina Shingo Fiddy found herself sticking out her thumb and hoping for a return of her California friends. The first vehicle stopped.

"Hello Fiddles," said Gorble Gote, grinning around a short, well-chewed cigar. "I thought you drowned."

"Hello Gorble! Islands don't drown. Are you going my way?"

"Sure am. Hop in."

She climbed into the front seat. "I'm going back to Wintry Hope," she told him. "I was planning a trip abroad but I couldn't stay away. You know, I very well couldn't. I'm still Miss Wintry Hope. My reign has never ended."

"You don't say."

She took out her tiara and arranged it in her hair. "Miss Wintry Hope 1945, and there hasn't been a pageant since so I've never handed on my crown. 1945 was the year World War II ended. That shows you the power of great beauty. Helen of Troy caused the Hundred Years' War. I ended World War II. We must always use our powers for good."

He nodded, slowly, and sped up. Fiddy settled down, rested the back of her head against the seat, and watched the countryside pass. They met the Northumberland at Cleaving Antom and the vast shimmering river brought a deep pain to her heart. It didn't have to do anything at all to be beautiful, she thought. No wig, no gown, no makeup. It wore only its diamonds, sparkling in the sun. She watched it, unable to shake her gaze away as they drove along the coast toward Wintry Hope. She noticed the islands had grown thick and were threatening to lift. She dared not blink in case she should miss the moment they would lose touch with the water. It was such a tragedy, she thought, to have everything she needed in Wintry Hope, never desiring to be anywhere else.

At the outskirts of Wintry Hope, she snapped out of her communion with the Northumberland and told Gorble to stop. Wintry Hope was on its way to Sunday Mass and Fiddy intended to take the opportunity to announce her triumphant return. She made sure her tiara was secure and when Gorble came to a stop, opened the door and slid out. "I think people have a right to see me," she said and headed to the back of the truck. With some difficulty, she climbed over the tail gate and arranged boxes of empty beer bottles into a throne. She sat down with gracious dignity and signaled to Gorble. "Anon, you may continue, but slowly."

They entered Wintry Hope and Fiddy waved to families on their way to church. "Good people of Wintry Hope," she called in her finest British. "I do thank you for all you've been to me." A little girl attempted to wave back but she was stopped by her mother who took hold of her arm and pulled her into line with the rest of the family. "I have missed you all," Fiddy continued and sang her entrance hymn:

Believe me in my pain,
I am a slave to costly joys,
I languish for your love,
Have pity on me!

She waved gently, serenely, with dignity – not with the excited, jerking movements as a moron would.

Gorble's truck arrived at the church as Johnny and his family were entering. They stared at the scene with mouths agape. Gorble's truck pulled into the parking lot, came to a jingling stop and Fiddy disembarked from her throne. She blew a goodbye kiss to Gorble and ascended the church steps with slow, stately strides as she'd seen Queen Elisabetta do in *Don Carlo,* careful of her silver-blue gown and tiara sparkling in the sun. She approached a wide-eyed Johnny at the top of the steps and gave him her hand. "I've returned," she said, "to sing my solo. Where's Mirabella?"

Johnny was speechless. He stammered incomprehensibly.

"Never mind," said Fiddy moving into the church imperiously. "I'll see her in the loft."

MIRABELLA'S RUM WAS WARM, as she'd long run out of ice, but it loved her just the same. From her seat on the front steps of her trailer, the sunlight seemed like a bright fog around her. She watched the steeple of St Margaret's and waited for the notes to begin, announcing the beginning of the High Mass.

Everything, she noticed, was in full bloom. Even her geraniums, neglected for only a few days, were blooming profusely. The window box above her was barely able to contain the blooms spilling out of it, thousands of small scarlet explosions buzzing with feasting bees. There were no leaves, just blooms, the result of their years of contained potential finding sudden release.

She was happy even though it was her last glass of rum. She needed to be happy because she knew what waited for her when the rum was gone – nothing. She had no more responsibilities, no chores, no Fiddy, no job, no faith. How could she belong to God when she was in a state like this? She was free. She raised her glass. "To freedom." She laughed and took a drink.

The notes began. Wintry Hope seemed to go suddenly quiet as the music trickled out of the church and up the hills to her trailer:

The heavens are telling the glory of God
And all of creation rightly sings praise . . .

She took a gulp and listened carefully to the voices while savouring the rum. That was her choir singing. Her choir, and she felt injured that they were permitted to sing without her. She could make out the violins and trumpets, tenors, basses, altos and sopranos and over it all, the pipes of the organ blending them together. The choir, like her geraniums, seemed to be benefitting from her neglect. She closed her eyes, swayed with the music and lifted a hand to direct them.

Perhaps, she reconsidered, they weren't as good as she first thought. Their timing was off, she noticed, with their last words before each rest sounding to her ears like a series of pistol shots. She shook her head. How humiliating for them. Without firm inflexible leadership, singers inevitably succumbed to the temptation to follow their own hearts into the song, lose themselves in the familiar rhythms and enjoy the hymn instead of focusing on technical excellence. Without a director, they were like oil spilled out on the ground to be wasted. They were random weeds to be plucked from the rows of a disorganized garden. Without a director, they were nothing.

And so they should be corrected. Mirabella finished the last of her rum, tossed the tumbler on the driveway and headed through the woods to the church. She avoided the driveway and chose a more direct route through the trees, charging like a moose through branches and alder clusters, across ditches and fallen spruce, through puddles and brambles in a straight line aimed at the church steps.

She arrived as Father Francis was beginning his sermon, staggered up the staircase into the choir loft and, to the surprise of her choir, stood before them covered with leaves, moss and twigs. "No. 51," she ordered. She snatched her baton from the bannister and waved it at them. "Now."

The choir stared back at her in horror.

"Come on," she slurred. "Backs straight, breathe, project, firm your stomach muscles, mouths open, tongues flat, an orange in the throat with an egg in the nose – give us the notes Virgil!"

They stood before her, frozen.

"Sing, damn it!" she ordered, frustrated they wouldn't start. Her voice echoed throughout the church and brought a halt to Father Francis' sermon.

Arthur stepped down from the third row. "Mirabella," he whispered, "this isn't the right time." He took her by the shoulder to coax her away.

She pushed away his hand. "No. 51!" she shouted. "Give us the notes!"

"You're drunk," Arthur whispered. "You're disrupting the Mass." He was joined by Johnny who had heard the commotion from the church below and arrived from the stairs on a full sprint. They pleaded with her to leave with them.

"Sing, damn it," she ordered. She tried pushing past Arthur

and Johnny to her director's position.

"I do say, Mirabella. You've gone and done it this time."

Mirabella stopped. She listened carefully for the voice she was sure she'd just heard. Johnny and Arthur continued to plead for her to leave the loft and she held up a hand to shush them. "Who said that?" she asked.

"I didn't hear anything," said Johnny.

"It was just an echo," agreed Arthur.

Mirabella noticed they were standing, conspicuously, between her and the front row of sopranos.

"Move," she growled.

"Yes, move," Fiddy chirped. "And I do say, Johnny, drunk or not, you should give the old girl a chance."

Arthur and Johnny stood aside and Mirabella searched the front row of sopranos, finding it difficult to focus properly. She soon spotted her: gowned in silver-blue, with pink boa and twinkling tiara, as proud as a calico cat, the sheets for No. 51 open and ready before her, an island arisen from the depths of the Northumberland. There she was, Fiddy Washburn, standing atop her stilettos in Mirabella's choir like a mountain kingdom. Mirabella studied her in disbelief.

Fiddy flashed a superior smile. "It's a miracle, dearest, isn't it? I'm here and ready to sing. Sound the trumpets, if you please."

Mirabella said nothing. Her mind, slowed by the rum, was failing to compute.

"Mirabella, darling, it's time for us to sing."

Still nothing.

"Or I could just sing my solo."

A thick mist of confusion seemed to have closed in on Mirabella. She couldn't breathe. She couldn't calculate what had happened and fit the pieces together with her impaired mind. Fiddy hadn't drowned? Fiddy had somehow evaded her at the beach, evaded a dozen search parties and survived on her own for almost a week? Impossible. And yet there she was in the front row of sopranos, ready to sing as always.

"Goats and monkeys, Mirabella. You must get hold of yourself. The people are waiting for a performance."

Mirabella simply stared at Fiddy, unable to move. Her hands hung uselessly at her sides as denied emotions struggled against each other for control. She struggled to bring order to the disorder. She struggled to list what had happened.

Fiddy wasn't dead.

Mirabella hadn't killed her.

Fiddy had caused chaos in Wintry Hope.

Fiddy had caused chaos in Mirabella.

Fiddy had been irresponsible. Fiddy had been impractical. Fiddy had duped Mirabella into feeling sorry for her. Fiddy had caused Mirabella her job. Fiddy had caused her to fall into temptation. Fiddy had caused her to break ten years of sobriety. Fiddy had driven her to drink.

Anger. Fury. Rage.

Mirabella found her voice and it trembled. "I don't give solos to fatheads."

Fiddy looked momentarily bewildered, then recovered and gave a gay chuckle. "I'm your best soprano."

"You're a fathead."

"Don't be a bore, Mirabella, it's time to sing."

"Fathead."

"It's time to sing," Fiddy implored.

"Your head's too fat for you to sing."

"It's not fat!" Her eyes were swimming. She pulled some strands of hair down from her wig to cover some of the forehead.

"Fathead."

"I'm not fat!"

"Fathead."

"I'm not –"

"You are. Your head's so fat it makes you look like a retard."

There it was. That horrible word. Fiddy took in an involuntary breath and cried out. "I'm not a retard!"

Her voice echoed throughout the church and the echoes came back like the voices on the playground of her childhood: *Retard! Retard! Retard!* She shook her head, trying to free herself of the insult. "No, no, no!" she cried, but another sound came back with the echoes: laughter.

Mirabella continued her taunts. Fiddy closed her eyes, covered her ears and cried to keep out the echoes. *Pulling a bit of hair over it doesn't help . . . it's huge . . . it's all anyone can see . . . it's what everybody calls you . . . fathead, fathead, fathead . . .*

Fiddy sang out a long soprano note to push them back but the waves continued. She sang louder. The taunts came louder. Mirabella stabbed and Cleopatra perished. Madama Butterfly fell. Marilyn Munroe and Meryl Streep were slaughtered. Audrey Hepburn gave her life up to the rapier. They all fell, their white necks crossed with blood. Then the sword came for Desdemona Pacifico-Rossini.

Fiddy resisted with all the notes she could muster but in the end even she could not deny that it was shrieking she heard, not singing. The opera was over. The *duet grotesque* was at its climax. There were no notes left. The opera was at full stop. The sheets of music went from her hands and she flew at Mirabella. They toppled toward the railing. Mirabella punched at the wigged head and tried to avoid the momentum of the body launched against her. Had she not been disoriented by the rum, she'd have easily sidestepped Fiddy and allowed the songbird to fly over the railing to her death. But she was caught by the clinging arms. She toppled back, off balance, against the railing. Her back broke through and they teetered at the edge of the loft. Screaming, they fell.

[TWENTY-FIVE]

'Spring Beauties! I had almost forgotten how lovely they are. They only open their petals in sunshine so it is no use to pick them for a bouquet, for when out of the sun they close tightly and their beauty is lost.'

– V.A. Gillett: Jan, *Where Wildflowers Grow*

MIRABELLA AND FIDDY FELL through the air like two animals clawing at each other and landed on a pew between Hector Gillis and Mrs. Crowe, who were fortunately deaf enough that they weren't startled into cardiac arrest by the boom. Being underneath, Mirabella bore the brunt of the fall, breaking both arms and both legs. Fiddy survived with whiplash.

Four days later, Fiddy was waiting at the trailer when Mirabella was released from the hospital. Johnny arrived with her, wheeled her into the livingroom and parked her beside the chesterfield. "I'll pay your salary until you've recovered," he told her, speaking in a loud voice as if Mirabella had become partly deaf in the accident.

Mirabella stared ahead miserably from between the casts and failed to respond, even to refuse the offer.

"That would be just fine," intervened Fiddy. "You can pay in cash. She can't sign the cheque over to me and I'm the one who will be buying the groceries."

A fierce glance from Mirabella but still she said nothing.

Fiddy looked at her with deep pity. "I hope her voice wasn't harmed in the fall," she said, her forehead creased in worry. She stepped over to Mirabella, leaned down so that she was level with her face, and spoke loudly. "ARE YOU OKAY DARLING? DON'T WORRY. I WILL TAKE GOOD CARE OF YOU. WE WILL HAVE LOTS OF FUN TOGETHER. THIS IS YOUR HOME TOO."

Mirabella's eyes were cool, malicious flames fixed on Fiddy's close face. Still, she said nothing and remained motionless, a slim abdomen between the thick arms of white plaster – a Preying Mantis ready to leap. Her jaw was locked shut so tightly that a vein in her right temple throbbed.

Fiddy straightened. "I don't know what's the matter with her," she sighed. "But I'll cheer her up in no time. Maybe I'll throw a welcome home party. I could have everyone over to tour the trailer. Everything here is so . . . quaint. It will be a while before she's able to climb the stairs to the choir loft so I'll be holding choir practice here." She turned to her patient. "WON'T THAT BE NICE, DEAREST? I WILL FILL THIS TRAILER WITH SINGING ALL DAY AND ALL NIGHT LONG."

No response except for the venomous stare.

Johnny lost a valiant struggle to hold back his smile. "Let me know if you need anything," he said and headed out before Mirabella saw it.

Fiddy sat down in her chair across from Mirabella. "Is there anything I can get you, Mirabella?"

No answer.

"A drink of water? Some pink lemonade?"

No response. Mirabella turned her head and looked out the window.

"A spoonful of green-gourd-marmalade-sauce?"

No response.

"Rum and coke?"

Mirabella moved her head slowly from the window and fixed a dark gaze on Fiddy, who had to shrink away from the coldness. Avoiding Mirabella's stare, she looked out the window. The crow landed on the lawn and pecked at the sod. The grass was brown under the relentless midsummer sun. The hardwoods swirled in the hot breeze. The distant Northumberland was spotted with a few white boats. The crow moved to the garden, selected a worm and flew away.

"You'll have to talk to me sooner or later," said Fiddy, turning back.

Nothing.

"You can't even go to the bathroom by yourself," Fiddy pointed out. "You can't dress yourself. You can't take a bath. You can't make my meals. You can't clean. You can't dance. You can't twirl in the middle of the kitchen floor. You can't work. You can't do your needlepoint. You can't make your bed or empty the garbage." She waited for a response. "You can't stab me with a fork."

Nothing.

"You're useless. All you can do all day long is watch me live my life and try to derive some enjoyment from it. The doctor said it will be at least six weeks before the casts on your legs come off. You can't just sit there all day doing nothing. You might not be able to sing, but at least you can talk."

Nothing. Fiddy leaned ahead in her chair and looked carefully at Mirabella. Maybe she really did hurt her voice in the fall, she thought. Or maybe she was saving it for a performance. Mirabella's eyes were locked on the window.

"I know what you need!" Fiddy shrieked. She stood up. "I'll be right back." She ran to her bedroom and returned, concealing something behind her back. She cleared her throat. "I have a presentation to make," she announced in an official voice. "Due to other commitments and for *tragic* personal reasons, the currently reigning Miss Wintry Hope is unable to fulfil her mandate." She took her hands forward to reveal her tiara. "Therefore, I present the runner up, Miss Mirabella Stuart, with the title." Fiddy stepped closer to Mirabella and raised the tiara above her head.

"I don't want –" Mirabella protested and moved her head away to avoid the tiara. "I don't want your stupid tiara!"

Fiddy struggled to follow Mirabella's moving head but managed to plant the tiara.

"You must use your reign to accomplish only good," she advised. Then she proclaimed: "Mirabella Stuart, I crown you Miss Wintry Hope." She stood back to study Mirabella. The tiara was lopsided. Mirabella's nostrils flared with each breath and she glared at Fiddy like a pit bull. Fiddy's eyes misted.

"Of course, you must remember," Fiddy added delicately. "It's only yours until you get back on your feet. Then it's mine again."

Mirabella shook her head in an attempt to knock the tiara off but only succeeded in making it more lopsided.

"See you later, dearest," said Fiddy and she pranced across the kitchen floor toward the door. "I'll be back to feed you later." She took the keys to Mirabella's car from a hook next to the door where Johnny had hung them. "After I come back from my drive."

"YOUR WHAT?!" Mirabella screamed but Fiddy was already gone.

DRIVING A CAR couldn't be much different than driving a bulldozer, Fiddy thought, as she pulled out of Mirabella's driveway with a roar. The new tires, which Johnny had bought to replace the old bald ones, scattered pebbles across the lawn. The *Park Lane* flew down the driveway with a cloud of dust rising, then languishing behind. She careened onto the highway, rolled down her window and laughed like Dixie Lee in the *Dukes of Hazard*.

She went down Thism's Hill, past the park, past St Margaret's church, past the community centre, past the ballfield and turned into the driveway of Applefern Mansion. She came to a skidding stop at the mansion and leapt out of the car. Walking across the front lawn, she waved to Johnny and his family, who were just sitting down to dinner. They didn't wave back, even when she put her face up to the windows in an attempt to see who the black-suited dinner guests were. She smiled so they would notice her. A wide smile. Sunshine on your face. Show them your teeth. Beautiful.

At the edge of the east lawn she followed a path to the beach and crossed a short section of sand to another path leading to the highest point on coastal Wintry Hope: an uprising of rock overlooking the Northumberland. She started climbing, finding the way difficult in her high heels. She took them off and carried them one in each hand, and as the path became steeper, used them to claw her way up the lichen covered rock. Near the top, she was getting tired and had to stop to rest. She could do it, she told herself. If Scarlet O'Hara could do it, Desdemona Pacifico-Rossini could do it.

She did make it to the top and took in the vista: the mansion, the marsh, St Margaret's church, even the brook in the far distance where it trickled down the shale to the beach. Smooth, curvaceous Northumberland swells coursed toward the beach from the invisible horizon like splendid muscles curling. As they neared the beach, she watched them rise, unfurl, show their white lips and teeth, open their mouths in a groan, slide against the pebbles, give up their guts of froth, and die.

"Hear this, pebbles, mountains and storms!" she shouted. She heard her voice echo throughout her kingdom of swamps, shrubs and hills. She hoped all her faithful subjects, especially Mirabella, heard her, because she did not intend to repeat herself. She took in a deep breath and sang out as loud as she could, as high as she could, to every part of the kingdom, in a blast of decibels: "I AM NOT A WAVE!"

FOR THE NEXT SIX WEEKS Mirabella sat lifeless in her wheel chair in the corner of the livingroom, unable to feed herself, unable to swat a torturing fly, unable to correct the plastic mats that were moved out of place from time to time. She spent hours sitting in indoor dusk contemplating her humiliation and could find no way of escaping the conclusion: Fiddy had won all. Mirabella had lost all. Fiddy's buoyancy had defied everything to prevail. Mirabella's intellectual strength and physical powers had annihilated only herself.

As a result, she came to understand apathy, an emotion hitherto foreign to her way of thinking. With nothing alive in her anymore, she began not to care about the crooked mats, Fiddy's lipstick-stained teeth, the overgrown strangled geraniums peering in from the window. Her soul's wasteland allowed every wind to blow over it with the tumbleweeds, the clouds of dust, the dirt.

Is this how everyone else lived, she wondered? The apathy that had taken hold of the world, in which people had ceased caring about anything except watching television – was this her future? She shriveled inside herself. She continued to descend into depression. She found herself in the darkest of places, where the heart either turns to ashes – or learns humility.

Even after the casts were removed, Mirabella remained in darkness. Fiddy continued to be the duchess as Mirabella claimed she was still too weak to return to work at Applefern or even to run her own household. She sat for hours looking out the window at sailboats coursing up and down the Northumberland. The islands on the horizon were thin brown lines.

She was so weak in spirit that she didn't object to the humiliation of being carried up the steps to the choir loft, which Johnny and Arthur did for her in the hopes that an experience of the choir would revive her. On a hot Sunday in September they sat her in her wheelchair in front of the choir. The choir looked at her hopefully. They wouldn't have minded even if she barked at them when they made mistakes. But she merely sighed, shifted her weight uncomfortably and looked at the windows as the opening hymn commenced, the director's baton lifeless in her lap. She didn't join in the chorus. Even when the *Gloria* had to be halted for mixed up timing and begun again, she remained unresponsive.

The Mass inched forward. Father Francis, his face flushed red from the heat, floundered through his sermon. "It wasn't Ignatius or Irenaeus," he said, trying to remember the name of the correct Church thinker but unable to focus the strength of his mind on the matter. He leaned against the podium and aimed his face at the heavens, chasing elusive thoughts. "It was . . . someone else . . . I think."

They waited, in a collective sigh, for Father Francis to recall his thoughts. The church was quiet. The babies were asleep in the heat, with their parents gazing at them longingly, as if wanting to join them. Outside, Wintry Hope was silent. Not a breath of wind pulsed through the open windows. The coast was mute of waves and the Northumberland simply waited with muscles flexing. It was as though Wintry Hope, its birds, trees, insects and fields had all been hushed by an eclipse.

Breaking the silence, one of the violinists near the back of the choir, where no one could see him, accidentally struck his violin. A dull groan echoed throughout the church. He whispered an apology but his neighbouring instrumentalists, all hot and glum, simply aimed their hollow souls forward, as if considering throwing themselves collectively over the unrepaired opening in the balcony in one final act of discordant mass suicide. As Mirabella and Fiddy had proven, however, the plunge was not a guarantee of death.

"Maybe it was Edith Stein," Father Francis proposed, but shook his head and fell back into his thoughts.

The muggy silence continued. In the choir loft, the sopranos fanned themselves in perfect unison. Except for Fiddy, they avoided looking at Mirabella who sat before them as if dissolving in her wheelchair.

Fiddy watched her and wondered what could be so interesting on the floor to have captivated Mirabella's long unwavering attention. Then, she heard, so distinctly it could have come from the organ, the first notes of No. 51. She whipped her head toward Virgil but he was watching Father Francis and seemed not to have noticed the notes. Fiddy looked at the rest of the sopranos. Their song sheets had all stopped mid fan and they were looking at each other in confusion. They had heard the notes too.

They waited. All eyes fell on Mirabella who continued her vigilant gaze. While they watched her, the notes came again, eight strong notes that began the No. 51 chorus, from somewhere within Mirabella. The sopranos couldn't be sure it was her or not, as her lips remained tightly shut. But then, like an ancient statue breaking free after centuries, Mirabella's head moved and she faced them.

"No. 51," she said.

They stared at her in disbelief.

"It's not time to sing," whispered the soprano closest to her.

"It's time," said Mirabella and slowly, with some effort, she tried to get up. Her legs moved the pedals out of the way, straightened, she pushed up from the arm rests and began to rise. Then she was before them, hovering more than standing on her thin weak legs. She raised the baton. "No. 51," she ordered.

A wave of dismay moved through the ranks. Arthur wiped his brow with a handkerchief and gestured toward the altar. "But Francis isn't finished," he said.

"No. 51," she commanded again. She tapped the baton on the railing. "Now."

They stared back at her.

"We've been practicing it for two years," she said. "If you don't sing it now, I'll make sure you never do."

Fiddy stood up and opened the song sheets. Among the others, however, panic prevailed. Near the back, an unfortunate violinist dropped his violin and shrieked. The altos and tenors looked at each other like frightened chickens. One of the altos wondered aloud if Mirabella had been drinking again. Others looked upwards, as if wishing they could flee to the safety of the bell tower to roost. There were high-pitched gasps from the first sopranos. The basses, however, stood up, stuck out their chests and chastised the others for being cowards. A fight nearly broke out with the insulted tenors, who stood to protest. The ranks buzzed with pandemonium.

"Quiet!" Mirabella hissed. "You're a choir, not a barn yard. Stand up and get ready to sing."

They all stood.

"You too Virgil."

He nodded, let his fingers find the correct keys and waited for her signal. She leaned against the bannister for support and surveyed her choir. The children were nearly in tears. Two of the tenors were scrambling on the floor looking for sheets of music among the second sopranos who were stomping their feet in warning like nervous cows.

Mirabella lifted her hands. "Ready . . ." They looked up just in time to see her give Virgil the signal.

The first notes pined from the top of the organ's brass pipes, the bows of the violins stroked, the church breathed and something like a flash of light leapt from Mirabella into the singers. They took a collective breath and sang:

Worthy is the Lamb that was slain,
and hath redeemed us to God by His blood!
To receive power, and riches, and wisdom,
and strength, and honour,
and glory and blessing . . .

They didn't know if it was because they'd gone six weeks without Mirabella's direction and were now hearing what they'd forgotten, or whether there was now a difference in their blend of voices. They had no time to think about it. They couldn't look around to see if they'd somehow been joined by invisible others to fill out the sound.

They couldn't afford to look anywhere other than to Mirabella.

Her right hand sent the sopranos to the rafters and from there into the sky. Her left hand wove together the harmonies of the altos and tenors and sent them across sloping hills, plains and marshes. The basses she ordered into the earth to shake the foundations of the mountains, to move those who never dared to move. Her directing was a dance of light and sound. The violins wept of endless thirst. The drums were a marching army. The basses had toppled the mountains. Crumbling, the rocks were falling around them. They would all be buried.

Then, the earthquake. The sopranos surged, the flutes awoke, and a spot of hope opened up, like a distant star coming brighter:

Blessing and honour, glory and power,
be unto Him, be unto Him
that sitteth on the throne,
and unto the Lamb, for ever and ever . . .

The trumpets arose from the darkness and announced the King. A thousand notes rose higher, racing like children through the hallways of the palace, seeking the throne room with rejoicing.

Forever! And ever! Forever and ever!

And then, just when they thought they could go no higher, they found the throne room and stood before the great doors in silence. Mirabella's dancing ceased, her arms fading at her sides. She stood before them lifelessly, only her eyes showing them her thirst for more. Always more. It would never be enough to fill her, not until she could throw open those doors and step inside.

The silence, as loud as the music had been, held the church. The choir stood looking forward with longing, and they knew that as high as they had reached, the most they could do was to point to the majesty and no further. Mirabella lifted her hands once more and they sang out all that was left to be sung:

Amen! Amen! Amen!
Amen! Amen! Amen!

When it was finished and every echo had fled beyond the church into Wintry Hope, Mirabella folded herself up and shrank back into her wheel chair. She nodded at her choir and let a small, approving smile escape. "That was good," she said, so suddenly, so miraculously that even those who heard it refused to believe it.

Fiddy, however, heard it, believed it and cried like an orphaned goose.

MIRABELLA INSISTED on driving herself and Fiddy home, leaving the wheelchair empty at the back of the church, as if testifying of a miraculous healing. Fiddy was both happy and apprehensive about the newly arisen Mirabella. She refrained from chattering and simply watched Mirabella carefully on the drive home.

At the trailer, Mirabella immediately set to work. She trimmed the gangly geraniums and painted the trim on her doorstep, sitting down frequently to rest. She inspected her garden, in which someone had planted carrots, potatoes and beans during her convalescence. She had the strength to plant a bed of gourds and hoped it wasn't too late for them to bear fruit.

She defrosted a casserole for supper, of chopped turnips and parsnips in a maple sauce, which Fiddy dared not complain about, although she did have the courage to refuse nine offers of green-gourd-marmalade-sauce. Mirabella cleaned up after supper and sat down on the chesterfield to read a newspaper with a cup of decaffeinated tea while Fiddy watched from her corner chair, blowing on her tea to cool it. A squall moved in from the northeast and pelted sheets of rain against the trailer. Fiddy finished her tea and started working on her nails, continuing to keep a wary eye on Mirabella. Mirabella said nothing. Fiddy sighed. Only the rain shouted.

Finally, Mirabella put down the newspaper. "I'm glad I had time to figure things out," she said suddenly. Thunder echoed from the highlands, across Wintry Hope to the strait. "In fact, I think I've figured you out."

"Really?" Fiddy tried not to sound interested.

"Yes. I think I know why you keep going. Even though you have no talent, you can't sing, you can't act, and everyone knows it, you keep on going, despite everything."

"I do keep going, don't I?"

"Yes. And I think I know why. It's those silly dreams you

have."

"Dreams change everything, dearest."

"I see that now. They keep you going even when the universe is against you."

"I will always find a way."

"And so I think I should do the same."

Fiddy made no effort to conceal her delight. "Oh Mirabella!"

"Indeed, it's time I had a dream of my own."

"Darling, you must tell me what it is!"

"It is a great dream. An ambitious dream. And I will need your help to achieve it."

Fiddy's delight doubled and tripled, to the point of weeping. "I'll do anything," she said fervently, "anything!"

Mirabella opened her mouth to tell her more but was interrupted by a loud number of desperate knocks at the door. They looked at each other in surprise. "Who on earth would be out in this rain?" Mirabella got up to answer it with Fiddy following closely behind.

Mirabella opened the door cautiously and they both peered out. "You!" shouted Mirabella.

A drenched and shivering Garden Twinkle stood outside blinking her eyes against the rain. "Please," she wept, "I have nowhere to go." Her soaked tent was wrapped around her and she teetered under the weight of it. "Please, I want to live in Wintry Hope!"

"Get away you vile thing," said Mirabella and slammed the door in her face and locked it. She went back to her place on the chesterfield. "As I was saying, I have an ambitious dream – Fiddy, stop that!"

Fiddy was opening the window. "You can stay there!" she yelled to Garden and pointed toward her own property. "That's my property – I own the little shack – you can stay in there!"

Then Mirabella caught her around the waist, pulled her from the window, slammed it shut and pulled down the blind. She turned on Fiddy. "What did you do that for?"

"She's my friend."

"She's an extremist who would put us all in jail if she could."

Fiddy shrugged. "Maybe everyone should be in jail."

"You can't encourage people like that."

But Mirabella did step back to the window and peeked out between the blind and the glass. The rain blurred even the darkness but Mirabella could make out the wrapped mass trudging across the lawn, dragging parts of the tent and a sleeping bag behind her. She disappeared in the darkness but moments later a dim light flickered from between the cracks in the boards of the dilapidated shack. "She has no brains," said Mirabella. "If she stays there, she'll die of cold."

Fiddy sat down and resumed working on her nails. "There's mice and nests of snakes in there too."

Mirabella went to another window to get a better angle. "She has a light of some kind, the fool. Why on earth doesn't she have any sense?" She went back to the first window. "Why doesn't she just go home?"

"Maybe she has no home. She said she wants to live in Wintry Hope."

Mirabella went to the kitchen window. Then to the door. She sighed. Finally she put on her raincoat and rubber boots and went outside.

Fiddy leapt from her chair and went to the window to watch.

A few minutes later, Mirabella returned, coming across the lawn dragging Garden Twinkle with her. Fiddy hurried to her chair and pretended to be working on her nails.

"I suppose you want something to eat," Mirabella said on entering.

"That would be nice," sighed a defeated Garden. She dropped her outer clothes on a plastic mat Mirabella placed on the floor for the purpose. "I'm a vegetarian."

"A vegetarian!"

"Yes. Kind of."

"I have no vegetarian foods. I have only some leftover turnip-parsnip casserole."

"That would be fine."

Mirabella quickly assembled the meal and placed it before Garden, together with several jars of condiments. She invited her to partake of them.

Garden looked at the food skeptically. Fiddy mouthed a silent warning not to eat the green-gourd-marmalade-sauce but Garden couldn't make out the strange formula on Fiddy's lips. In any case she said she'd start with the casserole, took a bite and nodded to the hovering Mirabella. "It's fine."

Satisfied with her effort, Mirabella sat down again at the chesterfield. "As I was saying," she resumed, "I believe the key to triumph in this life is to have a dream."

"True," said Fiddy, her attention now divided between her nails, the newcomer and Mirabella.

"And my decision has been confirmed, I dare say, by Providence."

"That's how it always happens." Fiddy stopped her painting and focused exclusively on Mirabella. "Tell us your dream. Unload your heart of its burden."

Mirabella winced but continued. "It's a grand dream, a dream that will –"

"What's this?" Garden suddenly blurted.

Mirabella and Fiddy looked. Garden held up a jar of green-gourd-marmalade-sauce.

Mirabella sighed. "It's green-gourd-marmalade-sauce. It's good for you. Nothing but puréed green gourds and some other ingredients, none of which were derived from or used to harm animals."

"It's the most delicious thing I've ever eaten."

"You don't have to make fun of it," said Mirabella. "If you don't like it, don't eat it."

"No, I'm serious. I love it." Garden looked at Mirabella earnestly. "Can I have some more?" She looked from Mirabella to Fiddy and back again, wondering why they were gazing at her in stupefied astonishment. Then, suddenly, Mirabella was at her side with a dessert dish, spooning green-gourd-marmalade-sauce into it with a spatula.

"It is delicious, isn't it?" Mirabella said giddily. "I have a few extra bottles if you're interested in more. It really is good, isn't it? Help yourself."

"Quite lovely," said Garden. "They would love it at the APT Society. What do you do with the seeds?"

Mirabella thought carefully. "I mail them to South America where they can be dispersed into their natural environment."

"I'll have some more." Garden stuffed a spoon of it into her mouth, closed her eyes and moaned with pleasure. "Delicious."

Somewhat dazed, Mirabella returned to the chesterfield and sat down. Deep in thought, she watched as Garden greedily ate the sauce. "You know," Mirabella said cautiously, "if you'd like to stay here in Wintry Hope for a while, you'd be welcome to live here."

Garden paused, swallowed and nodded.

"You can have Fiddy's room."

Fiddy bolted to her feet. "That's not fair, I was here first!"

"You can sleep on the pullout."

"But my back!" sputtered Fiddy.

"It's okay," chuckled Garden. "I'll sleep on the pullout. I don't mind."

"Are you sure?" asked Mirabella, her voice genuinely concerned.

Garden nodded ahead of another mouthful of sauce.

Fiddy sat down, grumbled a threat under her breath and gave Mirabella a most unimpressed stare.

"Thank-you," said Garden, swallowing, "and the marsh thanks you."

"The marsh?"

"I'm undertaking an intensive study of it for my doctoral thesis." She told them about the white iris, its probable extinction and her search for it. "But you can never know," she concluded, "whether it is for sure extinct. You can never know when all hope is lost."

"Indeed," said Fiddy.

"Logically speaking, it's almost impossible to prove a

negative," said Mirabella sensibly. "But it is good to have a dream. I have a dream now too. I was just telling Fiddy about it and how it appears that when the dream forms, Providence steps in to provide what is needed. You have both been delivered to me by the hand of Providence, I believe."

Formerly enthusiastic about Mirabella's announcement, Fiddy was now more reserved. "And, prithee, what will Providence have us doing?"

"You will begin by paying rent."

Fiddy opened her mouth to object but Mirabella quieted her with a glance. "Half of your social security cheque."

"I'm too young for social security. You must be referring to my royalty cheque." She whispered to Garden: "It's Merv Griffin's way of saying thank-you."

"My mistake," said Mirabella.

"I have no money and no income," said Garden.

"You can learn to make crafts," said Mirabella, as if the plan were already worked out. "I'll teach you to do crewel work. We'll sell them in Tina Shingo."

Garden looked at her uneasily.

"So, my love," said Fiddy with a superior air, "what is this dream we're helping you with? To become a landlady?"

Mirabella leaned back into the chesterfield and a faraway look came over her. "Not at all. Far more ambitious than that. My dream will be more exhausting than anything I've ever done. It will take everything I've got, all my energy, all my resources, all my talents."

"That sounds like my dream," said Fiddy, her attention recaptured.

A sharp look from Mirabella. "My dream is beyond even your dreams. My dream will take everything, every cell and fibre of my being, all of my intellectual and creative powers, my talents, my money, every penny of my savings, everything I can possibly offer."

Fiddy moved to the edge of her seat and was growing excited.

"Even with a good deal of luck," continued Mirabella, "I will probably face total financial and emotional ruin."

Fiddy could hold herself back no longer. "I know what your dream is! You're going to stage an opera!"

"No, you idiot," Mirabella spat. "I'm going to launch a lawsuit."

"A what?"

"A lawsuit. It's been almost twenty years since my brother died and his estate has never closed. I objected at the time and so it's still open."

"This is a very strange dream," said Fiddy, pushing herself back into her chair. "What are you going to do, dig up his body?"

"No, I told you I'm going to launch a lawsuit."

"Against your dead brother?"

"Against the person who stole my inheritance."

Fiddy strained hard, trying to think of who it was who had managed to run off with poor Mirabella's inheritance.

Mirabella smiled and her bleached teeth sparkled. "I'm going to sue Johnny."

"Oh my," said Fiddy. "You've gone and done it this time." She sighed. Johnny and his riches were surely doomed now, she thought. The mansion with its Gothic arch, marble floors and grand staircase, the gardens, orchard and pools, the luxury cars, the exotic shopping trips and vacations, all would come to an abrupt end, with Johnny, Martha and the children taking up residence somewhere in the swamp.

While Mirabella moved into the mansion. Fiddy thought carefully. "You know, Mirabella, I think I'll sue Johnny too."

"Me too," said Garden with her mouth full.

Credits

"Charity upholds . . ." from the *Catechism of the Catholic Church,* Concacan Inc. – Libreria Editrice Vaticana, 1994, for the English translation in Canada. Used by permission.

"Air is emptiness . . ." from POEMS by CS Lewis © C.S. Lewis Pte. Ltd. 1964. Extracts reprinted by permission.

"Obviously, a good choral ensemble . . ." from *Choral Director's Complete Handbook* by Lewis Gordon © Parker Publishing Co. Inc., 1977, New York.

"Oh, Adam was a gardener . . ." *The Glory of the Garden,* Rudyard Kipling (1865-1936).

"Ah, I laugh to see myself . . ." Marguerite, *Faust*, Charles Gounod (1818-1893).

Der Hölle Rache, aria from *Die Zauberlöte*, Wolfgang Amadeus Mozart (1756-1791).

"Where art thou death . . ." from *The Tragedy of Antony and Cleopatra*, Act V, Scene II, William Shakespeare (1564-1616).

"The heavens forbid . . ." from *The Tragedy of Othello the Moor of Venice,* Desdemona, Act II, Scene I, William Shakespeare (1564-1616).

"O thou invisible spirit of wine . . ." from *The Tragedy of Othello the Moor of Venice*, Cassio, Act II, Scene III, William Shakespeare (1564-1616).

"No torrents stain . . ." and "Pure stream . . ." from *To Levin Water,* Tobias Smollett (1721-1771).

"A love that can hardly be spoken . . ." Leonora's aria from *Il Trovatore,* Giuseppe Verdi (1813-1901).

"Sheep are very good . . ." from *Animal Sentience*, courtesy Compassion in World Farming Trust (www.animalsentience.com), Great Britain. Used by permission.

"Morning Has Broken" from the poem by Eleanor Farjeon © David Higham Associates, London, England. Used by permission.

"Good babysitters . . ." from *The Guide to Babysitting*, University of Illinois Extension, http://www.urbanext.uiuc.edu/babysitting/. Used by permission.

"Ostinato . . ." and "Cabaletta . . ." from The Penguin Opera Guide, © Amanda Holden, 1993, 1995, The Penguin Group, Ringwood, Victoria, Australia. Used by permission.

"What should you do if you are suddenly confronted . . ." from Backpacking, Joel F. Meier, © 1980, Wm. C. Brown Company Publishers. Used by permission of the author.

"In addition to their harsh calls . . ." from *Corvidae Calls*, by Raven J. Brown (www.shades-of-night.com). Used by permission.

"Chickens love to take dust baths . . ." from *Animal Companions* by PETA, People for the Ethical Treatment of Animals. Used by permission.

"The birds flew down . . ." from Desdemona's aria "Mia madre aveva una povera ancella," *Otello*, Giuseppe Verdi (1813-1901).

"Bladderwort includes . . ." from Roland's Flora of Nova Scotia, by A.E. Roland, revised by Marian Zinck, © Crown Copyright, Province of Nova Scotia, 1998.

"On the rose-scented wings . . ." Leonora's aria "D'amor sull'ali rosee," *Il Trovatore*, Giuseppe Verdi (1813-1901).

"Mine eyes have seen the glory . . ." from *The Battle Hymn of the Republic* by Julia Ward Howe (1862) © Shawnee Press, MCMXLIII.

"Believe me in my pain . . ." Morgana's aria "Credete al mio dolore," from *Alcina*, Act III, Scene I, George Friedrick Handel (1685-1759).

"The heavens are telling . . ." from *Canticle of the Sun,* by Marty Haugen © 1980 GIA Associates Inc.

"Spring Beauties! I had almost forgot . . ." from *Where Wildflowers Grow* by V.A. Gillett, Brunswick Press, Fredericton, New Brunswick, 1966.

"Worthy is the Lamb that was slain . . ." from Chorus No. 51 of *Messiah*, by George Friedrick Handel (1685-1759).

Sandy MacDonald

Born in Antigonish, Nova Scotia, MacDonald was raised in a fishing village of Arisaig, on the coast of the Northumberland Strait where six generations of his ancestors lived and worked as farmers and fishermen. His family founded a lobster distribution and processing company in which MacDonald worked as a teenager and university student.

He attended St. Francis Xavier University, receiving an honours degree in business administration and economics, and went on to study law at the University of New Brunswick, receiving his degree in 1998. He was called to the Nova Scotia Bar in 1999 after articling with the law firm of *MacIntosh, MacDonnell & MacDonald.*

With adequate fallback position firmly in place, he began his hitherto suppressed writing career, penning several books, short stories, collections of poetry and screenplays. *The White Iris* is his first novel.

Although he has visited most of Canada and the world's major cities, MacDonald continues to reside in Arisaig where he writes within full view of the Northumberland. He is currently working on his second novel in *The White Iris* series.